Praise for the novels of

# STEPHANIE CHONG

"Hauntingly beautiful, Stephanie Chong's
*The Demoness of Waking Dreams* boldly turns the
classic struggle between good and evil into a lush,
unpredictable love story. Angels and demons collide
in Venice, which is as much of a character in this book
as Brandon and Luciana. I'm anxiously awaiting
the next book in the series!"
—*New York Times* bestselling author Stephanie Tyler

"Chong delivers a wicked tale of a sexy guardian angel
battling for a not-so-lost demon's soul."
—*New York Times* bestselling author Caridad Piñeiro

"Stephanie Chong taps into a delicious fantasy
older than time, spinning it masterfully into a sexy,
moving tale that feels fresh and new.
I am sincerely her newest fan."
—*New York Times* bestselling author Maggie Shayne

"Mix a spirited angel with a sexy demon,
and you get one heavenly read!"
—*New York Times* bestselling author Kerrelyn Sparks

*Also by Stephanie Chong*

WHERE DEMONS FEAR TO TREAD

*Look for Stephanie Chong's next book
in the Company of Angels series,
available September 2013.*

# THE
# DEMONESS
# OF
# WAKING
# DREAMS

## STEPHANIE
## CHONG

HARLEQUIN®
entertain, enrich, inspire™

Recycling programs
for this product may
not exist in your area.

ISBN-13: 978-0-7783-1314-4

THE DEMONESS OF WAKING DREAMS

To Valerie Gray,
*la miglior fabbra.*

Was it a vision, or a waking dream?
    —John Keats, "Ode to a Nightingale" (1819)

# Prologue

*Chiesa del Santissimo Redentore*
*Present Day*

*Who will it be?*

In the austere marble interior of the Renaissance church, Luciana Rossetti stood watching the opening ceremony of a festival she despised. Dusky light filtered down through the soaring windows, dimly illuminating the bronzed crucifix that loomed high above the altar. At precisely seven o'clock in the evening, the priests started their solemn procession up the nave, to the front of the church.

*Yes, a priest would make a fine sacrifice,* she mused, imagining those ornate robes of cream and gold, spattered with scarlet.

*Or easier pickings? A member of the wide-eyed crowd of worshippers and tourists?*

It hardly mattered to her. She hated them all equally.

Besides, every human being ended up in the same place, eventually.

Dead and buried.

*Idiotic mortals,* she smirked to herself. *You have no idea what the afterlife really holds. If you did, most of you'd run screaming down the aisles of this Church of the Most Holy Redeemer right here and now.*

A single bead of sweat trickled down between her perfect breasts, dripping into the bodice of her silk dress. Her pale emerald eyes pressed closed for a moment, shutting out the sunlight warming her face. Unlike this crowd of fools, she had not come to celebrate the Festa del Redentore, the *Festival of the Redeemer.*

No, she came for darker reasons entirely. To pay tribute to a darker force.

Luciana Rossetti came to hunt.

From amongst the revelers crowding the church on this hot July weekend, she would select her annual sacrifice. A single victim, exchanged for certain privileges and freedoms granted to her within the demon world. An offering delivered to the Prince of Darkness.

An eye for an eye. A tooth for a tooth. *A soul for a soul.*

The head priest at the pulpit droned on in Italian, sermonizing about forgiveness.

About redemption. About salvation.

"We give thanks to our Lord Jesus Christ for the salvation he brought to Venice, in saving our most serene city from the plague in 1577. In loving gratitude, we citizens of Venice built this church," he said.

*Salvation,* Luciana thought, *is a funny thing.*

Fifty thousand people had died during that bout of plague. One-third of the population was wiped out, their bodies dumped into mass graves. Half a century later, the plague swept through Venice yet again, returning to reap another eighty thousand souls. However, the priest didn't bother to mention that. What could one expect from a man wearing a medieval headdress, so obviously stuck hundreds of years in the past, roped into rituals and incantations.

*If that's salvation, I'll take the alternative,* she thought.

Behind her, someone muttered in a low voice, grumbling discontentedly about something that Luciana could not hear. Turning, she saw it was an old woman in the pew one row back. An old grandmother standing with her family. On seeing Luciana's face, the old woman's wizened features contracted with fury. Her voice broke the silence of the crowd, shattering the air of reverence with a cry.

"*Demonessa!*" the old woman shrieked, pointing her bony finger at Luciana. "*Una demonessa nella casa di Dio!*"

*A demoness in the house of God.*

Every soul in the church froze, turning to stare in the direction of the crazy old *nonna* who was carrying on in such a way. Luciana shifted under the scrutiny, put on her most pious smile and tried her best to look as innocent as a dove. Standing at the end of the pew, she tensed herself to flee. Hoped that wasn't necessary.

Humans rarely recognized her.

But once in a while…once in a very long while…

"*Mamma! Basta!*" shouted her son, a balding man of about fifty who flushed red with embarrassment as he ordered his mother to stop. To the entire congregation, he rattled out a flustered apology involving Alzheimer's and missed medication. Then he dragged the old woman away, with the old bat spitting and shrieking as she was pulled down the long nave and out of the church.

Mutters of sympathy came from those standing around Luciana: "*Strega pazza…stronza vecchia…*" *Crazy old witch…*

*Gesù Cristo,* the demoness swore to herself. *Humans. What a pain in the ass.*

Outwardly, Luciana smiled and shrugged.

The ceremony resumed. When the tedious incantations and rituals finally ended, the clergy paraded down the center aisle past the congregation, on their way out of the church. A few of the priests caught Luciana's eye, eager to see who had caused all the fuss. She gave them each a pious little smile. But most of their gazes dipped lower, to her glistening cleavage.

*Men of God are still men, after all,* she thought.

The crowd dissipated, flooding out into the early evening. Toward the picnics and the celebrations, the boats decked with garlands of flowers and leaves, balloons and paper lanterns. There would be music and dancing, and once the sun went down, fireworks.

In the emptying church, Luciana lingered. Sauntering toward one of the side chapels, she knelt in mock prayer on the cool marble, even as she cast a furtive gaze over the thinning crowd.

*Who will it be this year?*

*Who among them will be the chosen one?*

Tonight she had a craving for a handsome young man. One man, whose life she would transform for one spectacular evening. Whose most secret fantasies and wildest desires she would fulfill in a single night. One man who would play with her the game of seduction. One man whose life would end before the rising of the sun.

She turned, her gaze catching upon a man who stopped her cold.

*Chi è?* She had to stop herself from saying it aloud: *Who is that?*

*Tall, dark and handsome.*

Yes. But those three words weren't the first that flooded into her consciousness.

*Dangerous. Wild. Angry.* Those were the words rushing through her mind.

He was sculpted more solidly than a Michelangelo, the muscled bulk of his toned arms etched with tattoos. Close-shaven dark hair, the cut of a military man or the like. Shaved purely for functionality and not aesthetics, she sensed. Light gray eyes, focused and intense. Eyes the color of rain. The aura of a restless ocean. His looks contrasted starkly with the preening *mammoni,* the mama's boys who seemed to proliferate in Venice.

He was beautiful. No pretty boy, this one.

The set of his broad body, the confidence of his stance marked him as foreign.

Not Venetian. Not Italian. Not European.

*Not human.*

The thought startled her. Although why it should, she didn't know.

Overhead, a single bird circled the church's dome. A rapid flutter of wings and a tremulous coo, lonely in the empty space. The tourists beneath craned their necks and pointed upward. Luciana glanced ceilingward, too. It was only a pigeon, one of the filthy winged rats that had infested Venice for centuries.

Still, the noise set a doubt churning in her mind.

The sound of wings often heralded the arrival of another sort of flying nuisance.

His face was as beautiful as any immortal she'd seen. She closed her eyes, directing her energy toward him. And waited for the signs. For the deep knowing. For the sensation of power, immortal and extraordinary, which emanated from all divine beings.

The flare of energy came. No mere internal sense of

intuition. But a hit of energy, a palpable shock that blew through her. Rocked her backward and almost pushed her off her feet.

*Angel.*

In that same instant, a flock of pigeons swept through the open doors of the church. They rose to join the one circling overhead beneath the dome, the single bird suddenly multiplied into a wild clamor of cooing and wing beats that filled the rounded space.

The noise of the pigeons and the voices of the tourists blended into a cacophony, shouts in a tangle of languages: Italian, English, German, Japanese…and a dozen more, all the people pointing and staring at the circling birds overhead. But the thunderous flutter of wings and human voices melded into a flat buzz that quieted before it faded away entirely.

At least to her ears.

Luciana was aware of only him. The first man and woman, meeting in a wild garden paradise. Or the last man and woman on earth, standing on an arid plain at the end of time.

Angel and demon.

Sworn enemies.

They stood in the chapel, and his gaze remained steady. Eyes locked on eyes. In that moment, Luciana felt the rush of centuries blow past her. Felt as if she had been made new again simply by the presence of this man.

Who seemed to peer into the depths of her very soul. Just as she saw into his.

For an instant, she forgot about the hunt. Forgot about revenge and her desire to obliterate the Company. Her mind went blank, and the only thing she knew was that moment, standing in the now-quiet chapel with the last rays of sunlight on her face.

*With him.*

If he were a human man, she might have been able to leave him to his precious Redeemer. To allow him to walk out of the church, out into the thronging festivities among the Venetians, to experience the city's pleasures. To watch the fireworks, drink some cheap Prosecco and then tomorrow morning, to leave.

*To live.*

Then, as quickly as the moment had begun, it was over. The noise of the birds overhead and the clamor of the crowd rose to a deafening roar, the humans now pushing each other to get away from the chaos. And Luciana came crashing back into the present moment, back to the reality of standing here in this too-hot church that she hated.

Back to the reality of exactly how much she hated this man and all his kind.

She would destroy him. She *must* destroy him.

She had never sacrificed an angel before.

What better way to pay homage to the devil? Yes, this man would make a fine offering. She curved her lips into a smile honed over centuries, a smile she knew spoke of pleasure, without the need for words, beckoning to him across the rain of gray feathers that littered the air around them.

*Screw redemption,* she thought. *Let the hunt begin.*

# Chapter One

*One day earlier*

"Welcome home, *baronessa*."

Luciana Rossetti's private boat waited at the dock of the Marco Polo Airport, and her driver helped her descend from the dock into the polished mahogany vessel. The water shimmered, early morning sunlight glancing off the surface of the lagoon. "Thank you, Massimo. It's good to be home."

"No luggage, *signora?*" the driver asked.

"I made an unexpected departure from America," she answered, settling into a seat at the rear of the boat. She leaned against the tan leather upholstery, relaxing at last. Inhaled deeply. And exhaled a sigh of pure relief.

*Unexpected departure* was an understatement. *Narrow escape* was more like it.

But at the moment, words escaped her. Mere language could not begin to relate what had happened in the past three months. She simply lacked the energy to explain it all to Massimo.

"Is everything all right?" Massimo asked as he steered the boat, navigating out into the lagoon. If anyone could sense when something was amiss with her, it was him. He was her *maggiordomo,* her steward, her right-hand man, and he had been for the past two centuries. He glanced backward now, brows drawn together as he scrutinized her. "You look tired."

"How many times have I told you not to say that, Massimo? No woman wants to hear it, even if it's true," she said, narrowing her eyes at him. "I'm *fine*."

She was not fine.

She closed her eyes and leaned against the leather. Perhaps with a little bit of time, she would be fine. But right now, she was absolutely exhausted. Utterly depleted.

*But still alive.*

"Everything is perfectly *fine*, Massimo," she lied again, repeating the word for emphasis. "I had a brief run-in with some enemies, but suffered no permanent damage. There is only one thing of importance. I have made it home in time to attend this year's Redentore Festival."

"Yes, of course, *baronessa*." Massimo's handsome face lit with a smile. "You are a strong woman. And you have the support of your humble servants, we Gatekeepers. Do you think you will have enough strength for the hunt?" he asked, clearly worried. "If you don't, I can assemble the staff. We can take care of your responsibilities if you wish."

"No, Massimo," she said, rubbing her temples.

Her Gatekeepers, low-ranking demons in her service, all happened to be young, Italian, male and pretty to look at. They were competent enough in their roles as housekeeping staff and minions for errands. But she didn't—*couldn't*—trust them to carry out her work.

"Don't concern yourself," she said. "I need a few hours to rest. By tonight I'll be completely recovered. Tonight is an eternity away. There is no need for the staff to take over a job that I am perfectly capable of doing myself."

Massimo nodded, concentrating on steering the boat as they entered the Grand Canal.

"A job that I am *obligated* to do myself," she added.

Moments later, the boat passed into the shadow under the Rialto Bridge, and her head began to ache. The bridge invariably brought back agonizing reminiscences of the man who had just caused her impromptu departure from America. Because over two hundred years ago, she had met her ex-lover here. When she'd been barely seventeen years old, still innocent. Still fresh. Still human.

Before Julian Ascher had ruined everything.

Pain, white-hot and sharp, seared between her temples. Her fingers curled around the little glass vial hanging on a delicate gold chain around her neck. The single object she had managed to salvage during her rapid departure from America. The contents of that little vial would help her achieve her heart's most fervent desire.

*Revenge.*

She had gone to America to get revenge. And she had failed miserably.

Luciana's plan had been to make Julian Ascher pay for all the things he had done to her. For getting her into the insufferable business of being a Rogue demon in the first place. When that plan had failed, she had nearly managed to kill the fledgling angel he was screwing— a moronically innocent girl called Serena St. Clair. And after failing to finish that kill, too, Luciana had only narrowly escaped capture at the hands of the Company of Angels.

And then she had returned home.

Exhausted. Depleted. *But still alive.*

*Julian Ascher will pay,* she thought. *The Company of Angels will pay.*

Luciana would have vengeance on them all. Inside of her, a dark alchemy had transformed this longing into a substance so hard and so sharp, it might have cut diamond. Once she finished with her annual hunt, she would turn her mind to completing her revenge.

At the thought of it, she smiled.

The boat cruised out from under the bridge, back into the sunshine.

Luciana tilted her face upward in the humid air, gazing at the palazzos lining the waterway in their elegant decay. The day was still new. The possibilities, endless. The winding streets of Venice teemed with people, already beginning their preparations for tonight's festivities.

"You're looking better already, *baronessa*," Massimo said, smiling back at her.

"Thank you, Massimo. The city is a balm to my soul," she said. "And the Redentore Festival always brings me such joy."

The fireworks display and homage to the Virgin Mary marked the height of every summer. Boats decked with garlands would crowd St. Mark's Basin for the pyrotechnic spectacle. Restaurants and bars would overflow with drunken patrons. The canals would stream with locals and tourists alike, come to watch and to party.

Venetians were masters of celebration. They had been honing the art of revelry for centuries. Looking up from their preparations, a boatful of shirtless men whistled as they watched her boat speed past.

*"Che bellissima!"* one of them shouted. *"Ciao, bella!"*

*Ah, sì.* The catcall. That was another thing Venetian men had mastered.

Normally, she simply ignored such men. Had been doing so since adolescence, when her womanhood had begun to flower. This time, she gave them an enigmatic little smile and called back, *"Te lo puoi sognare!"*

*In your dreams...*

*Across an ocean, the full moon shone brightly on a night that was just beginning.*

*Brandon Clarkson was deep undercover in the seediest area of downtown Detroit. A greasy sheen covered his body from not having showered in days, a stale feeling of exhaustion hung in his lungs. His ripped jeans and leather jacket, unwashed and overripe.*

*To look at him, you would never guess he was what he was.*

*A cop.*

*Not one of the drug dealers he had been tracking for months.*

*He slid into the dark alley, following the criminals he was on the verge of catching. He was close, so close. Knew they were here. Sensed their heartbeats nearby, could feel their breath mingling with the cool night breeze. The scent of them hanging in the air, alongside the smell of urine and garbage rotting in the darkness. The skitter of unseen vermin, animal and human, hidden in the shadows, surrounded him.*

*Something in the pit of his gut called to him, a little voice whispering urgently that something wasn't right here.*

*There's trouble...*

*His brain overrode it, with a message that was loud and clear.*

You've been hunting these criminals for the past six months. This may be the only chance you'll ever get.

*It was time to put these scumbags away. He knew their habits. Knew the sheer volume of their trade. Had seen a warehouse's worth of heroin and cocaine pass through their hands, enough to keep the entire city of Detroit high for a week.*

*He stepped forward, moving farther into the alley, holding his handgun at eye level, ready to shoot.*

Tonight's the night, *he told himself.* This ends right here.

*He heard a noise behind him. A few quick footsteps striking on the pavement. A pop so loud he thought his eardrum might have erupted. And then his spine exploded. He felt a burst of pain that seared and radiated, like magma surging in his vertebrae, more intense than any pain he had felt in his life. A burst that could only be a bullet.*

*He fell, the structure of his body ruptured, the sturdy architecture of flesh and bones shattered in a single instant.*

*Heard the footsteps nearing.*

*A pause.*

*He was dying. He knew it. Sprawled on his side, he could almost feel the life seeping out of him through the hole blown in his back. He shoved his hand in his pocket. Pulled out the old silver pocket watch he had carried every day of his job, ran his fingers over the raised engraving of Saint Michael on the back.*

*To the patron saint of cops and warriors, Brandon whispered a request for help.*

*"Saint Michael the Archangel, defend us in battle. Be our protection against the wickedness and snares of the devil..."*

*He held the old watch against his heart, felt the wetness soaking his shirt. Realized it was because the bullet had blown clean through his body. He was bleeding out, left to die here on the filthy pavement of this alley.*

*Heard the scrape of a shoe near his ear, so close now.*

*A second explosion as another shot slammed into the back of Brandon's skull.*

*Death came instantly. But the last sliver of his human existence, less than a fraction of a breath, stretched into an eternity that seemed to encompass his entire life span.*

*The last thing he saw through his human eyes was his watch, its second hand clicking its last tick.*

*All of time seemed to hover in a single instant, packed into the space between those two black lines that demarcated one second from another.*

*And in that second, the summary of his human experience poured forth in his mind.*

*Every image he had ever experienced, all flooding into his memory in a simultaneous rush. Emerging out of his mother's body, into the cold light of a hospital room...his infancy and childhood in a run-down suburb of Detroit...roughhousing with his brothers...front yards full of rusted-out cars and tall weeds...his high school sweetheart, Tammy...the police academy...his wedding... their first home...lovemaking in the afternoons...*

*All rushing through him and past him, as if he were being sucked backward through a tunnel.*

*And now, this.*

*The moments of his death were literally the worst moments of his life. In them, he felt loss, sorrow, regret, fear. Swirling together like a black hole in the cosmos. Nothing that words could ever describe, the feeling was so much more intense than language, which failed utterly to scratch the surface of that experience.*

The experience of intense suffering.

*Enough for a lifetime, compacted into the last fleeting scrap of consciousness.*

What a shitty way to die, *he thought.*

*Those were the last words that ran through his human mind.*

*He spiraled upward, flying out of his human body.*

*Looking down, he saw his mortal form sprawled on the ground, bleeding out onto the dirty pavement in the dark of night. Over his now-lifeless body, the killer leaned.*

*Brandon could only see the killer's back as the man bent down to remove the object enclosed in the curled hand of the corpse. The final impression of Brandon's human experience was one of absolute injustice. Not only had the killer taken Brandon's life, but he had also stolen Brandon's goddamned watch.*

*Fortunately, Brandon no longer cared. Detached from his human body, he spun upward.*

*Into light, he had been born. And now in death, he returned to light again. But not the light of the human world. Not a cold light this time, but reaching toward the warmest and most joyful light he had ever known.*

*Reaching, reaching, upward, upward...*

*To hang in the cosmos for a single, shining, glorious instant. An instant as long as eternity and shorter than the blink of an eye. But he knew he could not stay there forever.*

*Not yet. There were things to be done.*

*And then falling, plunging downward at a dizzying velocity, traveling faster than matter.*

*Because he, Brandon, was constructed of pure light.*

He landed with a jolt, the light of his soul crashing back into his physical body.

Lying in bed. Howling a keening cry of mourning for the life he had just lost.

Just as he did every time he woke from this nightmare.

Every single fucking night for the past ten years, he awoke shivering in terror.

Thanking God that it was only a dream.

Because the first time it happened, it hadn't been a dream.

*That time, it had been real.*

Three o'clock in the morning.

That's what time his bedroom clock read.

The clock that existed in real time. Not dream time.

He shut his eyes against the memory of his death. Brought himself back to the here and now. Dragged in one long breath, and then another. Beneath him, he felt the damp of the sheets. Soaked through with sweat. The throb of adrenaline still coursing through his body.

In the darkness of his room he lay, recounting the facts to himself.

He, Brandon Clarkson, was no longer human.

But he had been, once.

It had been ten years since his human death. Why he revisited the scene of his own death every night, he wasn't entirely sure. He would have taken it for a curse if he had not been reborn as something other.

*Angel.*

Immortal, but sent back in a human body. With all the same problems bound up with physical incarnation. Fatigue. Stress. Insomnia.

*Nightmares.*

Reaching for the lamp beside his bed, he switched

on the light. Blinking a few times, he squinted in the brightness. He got up and wandered around his apartment. The sleek modern loft in a historic Art Nouveau building was a world away from the alley where he'd died. He stood at the window, looking down at the river thirty stories below, shimmering gold in the hot July night, downtown city lights aglow on the surface of the water.

Not the Detroit River, but the Chicago River.

*Not Detroit,* he reminded himself.

Not Detroit, where he had been born. Where he had lived. Where he had died.

*I'm in Chicago.* Where he now worked as a Guardian in the Company of Angels. Where he had been promoted to supervisor, overseeing his own unit, after his preliminary training in the Los Angeles unit.

Chicago was a world away from his human existence. A lifetime away.

In the kitchen, he stood in front of the fridge, reading the words of the decade-old newspaper clipping he kept hanging there. His human life, boiled down to three paragraphs, black ink on yellowing paper.

Slain Officer Killed in Gang-Related Shooting

28-year-old police officer Brandon Clarkson was fatally shot in Detroit's downtown core on Saturday evening while investigating gang-related activities. Police say he died immediately from his wounds.

A memorial ceremony was held at Campus Martius Park, during which Clarkson was posthumously promoted to detective. His partner, Officer Jude Everett, was also promoted for his "extraordinary bravery" after capturing the man accused of gunning down Clarkson.

Clarkson had served seven years with the Detroit police force. He is survived by his parents, three brothers and his widow, Tammy.

As he read the words for the three-thousandth time, the old darkness rose in him, bitter and familiar. Somewhere deep inside him, the feeling that he wasn't entirely good. Not like most of the other members of the Company, whose pure-hearted goodness was beyond doubt.

Death had made him angry in a way that he had never been in his human life.

Brandon Clarkson had been born with an eerie sense of how he wanted to live. He had come into this world knowing exactly what he wanted to do.

*Serve and protect.*

He had lived fast. He had loved intensely. But if he had come into the world on a mission, he had left the world in service to that mission. He had been sent back as a Guardian, essentially to do the same thing he had always done. To chase down the most dangerous criminals on earth. To catch the most corrupt beings in existence, humans and demons alike. *To protect those who could not protect themselves.*

Now, here he was a decade later.

With one tiny problem.

The nightmare.

Of an endlessly recurring human death that made him feel like some character in a Greek myth. Like Sisyphus pushing the same rock up a hill, over and over. Or Prometheus having his liver pecked out by an eagle every day. Destined to relive the same hellish fate time after time.

*"Let it go,"* his superiors, the Archangels, had told him dozens of times.

Somehow, he could not.

*Not everyone dies young,* he thought, pacing around the apartment.

He did what he always did when he caught himself trapped in his own self-pity. Struck a match and lit one of the candles on his coffee table. Arielle, his former supervisor, had told him, *"Light a candle when you need help letting go of the resentment at having to leave your human life."*

Three thousand eight hundred and ninety-four candles later, Brandon was still waiting for the night his pain and resentment tapered out into wisps of smoke. Burned away like those many cylinders of wax.

On his dining-room table, his cell phone vibrated, jarring his attention away from the yellow flame. It was a message from Michael, the patron saint of cops and warriors himself. From the Archangel who was now his direct boss. The words he read on the phone's screen made him frown.

You have a new assignment. Return to your unit head-quarters immediately. Assemble your unit and con-tact Arielle.

Brandon pinched out the flame of the candle with his bare fingers. Then he headed out the door.

Heaven had called.

# Chapter Two

*If humans knew the extent of the unseen elements at work in the world, it would probably drive most people bat-shit crazy.*

Behind the wheel of his self-modified Dodge Challenger, Brandon sped through the empty streets of downtown Chicago, blaring the stereo so loud he could feel the guitar riffs buzzing in his bone marrow. He made the fifteen-minute drive to his destination in ten.

Punching his code into the electronic security system, he entered the mirrored-glass office tower. Took the elevator up to the forty-seventh floor. The office might have been just another upscale business—a law office or a consulting firm.

Instead, it housed the city's unit of the Company of Angels.

He unlocked the massive glass front doors, slid them open, flipped on the lights. One by one, the other Guardians began to trickle in. Every seat around the circular boardroom table was filled, all thirty angels assembled. Brandon clicked on the plasma video screen to start the three-way conference call with Michael and Arielle, along with the thirty angels in the L.A. unit.

"Guardians, a very serious situation has developed," Michael said.

The Archangel's image appeared on one-third of the screen, his luminous wings spread behind him, iridescent and beautiful. But the wrinkles in his face were deep set with worry. The words he spoke brought a hush over the two units of Guardians present. All pairs of jeweled eyes watched, riveted to the screens as Michael continued.

"Luciana Rossetti has escaped."

The name meant nothing to Brandon. One-third of the screen showed the L.A. unit, and on it, Arielle's face registered the smallest twinge. A tiny flicker of annoyance passed over her habitually neutral expression. In the ramshackle legal-aid clinic that served as the L.A. unit headquarters, she sat at the head of her boardroom table, her posture ramrod straight, her blond hair as perfectly coiffed as ever.

But she had definitely cringed. Brandon had seen it.

"Luciana is a Rogue demon," Michael said quietly. "As you all know, Rogue demons are not ordinarily at the top of the Company's priorities. They rank in the middle of the demon hierarchy. However, Luciana Rossetti is in possession of an extremely dangerous poison. A poison that could cause serious harm to every one of us."

There was a long, horrified pause before the angels began murmuring to each other.

Arielle spoke over them, her smile unnervingly calm. "With all due respect, I don't understand why the Chicago unit needs to be involved in this assignment."

Behind her, the thirty angels of the L.A. unit nodded, settling back into quiet.

Michael said, "Every city in the world has a unique unit of Guardians dedicated to protecting it. We all know that. But Brandon's approach is different. We

Archangels contacted Brandon because we thought the assignment could benefit from his particular approach."

*No hand-holding. No babysitting. No New Age bullshit.*

The total opposite of Arielle and her crew.

"The L.A. unit is totally capable of handling this assignment. Luciana Rossetti escaped on my watch," Arielle said in that infuriatingly neutral tone of hers, which he had endured for three years under her supervision. "The L.A. unit has this covered."

"What's your plan?" Brandon said tersely. "Are you going to hold a yoga class and hope the target shows up? Break out the acoustic guitar, start singing a round of 'Kumbaya' and pass a communal joint?"

Behind Brandon, some of the angels in the Chicago unit snickered.

"Stop," ordered Michael. "I didn't call you in to start an argument."

"Does Brandon even know who Luciana Rossetti is?" Arielle said to Michael. "He doesn't even know who we're talking about."

"Then we'll show him," said Michael.

On the video screen, a full-color image of the demoness appeared, a grainy image, captured from afar. Whoever had snapped the picture had caught the target in a bad moment. Or perhaps she only had bad moments.

Yet, she was undeniably beautiful. In the photo, she was suspended in midturn, tendrils of dark hair whipping in the wind around a face whose full lips and haughty, defined cheekbones could have graced the cover of *Vogue Italia*. But what caught Brandon, what made him literally stop and stare, was her glittering green eyes, so vibrant and snapping with life that they seemed to leap off the screen.

A shiver ran through him.

In both boardrooms, there was a pause and a hush as the angels looked at her picture. Behind Brandon, one of the male Guardians let out a low whistle.

"Enough," Brandon said, cutting off the inappropriate behavior by holding up his hand.

Michael switched the image back to the live video stream.

"Luciana Rossetti," Michael said, "is no ordinary demoness. She's fiercely independent and fiendishly clever, like all Rogues. But she is much more than that. She is a poisoner par excellence and a Mata Hari of the demon world. She escaped from the Company a few days ago. She's dangerous in her own right, but she has risen to the top of the Company's Most Wanted List because she has created a poison with which she killed another demon."

*If it can kill a demon...*

*It can kill an angel.*

Every angel in both Los Angeles and Chicago fell silent.

Michael continued, "We need to catch Luciana before she uses this poison again—on our kind. Or worse, before she manufactures another batch of it and distributes it among the demons. She has the ability to unleash a weapon of unparalleled power. It would give them an edge over us. An edge from which we might never recover."

Both units were still for a moment, as though the earth had stopped its rotation and for a brief moment the world seemed to come to a halt. Every one of the angels was thinking the same thing, Brandon was certain.

*If that poison got into the wrong hands, it could mean the end of our kind.*

"Furthermore, we have also received word that Archdemon Corbin Ranulfson is planning to retaliate," Michael continued. "Some of you may not know, but Corbin was recently defeated by the Company and lost his empire's flagship hotel. If Corbin strikes at us, he will strike to destroy. He is one of the most powerful demons in America. We believe that he was weakened in the last attack, but may be seeking to recover some of his lost powers. Three days ago, Corbin was sighted in hell, but word on the street is that he has been seen again, on the surface. We have every reason to believe that Corbin will search out Luciana. For the poison."

"Is he connected with her?" Brandon asked.

"She's his lover," said Michael. "Luciana is our only link to Corbin. And we believe she has returned to Venice. We must bring her back to America."

"We've got to find out what she's done with the poison," Arielle said, "and pump her for whatever information is inside that evil head of hers. I think this is a case for disposal."

*Disposal.*

The word sent another hush through the conference rooms.

"*Disposal is the term we sometimes use in the Company when an individual is to be returned to the divine,*" Arielle had told Brandon, back when he was a fledgling angel, training under her. "*Technically, the soul never dies. Energy is neither created nor destroyed. But a disposal means that a person no longer has a distinct identity.*"

Luciana would cease to exist.

As a rule, Brandon didn't agree with disposal. Normally, Arielle didn't, either. If she was so set on disposal in this case, he wanted to know why. But there was no time for that right now. First, he needed to catch the demoness and bring her back to America.

"Michael, please email me the rest of the file via secure transfer," Brandon said. "I'll go to Venice myself. And I'll finish briefing myself on the plane."

"Why you?" Arielle ground out.

"I can get the job done," he said.

Not a single one among the sixty angels disagreed with him. He disliked being arrogant in any way. But time was of the essence, and in the past he had found that it paid to be up front with Arielle.

Michael nodded.

Arielle shook her head, clearly frustrated. "Fine, do it your way. Of course, you'll work with members of my team. We were the last ones who saw her, and—"

"I work alone," Brandon stated.

Every angel in the Chicago unit knew that.

"As a supervisor, I'm a leader and a team player," Brandon explained. "I foster an environment of trust, so much so that my unit virtually runs itself. There is rarely dissent among my team. We all consider ourselves equals. I'm available for mentoring when the younger angels need guidance. I manage, but I don't micromanage." He paused, cleared his throat. "But in the field, it's a different story."

When Brandon Clarkson worked, he was a lone wolf.

He went undercover alone, and he never took anyone with him. After the trauma of his human death, he would not put another angel at risk the way he risked himself. He would never allow anyone to suffer as he had suffered.

"I'm going in alone," he said.

Arielle blinked rapidly, her mouth pressing into a line so flat it almost disappeared. Then she said, "This matter is far too important. You'll need backup. Won't he, Michael?"

Brandon crossed his arms and stared at the video screen as intensely as he would have done if they were standing in the same room. "Arielle, if I have to clean up your mistakes, I'm doing it on my own terms."

"There are rules in the battle between angels and demons," Arielle shot back. "Rules that cannot be—"

"Broken?" Brandon finished. "My ass. Rules are made to be broken."

"Stop!" Michael ordered. "The Company must remain strong. There is no point in bickering amongst ourselves."

"At least call Infusino, our contact in the Venetian unit," said Arielle. "He can help."

"I don't need help," Brandon said. "I will handle this alone."

Arielle's eyes flickered with determination, and he knew she was about to launch into an extended rebuttal. He had been the victim of Arielle's long-winded speeches in the past. He wasn't going to sit through another one tonight.

He cut her off at the pass, pushing the button to cut off video feed from the L.A. unit.

One-third of the screen went black. He shouted into the speaker, "Sorry, Arielle. Technical glitch. Michael, I'll talk to you when I'm back on American soil."

"Wait," said a male voice Brandon did not recognize. "I'm Julian Ascher, the newest member of the L.A. unit."

Around the table of the Chicago unit, the Guardians looked at each other with raised eyebrows. Julian Ascher, former Archdemon, had just been converted into the Company after almost two hundred and fifty years. He had been brought in by one of Arielle's underlings, a neophyte angel whose innocence and naïveté were unmatched in the Company. Not everyone had agreed with Arielle's tactics, and her scheme had been the subject of debate within the Company lately.

*Don't judge,* Brandon reminded himself. *It's not your job to judge.*

"Just listen for a second," Julian said. "Although I'm not proud of it, I was once Luciana Rossetti's lover. I have certain information about her that will help you track her down."

"Let's hear it," said Brandon, listening.

"Luciana has a deal with the devil that keeps her out of hell. Every year, she has to provide a human sacrifice to pacify the Prince of Darkness. She'll be at the Redentore Church tomorrow night, at seven o'clock in the evening. Without fail, she selects her victim from that church. You'll find her there. But be careful. Luciana is extremely skilled at using men to get what she wants. She will stop at nothing"

"Duly noted," Brandon said. "Thanks for the advice."

"Bring Luciana back as quickly as you can," said Michael. "And don't be afraid to call for backup if you need it."

"Good luck," said Arielle as coldly as the last time they'd spoken.

Brandon was intimately familiar with exactly how cold Arielle could be. But in any case, he had no time to worry about Arielle and her moods right now.

*Right now, I've got a job to do.*

To Luciana, walking into Ca' Rossetti was like walking into a jewel box.

In the high-ceilinged *piano nobile,* the main floor of

Ca' Rossetti, her staff of Gatekeepers scrambled to assemble to welcome the demoness home. The heels of her shoes clicked on the marble floor as she inspected the condition of the palazzo. Every surface sparkled, from the intricate mosaic floors to the Murano chandeliers. The walls were adorned with rich swathes of silk damask and lavish murals. Every square inch of floor, every gilded table, every lacquered cabinet and crystal vase, every cornice and curlicue was polished and shining.

"You've done your job well in my absence," she noted, casting a particular eye over the sprawling interior.

The Gatekeepers snapped into a neat row, identically clad in their working uniform: jeans and snug black T-shirts. Each taller, darker and more handsome than the last. There in the main hall, she nodded.

"Giancarlo, Antonio, Federico, Cesare, Salvatore, Massimo," she greeted them each as she inspected the line. "Thank you all. You may return to your duties, and I must return to mine. There is precious little time left today, as I must prepare for tonight's hunt."

She turned, ready to ascend the staircase to the second floor.

Just then, a female scream from the rear of the palazzo pierced the congenial atmosphere. The suffering in that sound was palpable; it was like an animal keening in pain. Luciana stopped. Her gaze tracked downward, to the bloody footprints glistening on the marble floor hidden behind one of the Gatekeepers. To the gray-skinned goblin the size of a small dog skittering along the edge of the wall, cackling to itself and dragging a woman's shoe. More blood seeped from the heel of that shoe, trailing a thin, scarlet line across the otherwise-immaculate floor.

Not a muscle twitched among her staff.

Not a single eye blinked.

They were hiding something. Or more precisely, some*one*.

Luciana maintained her smile.

"Whatever—or more precisely whomever—you've got back there," she said, waving a hand in the direction of the scream, "just make sure you clean up the mess. Now if you'll excuse me, I have work to do. Come, Massimo. I need you to unlock my workroom."

He dutifully followed along behind her as she mounted the stairway, the white marble overlaid with rich red carpet cushioning her footsteps.

"Did you happen to conclude your business with Julian Ascher while you were in America, *baronessa?*"

She closed her eyes briefly, fingertips skating along the carved stone balustrade of the curved staircase. The stairs teetered beneath her momentarily, the world tilting on its side. Every muscle in her body contracted. Her jaw tightened and her stomach threatened to expel the meal she'd just consumed.

"Don't speak that name in my presence again," she hissed, unable to contain her fury.

"Yes, of course, *baronessa.* I'm so sorry, I…"

She was held together so tightly it ached; she felt the pressure of her gritted teeth and wondered if they would break. Then she turned back to face Massimo and said, "If you must know, Julian has joined the angels."

"Do you mean he died?" Masssimo wondered.

"No," she said, pivoting to glare at him. She pressed her lips together for a long moment. "He was—" she paused before sneering out the word "—*redeemed* and joined the Company of Angels."

The Gatekeeper kept his own mouth shut, knowing better than to ask more questions.

She turned and continued up the stairs. Tried not to think about him, although that was impossible.

"Would you like to lie down for a few hours, *baronessa?* Perhaps you should rest."

She had work to do before tonight. She touched the little vial hanging around her neck.

"There's no rest for the wicked, Massimo."

All over Venice, people were preparing.

Luciana had her own preparations to make. Her own offering to procure. Her own homage to pay.

And it was not to the Redeemer.

On the third floor of Ca' Rossetti, Luciana strode the length of the hallway to a small room at the end.

Despite its size, it remained one of the demoness's favorite rooms.

The windows overlooked the Grand Canal, and the eastern sunlight poured in during the late mornings. Outside, passersby floated along the canal in gondolas and vaporetti, on transport barges and fishing boats, completely unaware of what went on within. What had been going on for centuries.

The fine art of poison.

"You've kept everything in the prescribed conditions, as I instructed?" Luciana asked Massimo as he unlocked the workroom door.

"Yes, *baronessa*," the Gatekeeper nodded.

"Thank you, Massimo. You may return later."

"If it's all the same to you, *baronessa,* I'll stay to assist you."

She suspected he wanted to stay to keep an eye on her, but after her ordeal, she needed solitude to clear her head. To think. "I'm *fine*. I'll call for you if I need assistance."

She gestured for him to leave with a wave of her hand.

He hesitated, but bowed a little and retreated.

She cast an eye around the tidy little room. Yes, the Gatekeepers had done their job maintaining her work space. Dried flowers and plants, belladonna flowers and narcissus bulbs hung from a ceiling rack, awaiting her return. A glass flask and burner set up for distillation stood on one side of the worktable. On the other side was a carefully organized and labeled stand of bottles and vials: *scorpion, tarantula, black-widow spider.*

*"Buongiorno, bambini,"* she called, bending down to peer into a sectioned glass terrarium, where a pair of green mambas slithered. Two pairs of beady green eyes fixed on their mistress, forked tongues darting out in greeting.

Among other toxins, the mambas' venom had contributed to the contents of the tiny glass vial around her neck. The liquid in this little vial had taken her months to distill, the rarest of poisons in a perfect combination that had already proven it could kill a demon. Its first victim, a low-ranking demon who had worked as a bell-boy in Las Vegas, had gone down quite nicely.

The contents of this vial, administered to a human victim, would quite literally be overkill. Unclasping the chain from her neck, she transferred the vial of poison into the hollowed-out bottom of a gold lipstick tube, which she slipped into her pocket.

That poison must be saved for another purpose.

A purpose that would make everything worthwhile in the end. All the hard work and suffering. All the humiliation, the pain she had endured. All the risks she had taken, the waiting games she had played.

Her enemies, old and new, would perish screaming her name.

Her name would echo in their minds as they burned in the depths of hell forever.

"Soon," she cooed to the snakes, "but not tonight."

She prided herself in choosing precisely the correct poison for every occasion, and distilled them herself. Through poison, one could achieve results that could not be accomplished through other means. The legacy of poison in Italy's noble houses—the Borgias, the Medici family—was almost an art, too valuable to ignore.

She perused her choices amongst the rows of bottles and vials.

*White arsenic.* The poison of choice for the Borgias. Too slow acting. She would need something faster tonight.

*Hemlock.* The poison that had killed Socrates. But it was positively antiquated.

*Strychnine.* Entirely too melodramatic. It caused a good deal of unnecessary thrashing and convulsing. Sometimes she enjoyed that, but she could do with something a little simpler for this evening's purposes.

Luciana picked up a clear bottle of liquid, held it up to the light.

*Cyanide.*

*Perfetto.* The perfect poison for the occasion. Clean, effective and incredibly fast acting. Timeless and classic, the Chanel perfume of poisons.

She decanted a small amount of the cyanide into a second glass vial. *And just like perfume,* she thought as she strung the second vial on the gold chain around her neck, *a little goes a long way.*

* * *

Brandon watched the lights of Chicago recede beneath him as the 747 lifted off from the ground, several hundred tons of metal, passengers and cargo rising into the air.

*Every act of flight requires a leap of faith,* he knew.

A bird, every time it flies, must leap. Must commit itself to the air and trust that its wings will carry it aloft. The same with a plane, barreling along the runway to launch itself airborne. And just like flying, every mission required a leap of faith.

*Leap, and have faith that the divine will guide you where you need to go.*

He had been operating along that principle for the duration of his existence.

And now, as he sat in his seat with the big plane shaking beneath him, the familiar anxiety niggled in the back of his mind. Fear of falling asleep. He reviled sleeping in public places, in the open where his inevitable nightmare might leave him vulnerable to prying eyes.

Still, he had no choice.

When the plane reached cruising altitude, he perused Luciana's file on his laptop, browsing through the documents relating to her case.

Now Brandon studied the series of low-resolution photographs. He found himself staring at her pale skin and vivid green eyes, mesmerized by the beauty of her face despite the expression of displeasure she consistently wore.

*"Beauty can be deceptive."* That was one of the first lessons Brandon had ever learned as an angel. Arielle had taught it to him. Despite her continual annoyance with him...despite his disagreement with her manage-

ment style…at the heart of it, Arielle knew what she was doing. She had told him, *"Don't equate beauty with goodness, even though it may seem angelic. Demons can also take the form of beauty. They like to mimic the divine. And demons are drawn to beauty. They love to defile it."*

Luciana was no ordinary beauty. She was exceptional. And apparently, she also loved to destroy exceptional beauty.

According to the file, her human life had been remarkably sad, scarred by family tragedies and betrayal. But reading through her lengthy history of misfortune, he felt nothing but disgust for her. She had been plagued by hardship, yes. But the choices she had made had been consistently bad. Tracing the steps of her biography, the more he read, the more horrified he became by the details of her grisly sacrifices, overwhelmed by the catalog of atrocities. He skimmed through a note in the file, marked History of the Redentore Festival:

Venice suffered from a devastating outbreak of the plague between 1575 and 1577, which killed more than one-third of the population. The Chiesa del Santissimo Redentore, or Church of the Most Holy Redeemer, was erected as an offering to the divine and a plea for liberation from the deadly disease.

On the third weekend in July, Venetians celebrate the Redentore Festival to commemorate the disappearance of the plague. A temporary bridge is erected on floating pontoons, leading from the main part of Venice to the Island of Giudecca, where the Redentore Church is located.

Every year, as Julian Ascher explained, Luciana chose to kill a victim at this festival.

*Why* she did that, Julian had not explained.

There must be a reason.

Brandon leafed through her file, looking for an answer. But if there was an answer, it didn't lie within the folder he had received.

He himself had faced difficult choices in life. However, at every turn, he had consistently made decisions driven by the desire to benefit humankind. Motivated by altruism. Geared toward forgiveness. Anything else lay beyond his realm of comprehension.

*"At their core, demons are just like us,"* Arielle had insisted, back when she had been his supervisor. *"They're just passionate beings who have made a big mistake. They don't recognize that their true nature is divine. It is our job to teach them that. To bring them back into the light."*

Not all of them wanted to come into the light. Not all of them were ready. Looking at Luciana's pictures, he was pretty sure this demoness was comfortable exactly as she was. Firmly ensconced in the dark, taking full advantage of all its powers and privileges.

With the file in his lap, he shut his eyes for a brief moment.

*And he stepped into the too-familiar landscape of his usual nightmare.*

*The same full moon illuminating the sky. The same cool evening breeze.*

*The same smell of urine and rotting garbage, the same dark alley.*

*And, yet, when he turned the corner to enter the alleyway, it wasn't the place of his death that he entered. Instead, he walked into an empty space, devoid of any-*

*thing, like an empty theater stage used in a minimalist production. No props, only a bare black wooden floor.*

*Into this blank space, the demoness emerged out of the darkness.*

*A wraith forming out of mist, she then solidified into a more concrete figure that seemed to Brandon utterly hypnotic. Out of thin air, her tall, slender body materialized with its impossibly lush curves. Skin so pale and so perfect he itched to reach his hand out and test the velvet texture of it beneath his fingertips, to hold the flawless curve of her cheek in his hand.*

*From the grainy photos, she stepped into living flesh, incarnated so vividly that he had no doubt that she was real. In an instant, he forgot completely that he had ever felt disgust for her. Looking at her, the sole emotion rushing into his brain, flooding into every part of his body, was desire.*

God in heaven.

"You're not real," he said, reaching for her. His fingers, roughened from his weekend mechanic tinkering, accustomed to the unforgiving motor parts of metal and rubber, caught on the silk of her dress. He reached out toward the fine porcelain of her skin to touch her face. Yet, he could not reach her. "You can't be real."

*So exotic. So beautiful. And, as she was in the photos, so incredibly unhappy.*

"You have no idea what you're doing," she said in a siren's voice, honey-soft and lilting with a Mediterranean rhythm. The rich and heavy vowels called to him despite the clear disdain of her message. "If you know what's best for you, you'll turn back now."

She vanished.

Left in the emptiness by himself, Brandon had no sense of space, no idea where to go. Intuitively, he knew *that if he stepped forward, he would walk back into the unavoidable dreamspace of his human death. But he had no choice. There was nowhere else to go. So he walked forward, felt his body shift into another place, enclosed by brick walls, suffused with the too-familiar scent of urine and garbage. He turned the corner. Into the same alley.*

*The first bullet exploded in the back of his spine.*

*The second, into the back of his head.*

He awoke, as he always did. In a cold sweat, feeling incredibly sad that he had died.

But there was something unusually disturbing about this dream.

Even more distressing than his usual nightmare was the fact that the dream had *changed.*

He had never seen that bare black space. Had never seen a woman in his dream.

"Heated hand towel, sir?" The flight attendant's normal, human voice jarred him fully into the waking world. He took the towel, wiped the sheen of sweat from his face.

Reminded himself again where he was.

*Not in a filthy alleyway in Detroit.*

On a plane, flying over the Atlantic, toward Italy.

To catch a demoness.

To find a woman he had not even met, who had already begun to invade his dreams.

Luciana looked up from her worktable, jolted out of her reverie. Her mind reached for the memory of the man she had envisioned, but his image faded too quickly to grasp.

A rumble, a disturbance blurred the air unlike anything she had ever felt before. She shivered.

On the edge of the table, just beside her hand, lay a feather.

She picked it up, examining it.

Dark gray at the tip, fading to dirty white at the bottom of the shaft. An ordinary feather, the kind pigeons left all over the city. Due to the city's recent measures to cull the population of winged rats, the flying nuisances infested Venice in fewer numbers than before. However, plenty of them remained.

Where this particular feather had come from was a mystery to her.

The window was closed, and the workroom remained sealed.

*How very curious,* she thought. *But no matter.*

Taking the feather between her thumb and forefinger, she tossed it in the garbage. Along with the vague feeling that it might be connected with the man in her dream.

*Who cares,* she thought. How many thousands of men's dreams had she invaded in the past? She did not even know. She was a virtuoso at this type of manipulation. An expert at navigating their desires. One more man would be as easy to discard as the rest of them.

She went downstairs to find her head Gatekeeper.

"Prepare the boat," she told him. "It is time to begin the hunt."

As the boat cleaved its way up the Grand Canal and out into St. Mark's Basin, the salt-tinged breeze off the Adriatic whipped through Luciana's hair. She closed her eyes, and the image of that single feather floated in her mind's eye again.

"Just there," she said to Massimo, pointing to a mooring post near the church.

She stepped up to the *fondamenta* beside the canal,

tilting her head to look up at the imposing marble facade of the church, at the monumental classical Roman pillars combined with the round lines of a Christian cathedral. People filed through the large open doors. Inside, hundreds of humans were gathering for the opening ceremony of the festival.

Eyeing the crowd funneling into the church, she wished she could cull the whole lot of them. Just get rid of them, like the city had done with the pigeons. Instead, she would have to choose just one, a single victim. It should not be a problem. These witless humans never seemed to suspect what was coming for them.

"Wait here for me," she instructed Massimo. "This shouldn't take long."

## Chapter Three

Brandon felt his lost humanity weighing on him as he entered the place he knew he would find her. Looking up at the marble facade of the Chiesa del Santissimo Redentore, he scanned the huge white building, looked at the figures decorating it.

*Why here, of all the sacred places in Venice?*

*Why not St. Mark's, the massive basilica across the canal?*

*Why not Carnival, the most famous of Venice's festivals?*

The questions flickered in his mind as he walked through the open doors and into the church. Inside, he slipped quietly into the back, blending into the congregation of humans come to pay homage to their God. Humans who brought their hopes, their fears, their dreams to this place of worship. His heart ached for them, for the suffering that humankind underwent.

No, he himself was no longer human.

The faint scent of incense drifted from the priest's censer, chants in Latin drifting with it: *et ideo cum Angelis et omnibus Sanctis gloriam tuam praedicamus...* The vague meaning of the phrase echoed in his mind despite the foreignness of the words.... Something about saints and angels, and the glory of the divine.

As he stood there in the church, images from his most recent dream drifted into his head. Images of her face, her body, her voice. And his body reacted, sensing her nearness. But he knew that he must fight against the failings, the desires, the weaknesses of the physical body.

*She is here.*

He heard the commotion when it began, the shouts of *"Demonessa!"* He saw the man drag his elderly mother out of the church. In the resulting scuffle, Brandon sneaked up the side of the congregation, moving toward the source of the conflict.

And he became all too conscious of his human desires.

He was still close enough to his lost humanity that he could not control the twitch of his cock in the moment he first saw her.

Dark hair tumbled down her back in a loose fall of curls. Green eyes the color of pale emeralds, of new grass, of springtime. Skin so fair it was almost translucent, glowing in the fading daylight that spilled into the chapel. She smiled, shrugging a little in innocence, appeasing those around her.

Brandon stood watching, transfixed.

When the ceremony ended, the church emptied, the congregation filing down the long nave and out the massive doors.

Luciana remained. She knelt in one of the side chapels, pretending to be praying, her head bowed in a graceful imitation of reverence, the last rays of sunlight swathing her lush body. If she was truly absorbed in prayer, she was issuing a request for help from the *other* side.

Murderer. Poisoner. Thief. Whore.

Too beautiful. Too evil. And entirely too easy to find.

*Beauty can be evil.* He knew that much. *But not beauty like this...*

Once this evening, she had already been named for what she was. By an old woman near the threshold between life and death, who everyone assumed was completely insane. That was the only other person in the building who saw the truth about Luciana. Who knew that she was not merely an innocent woman, not a pious beauty who had come to pay homage to the divine.

He neared, ready to approach her. He reminded himself why he was here. What he had been *sent* here to do. To find her. To capture her. To take her back with him. Back to America. Back to the Company of Angels.

Then he looked into those absinthe eyes of hers.

And felt himself falling.

The sensation reminded him of dying—not the painful part of passing over, but the feeling of elation. The bliss of rising up into a curtain of pure light, spiraling into a feeling of absolute peace. He had never experienced it while embodied in a physical form before. But here he was, in the midst of this church, with the crowd of festive Venetians and tourists still dispersing. He felt as though he might have been alone with her. He felt tremendous compassion for her, almost as if his heart were about to burst open. As if he could absorb all of her sorrows from that one glance.

For she was full of suffering, although she bore it behind a veil of pride and a noble bearing. Yet, there it was, an unfathomable sadness that made him yearn to fold her in his arms and wrap her in pure joy.

More sorrowful than the Pietà.

Full of grace, more than a demon should ever be.

And then she saw him, and her entire countenance changed.

He had never known that the color of fury was green, but looking into those eyes, at that moment, he was sure of it.

*The hottest fires of hell must be green.*

It chilled him for a moment, the depth of what he saw in those eyes. The lightning-fast change of emotions flashing in those verdant depths, a chameleon change so quick that it seemed he was looking at a different woman entirely.

Not an innocent and pious beauty.

But a dangerous and malevolent killer.

Which, in fact, she was.

Around them, in the silence, rose an unspoken challenge, a whisper so loud it seemed to ricochet off the walls of the church, louder than the wings of the birds that circled overhead.

*Nothing is sacred. If you want me, come and get me.*

She stood, pivoted her tall, slender body in a graceful turn. The rose-colored silk of her dress fluttered behind her. He knew he had no choice but to follow. It was a compulsion that was partly born from his duty to the Company. Partly born from the importance of the mission on which he had been sent. And partly to do with raw desire.

His silent words of prayer ascended to the dome of the church, to meet the last burst of sunlight pouring down through the apertures above.

*Give me the strength to accomplish what I need to do.*

In the same instant, the thought that ran through Luciana's mind mirrored Brandon's prayer exactly.

The demoness's prayer, however, was headed in the opposite direction.

Beneath the noise of the pigeons, angel and demoness circled each other, their steps striking on the marble floor. Pivoting in sync as if partners in a choreographed dance, the energy of their bodies was as palpable as a magnetic force. Opposite poles ruled by an invisible current, as highly charged as electricity.

The message, one to the other, was a challenge issued as plainly as a slap in the face: *game on.*

Physically, there was no question who would win.

He was well over six feet tall and all hard, lean muscle. In the set of his body, she read the movements of a warrior.

Yet size was not the primary concern when it came to her hunting skills. She had taken down bigger prey before. Brigadiers, marshals, generals, admirals. Career soldiers often had the most vulnerable spots, if you knew where to push. Oh, there was so much more at play than mere physical strength.

Luciana was an expert at seduction. She had other weapons at her disposal, but temptation was her weapon of choice. Centuries ago, she had mastered the one rule that all great seductresses, from Mata Hari to Madame de Pompadour, from Marlene Dietrich to Madonna, all knew. *To truly seduce a man, you can't just grab him by the* cazzo…*the cock… You've got to get inside his head.*

The demoness scanned her opponent, assessing. The energy radiating from him was raw and full of exuberance, but it was young energy that pulsed in the space between them. But there was more than that.

*Power.*

That was what made her pause.

Power emanated from him, like the subtle presence

of pheromones, intangible but sure, rising almost as visibly as the early morning mists that hung above the lagoon. It was there, innate in his stride. Built into his stance. It had nothing to do with wealth or materiality, and everything to do with attitude. A man could be as poor as a dirt farmer, yet still have power if he was his own man.

Yes, *power.*

Wherever he came from, whoever had sent him, this man had it. But his power lay beyond mere physical strength. There was a keen intellect behind his tough facade, those gray eyes sharp with latent intelligence. But not with experience.

In human years, he might have been in his late twenties.

In the ways that counted, he was a mere infant.

"Barely a decade past your human expiration date, I'd guess," she said.

She took a step sideways. Across from her, he mirrored the movement.

*Are you alone, or are there others?* she wondered.

She goaded him a little, prompting, "You're what they sent after me? Disappointing. Where's the rest of your Company of Assholes?"

He didn't react, pacing toward her. Didn't need to say anything—his face said it all. *Do you really think I'd need help?*

"Are you mute on top of it?" She laughed. "How sad."

"I came to collect you, that's all," he said, a low growl, the intense focus of his gray eyes as cool and flat as the surface of a rainwater pool.

"American!" she said, barely bothering to feign surprise. "You must be one of Arielle's."

"I *am* American. But I don't answer to Arielle," he said.

*Ah, there it is,* she thought. The edge to his equanimity, the tiny flint of an angry spark in the flatness of his rain-gray eyes. The trick was to feed that spark, to fan it into something that would *burn.*

"Haven't you ever heard of asylum?" she said, keeping her own voice as even as she could, although she could hear the tremor in it, a snag in its usual velvet. "You can't arrest me in the house of God."

His answer was immediate and unflinching. "The doctrine of asylum arose in England, and it was never widely used in Italy. It certainly hasn't applied to major crimes for centuries. Quit stalling. You can't talk yourself out of this."

He took a step toward her, clearly expecting her to back away.

Instead, she drew up and took a step toward him, holding herself straight, looking him straight in the eyes.

"Perhaps I've come here to repent my sins," she taunted. She licked her lips, looking him up and down. "If only I could find someone who would hear my prayer."

"Unlikely."

"How can you be so sure?" she whispered.

She was so close she could see clouds gathering in his eyes. She imagined that she smelled rain in the middle of a summer so flawless that not a drop of precipitation had fallen in forty consecutive days. She felt the sensation of a coming storm so tangibly that she shivered.

In the distance, thunder rumbled.

He reached for her.

What grazed her wrist wasn't his fingers, but steel. The rounded edge of a handcuff.

She snatched her hand away with a millisecond between herself and captivity.

The coldness of it shocked her. Not again. Never again.

In that sliver of time, she fled down the nave of the church and slipped out the door. Weaving through the crowd of humans, Luciana realized she had made a mistake in thinking she was a match for this man. For when she came out of the church, she saw something totally unexpected.

Massimo was not there waiting for her, as he should have been.

Her boat sat empty, tethered at the edge of the *fondamenta,* bobbing in the canal.

She glanced behind her.

The big angel came barreling out of the church, bearing toward her like a freight train. His face was contracted not with anger, but with absolute focus. Sheer determination.

The look of a man who would not let anything stand in his way.

The ground shook as he thundered down the stairs toward her, a minor earthquake shaking the pavement beneath them. For a moment, she thought she might have imagined it, but the humans felt it, too, scattering in every direction and grabbing for the security of anything stationary: railings, statues, each other.

Luciana looked around, but could not find a solid object to hold on to. So she did the next best thing.

She ran.

Damn, she was fast. Faster than Brandon had anticipated.

The Gatekeeper in the boat had not been such a problem at all. Although he was a big man, he was slow and easy to ditch. And likely still swimming his way back from the middle of the Adriatic where Brandon had dropped him.

Luciana herself was a different story entirely.

She glanced at him, looked at her empty boat, and in a quick shimmer of movement, she was gone.

No time at all was how long it took the demoness to disappear into the crowd. Dissolving into the fading sunlight. Outside, in the golden light of early evening, Venetian families gathered in throngs. Picnic feasts spread on white-clothed tables lined the walkways beside the canal. More revelers flooded back across the pontoon bridge toward the main part of Venice.

Amidst the rush of the celebrations, Brandon stood still.

Closed his eyes, willed himself into quietness.

Asked for guidance in order to track her.

*I must find her. Must not let her escape.*

He felt the movement of her dark vibration, deep in his bones, slightly to the west of himself. When he opened his eyes, he spotted her turned face in the distance, dark hair streaming in the wind as she crossed the pedestrian bridge.

Without hesitation, he took off after her.

She moved much faster than any human, slipping easily among the crowd with the lightness that might have belonged to a ghost. But she had a body. He was sure of that. Without even touching her, he had felt the pull of that body back there in the church, remembered the feel of her almost as if he had held her. Trailing her at a distance, fifty feet back, he could detect the dark energy of her, the density of her physical incarnation.

She glanced back, searching for him, undoubtedly

sensing him following. He ducked behind a pillar, waiting until he felt her attention pass over him. After a long pause, she moved onward, farther into the city.

Luciana crossed the square in front of the basilica of St. Mark's in a blink of an eye, moving rapidly through the dense gathering of tourists who stood gazing up at the famous domes. She wove into the streets behind the church, farther into the tangle of passageways that might as well have been another universe.

Everywhere he turned, eroding stone angels and crumbling saints looked down. With their peeling gilt wings and chipped halos, they seemed to cheer him on, lending him strength as he pursued the fleeing demoness.

How long she ran, he wasn't sure.

The sun disappeared, tucked into the sea as night settled over the celebrating city. Brandon lost track of time as she twisted and turned through the streets. He followed, focused only on her. On keeping the flicker of her hair, of her dress, in sight.

On the dark pull of her, urging him onward.

Turning the corner, he nearly lost her, the only clue to her a tiny corner of silk rippling, leaving empty air behind it.

He pursued.

Above, he read the street name stenciled in black on the cracked white cornerstone on the nearest building.

Rio Tera dei Assassini.

He stepped into it. And felt himself stepping into another realm.

From doorways and cornices, tucked into the designs on the buildings, eyes watched. Dozens of eyes, glistening in the darkness. Lingering figures turned to stare. Not human. Not mortal. Not even demon. Merely goblins, skittering along like oversize rats, cackling to themselves, their wizened skins the color of dirty stone. And ghosts, flickering low in the dimness, their tenuous connection with the earth merely an imprint on the place where they had died. Lost souls, unable to leave the place of their death.

Nobody had to tell him that people had been murdered here, or how many. He knew it in his gut, from the part of him that remembered what it was like to die. He saw it in those eyes. Felt the chill of death that permeated the cobblestones beneath his feet. Sensed the memory of traumas held within these streets.

The dark souls who watched him now...not one of them even registered who or what he was. These creatures were simply too stuck in their own despair to register an angel in their midst. He saw that in the eyes glimmering in the darkness, glinting with moonlight and suffering.

*Keep moving, Guardian,* he told himself. *You can't lose her now.*

At the end of the alleyway, he spotted her dress again, a fleeting wisp of pink.

He followed, then paused at the mouth of an alleyway that led nowhere, a dead end that closed in on itself. He found himself standing in the light of a failing streetlamp, peering into the alley. Overhead, the view was obstructed by the buildings. He could not see the moon.

At the end of that small, enclosed space, he could hear her, the sound of her heart thundering, her fear louder and more palpable than his.

*Focus,* he told himself.

Dead ahead of him, he could sense her, the vibration of her body and the emanation of dark energy pulsing from her. Of fear. He leaned toward it, barreling down the straight alleyway into darkness.

The walls of the narrow buildings rose above him like a tall cage.

For a moment, the cobbled passageway seemed to tilt beneath his feet, the darkness of these alleys too similar to the scene of his human death. A second of vertigo, the sensation of tightness escalating as the space between the walls seemed to constrict, the smell of urine and garbage filling his nostrils.

His heart pounded from the physical exertion and from adrenaline.

Panic shot into his bloodstream, his heartbeat escalating to a thunder.

Venice was closing like a trap around him.

He closed his eyes.

*Venice,* he told himself. *Not Detroit.*

She turned then.

In his dream of death, there was no woman.

*Not a dream. Reality.*

She ran up a small flight of stairs leading to a weathered old door, the skirt of her rose silk dress fluttering. And he followed.


Luciana's heart pounded and her feet screamed. How long had she been running?

*An hour? More?*

The angel tracked her through the maze of streets. Streets so familiar she could have navigated them with her eyes closed, drawn to her destination by the invisible pull of memory. Yet, never had she fled down these streets with such fear in her heart, pounding at every turn. Into the Street of Assassins. Into the one place in

Venice where there would be others of her kind. Where she had the greatest chance of finding help.

Behind her, a gale force gathered and drew her backward, like a tornado threatening to uproot a tree. Resisting that force, Luciana reached for the old brass doorknob in front of her. She stretched, her fingertips grazing the cool metal.

Now, pulled by that unseen power, she turned to look back at the angel who had followed her into the heart of demon territory.

Light radiated from his body, illuminating the alleyway. Around him, an aura glowed unlike any she had seen before. She winced in the brightness of it, raising her arm to cover her eyes.

Turning to look back had been a mistake.

A last burst of energy pulsed from him. She felt herself propelled backward toward him.

She made one last, desperate grab for the doorknob. This time, she closed her fingers around it. Twisted with every ounce of energy she had left in her. Yanked the door open.

Stumbling into the shop, she looked for cover.

Because she knew she only had moments before that force came in behind her.

Relentless. Unstoppable. And about as easy to hide from as a heat-seeking missile.

The shop the demoness had entered was a glass studio.

Lit by halogen lights, the window display illuminated the dark street. The colors of goblets and wine decanters, of ornaments and jewelry sparkled in the night.

He pulled open the door and followed.

Inside the dark gallery, shelves of more glassware sat

in tranquility, moonlight from the front windows and the lit shop display spilling into the store. In the quiet space, not a soul moved.

*Where the hell is she?*

He stood, listening. Waiting.

Edged deeper into the shop. His hand went automatically to the holster he no longer carried, touched the empty spot and felt only a wave of utter nakedness without a firearm.

And then suddenly the air was full of flying glass. Objets d'art veered toward him in a spectrum of colors as the demoness began hurling items from the shelves. Broken shards rained down on him, their colors catching the moonlight in the seconds before he closed his eyes. He covered his face with his arms, boxer-style. Felt the first impact of glass against his skin, sharp edges slicing into his forearms as it shattered.

The pain bit into his body. He kept moving through it. Toward it.

Knowing he must push through this temporary torture to stop her.

Forward, blindly stumbling. Beneath his shoes, the crunch of glass. Around him, the sound of smashing. He felt the blood dripping down his arms, the pain radiating from the shards slicing into his flesh.

Then all motion stopped.

Silence. Stillness.

Around the shield of his own forearms, he hazarded a glance.

There she was, backed into a corner. The shelves around her, empty. Eyes wild and gleaming, she fixed her gaze on him. Even in that moment of rage, he saw beneath it to her fear. She was like a cornered animal, defending herself.

So dangerous, but so very vulnerable.

She picked up the last object near her. She rushed at him then, her hand raised. In it, a long, thin silver blade glinted in the moonlight.

A glass-handled knife, the kind you might use for cutting bread.

She lunged forward with it. She missed, but the knife's teeth slashed menacingly close to his skin. She made another pass. This time, he felt the serrated blade bite into his abdomen, slicing through his shirt, through a layer of skin to the muscle beneath.

He grabbed past the knife, catching her wrist.

Squeezed until she gasped and released the blade.

With his other hand, he went for the pressure point at the side of her throat. Jammed two fingers into it. With the momentum of her own attack, he swung her body past him. Took her down cleanly in one broad sweep, as though they were partners in a dance, a tango dip. He held her suspended a foot above the floor.

Poised above the broken glass.

"If you're nice, we can do this easily," he said.

"Nice girls finish last," she said. "You have no idea who you're messing with, but you're about to find out. I'm going to send you straight to hell," she hissed. Hauling in a breath, she screamed, "*Diavolo!* Prince of Darkness, aid me now!"

There was an eerie silence into which Brandon smiled, looking down at her.

"I guess he's not coming," he said.

He felt the hard jab of her knee connect with his groin. Pain seared through him.

He dropped her.

She cried out as she hit the floor, the broken shards grinding into her back. Her hair spread on the floor, a dark halo around her, mixed with shards of glass catching the moonlight. Her eyes, bright and deadly, glittered like the glass scattered around her. A thousand times more mesmerizing.

Glaring up at him, she gasped, wincing from the pain. "Who the hell are you?"

"Nobody," he said.

"Tell me your name. You owe me that, at least."

"Brandon Clarkson."

"Well, Brandon," she said. "You may have won this round, but I warn you that the fight is far from over."

Her curves were distracting. Her sensuality, lethal.

*Do your job, Guardian,* he told himself.

He hauled her to standing. The back of her dress was shredded from the broken glass. His arms, too, were bloodied from their fight. Still, she struggled.

From his back pocket, he produced the handcuffs. Snapped them on her wrists.

The hiss she let out was like the sound of a cat being skinned alive.

He patted down her clothing, searching for concealed weapons. Slipped his hand into her pocket. Took out a credit card and a tube of lipstick, looked quickly at both and put them back. Ran his hands up her legs, under her dress. Tried to ignore what he felt there.

"This is assault," she said coolly. "I don't know who you are, but you are violating my rights."

"Human rights are reserved for human beings. You forfeited them when you ceased to be mortal."

He held the glass vial dangling between her breasts. Yanked. The gold chain broke. He shoved the object in his pocket.

He grabbed a silk shawl from a display stand at the front of the shop and wiped the blood from his forearms, then tossed it around her shoulders to hide the damage. Not that a human bystander's opinion mattered at this point. But still. A bloody shawl was better than her back, shredded to ribbons by the glass.

He tugged her along. "Come with me."

"Where are you taking me?"

"Somewhere you won't make more trouble."

Luciana realized she had made a grave error. Her hands bound in the darkness, he hauled her back down the Street of Assassins.

She could feel the blood dripping down her back.

Every soul stopped to look. Every motion in the street stilled. Not a single being moved, not a goblin or a ghost. They cowered in his presence. It was as if they believed he was too powerful to touch.

And then they swung back into action.

This man was no rookie. The energy pulsing from him made her weak, and it sent a signal to every soul on this street: *don't dare to cross me.* She reeled from that power, feeling her own energy sapped, draining away. She stumbled in the street as her heel caught a cobblestone, fell to her knees as the asshole angel dragged her along.

He looked down, merciless.

"You brought this on yourself," he said.

*"Stronzo di merda,"* she whispered, biting her lip against the pain. *I will not cry. I will not cry. "Brutto figlio di puttana bastardo."*

"What?"

"'Ugly bastard son of a whore'—"

"I get the drift," he said. "Next time I won't bother asking for a translation."

"I am a baroness and a noble daughter of Venice. Do you have any idea who I am?"

He knelt, brushed her hair back, his hand wet with blood, hers or his, it no longer mattered. In her ear he whispered, "I know exactly who you are. And I know exactly what you've done."

A wave of shame washed over her; shame like nausea, rocking her to the core.

Or was it the pain from the glass embedded in her back? She could no longer tell.

He hoisted her up, heaved her over his shoulder like a laborer hauling a beam of wood in the Arsenale. Her body screamed. She didn't have the energy to fight anymore.

He spoke her thoughts aloud. "You can scream all you want. The creatures here won't help you. They're too chickenshit. Any human would be completely ineffectual. Nobody here can do anything for you."

He was right.

Not because anyone or any*thing* here knew who or what he was.

Simply because they could sense his power.

She would have to think of a way out of this herself.

She would get herself out of this situation.

Just as she had always gotten herself out of every situation in the past.

*And once I have, I will make him pay.*

## Chapter Four

When he set her on her feet again, they were standing in front of a shabby pensione. Luciana looked up at the weathered awning, and then her eye caught the relief carved into the stone on the wall beside the door.

San Giorgio slaying his dragon.

*Just another martyr in this city carved full of them,* she thought viciously.

According to legend, Saint George had killed the dragon that would have devoured a village. All over Venice, there were statues and images of him. His was an image that the angels sometimes used to communicate with each other, marking doorways and buildings.

Here, she knew exactly what it meant.

The angel had brought her to the Company safe house.

Talk of this place had existed amongst the demons of Venice for centuries. Stories of a hideous old guesthouse with such a carving by the doorway—she'd heard them all, but had never seen it or known its location.

A laugh escaped her now as she looked at the crumbling figure. "That's how you see yourselves, isn't it? You Guardians think you're all dragon slayers. Kill the monster and save the village. I have news for you, *mio caro.* The world has changed. The village no longer wants to be saved," she told him. "The monster is too much fun to have around."

He said nothing, but hefted her over his shoulder again. From her upside-down position, she saw the faded carpet, the worn furnishings in the cramped foyer.

Brandon exchanged a few words with the concierge, took a key that was handed to him. From behind the simple counter, the man also passed him a duffel bag and a bottle of vodka.

Up the rickety elevator, into a hotel room.

He pushed her inside.

The room was shabby and spare, barely more than a backpackers' hostel. There was a narrow bed that would barely fit two people. A doorless space with a curtainless shower served as a bathroom. He dragged her over to the bed, unlocked one of her wrists—only to relock it so that she was secured to the cheap wrought-iron frame with her wrists bound together. Double-checking the cuffs, he ensured that her wrists had enough circulation. Then he stepped away, apparently satisfied.

He left her in this position, with her arms locked behind her, sitting at the top of the bed.

"It's no surprise that the Company of Amateurs would favor such a run-down dive of a *pensione*," she said. "There are palaces all over Venice. The streets are literally lined with palazzos. And this is the place you choose. Tell me, why do you angels always choose such dingy accommodations? You all seem to think there's something noble about living in poverty."

He eyed her up. "Deal with it, *principessa*."

She jerked so hard that the metal cuffs clanged against the gilded curlicue of the bedframe.

"Don't ever call me that again," she said. "You have no idea what you're playing with. You have no idea who I am. And whatever they told you, those angels of yours…whatever Julian Ascher told you is a pack of lies."

"Whatever."

She said coyly, "Are you going to punish me?"

"It's not my job to punish you," he said evenly. "I told you in the church—I merely came to collect you."

"Too bad," she pouted. "You're missing all the fun."

He whipped the shawl off her back.

She flinched, but willed herself, *Do not cry.*

"If you're planning on raping me, you'll never get away with it," she said sullenly.

"Believe me, I would never do that. That's not how I operate. But I will gag you if necessary. And for that, all I've got are old socks," he said, mildly amused. "So I'd keep my voice down, if I were you."

Without speaking, he inspected her wounds. He touched a spot.

*Don't cry,* she told herself.

"What is this, some kind of divinely charged handcuff?" she grumbled, twisting to stare down at the curved metal and willing the tears not to fall from her eyes.

"No, ma'am, just plain steel. I like to do things the old-fashioned way."

"Old-fashioned," she said. "You have no idea what that means. Aren't you worried that I might dematerialize?"

"If you were capable of that, you would have done it by now. You're bound to your physical body."

"Doesn't take a genius to figure that out."

She jerked against the cuffs again, shaking the bed. He looked down at her, bored. "I wouldn't do that if I were you. You're just going to injure yourself further."

She glared back at him, letting the hatred flash in her eyes. So she was at the mercy of this lout. She had never been in such a position before.

A position of total vulnerability.

She had negotiated, surely, had bartered her body to gain advantage in countless situations. But handcuffed and held against her will?

*Never.*

It infuriated her, as nothing had before. She had gotten herself into—and out of—many situations before. But she had never allowed a man to render her so completely helpless, as this one had.

She watched him as he moved around the room, digging through his bag for a clean change of clothes.

He went into the doorless bathroom. She wondered if the unmannered American barbarian was going to open his fly and piss right in front of her. Instead, he went to the dingy sink and began to wash the blood off his forearms. His gray gaze stayed trained on her, ensuring she remained chained to the bed.

He examined his wounds, whipping his bloodied, torn shirt over his head and checking himself over for major damage.

Brandon had the body of a warrior, tattooed like a man who had seen many battles—each one had been etched on his skin, the story of his bravery mapped out in dark ink.

Right over his heart was a tribal design, a swirling dragon whose body extended to his biceps. From there, at the top of his left arm, the design continued with a tree of life, the branches stylized in a Celtic pattern with four interlocking corners. On the other arm, an ancient Mayan sunburst. Continuing down the sleeve of that arm were bands of tribal designs and different types of animals, some real and some mythical. Lions, snakes and eagles intermingled with griffins and phoenixes. So many different creatures and symbols, all of them rendered in monochromatic shades of black and gray ink, creating an impressive aesthetic harmony on the canvas of his skin.

He turned, bending to inspect the cut she'd inflicted on his abdomen. Giving her a full view of the most impressive tattoo of all.

The huge tattoo stretching across his back was a massive angel rendered in black and gray. Feathered wings extended from the lines of a human body, the wing tips of the tattoo outspread along each of Brandon's shoulder blades.

A tattoo that might simply be a decoration on any other man.

On him, the tattoo was like the divine staring her in the face.

She had always known this day was coming, the day of her reckoning. After all the crimes she had committed, she supposed she deserved it. What a strange manner of capture, though, to end up strapped to a bed in a cheap hotel.

She turned her gaze away, unable to look.

*"Oh, Dio."* Oh, God.

The words slipped off her tongue, not a prayer, but a profanity.

"Those aren't just ordinary tattoos, are they?" she said.

He didn't answer, just looked at her with those dark gray eyes of his, as dark and foreboding as the ink on his body.

"What do they represent?"

"Assignments."

He didn't bother to elaborate, and she didn't ask. The explanation was clear enough. The ink sprawling over his skin told the stories of the people he had rescued. People he had helped.

"What happens when you run out of skin? Will you stop getting tattoos?"

"I don't *get* them in the ordinary way. Not from a tattoo parlor or a tattoo artist."

"Where do they come from, then?"

Looking into his gray eyes was like looking into the depths of the ocean. "They just appear. Each one appears after I've finished an assignment."

"And if you don't finish?"

He shrugged, the taut muscles of his shoulders contracting. "Hasn't happened."

"Were you sent to get rid of me?" she blurted, almost hysterical, wondering exactly what would appear on the canvas of his skin after he had dealt with her.

"Like I said, I was sent to collect you. That's all," Brandon said. "Violence isn't my preferred working method."

"What the hell does that mean?" she asked quietly.

"It means I have no present intention of harming you," he said, equally quiet. "If you cooperate, you'll spare yourself further injury."

He moved around the room, unpacking his duffel bag. She could not help but gawk at his tattoos, her eyes flickering furtively over the intricate maze of ink and flesh, reading the story marked on his body, the symbols that proclaimed who and what he was.

That was when she realized there was no point in fighting him.

She would have to use other means to get what she wanted.

* * *

He pulled a clean shirt over his head, grateful he'd sent his bag here from the airport. He felt Luciana's gaze travel along the lines of his body. Gave her a long, hard stare just to warn her. She sat at the top of the bed looking ever the princess who had been captured.

*She's a demoness,* he reminded himself. *It doesn't matter how beautiful she is. She is evil. She is extremely dangerous.*

"Whatever Arielle told you about me is completely untrue," the demoness said smoothly. Something in her tone had shifted, as though an idea had clicked in her head. He turned to glance casually at her, and he saw it in her eyes, too. The wheels were turning in that dangerous mind of hers. "Especially if she's getting her information from Julian Ascher these days. I heard he's one of you now."

"Why are you so hell-bent on revenge against Julian?" he asked.

"Haven't you ever wanted revenge on someone who hurt you? I injured you," she said softly. Her entire demeanor had shifted now, her tone placating with a vulnerability that *must* be calculated. "Don't you want vengeance?"

Brandon gave her a hard look. "You ask a lot of questions. I already told you, I'm just here to do my job. There's nothing personal about it. So, no, I don't want to avenge myself."

"Everything is personal. You can't haul me into a room, lock me to a bed and say there's nothing personal about it."

"Absolutely. Given those cuts on your back, I wouldn't say you got off easy. Let's call it even."

She gave a vicious yank on the cuffs, her temper flaring again. "We are far from even. You will unlock these vile things. You will let me go. Then we will be even."

He said nothing, but turned his attention to her back.

"We should get this broken glass out of you."

"It will heal," she ground out.

They both knew that was true. Immortal bodies of angels and demons healed quickly, but not instantaneously.

"If we don't take care of it now, the wounds will take longer to heal," he said.

He unlocked the cuffs, readjusting her hands so that they were bound in front of her.

He dug in his shaving kit, got out a pair of tweezers. Poured vodka over them.

When he eased away the fabric of her dress, the rose silk was crimson with blood. Even he winced at the sight. Her back was slashed with multicolored fragments of glass embedded in her skin.

"This will sting."

With a facecloth, he dabbed some of the vodka on her.

He felt her body react.

"I've burned in everlasting hellfires. You think this is anything in comparison?" she said. She was bluffing. He could hear the bravado in her voice. Finally, she said, "Give me some of that vodka."

He found a glass. Poured her a shot. Tipped it into her mouth as she tilted her head back.

"Give me another one." She downed that one, too.

He sat down behind her and cut away the silk of her dress where it was soaked with blood.

And started digging the shards of glass out of her back.

Piece by piece, he placed them all in the little tumbler on the nightstand. Until that little glass was full of jagged shards, covered with her blood.

He pressed the damp towel on her back. By the time he finished, the healing process had already started, the wounds beginning to close. Even when it came to demons, there were miracles to be had.

Outside, a noise popped.

The first firework shot into the air.

A long whistle shot up through the buildings, followed by the boom of its detonation and a series of smaller blasts. From tinny radio speakers in neighboring windows, the sound track of the fireworks floated, the Italian opera music lush and rich despite the surroundings.

"At least open the window," she said softly. "This pensione might be cheap, but the location is good and it probably has a view."

Brandon went to the window and opened it.

A panorama of red-brown terra-cotta rooftops spread out before him in the pale moonlight. In the buildings all around, Venetians hung from every balcony, every windowsill and rooftop. Below, the bay was crowded with boats of every shape and size. Each of those boats in turn was filled with cheering Venetians. And every single person craned up to look at the spectacle of light in the sky.

Her face was upturned toward the dazzling night sky, her pale skin awash with the reflection of colors. A face that, even in her misery, was lovelier than the display of fireworks. More beautiful than this magnificent, decaying city.

And he, her captor, wanted to wash her misery away.

The fireworks blasted outside the window. For the second time that evening, color rained down. But this

time the accompanying noise echoed in the sky, rico-
cheting inside his mind like the slowed-down gunfire.

In the dark, he flinched. His back twitched, his
breathing constricted for a moment, his body remembering its human wounds. Physically, he had healed.
But the memory of the scars remained, triggered by
the sound.

She must have seen the pain pass over his face.

"What's wrong, *il mio angelo?* Did someone shoot
you once?"

He willed himself back to detachment, told himself
to forget about the pain.

But she pushed onward, pressing her way deeper into
the wounds. "Is that how you died? My condolences.
Death is a bitch, isn't she? You know...I can take your
pain away. I can make it feel better. In fact, there's a
whole world I could show you, if you let me."

He checked for the watch. His pocket was empty.

*I'm awake.*

He paused momentarily. God, she was beautiful.
Temptation at its finest.

"First, I don't know what the hell you're talking
about. Second, there *is* no pain," he growled, pushing
her hands away. "Don't presume to know what goes on
inside my head."

"Whatever you say, *tesoro.* Lie to yourself if you
want. I can give you so much pleasure. I know you desire me."

With the colors exploding overhead, she tilted her
face up toward him and her eyelids fluttered shut. Expecting him to kiss her.

Looking down at her upturned face, a strange sense
of peace washed over him. She was like a child play-

ing at being bad, a little girl playing the villain's role in a game of dress-up.

*No, wait,* he told himself with a shake of his head. *Make no mistake about it. This woman is dangerous.*

He did not kiss her, but instead reached down and stroked the curve of her cheek.

Her eyes popped open, a shock of verdant brightness. She did not wince; her eyes darkened to a cold shade of green, their glitter a menace, hard and rare.

"I'd seek pleasure with you when hell freezes over," he said.

"If you let me go, I'll make it very worth your while," she breathed in her sultriest voice, arching upward on the bed to give him a good view of her ample cleavage. "What is it you want, angel?"

"Nothing," he said, staring her down. "And there is no way you could tempt me into letting you go. I was sent to collect you, and I intend to complete my mission."

She smiled, lowered her eyes demurely, then raised them again to peer out at him through half-closed lids. Very coolly, she said, "I take that as a challenge."

*Ignore her and keep your mouth shut,* he told himself. *Just do your job, Guardian.*

It wasn't as if he had never heard the promises of demons before.

Hell, it was practically par for the course in his line of work.

So why was this one so compelling?

Outside, shouts of appreciation and applause signaled the end of the fireworks. *"Uno spettaculo!...Che bello!...Bellisimo!"*

"I could make all of your wildest fantasies come true," she taunted from the bed. Ran her tongue over her top lip, suggesting what those fantasies might be. "Whatever you desire. However you desire it. Don't tell me you haven't imagined coming in my mouth. In my—"

"Enough," he ordered, cutting her off.

Instead of finishing her thought, she laughed, and he realized maybe that was worse.

Because when he heard that sound, he had an irresistible urge to jump on the bed and take advantage of her, chained there like a medieval maiden, offered to some dragon in order to placate its fiery appetites.

Only she was not a maiden. Not the princess. She was the dragon.

Not only that, but somewhere deep inside his gut, a flame was growing within him.

*Ignore it,* he ordered himself. *Just do your job and don't let her get to you.*

"Am I seriously supposed to sleep like this?" she said, frowning up at him, her lips set in a pout. "Aren't you going to let me go?"

He did unlock her wrists, but only for an instant, to change her position.

"I'm taking you back to America tomorrow," he said. Then he ordered, "Lie down."

"Make me," she said.

He shook his head. "I really wish we could do this the easy way."

In two seconds flat, he had her lying on her side, with her hands bound over her head.

"And where are you going to sleep?" she grumbled.

He threw a pillow and a blanket on the floor. It wasn't comfortable, but he'd slept on far worse before. From the floor, he could still see her, even if she was lying flat on the bed. He didn't dare turn his back on her, but

wished to God he could. Momentarily, he thought of
turning her over to the concierge for the night. But there
was no way he could delegate his responsibility for her.
This was *his* mission. *His* obligation.

"Be quiet and go to sleep," he ordered.

"No *coglioni*," she muttered.

"What?"

"No *cajones*. You Americans. All talk," she said
coolly, "and no action."

He would not let her bait him.

She turned her back to him, the tumble of her dark
curls on the white cotton bedsheet, the exposed curve
of her neck so appealing, so irresistible—it seemed to
call out *touch me* in the dim light—that he didn't know
how he would get through the night without reaching
out to skim his fingers along it.

He turned off the lights and lay down on the floor.

"Good night, *principessa*," he said mockingly.

He heard her stir, felt her glaring at him in the darkness. "What is it they say in English? Oh, yes, I remember the phrase I was thinking of. *I hope you burn in the
fires of hell forever.*"

On the floor, he smiled. He had to hand it to her.

The woman had *coglioni*.

Luciana stared out the tall windows of the shabby
little hotel room, into the darkness. It was so late that
it was early, the revelry of the party finally died down
now. Nothing could be heard but the quiet sound of the
canal waters lapping against the rotting brick of this
crumbling pensione.

*Failure.*

Somewhere out in the darkness in front of the Redentore Church, the devil's ferryman waited, floating

in his black funerary gondola, watching for her to arrive with the sacrifice she had promised.

The sacrifice she had now failed to deliver.

The tall, dangerous warrior of an angel who now lay beside her. Who looked more demon than angel. Who seemed to act out of pure animal instinct more than reason. Whoever had sent him had known exactly where to hit her, and how.

Inside her, rage and exhaustion swirled. Not only from having aborted a failed hunt, but prior to that, from months of striving to attain revenge that she had not reached. This thug among angels made an unlikely nurse. His hands, so big yet so gentle on her back, were a contradiction unto themselves. The moment he touched her, the pain dissipated. She felt strangely at peace.

The feeling was so odd to her.

Peace.

*Is this what Julian Ascher felt with Serena?* she wondered.

For now, she was utterly and completely at his mercy. But it was only a matter of waiting. She would find a way to escape, even now when her strength was at its lowest.

"I will think of some way to get out of this intolerable situation," she snarled in the darkness. "I always do. And when I do, I will have my revenge on you all."

Sooner or later, the devil would come calling for the sacrifice she owed him.

And when he did…? Oh, what a sacrifice it would be.


*Better to stay up all night than to fall asleep for even an instant in this woman's presence.*

Brandon had endured countless nights of sleeplessness. But tonight, after all that he had gone through, his physical body reeled from the effects of exhaustion. From the moment he lay down, even on the hard and uncomfortable floor, he fought sleep.

Sleep was a tyrant. Sleep was his enemy.

If he fell asleep, he risked falling back into the dream. Or worse yet, falling into another dream of *her*.

Sometimes being too close to his humanity was a very bad thing.

The urges of his body raged as he lay mere feet from her, silent and still.

In the darkness, he could sense her seething, her anger and frustration almost tangible. He could almost hear the wheels turning in her head. Could almost feel her plotting her escape.

Tired of staring at the luminescent reflections from the water dancing on the ceiling, he closed his eyes for an instant. Only a second, to rest his tired eyelids.

And lapsed into sleep.

Only for an instant, then jolted awake again.

*When he opened his eyes, he saw the full moon through the French doors of the hotel room. How strange, he thought, since the moon had appeared as a mere sliver earlier in the evening.*

*Was he dreaming? No.*

*He was not in his nightly dreamspace. No smell of urine and garbage. No narrow alleyway. Just the same dingy hotel floor where he'd lain down a moment ago.*

*He breathed a sigh of relief. Coached himself to inhale. Exhale.*

*But when he turned his head to look at the demoness, she was no longer attached to the bed.*

*Somehow, Luciana had freed herself from the bonds of the handcuffs. Had done so silently, in that single blink of unconsciousness. Now, she stood by the side of the bed, looking down at him, a glimmer of triumph in her eyes. Slowly, she knelt beside him. Levered one of her long, slim legs over his prone body to straddle his hips.*

*He lay still, flat on the floor. Not daring to move. Not daring to even breathe.*

*She took his hand, guided it to her breast.*

*He started to pull his hand away, then stopped.* Let her. *Fascinated, he watched his big hand as it covered the large, firm globe of her breast over the thin layer of her dress. Watched his fingers as they tweaked the pert nipple through the silk. Watched his hand as it traveled down her flat stomach, slipped up under the hem of her dress. Up the smooth skin of her thighs, to touch the front of her panties, a scrap of lace that seemed like it might melt away at any second.*

*God, she felt good.*

*He whipped his hand away from her and she laughed.*

*Lowering herself directly over him, she rocked slightly, pressing the most intimate place of herself against his groin. Leaned down over him and whispered, "I asked you if you had imagined your cock in my mouth. If you had imagined it in other places. And now, it seems you'll get to experience that."*

*Slithering down his body, she popped open the button of his fly. Unzipped it, and pulled his jeans and boxer shorts down so that his erection sprang free, harder than it had ever been. With such gentleness, she caressed him, sliding her hand down the length of him. He was about to burst.*

*No.*

*He grabbed her hand, pressed it away from himself and held it there, squeezing hard. With more force than he should, he knew.*

*"You're hurting me," she growled.*

*"I told you I don't want anything from you," he said to her.*

*She wrenched her hand away. "Then let me go. You know you want to. This is all just a dream. There won't be any consequences."*

*"Forget it."*

*"If that's your decision, so be it," she said.*

*Something evil glinted in her eyes. Then the demoness disappeared.*

*And he found himself back in the same familiar alleyway, once again assaulted by the scent of garbage and urine. Walking toward his fate with his gun held at eye level, wondering where the hell the demoness had gone.*

Luciana slipped out of the dreamspace like a thief stealing away from the scene of a robbery.

When she awoke, she was still handcuffed to the bed.

On the floor, the angel still slept, twitching in his slumber, apparently caught in some nightmare. Whatever he was dreaming now was no concern of hers. How long he would remain asleep was entirely uncertain. He could wake at any moment.

And she would be caught forever.

She looked around wildly, hoping for some solution to present itself. If only she had a pick or even a hairpin…but there was nothing.

No alternative.

There was only one thing she could think of.

*Oh, God. Just do it,* she told herself. *Do it now, or you'll suffer worse consequences.*

She sat up in the bed, as much as she could without waking him. Braced her left hand against the wall. Closed her eyes. Took a deep breath in. And slammed her right hand against the left thumb with all the strength she could muster.

Pain seared through her as the bone broke. The quick "snick" sound it made was like a little twig snapping. She clenched her teeth to keep from screaming.

*Don't think about it,* she told herself, holding her breath as a wave of dizziness and nausea washed over her, threatening to sweep her off course. *It's only pain. Pain is temporary.*

The thumb gave way, and she slipped her hand out of the cuff.

She took one last look at the angel thrashing in his sleep. And hoped whatever nightmare had come to haunt him was a thousand times worse than the pain she had been forced to inflict on herself.

Brandon jolted out of sleep, spiraling from the shock of his fatal gunshot wounds, covered in sweat as usual.

But this time, his ear caught the scrape of a window opening.

His eyes snapped open. His hand flew to his pocket. No watch.

*I'm awake. Not dreaming.*

*Holy shit.*

The last image he had of the demoness was of her standing on the windowsill with the handcuffs dangling from one wrist, the glint of moonlight flashing off the metal. Her face turned toward him, green eyes fixed on him.

"You may catch me, but you will never hold me," she said, her hair whipping in the wind, wild and dark as she slipped out the window, to freedom.

"Luciana Rossetti has escaped. The safe house has been compromised," Brandon said to the Guardian on concierge duty. "It's my fault entirely. I still have no idea how it happened. I had her handcuffed securely."

The other angel, a distinguished older angel with gray hair and kind brown eyes, merely shrugged as he looked up from the desk, relatively unsurprised. "How do you think she has evaded our local unit here in Venice for so long? She is adept at escaping. Luciana is an extremely deceptive individual, something more of a legend than reality to most of us locals."

"How is it that she has been allowed to run wild for all this time?"

The concierge gave a short laugh. "She is the least of our concerns. She is not the only demon in this area. There are dozens of Gatekeepers here, just like in any city. We lack the time and the resources to take care of the likes of Luciana Rossetti. Demons are embedded in this city, as deeply as San Marco. Venice is a city of the divine and the profane, a city of beauty and vice. Both are drawn here, each by the other. I suppose we *Veneziani* have simply learned to accept that."

"I promise you, I will rid this city of her before I leave here," Brandon said gruffly.

"If you have taken it upon yourself to try to excavate her from Venice, I wish you luck. But no one will blame you if you don't succeed," said the concierge. "Now, if you care to gather your things, we will find you another place to stay tonight."

Clearing his things out of the room, Brandon surveyed the space.

The image of her perched on the windowsill was burned into his mind's eye.

*How did she manage to escape?* he wondered. *Was she real? Was she even here at all?*

The bed was empty but for a rumple of sheets, showing no clue as to who had lain there.

But on the nightstand stood the tumbler full of glass shards, mixed with her blood.

# Chapter Five

The clock tower at the Piazza San Marco tolled three in the morning. Luciana stumbled out of the pensione, staggering into the now-deserted square. In the moonlight, all was silent, Venice sleeping after the celebrations.

Far in the distance, on the Lido, the young Venetians would party into the night. On the beaches, DJs would spin techno music until the early hours of the morning. Every single year past, Luciana had joined them, dancing in another year of freedom on the beach until the sun rose, glorious and brilliant over the Adriatic.

Celebrating another year of demonhood, another year of renewed vitality.

Another year of power.

Not tonight.

*Tonight was a total and utter failure,* she thought, starting homeward.

After almost two and a half centuries of successful hunting during the Redentore Festival, Luciana Rossetti had failed utterly to fulfill her annual requirements.

She had been bested, once again, by the goddamned Company of Angels.

*But at the very least, I survived,* she thought. *And I escaped.*

Her hand throbbed.

The thumb was bent at a distorted angle. But at least the break was clean, and she was free. What had gone on in that godforsaken little hotel room was now behind her.

Around San Marco's square, a few stragglers wandered, stumbled, singing in deep states of inebriation. Any of them would have been easy targets.

Right now, Luciana didn't have the strength left to kill a fly.

She limped home on bare feet, barely noticing the roughness of the cobblestones beneath her soles. By the time she reached her palazzo, she staggered through the door with the last ounce of energy that remained in her body. Bloody and aching, she collapsed into a chair in the *portego,* cradling her broken hand.

"Thank you, lord of darkness, for my continued survival," she whispered. "For the survival of my household."

The house was silent, but then a door opened somewhere in the back of the palazzo. Massimo rushed out, his eyes going wide in the dim light at the blood. He blinked, swallowing at the sight of her crushed left hand and the handcuff still dangling from her right.

"You have returned, *baronessa!* But what happened?" he said. "We thought the worst. We thought you had been captured by the angels."

"I'm fine," she managed to squeeze out. "I *was* captured. But I escaped. I saw the boat when I came out of the Redentore, and you were not in it."

She ran the fingers of her good hand along the fine carved wood, consoling herself with the familiarity of the furniture. With its solidity, its real presence in the material world. She wanted to hug Massimo, flooded by protective emotion. The thought of losing him was almost like losing a child of her own, or a sibling.

Yet, for the centuries they had spent together, the formality of a noblewoman and her servant still stood between them. The invisible barrier of a class division that had all but been forgotten in the modern world still separated them, barely present but still palpable.

"I was attacked while waiting for you outside the church," the Gatekeeper said. "The attacker tied me up and dumped me in the middle of the Adriatic. I would have drowned had he not tied my bonds as loosely as he did. Once I swam back to land, I searched for you everywhere, but determined that the attacker must have captured you."

"He did. I was lucky to escape," she said. "Where are the others?"

"Still out searching for you."

"Call them in. The ordeal is over. Did you manage to see your attacker?"

Massimo shook his head. "He was too fast. I have no idea who it was."

"He is a member of the Company of Angels," she told him. "His name is Brandon."

The mention of his name passing through her lips made her feel faint; she closed her eyes as a sick feeling passed over her.

"How badly did he harm you, *baronessa?* Your hand! And what on earth has happened to your back?" he said, turning her so he could look at it.

He went to a drawer, produced a pick and quickly removed the handcuffs. She examined her crushed hand. Wincing at the pain, she set the bone of her thumb back into place. Held it there, willing it to stay.

"I'm *fine*," she insisted. "I will heal quickly. You know that. The immortal body always does."

He gave her a long, scrutinizing look.

She was not fine. Yet, he knew better than to contradict her.

"What about the hunt?" he enquired. "I trust you delivered your annual sacrifice."

For the first time in two centuries, she could not answer in the affirmative.

His face blanched to a very pale shade of white.

In his green eyes, she saw her own fear reflected back.

"Perhaps the devil might still be mollified," he said quickly. "Perhaps it's not too late."

Luciana nodded. "Go out now and find a human. There's no time to lose."

His mouth thinned into a line; something fierce lit in his eyes. "That won't be necessary. We have a human in-house that might do the trick."

Luciana remembered the female scream that had interrupted her homecoming. The shoe with its trail of blood. She swallowed, remembering how she had wondered what the Gatekeepers had been doing with that woman, and why they had been keeping her here....

"The Gatekeepers have been keeping her as a plaything. It was the others, *baronessa.* I never touched her, I swear, and I—"

"Never mind the details," she said, waving her hand. "Just go get her."

Whatever the Gatekeepers had been doing on their own time was not relevant to Luciana. All that mattered was the possibility of fulfilling her obligation to the devil.

* * *

*"Keep away from that house, my darling girl."*

Those were the words Violetta Ravello's grandfather had whispered in her ear every time they passed the confection of stone and marble that sat adjacent to a beautiful courtyard on the Grand Canal.

"That house is even more cursed than the famous Ca' Dario," her grandfather would say. Both of them would shiver at the mention of the now-empty palazzo, whose owners inevitably came to tragic ends. "The gondoliers cross themselves when they row past it."

"Why?" Violetta would ask.

"No one quite remembers," he would say, furrowing his brow. "The only thing anyone can say is that it's evil."

How many hundreds of times she passed that palace, Violetta didn't know. But as she rode the vaporetto on the way to the opera house or to her singing lessons, she would look up at the ornate facade, hoping to catch a momentary glimpse of the beautiful men and the woman she sometimes saw through the stone tracery of the windows.

What fragments she managed to catch did not look evil to her.

To her, the palazzo looked romantic and wonderful.

Now, at twenty-one, she finally understood that it was not.

Her grandfather had been right all along.

Trapped in this house, she had become a victim of evil. Her mind had been corrupted by the whisperings of her captors. Reality had become distorted until she no longer knew what was real and what was not. She only knew that she hated the men who kept her here, who used her as their plaything, who forced her to take part in their perverse sexual games.

These men were not human.

These men were something other. Something evil.

"You will experience pleasure beyond your wildest imaginings," they had assured her, "if you'll just cooperate. If you'll do what we want."

She had resisted. Until she could resist no more.

Tonight, standing in the semidarkness of the *piano nobile,* she was quite sure she was going to die. The grand room was unlike the servants' quarters where she had been held prisoner during the past few weeks. Here in the dim light, the woman who stood in front of her was one of the most beautiful creatures she had ever seen. This woman Violetta had seen before, glimpsed through the windows countless times over many years. The woman was perhaps a few years older than Violetta herself, but she seemed a universe more sophisticated. She moved with otherworldly grace, drifting as if in a dream.

And yet, there was something strange about the woman's beautiful eyes.

Something inexplicably sharp and dark sparkled in the green depths of the woman's gaze.

"Here is the girl. Just the way you prefer them— young and innocent," said Massimo as he held her loosely at the elbow.

"What's your name, child?" the woman asked, her voice lilting, mesmerizing.

"Violetta."

The woman peered closer, grasping Violetta by the chin and tilting her face to and fro. "I know you from somewhere. You are..." Her lips pressed together in recognition. "I've heard you sing at La Fenice. You're a soprano. You sang the role of Tosca last season."

"Yes, that was me," Violetta said defiantly.

"You were quite good, for a singer so young," said the woman. "Quite a rising star if I'm not mistaken."

Violetta said nothing. She would not thank this woman, in whose house she had suffered such indignities. Who held her captive, who clearly intended to kill her.

"What is she doing here?" The woman looked not at Violetta, but turned her attention to Massimo, waiting for an answer. "What did you do to her?"

Silence.

Violetta could not bring herself to voice the things they had done to her. She had shut those things away in a little box, deep inside herself. To open the lid of that box would unleash a whirl of shame, rage, torment.

"How have you been torturing this girl, Massimo?" said the woman, narrowing her eyes suspiciously at him. "Normally I would never ask what you Gatekeepers do on your own time. But this is different. It's quite rare to find such talent."

"I did not take part," he said quietly.

Violetta turned to glare at him and thought, *But you allowed it to happen. You stood by as the others did what they wanted. You did not prevent them.*

"Let me go," Violetta demanded.

"That's not a possibility," said the woman.

"Then kill me," said Violetta, surprised at the fierceness that came out of her own mouth. "If you're going to do it, do it quickly. Don't stand around talking about it."

"You want to die?"

"I cannot remain alive in this house," she said. "And

if you will not release me, I would rather die and take my chances in death. At least then I might find some relief."

"The soul does not die, child," said the woman. "Death is not the end."

Violetta lifted her chin high. Stared the woman in the eyes. "Then I will find out for myself. The devil cannot hold a soul who does not deserve to be held. "

The woman hesitated, staring deep into Violetta's eyes.

Then, after a long moment, she said, "Unfortunately for you, my dear, that's not always true."

She picked up a knife from a nearby table.

Violetta saw the tightening of the woman's throat, the pause.

Felt the blade tremble, the point of it sticking at her throat.

Felt the razor-sharp tip of it, slicing into her skin.

Felt herself melt toward the floor, supported by the woman's arms.

She wanted to scream. But she clenched her teeth, willing herself not to make a sound.

*I will not give them the satisfaction of hearing me suffer. Not this time.*

A thousand feelings, a thousand images rushed through her mind as she began to die.

*Anguish. Regret. Sorrow.*

*The faces of her family, of her mother, father, grandfather, flashed before her...images of her smiling friends, her voice teachers, fellow singers in the opera company...all the scales she had ever sung, all the arpeggios and solfeggios and arias...all the hours spent practicing in her room at home...all the lessons she had ever had in little rooms in conservatories...endless rehearsals and performances on stages in theaters all*

*over Italy...the desperate desire to cling to all of these
people and experiences was what she felt in the final
moments of her life.*

With her last, choked breath, she thought, *If only I
could go on forever.*

And in the next instant, there was an immeasurable
pause, a single moment in which she knew, *I will.*

Violetta Ravello flung herself into death with all
the fervor of a burning monk or a martyred saint shot
through with arrows. In the name of all that was divine,
she placed herself in the hands of a greater power and
trusted in what was on the other side.

In the moment of her death, she heard a single, high
note, the sweetest music she had ever heard, sustained
like a beacon of light at the end of a tunnel built of
pure sound.

The noise was sickening as Luciana slid the knife
into Violetta's lamb-soft skin, throat slitting open like
butter. With one quick, deep stroke, she cut through
the girl's jugular and trachea. Blood rushed out of the
girl, streaming in a massive pool of scarlet that spread
across the marble floor.

Luciana wanted to weep for this poor, fragile human
girl.

Why, she did not know. She had done this before, so
many times. Countless times.

Had slaughtered so many victims without a single
moment of remorse. Had consecrated so many innocent
souls to the devil.

For such an emotion to plague her at this moment
was absolutely nonsensical.

She held the dying girl's head as Violetta closed her
eyes for the last time. Stroked the soft brown hair that
streamed down to the floor, the ends now wet with crim-

son. And whispered into her ear, "Rest in peace, my dear. Or as close to it as you can find."

"She's going so peacefully," Massimo commented. "Not like the ones who fight it."

Not like the ones who thrashed. Who cried and scream at the end. Who begged for mercy.

Luciana had seen it all, watched the death of each of her many victims. Big, small. Powerful, weak. Famous celebrities and reclusive hermits. Captains of industry and street sweepers. Of all the deaths she had seen, this young girl had died with perhaps the most dignity she had ever witnessed.

*Perhaps it was the right thing, after all,* Luciana thought.

In death, the girl was beautiful. Even more beautiful than she had been alive.

*Young. Tender. Innocent.* Preserved forever in the glorious, innocent state of youth.

Violetta, lucky girl, would be spared the agony of life. Spared the continued abuse and torture at the hands of the Gatekeepers. But also, spared the agony of making impossible decisions and ridiculous sacrifices.

"You, child, are dying in your prime, at the pinnacle of your talent, with the world laid open like an oyster before you. You will never know the decline of your beauty or your potential," she said to the shell of the girl, almost emptied of life.

Yet, Luciana felt a tremor of regret.

Perhaps because the girl's potential would never be realized to its fullest.

Perhaps because in the afterlife, Violetta would most certainly continue to suffer.

The demoness laid a hand on the girl's forehead, comforting her as she eased into the final stages of death. The most vulnerable point, as the soul separated from the body.

"Now," Luciana said to Massimo, putting her good hand out.

He placed a syringe into it. Luciana inserted the needle into the dying girl. She removed a length of blood, drawing out enough to fill the plastic tube.

"This must be done quickly. Just as the soul is releasing from the body. This is the vital ingredient I have been collecting for my poison," she said.

Massimo looked at her, brow furrowed. "Blood?"

"What I gather from my victims is much more than just blood," she told him.

"How?" he puzzled.

"It is the essence of death itself."

The rare kind of terror that arose only during a person's last moments on earth.

Even if Violetta's death was a quiet one, Luciana knew the feelings coursing through her. Even if she did not scream and thrash, beneath those closed eyelids, in the girl's mind, the fear of the great unknown would spin until she reached oblivion.

*I know because I remember that myself,* Luciana thought.

She held up the syringe, bright red in the dimness, as the girl lay fading on the floor. Trapped in the scarlet liquid, the essence of death would be distilled into Luciana's concoction later.

"Take this upstairs and put it in the workroom. Then take the body, and go out to the requisite meeting place. There is a chance that the conditions for this year's hunt might still be satisfied, even though I am late," she told him. "And get the others to clean up this mess."

There was a glint in his eye, deeper and more powerful than she had ever seen before.

"Out of curiosity, why didn't you poison her?" he asked.

"Poison is an art. There's a time for subtlety. Then there's a time to get the job done."

"It takes a brave woman to kill like that, *baronessa*. The girl would have suffered, otherwise," he said.

"Killing has nothing to do with bravery," Luciana told him tersely. "Especially not killing like this."

Fury burned through her. How the Gatekeepers could have kept such a person in the house without her approval—well, it galled her. But she would deal with them later, when she had the luxury of time to do it properly. Not now.

"Of course, *baronessa*," was all Massimo said.

She followed him up the stairs. But while he headed to the workroom, she retired to her bedroom. In her private bath, she ran the water in the huge marble tub for herself. Rummaged in the drawer and found a bandage to bind her crushed hand.

When that was finally done, she removed the lipstick tube from her pocket. How that had survived the evening intact, she didn't know. She set it on the countertop of the marble vanity. She stripped off her bloody, ruined dress, tossing it on the floor. Then she sank into the warm bathwater, wincing slightly as it lapped over the gashes on her back.

The residual pain was fading, even if her memory of the angel's touch was not.

Thank God the night was finally over.

*Why did it all go so wrong?*

She had killed countless young girls, many of them younger than Violetta Ravello. Had always enjoyed the process. The draining of the blood. In the past, she had felt no guilt. She had felt nothing. Exactly as she had explained earlier this evening, she knew that death was not the end. Pain was fleeting.

And she, Luciana, had fared so much better as a demoness than as a human.

In her afterlife, she had gained power that she had never imagined before.

She had reveled in the deaths of the innocent, as if somehow it could profane the name of God. While she had drained their bodies and bathed in their blood, she imagined that she was giving these girls the same opportunities that she, Luciana, had achieved through death.

But this time, thinking about the child who lay dead downstairs, Luciana wanted to retch.

Perhaps because she knew that Violetta should be on her way to heaven. Instead, the girl was headed in a different direction entirely.

At the slight creak of the old door, Luciana called, "Is that you, Massimo? I told you never to interrupt my baths. If there's some problem, I'll be down in a moment."

At the soft laugh behind her, she froze.

She looked in the mirror. The person she saw reflected there was not Massimo.

His amber eyes glowed in the dim lighting of the bathroom, the steam rising around him as though he had risen freshly from hell itself. His blond hair was as immaculate as ever, his face as classically handsome as ever, but his Nordic good looks put a chill through her.

Even in the heat of the bathwater, she shivered.

Corbin Ranulfson had come out to play.

He was one of the most powerful Archdemons in

America. Arguably *the* most powerful demon on earth, before Julian Ascher had knocked him down a few rungs on the demon hierarchy. And she had used him. Luciana had endured Corbin's companionship and his perverse sexual tastes for months as she schemed to get closer to Julian Ascher.

Whatever Corbin was doing here, his arrival did not bode well.

"No, my dear. Massimo's not back yet," he said, coming to loom over the bath. He dipped his hand in the water, swirling it as he perused her body beneath the clear surface where the bubbles separated. "Plain water this time? I thought you preferred to bathe in blood. The blood of young girls, like Elizabeth Bathory. If I understand correctly, there was one downstairs that might have served nicely."

Admittedly, she had previously made a practice of bathing in blood. It was something she had done from time to time, partly to keep up her reputation. Especially when one traveled in circles with the likes of Corbin, terrifying behavior was necessary to avert the bloodlust of other demons. To keep them from attacking oneself.

However, right now, all she wanted was to cleanse herself of blood, not cover herself in it.

"I heard about your little encounter in the glass gallery on the Street of Assassins. I would have come sooner, but I was detained elsewhere," he said, and she knew what that meant.

Detained by their boss, in the bowels of hell.

"I was released only on the promise that I would accomplish a certain task," he said. "My task is to keep you on track. As of midnight, you failed to deliver your promised sacrifice."

She swallowed, wondering what he had been sent to do.

In the past, Corbin had done barbaric things in front of her. She had seen him dismember a human woman and sink his teeth into her flesh as she was still alive. It had terrified Luciana then, but she hadn't said anything.

And now...

"The Company of Angels sent a Guardian after me," she said quickly. "I was unable to complete the hunt. But the problem has already been solved. The Gatekeepers had a girl here and we...I dispensed with her."

"Oh, my dear Luciana, that doesn't come close to the penalty you're going to pay."

"Fine," she said, swallowing down her fear. "If you want another sacrifice, I'll deliver a second victim."

"Not just any victim," he said. "Satan wants the angel."

"Impossible." She sat up then, covering her breasts with her hands. The water churned around her. The bath was so full that it threatened to slosh over the edge from the sudden movement. "No Rogue demon has ever killed a Guardian."

"You underrate your capabilities, my dear. I have faith in you. It will be easy. Here's what you're going to do. Let him believe you're interested in negotiating. Convince him you've had enough of your whoring, lying ways. Lure him into your home. And then..."

She swallowed down fear. "What?"

His hand shot into the water, seized the wrist of her broken hand. "Don't play the fool with me, Luciana. I know you. You're an experienced and heartless killer. You have an entire laboratory full of toys just down the hall. I'm sure you'll think of something."

He squeezed the bandaged hand, pressing the broken

bone so that it snapped out of place again. When she cried out in pain, he released her, letting her wrist fall back into the bath. This time, the hand began to bleed, seeping crimson into the water.

"You have one week," he said.

"You must be out of your mind," she said, cradling her hand, trying to stop the bleeding.

"Serena St. Clair *reformed* Julian Ascher in one week. He has utterly abandoned the demon hierarchy and has completely changed his ways, unfortunately for us. This task should be infinitely easier. We're not asking you to change this man's allegiance. We're asking you to kill him. Where is your precious poison? You can use that to get rid of him."

Her mind flickered toward the gold lipstick tube sitting on the marble vanity.

*Don't look toward it,* she willed herself.

"Gone," she said.

He sauntered over to the vanity, picked up the tube. "You mean it's not in here?"

He pocketed the lipstick, walked back over to the bath.

Then he leaned down to whisper in her ear. "Don't forget that I know all your tricks."

Then he pushed her head under water, holding her there as she thrashed. She tried to hold her breath until it was useless. Water flooded into her lungs, into her stomach. She started to black out, slipping to the edge of consciousness.

Only then did he let her up.

He bent down and murmured softly, "Don't ever forget."

"Wait," she said miserably, coughing out warm water.

"I have no more of that poison. How am I supposed to kill the Guardian?"

"You'll figure it out. You always do."

Then the Archdemon swept out of the bathroom, closing the door behind him as he went.

Leaving her alone.

A pawn of men.

Exactly what she hated being. Had slaved for centuries to get out of.

She laid her head against the side of the bath, soaked in the unwashable filth of that feeling, and she vowed to herself that she would do whatever it took—she would one day get revenge on them all.

*Luciana is still sexy, even if she's a manipulative bitch,* Corbin ruminated as he left her palazzo. *However, she's not the only whore in town.*

And then he went to discover what Venice had to offer.

In this city of excess, so much of what Corbin loved was so close at hand.

The night was not yet over. And there were infinite possibilities to explore.

Out in the middle of the San Marco Basin in front of the Redentore Church, Massimo and Giancarlo waited in the boat. In the bottom of the vessel, the dead body of the girl lay, wrapped neatly in a large swathe of black cloth.

"This is the appointed spot," Massimo said, "but we have never attempted a delivery so late. The *baronessa* usually sacrifices her victims well before the toll of midnight. She's a very efficient hunter."

"Not this year," Giancarlo said grimly.

"It was not her fault," Massimo said.

"I never said it was," the other Gatekeeper said quickly, his furtive gaze sliding to Massimo. "Don't tell her I suggested it might be."

They waited.

There was no sign of the black funerary gondola, no sign of the dark-hooded figure.

"Satan is not coming to collect," said Giancarlo.

Massimo looked down at the black cloth that lay in stillness on the bottom of the boat. Tried his best not to imagine the body within, stiff and cold. Tried not to imagine her face, her brown hair spilling on the floor of the palazzo in the pool of her blood.

"You missed out," Giancarlo said. "That girl was a fantastic lay."

"Don't speak of her like that. Have some respect for the dead," Massimo said.

Giancarlo snorted at the wistful look on Massimo's face. "Better to die young and leave a beautiful corpse."

That was something both of them knew firsthand.

Returned to earth and preserved at the age of their deaths forever.

By the time the sun began to rise, the Gatekeepers realized they had come far too late. What would happen to the *baronessa,* Massimo didn't know. He genuinely worried for her. In two centuries, had never seen her this worn, this tired.

"What should we do with the body?" Giancarlo said. "Throw her overboard?"

Massimo looked over the edge of the boat, into the water. Here, in front of the Redentore Church would make as fine a resting place as any. "All right."

They weighted the corpse with the concrete blocks they had brought for such a situation, though had never needed until tonight. Then they tipped her over the edge, slipping the body into the water with a little splash. The top of the cloth she was wrapped in came unraveled. Massimo watched as her brown hair drifted downward in the water. The last tendrils of it seemed to reach up toward him as the girl disappeared into the depths of the canal.

Once she was gone, he started the motor and headed home.

"The job's done," Giancarlo said.

But not done well. They didn't realize the extent of it until they returned to the palazzo.

Where the girl was waiting.

Not the full body of her, just a flicker of her spirit, floating in the window near the place where she had died. Her voice, ghostly and beautiful, drifted out to fill the canal. The faint but sweet strain came from an aria that he recognized from Puccini's *Tosca,* the last role she'd sung.

*I lived for art, I lived for love,*
*I never did harm to a living soul...*

"The *baronessa* is not going to like this," Giancarlo said, voicing both their thoughts. "Not one bit."

# Chapter Six

*Sunrise over the Grand Canal*

Brandon awoke in the early hours of the morning, went to the window overlooking the fluid curve of water that sparkled in the pale light. Somewhere out there, Luciana was plotting.

The first place he started looking for the demoness was the last place she had run last night.

Rio Tera dei Assassini.

Even in the early morning, the sun was already blazing in the sky and a sticky heat was settling over the city. In the light of day, his destination looked as charming and as innocent as any other street in Venice. On the corner stood a bookstore stall with racks of Italian publications. There were a few souvenir shops, and restaurants with their colorful awnings. And of course, tourists milled about the street on this too-sunny day.

The glass gallery was not difficult to find. A few humans stood examining the glassware displayed in the window.

He pulled open the door and went inside.

The glass shop showed no trace of a struggle.

The shelves were restocked, every piece back in perfect order.

Not a drop of blood in sight. No stray shard of glass to tell the story.

The immaculately dressed shop assistant sauntered over to him.

"May I help you with something, sir?" she said in English.

*Does every single demon in Venice have green eyes?* he wondered fleetingly.

"I'm looking for a woman," he said. "Her name is Luciana Rossetti."

Nothing on her face moved but for the slight widening of her eyes, the barest recognition of the demoness's name before she recovered her composure. "I'm sorry, sir, I am not familiar with any person by that name. May I interest you in a handblown wine decanter? Although you will find many pieces of glass for sale in Venice, the artistry of our master glassblowers is unparalleled. The pieces are all lovingly crafted on the neighboring island of Murano, where all the factories were originally established because of the risk of fire to the wooden buildings of Venice—"

He cut off her sales pitch with a quick jerk of his hand and said quietly, too low for the others to hear, "I don't have time for a history lesson. I'm looking for Luciana Rossetti. Don't pretend you don't know where she is."

"Now look here," she said. He caught the demonic spark that lit in her eye, and her voice dropped to a hiss. "In Venice, we live in agreement, your kind and ours. Don't upset the balance."

"Then tell me, where's Luciana?"

"I haven't seen that bitch for years," she choked, spitting out the words. "She would not deign to enter this place."

She was lying. Brandon knew it in his gut, as surely as he knew his own name.

"I guess you won't mind if I search the gallery, then," he said.

The woman grabbed his arm. "What do you think you're doing? You have no right to march in here and start poking your vulgar nose into this business."

He held up his arms, the healing cuts still visible. "I have every right in the world."

In the shop's back room, he looked among the shelves. Nothing. Not a single hint of anything amiss. He stood for a moment, waiting in the stillness.

Then his eye caught the movement of a door in the very back of the shop opening, noiselessly. Just a tiny crack, a sliver of darkness that shifted. And then it shut again.

He looked down at the shop assistant. "What's back there?"

"Nothing," she said. Her eyes flickered to the customers inside the shop, perusing the glass. "Sir, you are disturbing our patrons. Please leave."

The humans looked over at him, whispering.

"The shop is shutting for an emergency right now. If you're interested in purchasing something, please come back later," he told them. He pulled open the front door and flipped the sign to *Chiuso*—Closed. As the humans scurried out, Brandon said to the salesgirl, "There. No customers to worry about."

He marched to the back of the store, hauled open that door.

"Wait!" the woman shouted. "You can't go up there."

Ignoring her, he peered into the darkness, up the staircase. "Oh, but I can."

Brandon charged his way up the stairs.

At the top, he entered the foyer of a grand space designed as an entertainment area, which looked as if it was waiting for a party to begin. Velvet sofas and sumptuous draperies furnished the space. A sweeping staircase led to yet another floor above, with a long row of closed doors behind carved balustrades overhead. Above it all, the high ceilings were hung with elaborate chandeliers.

One of those doors opened, and a girl peered down to call out, *"È lui un cliente, Carlotta?"*

"No, he's not a client. Not at this time of day," the saleswoman snapped in English, as she came barreling up the stairs after Brandon.

The noise prompted more doors opening. On the balcony overhead, girls in various states of undress came out of their rooms, gathering as they peered down over the carved banister. They clustered in a pack together, looking down at him, the collective hiss of their hypnotic voices, whispering, *"Angelo."*

Eyes burning bright in the dimmed light inside the brothel.

Because that's what this was, he realized.

A demon brothel in the middle of Venice.

The first girl who had spoken sauntered up to him, fingering her cleavage so that he had nowhere else to look. "I have a tattoo, too. Would you like to see it?"

She pulled her bodice open, flashing her breasts at him. He looked away quickly, pushed her aside without looking for the promised tattoo.

"Where is Luciana Rossetti?" Brandon demanded, calling up to the rest of the women. "Who among you has seen her?"

*"La Lucciola?"* one of them crowed.

They laughed, all of them, the sound of it like a siren's call, the promise and the smell of sex hanging in the air. Their nearly naked breasts, pushed up and mounded in corsets and clothing designed to accentuate their assets, shook with their laughter.

Behind him, Carlotta said smoothly, "Luciana is not here."

"What does that mean?" he asked gruffly. *"La Lucciola?"*

Hearing the sound of the Italian words coming out of his mouth, the demon women laughed louder. Some of them gripped on to the banisters, as if they might fall right off the balcony above.

Carlotta laughed, too. "It is a nickname she used here. It means 'firefly.' If you're trying to catch her, maybe you should try a net," she said, drawing her silk scarf teasingly across his face. When he swatted it away, she said, "You, my dear, could use some lessons on how to treat a woman. You might loosen up if you stick around long enough."

*"Enough!"* Brandon shouted.

Beneath them, the floor shook. The damask-covered walls and the antique furniture rattled. The chandeliers hanging from the ceiling trembled in a precarious circle, threatening to fall, sumptuous tiers of crystal shaking in a jangle of sound.

"Do you doubt the power of the divine to raze this madhouse to the ground?" he bellowed, bluffing. It was unlikely such a thing would actually happen. But none of these demon women knew that. "Tell me where she is!"

The entire group fell silent.

Terrorized.

The clink of the crystal chandeliers overhead was

the only audible sound in the room, before even they lapsed into stillness.

Carlotta's lip trembled.

"*La baronessa* would hardly sully her reputation in here," said the brothel keeper. "She hasn't been seen in here for years."

"But she was, once…"

"Yes. That bitch worked here once. She was once even more of a whore than she is now."

*Now that's an interesting bit of information that wasn't in her file,* was his first thought. His second thought was that it came as no great surprise. Yet, strangely, it stirred something in him, a sadness for her. Empathy for a demoness was not something he had ever thought possible before. Yet Luciana was a woman with some deeply hidden secrets, and despite his better judgment, they intrigued him.

*How did she end up here? Did she work here of her own volition?* A thousand questions flooded into his mind, but there was only one that was relevant here and now.

"Where is she?" he asked.

"In the deepest reaches of hell, for all I care," Carlotta spat.

"I'll give you one more chance to answer my question. Where is Luciana?" he said.

She smirked.

And he grabbed her by the throat and squeezed.

*There are rules governing the interactions between angels and demons.* Arielle's words rang in his ears as he watched this demon struggle as he held her by the neck. *Rules that must not be broken.*

Killing a demon without just cause was one of those rules.

He might not be allowed to kill her, but he could certainly take her as close to the precipice of death as his own conscience would allow. He tightened his grip a little more.

*Human lives are at stake,* he reminded himself. *If I don't track down Luciana, who knows how many people could die.*

Carlotta choked and grasped his wrist, trying to pry herself out of his hold.

None of the other girls rushed forward to save her. They stood frozen, but did not dare interfere.

Finally, he released Carlotta and she stumbled away.

"Tell me where to find Luciana," he said, looming over her.

"I didn't know you angels could be such bullies. Aren't you supposed to be a harbinger of peace?" she said, narrowing her eyes at him, rubbing at her throat.

"Now!" he thundered.

"Luciana's home is nearly impossible to locate."

"Why?" he demanded.

There was a hush in the bordello. Not a soul moved.

Carlotta swallowed, and the sound seemed to echo in every corner of the room. "Because it was erased from human memory."

"How did that happen?" he asked, relenting a little.

"Luciana was the daughter of one of the noble houses of Venice. The Rossetti family was once very well-known, as esteemed as any of the others inscribed in the *Libro d'Oro,* the *Golden Book* of the city's nobility. She was the last of her line. After she died and became a Rogue demon, she made a deal with the devil to protect her home. By his hand, her family's name was erased from the city's records. Her palazzo was hidden from the view of ordinary mortals."

"So how do I find it?"

"It is in plain view on the Grand Canal, although it is protected by dark forces. Any human who tries to remember the house simply cannot hold the details of its history in mind. Some of them may sense its demonic vibrations, but their minds are too weak to fully grasp what that house holds. However, we demons here in Venice know it well."

"You will take me there. Now."

She peered close, held out her hand. "If I'm going to take you there, I want to be compensated."

"How much?" he asked.

She named an ungodly sum. He agreed to it, saying, "I'll arrange for you to receive the money. You have my word."

*"Molto bene,"* she said, placated at last. "I know you angels are too self-righteous to break your promises. I will show you the palazzo. Once you have seen it, you will not forget it. We will have to wait until nighttime, to lessen the chance of being seen by her Gatekeepers. It will be easier in the darkness. But I warn you. If you do manage to track her down, you will never be able to conquer Luciana Rossetti. She is a scheming bitch, and she will find some way to destroy you or extinguish herself trying. She has survived in this world for centuries. If you think you're going to find some way to best her, you have another think coming. You'd better pray for a miracle."

Carlotta was right, Brandon thought as he looked at the house to which she had taken him.

*I need a miracle.*

The front of the house was only accessible by water, so she took him in a small motorboat that she drove herself. As they drifted slowly past, Carlotta's mouth pinched into a flat line as they looked up at the house. She hid her face behind the hood she wore.

"She will kill me if she finds out I have brought you here," said Carlotta.

The palazzo was fully lit, the lights reflected on the canal in front of it.

There was no sign of Luciana herself in the large, imposing windows.

But the air in front of Ca' Rossetti had a dark, shimmering quality that he had never seen before. Meticulously maintained, the palace was a confection of carved stone, its arched windows delicate and accented with gilt and brilliant blue the color of lapis lazuli. Even in the darkness, its pristine facade contrasted against the elegant decay of its neighbors, the other buildings weathered and crumbling from centuries of exposure to the elements.

As they advanced closer, Brandon noticed that the ornate entranceway was adorned with carvings of demons, their stony wings folded in repose. Half a dozen goblins, a small pack, perched on the corner of the concrete landing in front of the doorway, like water rats living beneath the palazzo. The creatures hissed at the passing boat, their red eyes glowing in the darkness.

The canal rang with the reverberation of a voice, singing.

"Did you hear that?" he said.

They paused, listening. Carlotta narrowed her eyes at him.

"You will go insane, angel. She keeps a nest of vipers as security guards," the brothel keeper hissed. "Even if you manage to get past them and capture her, you'll never pin her down. She will more likely destroy you before you destroy her."

Then she disappeared into the night, letting him off not far from Ca' Rossetti, standing on a concrete walkway. And he knew he needed to find somewhere he could keep an eye on Luciana.

Brandon wandered the alleyways behind the palaces surrounding Ca' Rossetti, looking for a place to set up surveillance. He found it in an abandoned palazzo across the canal from her, the windows boarded up.

He pushed open the door and entered, his eyes adjusting to the darkness.

*Skitterings of unseen vermin and the scent of urine. High walls and a narrow space.*

*Am I dreaming?* he thought. *No.*

*Not Detroit.*

*Venice.*

Not an alley.

But rather, the ground floor of a once-glorious noble house. There was a single long room stretching the depth of the palace, completely empty of furniture. The fixtures dated from another century, but which one, he could not even guess. The windows in the back looked very old, made of dusty, nearly opaque glass like round bottle ends fused together in the large frames.

He climbed the stairs to the second floor, which opened into a room that might once have been a ballroom or a grand dining room. Moonlight flooded in through the huge windows. The peeling frescos, smudged images from a distant past, stood disfigured and unrecognizable now. Ornate doorways and ceilings, the plaster broken and chipped, were fallen away in sections in some parts.

He found a spot in front of the window that was well hidden, unseen from the outside. From this vantage point, he could see Ca' Rossetti across the street, as meticulously maintained as this palace had been neglected. Here, he had a view of not only Luciana's front door, which opened directly onto the water, but the side entrance, as well.

And he settled in to watch.

Luciana sat in her workroom, hunched over the table. The cuts on her back had almost healed. Her left hand still throbbed. But she had reset the bone, and in another day or so it would be back to normal. Sitting still was far from comfortable. But there was much work to do.

Massimo hovered over her shoulder, watching carefully, absorbing every word that she said.

"Ordinary poison can harm an immortal body temporarily. But it is not enough to kill an angel or a demon, as you know. However, the poison *I* created proved effective on a low-ranking demon," she said. "A bellboy working for Corbin Ranulfson in Vegas."

"So what is the problem?" Massimo asked.

"Corbin stole the last dose of my last concoction," she said. "We must make more. To do that, I'll need your help."

She held one of the vipers just behind its jaws, grasping its head in her gloved hand as she held it over a venom-collecting receptacle. It bit into the plastic-covered glass funnel, the venom squirting down into the jar below.

"This must be done with a very delicate touch, Massimo. The utmost care must be taken not to damage or traumatize the animals during this process," she explained. "A good craftsperson always takes proper care of one's materials."

"Why do we even need these ingredients if we have the essence of death collected from the girl?" he asked.

"We need to build a poison that will kill not only the spiritual, but the physical body. We could use any poison as a base, but I like to combine several different ingredients. Snake venom, cyanide and botulinum, for instance, make quite a nice combination. Along with those toxins, we use the essence contained in the human blood."

She put the viper back into its habitat. She withdrew another snake and handed it to the Gatekeeper. "Now you try it." As he performed the same movement, she nodded. "That's it exactly. It's time you learned these techniques. There must be someone who can carry on these ways."

*Just in case I'm captured,* she thought.

"Poison may seem like an antiquated way to end a life," she explained, "but poison means power. There are demons who are capable of ending a human life just by snapping their fingers. However, we lower demons must find our own ways to amass power. Creating a poison that can end the lives of immortals has given us a distinct advantage. But we need more of it. If we can make large quantities of it, we can create a commodity that will be extremely difficult—perhaps impossible—to trace. There are rules in the interactions between angels and demons."

"Rules that cannot be broken," Massimo said wearily. He had heard it a thousand times.

"But they can be bent. Angels and demons are not allowed to kill each other. That is the first and most important rule. Everyone knows that. If that rule is broken, then the balance between heaven and hell will be disrupted, and all-out war will be waged on the earth. Humans will be caught in the middle. But if the angels can't track who's responsible for the killings, there's no accountability, no one certain to blame. Poison may be our way around the rules. We will be able to bargain with the rest of the demon hierarchy. We will have a commodity that could affect every immortal in existence. Every creature in existence."

"Yes, *baronessa*," said Massimo.

"If we can control the demon hierarchy, then the world is ours. We won't even have to worry about killing the angels ourselves. And no one will ever be able to hurt us again."

That was the goal. To insulate herself and her Gate-keepers from pain.

The window was shut, and even though it was unbearably hot outside, the modernization of Ca' Rossetti meant that the air-conditioning inside kept everyone cool.

Luciana looked up from her work, rubbing the back of her hand against her forehead.

*Feathers.*

Pigeon feathers. Not just a single feather this time, but several of them. They sat on the corner of the workbench. She dropped her arm, and the change in the air blew them off the table's edge, where they drifted onto the floor.

"You didn't open the window this morning, Massimo."

"No, *baronessa*."

His eye caught the feathers, and he frowned, puzzled. "Where did those come from?"

The angel was watching them.

From where exactly, she could not say. And how he had found her, she did not know.

But he was close.

She got up and went to the window, peering across the canal. In the darkness, the Grand Canal looked the same as it had every night for the past two centuries. Yes, it had shifted slowly over time. The boats had become equipped with motors and fashion had changed. The old Venetians had slowly died out, and the place had become flooded with tourists. Other than that, the same buildings had stood for centuries, sliding slowly into decay.

Except that in one of them, an angel sat watching her.

The most likely location was slightly to the right.

"Come here, Massimo, and tell me if I'm imagining things," she said, pointing to the only abandoned building within view. "Is it me, or is there movement in that house?"

For the past fifty years, it had been boarded up, left to rot slowly because of the impoverished state of the family who owned it, who could not afford its upkeep.

Massimo didn't respond, but Brandon was in there. She could feel him.

In the space of their short time together last night, some strange connection had been forged between them. A connection that she neither welcomed, nor would she tolerate.

She would have to find some way to break it.

"Massimo, take off your gloves and go downstairs at once. Make sure all of the doors are securely locked, and the outside gates, as well. Alert the other Gatekeepers. We are under surveillance."

"But there's just one man, isn't that right, *baronessa?*"

"Just one angel," she corrected. "And a very dangerous one."

Luciana sat looking at the light that spilled over the canal. A lone gondolier rowed in the dark of night, singing of the moon and of lost love.

On the other side of the canal, Brandon sat at the window, listening to the melancholy sound of the singing boatman.

*Die my human death again, or be seduced by Luciana in my dreams.*

The choice wasn't even his. But, God, if he had to pick between them, he didn't know which was worse. He lay on the hard concrete in the abandoned building, waiting for one of them.

*Come, sleep. Come, dreams. Come, darkness.*

He closed his eyes.

*At the sound of female laughter, his eyes popped open again. The laughter was so low, so velvet that he thought simultaneously of vintage Chianti and very rich chocolate.*

*He was no longer lying on the hard floor of the abandoned house.*

*Now he was standing in the entrance to the same dark alleyway.*

*He saw the flicker of rose-colored silk. He followed.*

*He dug in his pocket for his watch and felt its familiar smoothness.*

I'm dreaming.

*Looking up, he saw the black letters stenciled on aging stone: Rio Tera dei Assassini. What he was doing here, he didn't know. All he knew was that he had to follow.*

*Through the door of the glass gallery. In the back of the shop, up the stairs.*

*The vast room sat empty. The chandeliers blazed now, illuminating the night.*

*A woman with dark hair curling down her back. The pale, perfect skin of that back completely unmarred, not a single scratch or scar on her. No blood, no glass.*

*Her hand outstretched behind her, motioned for him to follow.*

*Into a magnificent room with velvet furniture. The sound of the door closing behind him.*

*When he reached for his gun, it was gone. The shoulder holster where he normally carried it, empty. No matter. She was not the kind of enemy you could kill by shooting.*

*Luciana turned, resplendent. With a single motion, she shed her dress. It dropped to the ground, pooling at her feet. Beneath it, she wore merely a black lace bra and a garter belt attached to thigh-high stockings. It was not the clothing he noticed, so much as what it barely concealed. Or rather, what it failed to conceal.*

*Her body. Her impossibly long legs, slender and strong. The appealing, subtle curve of her belly. Her high, full breasts, dark nipples just visible through the fabric of her bra in the dim lamp-lit room.*

*Decadent. Sinful. And so, so right.*

*But it was her face that took his breath away. Those plump lips of hers that seemed to invite him to picture them wrapped around his cock. Her evergreen eyes, her glossy hair tumbling around her in a permanently just-been-laid way that women usually paid ungodly amounts to achieve.*

*"You went digging into my past," she said. "And you found your way here."*

*"It was the only lead I had," he said gruffly, feeling like he was apologizing.*

*"It's your dream. Your fantasy. You wanted to see me like this, didn't you?" she taunted, fingering a silk ribbon on her garter belt. "Isn't this what you went searching for? This is what you wanted to find."*

*"I'm not after your body," he said. "I'm only here for one reason. To collect you on behalf of the Company."*

*"So you keep insisting. But that won't fly. Not here, in your dreams. You're tempted, aren't you? And there's only one way you're going to scratch that itch. You know what Oscar Wilde said, don't you? The best way to beat temptation is to succumb to it." She laughed. Then she cooed, "Besides, it's just a dream. That's all it is."*

Was it? *His mind reached for the truth, unable to grasp it. He reached for the watch in his pocket and touched it again, just to make sure of what he already knew.*

I am dreaming.

*"La Lucciola," he said. "They said that was your nickname."*

*She laughed. "I should slap you for calling me that. Do you know what it means? It's the word for 'firefly.' Italians use it to refer to a common whore. Because streetwalkers light up the night, just like those small, bright insects."*

*"They told me..." He swallowed. "Carlotta told me—"*

*"So you met her. You believed what that old prostitute told you?" She laughed. "You angels are a gullible sort. And so horny, all of you. When was the last time you had sex? Real sex, I mean." She ran her finger down the curve of her breast, drawing his eye there.*

*He swallowed and saw her watch the movement.*

*She pulled him toward the bed. "Come with me."*

*"Your body is sacred," he said, shaking his head. "You need to treat it as such. I'm not one of your customers."*

*"My body hasn't been sacred for two hundred and twenty years. It may be a physical body, but it isn't human."*

*"It's still part of the divine," he said. He knew there was nothing wrong with sex. On the contrary. But sex without spiritual connection, even a fleeting one...*

*Even in his dreams, he knew better than to go there.*

*"It's just a dream. That's all it is," she cooed. "If you want a connection, I can give you that. Let me teach you some words in Italian. To speak my language, you must make your mouth very sweet. Watch me," she said, as if he could tear his eyes away from the movement of her lips, the suggestive and subtle flick of her tongue as she skimmed the tip of it across her upper lip, taunting. "Ti amo. That means I love you. Is that what you want to hear?"*

*"Don't invoke the concept of love. You don't even know me," he growled.*

*But in his pants, his cock stirred, rising to harden.*

*"Perhaps not. But I know that," she said, addressing his erection. "And it is just like every other of its kind on the planet, angel or otherwise."*

*His mind was scrambled in a thousand different directions, trying to decipher what was allowed and what was not. What he could and could not do.*

*"What is it you really want? Don't be afraid of your desires. It's just a dream."*

*Draping herself along a velvet chaise longue in deep burgundy, she reclined, allowing her legs to part. Fingered the edge of the bra, allowing her nipple to peek* out its lace edge. She reached for his hand, drawing it to her breast, his fingers and hers coaxing the heavy globe out of the fabric. The nipple hardened beneath his touch. He flicked it with his thumb, teasing.

"That's right. Give in to your desires. You've been pent up for so long. I know you have."

No one could have told her that, but it was a good guess.

The right guess, *he thought.*

*Unable to resist her, he sank to the floor before her, his knees cushioned by the thick carpet. Between her spread legs he bent, running his hands up her pale thighs. Inhaled the scent of her, musky and dark, calling to him. He kissed the inside of her thigh, brushed his lips against the soft skin there, and heard her moan in response. She touched his head, running her fingertips over the coarse stubble on his face while he explored the smooth skin of her inner thigh.*

*He felt her fingers skim over his broad, muscled back.*

"Il mio angelo," *she whispered. He felt her fingers brush over the tattoo of the angel, tracing over the dark gray lines, the pattern of the wings on his back as he touched her sex through the silk of her panties. Her fingers sprawled over the sinews of his back as she undulated, his arms hooked around her legs, holding her thighs open.*

*Gently licked with his tongue, opening her to him ever so gently.*

*There was something so exquisitely tender about this demoness, something he had never experienced with another woman.*

*He felt her tense.*

"Relax. Stop thinking and just feel," *he ordered.*

*"You were right,"* she said, sitting up a fraction. *"We can't do this. We should stop."*

This isn't part of my fantasy, *his brain argued.*

*He raised his head for an instant, registering the genuine shock in those green eyes of hers.*

*"Why now,* principessa?*" he said, drunk on the taste of her.*

*She pulled her legs closed, swept up her discarded dress from the floor. She stood and looked down at him as he knelt there still, her fiery green eyes blazing. "You must leave."*

Go, *his gut screamed.* Otherwise, she's going to kill you.

*He stood, bewildered, and turned to leave.*

*Opening the door, he passed through the doorway.*

*His body braced for the shock of stepping, for the three-thousandth time, into the familiar scene of his nightmare. For the familiar scent of urine and garbage, the alleyway. For the intense pain of the gunshots fired into his back, his neck.*

*But none of it came.*

Instead, he came slamming back into consciousness, into darkness, with his heart pounding as if it would explode inside his chest. On the hard concrete of a floor that somehow felt more real, the odor of the room and of his own sweat, somehow more intense than the sensations of the dreamworld.

And yet, he had not died in his dream.

Orienting himself, he checked his pocket.

No watch.

*Not Detroit. Not Chicago.*

*Venice.*

Not the brothel, but lying on the dirty floor of a condemned palazzo.

In the dark, he stilled, listening to the shift and creak of the old building, to the sound of a slow leak somewhere in the back rooms. Water dripped, drop by single drop. And every drop that fell pulled him further back to the reality of waking. He lay wondering if the weary edifice might possibly succumb to the pressure of its thousand years. Might suddenly collapse on top of him, burying him beneath the rubble of decaying brick and unwritten history.

He lay waiting for a break in the craziest assignment he'd ever been dealt.

Whether he was awake or dreaming, he hardly knew.

Reality and dream had become equally unfathomable.

Across the canal, the demoness lay in her bed, on her silk sheets.

Staring up at the splay of light shifting across the ceiling, wondering how the hell the angel had brought her so perilously close to the edge of letting go.

*I'm supposed to be the one seducing him,* she thought. *I'm supposed to be the one in control.*

And yet there, in his dream, *he* had made her completely forget herself for a moment.

She got up and paced around the room. Went to the window to peer out into the darkness, toward where he lay.

Nothing like this had ever happened before. She had never lost control.

But this time, it had seemed so real.

The dream had not been entirely good. There were things she would rather forget, things she had buried centuries ago that she had hoped would never resurface.

*Luciana, La Lucciola.*

She had not thought about such things for a very long time.

But still, there had been the beauty of *him,* the nearness of him, the realness of him. She put a finger to her lips, still able to feel the pressure of his mouth against hers, breath to breath.

She returned to her bed and wept tears that slid onto the sheets and stained the silk, marks that convinced her that she was in the physical world.

He was still here, in Venice, a stone's throw away across the canal.

But he might as well have been living in another century or another universe. Her world, although on earth, would always be partly sunk in hell. She closed her eyes and fell into the dark void of dreamless sleep, hoping that she would find some respite from the painful reality of waking existence.


In the past few weeks, Corbin Ranulfson had suffered the most intolerable humiliation of his existence.

On earth, he had lost his newest hotel to traitor demon-turned-angel Julian Ascher.

In hell, Corbin had been demoted and stripped of his power to dematerialize.

But he was determined to show the demon world that he would not be forgotten.

He had come to Venice in a massive yacht, which he anchored in the Venetian Lagoon, ignoring the human regulations forbidding it. From there, in the shallow waters of the Adriatic, he could view the comings and goings of the city.

He ordered Carlotta to make an appearance. When the courtesan arrived in his stateroom, she curtsied graciously. And he thought, *Luciana ought to take lessons.*

"What can I do for you, your lordship?" she stuttered.

Corbin grabbed her by the front of her elegantly tailored suit and said, "Very pretty. But let's dispense with the formalities, shall we? Now why is a whore like you cooperating with the Company of Angels? Why did you feel you needed to take that angel to Luciana's?"

"I needed to get him out of my establishment. I have a business to run. Girls to protect."

"And you thought that was the smartest thing to do?" He caught her by the throat.

Their eyes met. "Yes, Corbin. I did."

"There's something about you that reminds me of Luciana," he said.

"Men think all Italian women are the same," she said, rising to the bait a little. "We are either regarded as hypersexualized or not regarded at all. Not much has changed in the past two centuries."

For a long moment, he held her pinned against the wall. "You're a poor substitute for Luciana, but you might do in a pinch. Courtesan. *Cortigiana. Hora. Puttana.* A rose by any other name would smell as sweet, isn't that what they say?"

Her mouth tightened, but she didn't dare say anything.

"Deep down, all women are whores," he said to her, partly because he really believed it, and partly to see her react.

But she was well trained in her trade and simply smiled a simpering smile.

He slipped his hand down the front of her blouse, popping the buttons open. Grabbed her lush breasts, fingered the nipples roughly, then shoved her onto a nearby desk.

And then he opened his trousers and sank himself

into her, pumping forcefully until he came, thinking all the while about Luciana and how furious she had made him. When he was done, Carlotta stumbled away, adjusting her clothing. What he sensed in her was not uncommon in the women he fucked, a kind of emptiness and a barely concealed terror. Carlotta knew exactly what he was capable of.

"How long did Luciana work for you?" he said, zipping up his fly.

"As long as she needed. She had to clear her debt to the devil, once he let her out of hell. She was a very popular girl, but as soon as she worked off her debt, she left. It has been hundreds of years since she worked at the gallery. Hundreds of years since I've seen her."

"That many? I don't believe that for a second. You're a two-faced lying bitch, just like her."

"I take that as a compliment," she said, trying to make light of it.

It pissed him off. She would pay for that later.

In the past, no demon would have dared to contradict him. Since his last run-in with the Company of Angels, he was severely weakened. The underlings could sense it. In the past, Corbin would have taken care of this situation with relative ease, dematerializing in and out of dimensions with the same ease as a human walking through a doorway.

The run-in with the angels had left him stripped of that power. It had lowered his position within the ranking of Archdemons, knocking him from the top of a ladder he had been climbing for many hundreds of years.

Being unseated from that position left him furious.

Corbin had barely gotten out of hell this last time. He had bargained his way out, promising the Prince of Darkness himself that he would find Luciana and bring her back. That was a task he would accomplish with the greatest of pleasure.

*Oh, yes,* Corbin thought. *I will return Luciana to hell. I will reap my rewards from the devil. And once again I will walk amongst humans as the most powerful Archdemon on earth.*

He would claw his way back to the top if he had to.

Regardless of whom he had to destroy to get there.

# Chapter Seven

Very early in the morning, before the sun rose, Luciana crept out of the palazzo.

And she went back alone to the glass gallery. To gather information.

What a shame they had put everything back in its place, not a shard askance. The rows of glass stood, perfect and pristine. Glistening and still. Artful. Tasteful. And all restored merely one day later. When she had trashed the gallery, it had been enormously satisfying. Smashing all that beautiful glass had been such a liberating feeling.

Entering the back room, she pulled open the door and mounted the stairs.

"Mother of Lucifer, how I despise this place," she muttered to herself.

Once upon a time, when she had been a girl, there had been no need for such a facade. The brothel had been legal, and Venice had been the city of courtesans, famous all over Europe for the beauty of its whores. Prostitutes had vastly outnumbered noblewomen, far more visible on the streets of the city than gently bred girls.

As one of those gently bred human girls, Luciana never would have come here.

As a fledgling Rogue demon clawing her way out of hell, she had no other choice.

She'd paid off her debt to the devil through working here.

How Carlotta stood it here for so long, she did not know. Obviously, the woman fancied herself a sort of Veronica Franco, a member of the extinct breed of *cortigiana onesta,* the "honest courtesans" who once ruled Venice with their educated wit and their political influence. Once, the courtesans of Venice had entertained noblemen. Even the king of France himself had spent a night between Veronica Franco's thighs.

For Luciana, this place had been hell on earth.

To her, no matter how rich or powerful a client was, he was still a client.

Still a man who paid to bury himself between her legs.

A fleshy, drunken human man grabbed her arm and pulled her inside, saying, "Come on in, gorgeous. Join the party!"

*Party,* Luciana thought, *is a tame label for what's going on up here.*

To her, it looked like a full-fledged orgy.

And it had been going on for quite a while, Luciana guessed from the look of it. Women and men cavorted everywhere; in various states of inebriation, undress and copulation. She pressed forward, into the sea of exposed flesh, looking for Carlotta.

To find out what the brothel keeper knew about Brandon, and what she had *told* him.

Dressed in a low-cut crimson gown, Carlotta stood watching the spectacle from the balcony above. She smiled, showing white, sharklike teeth that seemed to have grown sharper since the last time Luciana had seen her.

"*La Lucciola!*" called the courtesan.

"*La Tenutaria.*" Luciana flung back the Italian word for *madam*.

"I hate that word," Carlotta said. "I told you never to use it."

"Likewise."

Every demon within earshot laughed, for all of them understood the reference. Luciana ignored them and mounted the stairway, glaring up at the courtesan. "I need to speak to you at once."

Carlotta simply laughed. "How did you know we were having a party, Lucciola? We're having such a wonderful time. You should join in. You never reached your full potential in this business, you know. There was so much more you could have accomplished."

"I don't do this anymore," Luciana gritted out. "I haven't for a long time."

They went into the silence of Carlotta's office, where a couple was in disarray on top of the desk. Carlotta shooed them away, settling into an armchair as they picked up the scraps of their clothing and hurried out the door.

"Really, why did you come here? Was it just to check up on me? Or did you come to scream at me for directing that big, strapping man of an angel toward your house? I hope he managed to find what he was looking for," Carlotta said.

"How much did he give you?"

Carlotta smiled, fluttering her eyelashes. "I don't know what you mean."

"How much did the angel give you to sell me out?"

The courtesan sighed. "There was a small sum involved. But I would have done it for free, you know. You're such a bitch. You only come to me to complain. Honestly, I don't know why you brought him here in the first place. Putting all of *us* in jeopardy while you keep your own household safe and sound."

"Well, you fixed that, didn't you? Ca' Rossetti is no longer safe, thanks to you. Don't forget what's at stake for you if my household is infiltrated," Luciana said, the threat hanging in her voice. "Need I remind you of all that has passed there?"

"No," Carlotta said, lapsing into silence. "But why did you have to come *here*?"

Luciana sighed. "Running here was the only thing I could think of to do with that angel behind me. I had intended to seduce him. This would have been the ideal place to accomplish that."

In fact, this *had been* the ideal place. In his dream.

But Carlotta didn't need to know that.

"Leading him to your home was the only way to get him away from *my* home," Carlotta shot back. "It was gratifying, even though I knew you would come poking around here afterward."

There were a thousand insults on the tip of Luciana's tongue. But she swallowed them down, knowing there was no use in squabbling.

"So what are you going to do about him now? It should not be difficult to seduce him, if that's what you intended. Get inside that head of his. For you, that should be easy. Are you still poking into men's dreams?" Carlotta said.

"It has been known to happen from time to time," Luciana said.

"How do you manage it?"

"I can't explain it. How do you see? Feel, taste, touch,

hear? It's the same for me with other people's dreams. I sense the same things I would in the waking world. I don't know how it happens. I only know that it does," Luciana said. "If I had a choice in the matter, I would steer clear of this man's unconscious mind. In fact, I plan to get rid of him entirely."

"If you don't want him, bring him back here. There are plenty of girls who would give him a free ride," said the madam. "Hell, I would take him myself."

"Ah, yes. I forgot how much you enjoy other women's things," Luciana said, looking pointedly to the ornate emerald drop earrings Carlotta was wearing.

The earrings Carlotta had stolen from her.

The emeralds had been in the Rossetti family for centuries, given to Luciana by her mother as a wedding gift. They had been the first item she had recovered when returning to Venice as a Rogue demon. When she had departed this godforsaken brothel, the circumstances of her departure had been rushed, to say the least. *I escaped,* the demoness thought. *The earrings did not.* They had ended up in Carlotta's lobes, and ever since then, *La Tenutaria* had refused to give them back.

"These earrings are mine, and they have been for a long time," said the madam. "You left them here when you departed. You should have been more careful if they were so precious to you."

"You're unbelievable," Luciana said, narrowing her eyes at Carlotta.

"You can see yourself out," said the madam with a dismissive flick of her hand.

Just as she opened the door, she spotted Corbin down below, ensconced in the arms of a pair of Carlotta's girls. She hesitated, turning back to tell Carlotta. "You had better be careful. Corbin is more dangerous than you can even begin to guess."

"I don't need your advice," said Carlotta. "I can take care of myself."

Luciana shivered, knowing just how dangerous the Archdemon was. However, if Carlotta didn't want to listen...

On her way down the staircase, Corbin grabbed on to her arm. "Where are you going, lovely?"

"I have business to attend to, Corbin," she said, "which does not involve you."

"Everything of importance involves me, *cara.* You had better get used to that."

She shook off his grasp and hurried down the stairs, back into the hot day.


The Company safe house had not been luxurious, but it had at least provided Brandon with some basic comforts. Here, in this condemned building, there was no air-conditioning.

Not even a fan.

No relief from the stifling heat of summer, the humidity.

Sweat trickled down his undershirt.

Across the canal, the shutters were closed on the demoness's palazzo, closed up and silent as a sepulcher. Yet within that mortuary stillness, he felt her breathing. Sensed her thinking. Knew, rather than saw, the plans being laid around polished tables within that house. The team of Gatekeepers in there with her, plotting.

He watched for hours. But across the canal, nothing moved. Not a flicker. Not a sound.

Nothing.

*Don't fall asleep,* he told himself. *Think of something else.*

In this city with no cars, the itch for the driver's seat crawled beneath Brandon's skin. The hum of acceleration vibrated in the marrow of his bones. His palms twitched to feel the familiar curve of a steering wheel. His foot pressed, seeking the resistance of a gas pedal and its resulting acceleration.

He closed his eyes and felt himself driving.

*Felt the instant of escaping the material world.*

*The moment of surpassing the limitations of the human body. Yet still totally within its confines. Hurtling forward at a hundred miles an hour, yet in total stillness. Veering along a deserted country road, completely alone. Totally connected, completely attuned to the divine.*

*Hand on the stick, he shifted into a higher gear.*

And felt a hand gently squeeze his thigh.

*Looked over into the passenger seat and saw Luciana there, green eyes brilliant and a slight smile on her lips.*

He jolted out of sleep, shocked back to the reality of his present situation.

Back to a city where there were no cars.

Only water, and the endlessly curving pedestrian walkways.

*And a demoness who's driving me completely crazy.*

He got up and paced around the perimeter of the room, trying to shake off the feeling of her hand on his thigh. Luciana was an enigma, a contradiction of elements combined within an elusive package. Her face could range from purely innocent to worldly wise in a fraction of a second. To him, she seemed both vulnerable and dangerous at once.

For a woman who had killed so many people, he

had never expected such breathtaking charm. She had a strong personality, certainly. But there was also the element of the chameleon about her. She would become what a man wanted. His waking dream.

He had to remind himself, for the hundredth time since his arrival, of what she was.

*Not a waking dream, but a walking nightmare.*

When Luciana arrived home, she returned to her workroom, settling down to once again dedicate herself to her formula. Late in the afternoon, she heard a faint sound of a woman's singing coming from the ground floor of Ca' Rossetti. It sounded like opera.

*Tosca, if I'm not mistaken,* she thought.

The Gatekeepers lived in an area of their own, on the third floor of the house, which had always been used as the servants' quarters. However as the head Gatekeeper, Massimo had his own converted apartment below, in a space that the Rossetti family had once used as warehouse space for their silk trade.

She never ventured into any of the servants' quarters, letting the Gatekeepers run themselves. Massimo kept them in line, and kept the house running smoothly. The work that traditionally fell to women, the cooking and the laundry, the polishing of the silver, the cleaning of the floors…the staff performed it all with surprisingly little complaint.

The only thing she asked was that the Gatekeepers practice discretion when it came to their carnal activities.

Out of sight, out of mind.

Even after the debacle with Violetta…. Well, she had let that slide. She had not disciplined the Gatekeepers after all, as she had originally intended.

However, tonight when Luciana went to investigate, she regretted that decision.

She held her ear to the heavy wooden door, listening to the soft sound of singing there.

And then Massimo opened the door.

Behind him stood Violetta. The girl drifted behind Massimo, indistinct and translucent, a disembodied spirit who glared at Luciana with large, otherworldly eyes. The demoness did not bother to ask why Violetta had come back to Ca' Rossetti. The reason was obvious.

"What are you doing, harboring her here in your rooms?" Luciana asked.

Massimo pushed Violetta behind him, placing himself between the two women. "Don't hurt her."

"What am I going to do to her now? She's already dead," Luciana said flatly, "and the devil wouldn't accept her soul as a sacrifice."

"I wanted to find some way to help her," he admitted. "If the sacrifice had gone according to plan, her soul would have been stuck in hell. But since the devil didn't take her, at least she was able to return to earth as a ghost. She deserves our help."

"Nobody benefits from pity, Massimo," Luciana said, shaking her head. "Really, you should have come to me once you realized she was here. There are some things that refuse to remain hidden. Well, Violetta, what do you have to say for yourself? Not so brave now that you realize what it's like to be dead, I see."

"I thought this would end and I would be able to leave this place," the girl gritted out. "I saw a light when I died. I tried to go into it, but I could not. Am I going to become a demon?"

"That's quite unlikely," said Luciana, sighing. "You must be able to guess that not every human becomes a demon or an angel when they pass over. There are exceptional circumstances."

*Circumstances that this child would neither be able to fathom nor endure.*

Luciana knew that instantly by looking at her. Had known it when they had sacrificed the girl. Violetta was too fragile. And altogether too good.

"You need to move on. Just let go," Luciana told her. "There's nothing holding you here."

"I'm not going anywhere. Not just yet," said the girl, a fraction more solid than she had been an instant ago.

"If you still had a body, I would give you a good shake," said Luciana. She had never encountered such a situation before. After all the sacrifices that had ever occurred within the walls of Ca' Rossetti, no soul had ever stayed around afterward. Each and every one of them had been ferried away in the devil's funerary gondola, after Luciana had delivered them in front of the Redentore Church. Now, she thought bitterly, *if only Brandon had not screwed up the hunt, everything would be fine.*

"Your stubbornness is commendable, but it's not helping you now. Find the light, and go into it," Luciana told her, making a shooing motion with her hands. Then, a little more gently, a little more cajolingly, she said, "That's what I would do, if I could."

"Why can't you?" Violetta asked.

"Why do you think?" Luciana snapped. "Use your head. I've killed people. A lot of people. Demons are not just allowed to leave when we feel like it. But you are. You should go."

"I'm not ready," said Violetta defiantly. "I still have things to do here."

Luciana threw her hands in the air. "For the love of

God, what *things?* There is nothing keeping you here except your own stubborn beliefs, and your own fear."

"There must be something we can help her do. Say goodbye, perhaps," said Massimo.

"No," said Luciana. "We owe her nothing. More important, we have no time to deal with this right now. We have much more pressing things to worry about. If you didn't notice, the angel is still out there. Watching us."

Violetta vanished, the wisp of her image trailing into vapor as she passed through the surface of the wooden door. Massimo's gaze followed her, and a small frown pulled at the corners of his mouth. He tried to hide it, but Luciana saw something she didn't like: the slight parting of his lips as he started to call after Violetta.

"You," she said, pointing at the Gatekeeper, "don't call her back here. Don't even think about her anymore. You've got to keep your wits about you. Love doesn't exist for demons."

"Yes, *baronessa,*" he said quietly.

"Forget the girl. Just let her go. We need to do something about this angel."

She peered out the crack in the draperies of Massimo's window, wondering if this perspective would afford her a better view of Brandon's hiding place. But outside, there was nothing but the empty canal, and across it, the crumbling palazzo sat dark and quiet. No movement.

"I need to go out," she said, shutting the curtain with a snap. "Being trapped in here is driving all of us insane. We must show the angels that we won't be kept penned in like animals."

She could feel Brandon's rugged energy from across the canal. Could almost feel as a palpable sensation the twitch of his hard muscles, the uncomfortable shifting of his big body. Itching to run, to grasp, to capture. To *do*.

You could not force a seduction, she knew. Especially not with a man like this.

A hunter must hunt.

So give him something to hunt.

*Someone* to hunt.

"Brandon is a man of action—that is one thing we know for sure. Undoubtedly if I leave this house, he will follow. I cannot stay in here a moment longer. I need to remember who I am," she said, more to herself than to Massimo. "I need to go hunt. And I will flush the pigeon out of his hiding place at the same time."

"Isn't that taking an unnecessary risk, *baronessa?*"

She smiled. "Not at all. It will serve two purposes. You know the expression in Italian—*Prendere due piccioni con una fava.* The English translation is literally 'to take two pigeons with one bean.' But the real equivalent is 'kill two birds with one stone.' That, my dear Massimo, is what I intend to do."

She smiled to herself.

The English had such a violent way of expressing the same idea.

But in fact, the English saying expressed precisely what she planned to do.

The sun had just set over Venice, casting the city into a dim light. Across the street, Brandon saw a shape flicker, the merest hint of a shadow moving. He leaned forward, peering closer. And saw the figure of the demoness leaving through the side entrance of the house, a hooded cloak drawn over her head. She looked around covertly, then made a quick dash into the alley behind the house.

He jumped up, running across the bridge after her.

He tracked her as she wove through the streets, her dark cloak trailing behind her. There was something different about her, Brandon thought. Something hesitant. Was she in doubt about what it was she wanted? And why had she left the house?

She walked in halting steps. Stopped. He saw her enter a doorway.

He followed the sweep of her cloak.

She turned.

And *she* wasn't Luciana.

The girl's face was paler than the living.

"Who are you? And where is she?" Brandon said, grabbing for her arm. "Where's Luciana?"

He found himself holding a fistful of empty cloak, the fabric draped from his hand as the girl pulled out of the garment entirely. She looked at him with an astonished stare, ghostly eyes flickering with slight anger in the dim light.

"If you're talking about the *baronessa,* I have no idea. She went somewhere, but I don't know where."

He looked at her closely, wondering why she had been inside Ca' Rossetti.

"What did they do to you in there?" he asked.

She shook her head. "That doesn't matter anymore. All that matters is that I need to finish what I have to do. And then I will find the light."

"That's right," he told her. "You've got to go into the light. They can't hold you, you know. If you did nothing to merit damnation, you are not the property of the devil," Brandon said.

"Of course I know that," the girl said, pulling herself up proudly.

"Let me help you. Tell me what I can do."

She stared at him, sending a chill through him. She opened her mouth to speak, as though she had gotten a flash of clarity, had realized something of great importance.

Then she vanished into thin air.

*I hope you find whatever it is you're searching for,* he thought.

God knew there were enough lost souls wandering the streets of Venice.

Brandon headed back into the night, resolving to take care of some unfinished business of his own.

As Luciana prepared to exit the palazzo, she looked out the window and saw the girl fleeing through the side door. And saw Brandon follow.

*I don't even need to flush that pigeon out of his hole,* she thought. *The girl has done it for me.*

Smiling to herself, Luciana waltzed right out the front door, stepped into her boat and drove up the Grand Canal to the Piazza San Marco.

The trip was a short one, and as she navigated her way up the canal, she wore a little smile on her face. Even after two and a half centuries as a Venetian, she never tired of this square, its beauty as stunning as when she had been a young girl.

Ah, yes, it felt good to be out in the open air again.

Back on the hunt.

She docked the boat at a mooring post and headed toward the action.

On this balmy midsummer evening, every table was packed in the big open-air square of the Piazza San Marco, every *caffè* full to capacity, crowds entranced by the many small orchestras playing classical music that wafted into the air. The vendors were out in full force, hawking every sort of Venetian souvenir to the hordes of tourists.

*Finding victims in San Marco is like shooting fish in a barrel,* thought Luciana.

She ordered a Cinzano and settled in to watch the crowd.

Across the pool of crowded tables, a tourist fixed his half-drunk gaze on her.

*Tourists,* she thought nastily, *are more annoying vermin than the pigeons we worked so hard to cull. So perhaps I'll do my civic duty tonight and rid Venice of one more nuisance.*

She smiled, enticingly. Waited for the tourist to come over.

Over the past two centuries, she had heard every pickup line imaginable.

*"Hai da fare per I prossimi cent'anni?"* What are you doing for the next hundred years?

*"Fa caldo qui, o è perchè ci sei tu?"* Is it hot in here, or is it just you?

*"Tu sei il mio sogno proibito."* You're my forbidden dream…

What came out of this one's mouth was no better than she expected.

"Was your father a thief?" he said in English.

"Yes. He stole the stars from the sky and put them in my eyes," she said with a roll of those eyes skyward, toward the stars from which they were allegedly stolen.

"You, too, are a thief, *belissima.* You stole my line."

"We Venetians are thieves at heart," she said, leaning forward to give him a good look at her ample cleavage. She widened her eyes as she looked up at him, and made her voice very sweet as she said, "Half our treasures are looted from religious wars. The facade of our most famous basilica of San Marco is a *miscuglio*...a medley of stolen columns taken from foreign temples. Inside, its altars are decorated with jewels filched from other cities, other churches. Even the famed Horses of San Marco, the four bronzed statues, were so famously robbed away from the Byzantine Empire. *Sì*, even the body of San Marco himself was stolen, his remains thieved out of Egypt by Venetian merchants in the ninth century."

Tourists loved this story. Just as they loved finding an authentic Venetian.

And like all the rest of them, this one ate it up.

He pulled out the chair next to her. "May I?"

"Only if you're in the mood for trouble," she said, running a suggestive finger along the edge of her neckline, along the top of one perfect breast.

He laughed, his eyes almost popping out of his head. "On the contrary. I think I've died and gone to heaven."

"Not exactly," she said. "However, a trip in the other direction can be easily arranged."

He laughed at the odd statement, thinking it was a joke.

*Well,* she thought. *Can't say I didn't warn him.*

He flagged the waiter over and ordered two Cinzanos. When the drinks came, she thought about how easy it would be, what a subtle movement it would take to poison him. A slight squeeze of the fingers could decant a single drop of poison into his drink, too quick for his feeble human mind to even detect.

Under the table, his hand rested on her thigh. Gave it a squeeze that made her want to kick him. Made her want to poison him right here in the square. To leave his dying corpse sitting in this metal chair, for one of the *caffè* waiters to find.

But to do so would draw undue attention to herself. To take a risk that she couldn't afford. Not right now.

Instead, she stretched her face into a tight little smile.

"Venice is so much more than a cliché for tourists," she told him. "You come here for the festivals. Buy a carnival mask, drink some Prosecco. Tour the palazzos and the churches. If you consider yourself very stylish, you might have a Bellini at Harry's Bar. But you will never get another chance to see Venice as the real Venetians know it. I would love to show you the secrets of my home. A part of the city that few other tourists have ever seen."

That part was no lie.

Before the night was over, he would take a tour to the bottom of a canal.

After all, how many tourists got to see *that?*

She pulled the tourist toward one of the waiting gondolas, allowed him to help her into it.

"Take a leisurely route," she told the human gondolier, rattling off directions that would bring them within stumbling distance of her home. "Listen," she said, leaning on the edge of the boat. "The gondoliers are singing *barcarole,* traditional folk songs. They sing all the time, but mostly popular songs from the South. 'O Sole Mio.' That is what you hear in the canals so often, and it is not even from Venice. But once in a while, you will find some who sing the old Venetian songs. How beautiful, no?"

But the tourist wasn't listening. He pawed her, clumsily running his hands over her, evoking nothing but disgust in her.

*Soon,* she promised herself. *Soon this will be over, and he will be lying underwater.*

Then, the most disturbing thought popped into her mind.

She found herself wishing Brandon's hands were running over her.

Wished it were Brandon's tattooed, muscled arms holding her. His beautifully curved lips brushing over hers, instead of this cretin human tourist's.

And when she opened her eyes, there *he* was.

Standing on the rooftop of one of the old palazzos, high above them, staring down at them. Silhouetted against the night sky by the moonlight, and there was no doubt why he had come.

Luciana gasped out loud.

"What is it?" asked the tourist.

"Nothing," she said, stealing a glance upward.

The angel was strolling along the rooftops as casually as any human might stroll along the *Mercerie,* shopping for goods.

Neither of the humans below—not the tourist nor the gondolier—gave a hint of even noticing.

In a flash, the angel was beside them, bearing down on them. He ripped the man away from her. Grabbing the front of his shirt, he stared deep into the tourist's eyes. Quietly, Brandon said, "Get out of the gondola now. Forget you ever met this woman. Your little adventure is over. You will not recall any of this. If you ever try to remember what happened tonight, you will only remember wandering among the streets of Venice, lost."

The human froze for an instant, in shock as the angel bore down on him.

*"Go!"* Brandon thundered, nearly pushing him clean out of the gondola.

In the calm water, the boat rocked.

For an instant, Luciana wondered if the whole contraption might tip into the canal, spilling all of them into the murky water. The tourist clambered out of the boat onto the *fondamenta* and took off without a backward glance.

Expert with his long pole, the gondolier steadied his craft. He frowned deeply at his two remaining passengers and opened his mouth to complain, but Brandon cut him off before he could speak.

"There's nothing out of the ordinary here," the angel said, staring deep into the mortal's eyes. "Please continue rowing, and pay no heed to our conversation."

The gondolier hesitated and his eyes blanked before he began absorbing the suggestion. Then he complied, and they continued to glide along the canal.

"You again," the demoness hissed at Brandon. She frowned deeply, leaning back on the velvet cushions of the gondola. Suddenly, she felt cold, the rush of adrenaline from the hunt seeping out of her, replaced by something else. The chill of exposure as Brandon stared at her. "You're ruining all my fun these days."

"I'm ruining your fun? You're the one invading my dreams, succubus."

"*Zuccolo.* You're completely crazy," she said. "I'm not a succubus. Why would I stoop to seducing men in their dreams when I am perfectly capable of doing so while they're fully conscious?"

"Then what did you do to my dream? How did you control it?" he demanded.

Her brow furrowed in the moonlight, peering at him in the darkness. "I don't know what you're talking about."

"You know exactly what I'm talking about."

"What you dream is your own business," she said, giving an exasperated sigh. "If you saw me in a dream, it was because you wanted me. Your unconscious mind is running wild. We can pick up where you left off...."

She ran her hand up his thigh. And felt his entire body tense. Yet, he didn't make a move toward her.

"They're your dreams, too," he said quietly. "There are details that I've never seen before."

"Perhaps you're simply imagining what my world would look like."

He grabbed for her wrist. She moved away, out of his reach. She leaned over the side of the gondola and trailed her fingers in the water, enjoying the flow of the cool water over them. Biding her time.

"You think you can just grab me again, barbarian? Think. I'll just escape, the same way I did the first time." Her voice dropped to a whisper, too low for the gondolier to overhear as she spoke in the angel's ear. "Besides, after our last little encounter in the flesh, I set up a little insurance policy. If I don't return to my home by a certain time, my Gatekeepers have instructions to distribute a large amount of very lethal poison among the demon hierarchy. The results could be devastating."

She smiled, keeping very still and very calm.

The trick to bluffing, she knew, was to believe your own lie.

*It's partly true,* she told herself. *If I don't return, in all likelihood, Massimo would do exactly what I said. He has all the knowledge he needs to master the art of poison by himself. Even if he is not quite ready yet.*

"You're bluffing," he said. "If you had a massive amount of that poison, you'd have used it by now."

"Would I? If you're willing to take the risk, you can find out for sure," she challenged back, staring deeply into his eyes. "If you don't believe me, take your chances. Slap the cuffs on me. Haul me away."

"You wouldn't dare release that poison," said Brandon. "You know you can't violate the rules between angels and demons."

"Rules are made to be broken. And if not broken, rules can be bent. Try me."

"What do you propose?"

"You should consider joining our side," she said, sliding her hand up his thigh, reaching upward. "I can feel something in you that's not like the rest of them. Something dark."

She looked up at him, letting her eyes do their work on him. She could see him struggling with his lust, the turmoil in those gray-as-rain eyes of his. Saw him clench the muscles of his tightened jaw as he fought to keep his cool beneath that tough-guy exterior.

"What will it take to get you to cooperate?" he said.

"Why should I cooperate?"

"Because you have the power to do the right thing."

"Don't talk to me about the right thing. You don't know what I've had to endure to get to where I am. You think Venice is beautiful and sacred. You don't know the *real* Venice," she said, her voice deepening into a snarl. "Can't you feel it? This city is steeped in suffering and death. Not two hundred yards from here, prisoners were tortured. There is an entire museum full of weaponry and torture instruments. I can take you down into the prison cells attached to the Doge's palace. We can take our own little trip to hell without ever leaving Venice."

"No, thanks," he said, staring her down.

"If you look closely, you'll see the underworld drawn on this city. Etched in the architecture. Gargoyles and gremlins crouching in corners, perched on cornices and tucked into the shadows beneath the eaves. A satanic lion's head is carved on a palazzo on the Calle Diedo.

On the facade of the *Ospedale Civile,* the 'City Hospital,' there's a sixteenth-century graffiti etching of a murderer holding a human heart after ripping it out of his own mother."

"If you're looking for hatred, it's easy enough to find," he said grimly.

"Never underestimate the presence of evil. Evil exists here. It is real. If you don't believe me, I can show you. Venetians used to believe there was a dragon living in the lagoon who could be pacified only by the oars of the gondoliers. Do you think that myth was founded on a superstitious fear, or do you think there was some truth to it?"

Around them, the water rippled as the gondolier's oar stroke pushed through it. Then the canal began to churn, and Brandon caught sight of an object surfacing in the dark water.

The long, lizard-scaled back of what looked like a very large snake.

Brandon blinked, his mind not trusting what his eyes were telling him.

He reached toward his shoulder holster for his gun, but neither were there.

Neither had been there for the past decade.

*Whatever it is, this is not a dream,* he thought.

Massive and furious, the dragon rose. Water poured from its body as it emerged from the canal to tower over the boat. The sheer bulk of it, as huge as a rhinoceros and as fast as an anaconda, hung over them. Its eyes, bright green and verdant like Luciana's, fixed on Brandon.

Who simply returned its stare.

Despite the pounding of his heart and his gut screaming at him to swim, to run, to flee however he could to escape this beast from the underworld.

But he looked back at the demoness and said in a calm voice, "Put it back. Whatever realm of hell you dragged that thing out of, send it back where it came from."

"Why should I?" the demoness grated out.

He didn't remove his gaze from her. "It doesn't belong in this world."

Twelve feet in the air, the animal opened its mouth and roared out a stream of fire that singed the air beside Brandon's head. The gondolier cringed in terror, hunching down nearly into a fetal tuck. Yet Brandon did not relent. He *could* not relent. His calm gray eyes remained fixed on her. For long moments, he stared.

"You can choose to destroy me right here and now," he said calmly, "but you know you'll start a war you can't finish."

He saw her mouth tighten, flattening into a frustrated line.

At last, the dragon gave a final heated sigh and slid back down into the canal.

Cowering, the gondolier remained kneeling in a ball at the back of the boat.

"Please continue," Brandon told him, urging the man up. "It was simply an illusion. Just a trick of the shadows."

For a moment, the gondolier's human mind wavered with the idea, not accepting it.

"Who would really believe that you saw a real dragon?" Brandon asked him. "It was merely a trick that my friend here conjured."

Luciana, too, began to cajole the man in Italian.

He smiled shakily, but once again stood and began to row.

"Are you happy?" Luciana said, sitting back against the cushions. "I should have ordered that creature to burn you into oblivion, where you belong. Really, why do you insist on spoiling everything?"

"That's my job," he said flatly. "It's my role to believe that everything and everyone in this world would choose goodness, given the choice. Even you. You can pull out every trick you've got up those lovely sleeves of yours, but nothing you've got can scare me."

"I may not be able to scare you. But a darkness resides inside you. It is your greatest vulnerability. If it doesn't frighten you, it should."

His heart began to race, more terrified of that truth than he had been of a mythical creature rising from the waters of an illusive city.

She leaned near, whispering in his ear, "I can fix that darkness inside you. I can give you what you want."

*You can't give me what I want,* he knew. *No one can.*

"Young lovers," said the gondolier, finally emerging from his shock as he mistook the nearness of his passengers for intimacy. "This is a city for lovers. See, we are coming up to the Bridge of Sighs. We Venetians say that if a pair of lovers kiss as they pass under this bridge, their love will last for all eternity."

The demoness's hand touched Brandon's shoulder, a light touch that was as fleeting as the landing of a butterfly's wing. The profound softness of that contact surprised him.

*How can a woman who just conjured a dragon out of the depths of the Venetian lagoon be so gentle?*

With her other hand, she pointed, and he shifted his gaze from her face for an instant, looking up at the ornate covered bridge that arched overhead. He turned back to look at her, watched the last play of moonlight on her face turning to shadow as they passed beneath the bridge. Utterly without thinking, he leaned forward and closed the distance between them. With a brush of his fingers on the side of her jawline, turned her face toward him.

*You're on a mission here,* said his mind. *You must retain all your faculties of reason.*

*Kiss her,* screamed his gut.

So he kissed her.

A mere graze of his lips against hers, a flutter of contact as light as her butterfly touch. But he felt it as a visceral jolt, that intimate connection of skin against moist skin, a shock that resounded in the depths of his being. He felt as though he had shifted into another reality, one that seemed as volatile and ephemeral as a dreamspace.

He felt her gasp.

Felt her lips part beneath his, felt her sharp intake of breath. Felt her mouth quiver against his before she went completely and utterly still. After a pause that seemed to last a lifetime, her breath escaped on a sigh so faint that it was almost outside the realm of perception.

*Am I awake, or am I dreaming?* he wondered.

The butterfly effect sprang to mind—the theory that something as light as a butterfly's wing could change everything. That the mere presence of one small insect could alter weather patterns. Could lead to the creation or the absence of a hurricane, for instance.

*What about a firefly?* he wondered.

Whether it could or not, a hurricane sweep of desire was building inside Brandon, generated by that kiss. That gentle contact had stirred an internal fire that flared and raged, aching to get out. It was a desire he fought against with all the discipline of his calling, wrestling with his unruly passions.

From somewhere deep inside himself, a little voice said, *Perhaps this kiss could change everything...*

He promptly dismissed the notion, laughing a little to himself at the ridiculousness of it.

And was brought back into the here and now by the action of Luciana's hand as it fell away from his shoulder in a jerky motion, almost as though her body had entered a state of shock.

"Why did you do that?" she said.

Her face had gone a pallid shade of white, even paler than her usual coloring.

Blinking up at him, she seemed flustered, confused.

To Brandon, she looked not as though she'd seen a ghost, but as though she *was* one. An apparition struggling to maintain her grasp on her earthly form, perhaps about to leave it. As far as he knew, she lacked the power to dematerialize. As bound to her physical body as he was to his, Luciana nonetheless looked like she might evaporate on the spot.

Instead of answering her, he kissed her again. As his lips descended onto hers, all thinking stopped entirely. And feeling took over.

# *Chapter Eight*

In Luciana's gut, panic rose.

"Stop," she instructed the gondolier. "I need to get off immediately."

Reaching into her purse, she flung a fistful of euros at him.

Then she took off into the streets, walking quickly, wanting to get as far away from Brandon as possible. Wanting to erase that kiss from her lips, the memory of it, the fact that it had ever happened. Wanting to erase the feeling that he had somehow trapped her into the most horrible thing that could happen to a woman like her.

*Love.*

Brandon followed, his stride even and unhurried, keeping up with her easily as she flitted through the passageways.

They passed beneath a carved relief of a dragon slayer with his spear.

He grabbed her arm, stopping her.

"San Giorgio," she spat out. "He is everywhere here in Venice. But where is he now? Will he help you slay the dragon and save the maiden? Do you even know which is which?"

*Do I know which I am?* she wondered. *Am I the dragon or the maiden? Am I both?*

"Right now, looking into your eyes, I can tell what you think of me," Luciana said fiercely. "That there is something fragile and innocent inside of me that needs to be saved. You couldn't be more wrong."

He didn't answer.

"Perhaps it's *you* who need to be saved," she taunted. "There is something dark within you. I can feel it. Something yearning for release."

It was very quiet here in the street, with the silence of sleeping Venice surrounding them.

He backed her into a dark doorway, beneath a stone arch that could have belonged to a private home, a shop or a restaurant—it hardly mattered to her which. All that mattered was *him*. He pressed into her, trapping her body against the door.

She felt a tremble run through her own body as his lips brushed over hers, gentle at first.

And then not gentle.

Seeking, demanding, a pent-up fire in him fiercely seizing her mouth. Burning.

As it was, pinned between his body and that door, there was nowhere to move.

Nowhere to go.

Yet inside, she had taken flight. The heady rush of desire—or was it his muscled arm—lifted her so that she was off one foot, her thighs opening for him, one leg lifting to ride his hip. His hands held her, lifting her off her feet entirely, bracing her against the door. His fingers dug into the backs of her slim thighs as he ground his hardened cock against the softest, darkest place of her. The only thing separating the most intimate joining was the barrier of their clothing, the zippered fly of his jeans and the thin silk of her panties.

Darkness. Her territory.

And yet, here on the familiar streets of Venice, she felt as though she were venturing on to new ground entirely, here in the arms of this man. Of this angel.

She slipped her hand between them, rubbed the flat of her palm against the hard, hot bulge behind the fabric of his jeans.

She wanted him inside her.

He groaned, throbbing in her hand, pulsing in her palm as though he might explode any minute.

*Power.* The balance had shifted back to her, the epicenter of her control held in the palm of her hand, in her fingers wrapped around this gloriously hard erection of his.

He kissed her, more deeply, a deep, guttural groan vibrating through her. His hand slid up her throat, caressing, his thumb rubbing against the pulse point there.

How easy it would be to simply unzip his fly, she knew. Free the hard length of him. Guide him to herself and open for him. And then feel him sliding into her, the girth of him filling that void inside her, the power of that connection shared between them in the most intimate way possible.

She opened her eyes.

*Madness. Absolute and unquestionable.*

*Yes.*


They stood in that darkened doorway, learning each other's bodies, the contact of each other so heightened and new, as though they had entered some other world.

The dark pull of her was an attraction that made Brandon think thoughts he had never even imagined before. Sensual images of the two of them flickered through his mind. Sweat-slicked in the height of fervor, joined in the most intimate and sacred of ways, their bodies moving together as they reached for the state of ecstasy.

As their lips met again, he resisted the urge to press farther, his body aching to push into hers, already flush against the door. No fireworks tonight, but the explosion of lust inside of him detonated.

Desire radiated through him, hot and pure. Slipped into his bloodstream faster than any poison. More potent than any drug. More dangerous than death itself.

Then Brandon broke off the kiss.

From the shadows of that doorway he saw a figure high above them, silhouetted by moonlight. Up among the statues on the top of St. Mark's Basilica, was the Archangel Michael.

Brandon saw him now. And so did Luciana.

The Archangel circled down from the dark heavens, wings outstretched, more monumental than any statue, more glorious than any painting ever managed to portray him. A myriad of colors undulated in his wings; a dazzling display of light poured from him as he approached, circling down from the sky overhead.

Brandon let go of the demoness. She ran, her dark hair swirling around her as she turned to look back at him, green eyes glittering in the darkness. The sound of her footsteps, quick strike of her heels on the uneven cobblestones, faded into the alleyway as she turned a corner and disappeared.

And Brandon turned to face Michael as the Archangel landed in the empty street.

The single being, aside from God himself, who had authority over him.

The one Brandon resisted the most.

On the night Brandon had died, Michael had answered his prayer. Lying there in the filth of the back alley, bleeding out on the pavement, Michael had drifted down to collect him. Not clad in the traditional armor with sword and shield, like the statues scattered around this city, or the old paintings that existed of him. But in a leather jacket and jeans.

There was a reason they normally communicated through text messages, not face-to-face.

*You guided me into the afterlife, ordained my soul into the order of the angels. And I never forgave you for it.*

"I haven't seen you in person for a while," said Brandon. "What brings you to this neck of the woods?"

Michael looked calmly in the direction the demoness had fled. "You need help."

"She was in my grasp," Brandon said. "I almost had her."

"No, Brandon," Michael said casually, folding his wings back down, taking on an appearance that was almost human. A glowing, ethereal human. "*She* almost had *you.*"

"Don't be ridiculous."

"I have come not just as an Archangel. Not just as your boss. But as someone who cares for you and is concerned for your well-being."

"I didn't know you cared."

*If you cared so much, why did you let me die?*

*If you cared so much, why do you allow me to suffer every night?*

The questions hung between them, as they always did when Brandon and Michael met.

"I do care. I care about you, and I care about this

mission. You must accept help. You have surpassed the point at which you can handle this assignment alone."

"She's just one demon."

The doubts began again in his mind, spurred on by the things Luciana had said tonight.

"Maybe I'm not good," he gritted, hating to say the words aloud to Michael. But there was no one else to whom he could turn for guidance. "There's a part of me that wants her. Wants the things I gave up to become an angel. Even a divine calling cannot make up for the things I left behind."

"I understand if you're upset about your human death. But haven't you seen that death is not the end? I've tried to show you that time and again. Each of your assignments has been leading to a point, which is to give you further wisdom about this world. Not everything is the way it appears. Nothing is static."

"What the hell does that mean?"

"It means you don't have all the information. You aren't meant to know the circumstances surrounding your human death at this time. You have been told that countless times since you were ordained. Leave it alone."

"What's the point of all this? Of being stuck in this physical body?"

"Being sent back in a physical incarnation allows you to continue to understand humans. For example, I, who am so removed from the earth and from physical form, cannot help them in the same way that you do."

"Those are crap reasons," Brandon said. "Basically, what your answers have taught me is not to trust you. And that *you* don't trust *me*."

"You know that's not the case. We trust you implicitly. Right now, that's not the issue. I simply came here to warn you. Luciana Rossetti is close to tearing a hole in your consciousness. You don't seem to recognize how much power she can wield, given the opportunity."

"Then why did you assign me to this case?"

"It's an opportunity for both you and Luciana to grow."

"Then let me do it my way," Brandon said. "Until you can prove to me that it's not working."

"You're not the one calling the shots here, Brandon. Don't let your ego get in the way of your mission," Michael chided. "I'm not going to micromanage you. But Luciana is very persuasive, and you are in grave danger of losing your grounding. I'm giving you two more days to do things your way. And then the Archangels will step in and take over."

Brandon didn't answer, but simply turned and walked away, leaving the Archangel standing in the quiet street.

Luciana slammed the door behind her when she returned home. Breathless, she leaned against it, grateful that she had escaped once again.

*From an Archangel. Impossible.*

Venice was full of their images. You could barely swing a cat without hitting a picture of a saint in this city, but they didn't expose themselves very often. At least not to her eyes.

In fact, the total number of times she had actually seen one before was zero.

The Gatekeepers were gathered in the front room, discussing heatedly amongst themselves. The conversation stopped, and they all turned to look when she entered.

"Violetta has not come back yet," Massimo said, pacing back and forth. "It was a mistake, sending that girl out there. She was not ours to begin with. She should never have been kept here. We should have found some way to help her pass on immediately."

"Stop worrying about her," Luciana snapped. "She's a ghost, not a lost puppy. We have much more pressing things to worry about."

"Where were *you* tonight?" he asked.

"I had a run-in with the angels."

"Angels, as in plural?" Massimo's green eyes widened.

She briefly recounted her encounter with the Archangel and fleeing from Brandon.

The Gatekeepers would never dare speak it, but a question hung in the air, poised among all of them.

*Why didn't you kill him tonight?*

"You must find a way to end him quickly," Massimo said quietly. "Without hesitation."

"Yes," she said, pressing her eyes closed, swallowing down the feeling of her own failure. "I know that."

"You've said many times that demons cannot love."

"Love has nothing to do with any of this," she said, her temper flaring. "Don't presume to think that it does."

"Of course, *baronessa*," he said.

With a bow, he departed, and she heard him go downstairs to his own quarters, close his door with a small sound. The other Gatekeepers, not knowing what to do without his guidance, dispersed to their own rooms, too, muttering to one another as they went.

Immediately, she regretted snapping at him.

Downstairs, Violetta began to sing, a soaring aria that spiraled up through the old stone. Eerie, but in its oddness, more beautiful than any human voice Luciana had ever heard. *So she made it back after all.* A strange sense of relief washed over the demoness, although why she should care about the girl, she didn't know.

*Massimo is right,* she knew. *My resolve is slipping.*

For almost two and a half centuries, she had navigated this city with finesse. Gliding through its streets and taking what she needed, relishing in her feats under the cover of night. She had climbed her way out of hell and rebuilt her household. She had maintained that household with all the dignity of the noble name to which she had been born.

Never wavering, never hesitating, never regretting.

Now, with the arrival of this interloper angel, everything had changed.

Luciana abhorred change. The angel would have to be fixed.

And quickly, because she was running out of time.

"You've got to sleep sometime," she murmured, peering out the window into the darkness, knowing that *he* was out there. "And when you do, I'll be waiting."

Across the canal, Brandon returned to the crumbling building, back to the windowsill with the boards stripped away. There was no point in hiding from her now—she knew exactly where he was. He would have to find a way to attack the demoness on another front.

Weaken her defenses without giving her the opportunity to weaken *his.*

And as he returned to his observation point, he saw exactly what he needed.

An opportunity. An opening.

*Her Gatekeepers.*

From what he had seen, there were six Gatekeepers in all, burly young men in jeans and black T-shirts. Because they looked similar and dressed identically, it was hard to tell how many there *actually* were. Now, through the palazzo's massive windows, he could see Luciana and her Gatekeepers pacing back and forth, immersed in a conversation that appeared to leave them all dejected. Then they dispersed, each going into different rooms.

*She's probably told them about her little run-in with me,* he realized.

None of them looked too happy about the discussion that had taken place.

It was exactly the kind of opening he needed.

Right now, her security system was on the brink of collapse.

He slipped out of his hiding place. Not far away, he found a rickety wooden boat tied to a mooring post and decided to borrow it. He rowed quietly across the canal, leaving his borrowed vessel tied loosely to her neighbor's landing.

The courtyard beside her palazzo was beautifully kept, spilling with roses, the scent of them overwhelming in the summer heat.

*Such a beautiful garden must be maintained by someone,* he thought.

There was a small shed in the corner of the courtyard. He went to it, easily picking the ornamental lock. Perused the gardening tools inside. And picked up a hedge trimmer.

Tucking it into the back of his belt, he circled the house quietly in the dark. Halfway up the side wall, he spotted a box near the roof that looked like it might contain some important electrical wiring.

He climbed up the ornate decoration, hanging on the edge of a balcony just below the box. Reaching for the hedge trimmer, he used the tool to pry open the box. Inside, the multicolored electrical wires curled in a thick coil.

He hacked through the cords.

Inside the house, the lights went off. The reflection disappeared from the surface of the canal, moonlight the only thing spilling across the dark water.

And Brandon waited. Silence.

Shouts from within the house began.

The demoness's distinctive honey-toned voice rang out. *"Massimo! Giancarlo!"*

The deep voices of the Gatekeepers, calling to each other in a rapid stream of Italian.

The side door opened.

Two of the Gatekeepers came outside to investigate, one carrying a toolbox.

The Gatekeepers might be slow, but Brandon could tell they sensed him out there as they stood outside the door, listening in the stillness, peering out into the dark.

It was the goblins under the house who gave him away. The evil little creatures screeched in high-pitched squeals, like alley cats in a fight. The Gatekeepers turned toward the noise. The one with the toolbox flung it open. He drew back his arm and chucked a wrench at Brandon's head like an anvil. The other one charged, head down like a bull.

Brandon caught the wrench in midair, pivoted like a matador to avoid the charging demon and brought the heavy tool down on the back of his assailant's neck. The demon fell like a rock.

In a split second, he was after the other one, throwing the wrench back and knocking the Gatekeeper's knees out from under him. The man groaned and Brandon held him in a headlock until he passed out.

One at a time, he hauled each unconscious body to

the little wooden boat and tossed them both in the bottom, securing their hands with his cuffs. Once he had rowed the short distance across to his own crumbling temporary abode, he still wasn't done.

He hefted them inside. It was only when he had them both arranged securely in a windowless little room in the back of the building that he checked to see what the demoness was doing across the street. She was standing in a window, holding a candle and peering out into the night.

*Come out and play,* he almost shouted across the canal.

Then he went to interview his new acquaintances.

In her workroom, bent over her extractions, Luciana continued working on her formula by candlelight.

Massimo pounded on the door. He called through it with a strained note in his voice that she had never heard before. "*Baronessa,* we have an emergency."

She opened the door, pulling off her gloves to rub her tired eyes.

"I can see that," she said, blinking in the darkness. "Have the Gatekeepers made any headway restoring the electricity?"

"No, *baronessa.* As you can see, we are still without power. But more importantly—" Massimo's face was drawn "—two of the Gatekeepers have disappeared."

"Which ones?" she said.

"Giancarlo and Antonio. They went outside to try to fix the outage."

Neither of them said anything. Giancarlo and Antonio were both strong young men. Certainly capable of holding their own.

She swallowed. "We don't know what happened to

them, but it doesn't make sense to assume the worst. If the Company of Angels got a hold of them, they'll likely just find a woman to fuck them into submission. That seems to be their main mode of operation."

Massimo managed a shaky smile. "True enough."

"We can't worry about them now. We have other things to focus on," she said. "Time is running out. We have a handful of days left to deliver our sacrifice. And if we don't…"

She pressed her lips together and swallowed. There was no use thinking about the consequences. They both knew what would happen.

"Do not fear, Massimo. See if you can repair the power outage. I must keep working."

She bent over the worktable, furious as she worked by the flickering light of a taper.

Brandon tried every interrogation technique he knew, short of torture.

After several hours of interrogating the Gatekeepers in separate small, windowless rooms, he was getting nowhere. He loomed over one of them, who matched him in size, chained carefully—with his hands separated from each other—to the foot of a rusted-out bed frame. The man glared up at him. His ferocious loyalty to his mistress was clear in his dark brown eyes.

"Why are you so loyal to her?" Brandon asked, crouching once more to stare eye to eye with the man. "She wouldn't do the same for you."

"You have no idea what the *baronessa* is like, deep down," the Gatekeeper growled, the first words he had spoken. "You totally misunderstand her."

"Then tell me."

"Your kind is always too busy judging to hear the truth."

"Try me," Brandon said, folding his arms across his chest.

*Silence.*

Brandon paced around the room, looking down at him, knowing that to hit him would be to lose the game. He wouldn't stoop to violence—not in this situation. He had already gone as far as he cared to go in that direction. So instead, he started talking. Talking absolute bullshit, saying the worst things he could think of about Luciana Rossetti.

"She's a whore. She's weak. She's mentally deranged. She'd sell her own grandmother to the devil, and probably did. She'd sell you Gatekeepers out if anyone ever offered her the chance." He continued, circling the room and ranting out every insult that came to mind.

"Enough!" The Gatekeeper lunged forward finally, yanking violently against his bonds. The entire bed frame clattered. "The *baronessa* is none of those things."

"We're not going anywhere, so you might as well talk. There's no harm in telling me why you remain loyal to her, is there?"

The Gatekeeper bunched his hands into fists and gave a growl of frustration. He considered it for a moment. Then he said, "We were orphans, all of us Gatekeepers. Lost souls living on the streets. We were no better off than the vermin you see crawling in the gutters, no better than the goblins living beneath the houses here. The *baronessa* gave us a roof over our heads, food to eat. She gave us a purpose."

"Killing people," Brandon said flatly.

"It is a small price to pay for our freedom. At least

her victims have a chance of redemption. What happens to them is temporary—they can't be held in eternal damnation. Not unless they're truly evil to begin with."

"You tell yourself that, to alleviate your conscience," said Brandon.

"You don't think the devil can hold the souls of the truly innocent forever, do you? If you believe that, then you're more screwed than I am," the demon growled.

"So you have a conscience, after all. I can help you. Just tell me how much poison Luciana has," Brandon said. "You know which one I'm talking about."

"I know no such thing," the Gatekeeper said.

"Don't play stupid. She has a poison that can kill immortals. She killed a demon in Vegas, a low-ranking bellboy. How *much* does she have?"

The Gatekeeper stared back, hate snapping in his brown eyes. "That, you'll never get out of *me*. What I will say is that the *baronessa* has the power to avenge herself on you, and all of your kind. And when she does, you'll regret you ever came here."

Brandon paced a little circle around the room.

"I've seen your kind come through this city before," the Gatekeeper spat. "In the sixteenth century, we called it the Inquisition. You think you can justify torture just because you tell yourself that you're on the 'right' side. You have no idea whether your side is really justifiable. Look at yourself. What makes you any different from me?"

"The fact that I haven't pummeled you into a bloody mess, like you would have done to me if the circumstances were reversed," Brandon said.

"You'd better pray that never happens," the Gatekeeper growled.

Brandon gagged the man quickly. And then he exited

the room immediately, without saying another word. Because he was an inch away from doing real physical damage to the demon.

Maybe the Gatekeeper was right.

Maybe there was a fine line between angel and demon, between just how far a person was willing to go in the name of the "right" cause.

*Maybe.*

Outside in the hallway, just for a second, Brandon leaned against the wall, sliding down it to sit on the floor. He shook his head, trying to clear the exhaustion out of it, and for a mere instant, let his eyelids drift shut.

*Just to rest my eyes. Just for a second.*

*And when he opened them, he checked his pocket, touched the watch.*

I'm dreaming.

*He stood by the edge of a swimming pool. The moon's reflection splayed across the surface of the water, and as Brandon looked into its crystalline blue depths, the pool looked so unbelievably alluring that the promise of diving into it was almost more seductive than the demoness herself.*

Almost.

*When he saw her, he realized how ridiculous that thought was. She wore her long, dark hair pulled back in a sleek ponytail. Her lush body in a tiny silver bikini seemed to Brandon like evidence of the divine if he'd ever seen it. The miniscule garment she wore seemed to have been designed to catch the moonlight, as though it had some power to draw light into it. And where light was drawn, so was the eye.*

"Buona sera. *It has been so hot in the city these past few days, don't you think? Why don't you take a little break with me?" she said, the coy slide of her green*

*eyes a calculation in seduction, the angle of her face
so shockingly lovely, the movement so simple and yet
so arresting.*

*Everything Luciana did was measured. Every ges-
ture, perfectly choreographed, every glance, perfectly
timed. It only seemed simple, he told himself, because
she had perfected it, had practiced it for hundreds of
years on hundreds of men. Perhaps thousands.*

Beauty can be evil, *he reminded himself for the hundredth time in the past several days. And for the hundredth time, his body answered back,* But not beauty
like this.

*She strode toward him, her skin luminescent in the
moonlight.*

Look away, *said his gut.*

That would be an utter waste, *said the rest of him.*

*In any case, he found that he could not tear his eyes
away, even if he had wanted to. Why he had thought
he had any chance of resisting her, caught up in this
world of dreaming with her, he had no idea. He was a
fool, full of bravado and good intentions.*

*Intentions he now realized were mere paving stones
along the road to hell.*

*As if he had a choice.*

*"Enjoying the show?" she asked, tilting her head
slightly as she walked toward the pool. "In case you
were wondering, they're real."*

*He flushed red, because he* had *wondered...*

*She ran a finger along the edge of one taut silver
triangle. Then she went to sit on the edge of the pool,
dipped her toe into the water. "Così buono, 'that feels
so good.'"*

*He rolled his eyes toward the darkened sky.*

*Somewhere up there, Michael and the rest of the*

*Archangels must be looking down and having a good laugh at his expense.*

"*Well, are you just going to stand around and watch? Why don't you join me for a swim? I know you must be hot. It would be such a relief just to take a little dip, wouldn't it?*" *She beckoned, holding out her open hand toward him.* "*Come on. You know you want to. We could even swim* senza vestiti."

"*What does that mean?*" *he said, feeling like a complete moron when the answer was so glaringly obvious. Still, he could not control himself. It was as if someone else was speaking for him, controlling his tongue here in his dreamworld.*

Luciana, *he thought wildly,* is gaining more and more of a hold over me.

*She smiled as though she understood everything perfectly.*

"*I could tell you. But why don't I demonstrate instead?*" *she said, reaching behind her neck. Two quick pulls of a silver string, and the top of her bikini fell away. He felt himself harden at the sight of her large, dark nipples.* "*See? Isn't learning Italian fun?*"

*His mouth was completely dry; he didn't even try to speak.*

"*Come,*" *she beckoned.*

*He found it impossible to resist.*

*He went to her, shedding his clothes along the way, dropping them onto the pool deck behind him. He came to sit beside her, lowering his own legs into the pool. After days of sweating in that abandoned building, he was ready to plunge right into the depths of the water.*

*Reaching up, she brushed the side of his cheek with her fingertips. He reached down to cup one of those glorious breasts, brushing his fingers over the nipple, feeling it tighten beneath his touch.*

*She kissed him. The sweetness of it was impossible. He pulled her into the water so they stood waist-deep, lifted her leg so it rode his thigh. He was just on the verge of entering her, of plunging into the sweet depths of her.*

When a voice came whispering through, shattering the moment of intense pleasure.

# Chapter Nine

"*Brandon, wake up.*" The whisper of a woman's voice, the teasing brush of her hair on his face lured him from sleep.

"Luciana?"

A delicate perfume filled his nostrils. A scent he knew well. Roses and a hint of vanilla.

Not a scent he associated with the demoness.

In the early morning sunlight, he blinked, dazed for a moment.

The eyes peering down at him were clear blue. Not green. The crease between them was one of profound concern. A flood of sunlight illuminated a halo of bright gold hair. The woman who hovered over him was so near that he almost flinched at her presence.

"You must have been in the middle of a nightmare," Arielle stated flatly.

Her intense blue gaze swept over his disheveled state, assessing in a single glance. What a sight he must look, sweat dried on him, unwashed and unshaved. Her dainty nose twitched slightly; her mouth pressed into a thin little line.

Yet, she knelt so very close. And lingered over him a little too long.

When she straightened to stand, the sunlight behind

her seemed to dim, and the intensity of her presence faded as she backed away. Dressed in one of her usual perfectly tailored suits, Arielle looked completely out of place in this dusty Venetian ruin.

*Luciana is...not your run-of-the-mill nightmare,* he thought, blinking hard. He rubbed his eyes, trying to erase the last remnants of the dream from his mind's eye. *But that's nothing you need to know, Arielle.* His former supervisor and ex-lover had never been privy to his dreams; they were not something he wanted to share with her.

Not in the past. And especially not now.

Heat flushed into his face. And he was a man who never blushed. But he felt like he was back in his bedroom in Detroit as a teenager, busted by his mother for "reading" a nudie magazine. He shifted uncomfortably, wondering if Arielle had noticed his erection. Luckily, in her presence, it shrank at an amazing speed.

"I came to help," she said. "You look like you could use some assistance."

"I've been in Venice for two and a half days," he said, irritated as he sat up. His body ached from lying on the hard concrete. He twisted, trying to stretch; he saw her eyes flicker over his bare torso. He chose to ignore that. "I'm not a rookie. I don't need you looking over my shoulder."

"I came for your own good," she said.

*For your own good.*

According to Arielle, everything she did was for someone else's good.

He had gotten his first taste of that ten years ago, when he had joined her unit in L.A. Arielle had taught him a lot. That was undeniable. Had let him follow her everywhere, had answered every question he ever had about being a Guardian. What's more, when he had been sunk in grief over leaving his human existence and his wife, Arielle had been there to comfort him.

But things had changed. At first, it was nothing he could put his finger on. Just a low-lying feeling in his gut that something wasn't quite *right* with Arielle. And then the real controlling behavior had begun. Checking up on his every move, constantly nitpicking over the tiniest details. And she never broke from that constant neutral tone of hers. Just outlined her criticisms with unwavering composure.

No matter what he said, she always insisted the criticism was *for your own good*.

After three years of it, he'd had enough and applied for a transfer.

Now, as she said it, those lips of hers pressed into an even flatter line.

"Things have gotten out of control," she said. "What are you doing, Brandon?"

"My job," he growled. "If you recall, the Company agreed that I would handle this assignment on my own."

"I know you've made significant contact with the demoness, and I know you allowed her to escape. Some members of the Venetian unit told me," she said.

Briefly, he recalled an image of the gray-haired, dignified concierge at the pensione. So he'd been ratted out. *But, why?*

"Venice is a small town," she said. "Word travels fast here."

She began to talk, and his head began to ache. She paced around the room, outlining a long list of reasons she had felt compelled to come here. Instead of listening, he watched her face as she rambled. Watched her eyes flicker over his body as he pulled on a shirt. There was something hungry in her gaze, and it irked him. More concerning, when she talked about Luciana there was a little spark in her eye that—if Brandon didn't know better—he would have pegged as hate.

But he did know better.

*Arielle is an angel,* he told himself, *and angels don't hate.*

"We need to pin this demoness down," Arielle continued. "To do that, we need to enlist the help of the local unit. I've contacted Israel Infusino, the Venetian supervisor. He and some of his team members will be arriving shortly. We're primarily here to—"

"Keep tabs on me," Brandon said.

She shook her head. "I only came because this assignment is so important to the Company. There's too much at stake here. We need to accomplish what's in everyone's best interests."

*My ass,* he thought. *What's your agenda?*

"What was that?" Arielle said, turning her head sharply toward a noise from one of the other rooms.

"I collected two of her Gatekeepers. I've interrogated them, but haven't gotten anything useful out of them yet."

"Collected?" said Arielle, her eyes going wide. "You're keeping Gatekeepers under arrest, without following Company protocol?" She shook her head. "This is completely unacceptable. We definitely need to call in backup."

"Fine," was all he said. "You're probably right about that."

She stood, looking around them in disbelief, as though she were trying to figure it all out.

"What happened between you and I?" she said softly. "It could be good between us again, Brandon."

*Good? Again?* It had never been good. What he wanted to say was, *Lady, you're on crack.*

He bit his tongue.

Out loud what he said was, "We're just different people, Arielle."

"You're a complex man, Brandon, with complex desires."

"Let it lie," he said gruffly. "And by all means, call in the local unit. You and I will tear each other apart if we're stuck working alone together."

A few hours later, Arielle returned with the Venetian unit, who moved in with their equipment.

"This is Infusino, supervisor of the local unit," Arielle said, gesturing toward the smiling gray-haired man whom Brandon recognized instantly. He was the concierge from the pensione. "He and his team will be helping us from now on."

"You didn't mention you were a supervisor," Brandon commented.

"You didn't ask," Infusino said.

The Venetian unit certainly did things differently.

They spread picnic cloths on the bare floor. Unpacked food and wine. They lit candles around the room, dispelling the foreboding atmosphere of the abandoned building. They chatted to each other in quick quips of Italian, laughing freely.

Luciana was the stuff of legends.

By the glow of candlelight, the Venetians spoke of her in whispers. The stories they told of her were like ghost stories about a mythical woman who did not exist. Rather than a flesh-and-blood incarnation of a woman who was across the canal at this moment, plotting the downfall of the Company and everyone it stood to protect.

*"...she bathes in the blood of young girls...."*
*"...she eats human flesh for breakfast...."*
*"...she has seduced half the men in Venice...."*

There was so much whispered gossip about Luciana Rossetti that Brandon had no idea what was true.

"One thing we know for certain is that for the past two and a half centuries, Luciana has managed to elude capture by our unit," said Infusino. "The secrecy around her palazzo has been unbreakable. Until you came along, Brandon."

The angels around him raised their glasses to him, various shades of eyes shining in the candlelight.

*Might as well invite the whole neighborhood over for an open house,* Brandon thought. *And who cares if the folks across the way happen to be our sworn enemies?*

Brandon was grateful for the creature comforts they had brought. He was appreciative of the companionship. But he still had a job to do. He finished his glass of wine and went to sit apart from the group, taking his customary place by the front window.

He shifted uncomfortably, watching.

Waiting.

"Why don't you sleep, Brandon," Infusino said, coming over to place a hand on Brandon's shoulder.

Brandon shook his head. "If I sleep, then the whole damn assignment goes to hell."

*Time is running out.* Luciana could feel it slipping through her fingers. Before sunrise, Luciana rose and went to her worktable, took stock of what she had left. *Not enough. Not strong enough. Not quick enough. Not deadly enough. Just...not enough.*

She bent her head to the table, touched her forehead to the old wood. Closed her eyes for a moment. And the regrets began to flow, pouring out like a torrent that threatened to wash her away. *If only I had more time...if only Corbin hadn't taken that damned vial of poison... if only I had never run into Brandon in the Redentore Church...if only Julian Ascher hadn't walked into my life at that moment over two centuries ago, near the Rialto Bridge...if only...*

The noise behind her made her start.

"Apologies, *baronessa*," Massimo said, bowing slightly.

She frowned. She was going insane; it felt like she had spent years in this workroom, trying to create a poison that would kill an angel as powerful as the one she could practically feel breathing from only a few hundred yards away.

"Wait, Massimo, I need your assistance."

"Yes, *baronessa*. It would be my pleasure."

"Go catch one of the goblins. I need to test this formula."

He was back shortly. She administered the shot. The goblin lay down, frothing at its ugly little mouth. But in the next instant, the creature popped back up again, choking a bit. A white froth smudged the edges of its mouth, but it was still breathing. It stood up, cackling to itself before it hopped off the table and scurried under a workbench.

The poison had failed to kill it.

Luciana put her head down on the worktable, closing her eyes for a moment. *If only...*

"What has gone wrong with it, *baronessa*?" Massimo said, stopping her thoughts. "Whatever it is, I'm sure we can fix it."

Opening her eyes, she sighed. "Most likely, the blood from Violetta's death wasn't strong enough. She died very quietly, which isn't the usual way I collect blood. It's possible that goblin might die within the next few days. But if it does, it will probably have a very gentle passing. However, that's only a guess. What's gone wrong with the poison is not entirely clear."

What had gone wrong with *herself* was infinitely more troubling.

She knew exactly what was wrong with her.

It was tall, dark and American.

Luciana could feel him. Closer and stronger than she had ever felt him before.

*Where are you?* she wondered.

"In any case, Massimo, we must work to find a solution. Either we must find another victim, or bolster the formula with another ingredient. Either way, we must work quickly. There is no time to squander."

Massimo went to peer through a crack in the shutters. When he turned back to her, his face was ashen.

"What is it?" she demanded, and went to look for herself.

Across the water, the abandoned palazzo was no longer abandoned.

Luciana saw the light coming from within, noted the figures moving in the darkness.

Massimo said, "He is no longer alone."

*Don't fall asleep,* Brandon told himself repeatedly. Sitting in his observation point at the window, staring at the closed palace across the canal, Ca' Rossetti seemed like a mausoleum. *Do not sleep. Not now.*

Not simply because of the dreams themselves.

But because now, an entire unit of angels was here to witness them. Including Arielle.

"You must sleep," Infusino coaxed, shaking his head

as he watched Brandon fight to stay awake. "Your physical body is completely exhausted."

Brandon closed his eyes and leaned his head against the windowsill. Just for an instant.

"Don't let me do anything, go anywhere..." he muttered, feeling Infusino's shoulder supporting him, guiding him to a cot the Venetian unit had set up in one corner of the big, dusty room. "If I start talking in my sleep, wake me up."

He lay down on the cot, his gaze focused on the ceiling high above, on the peeling remnants of painted angels who seemed to laugh down at him.

Around him, a haze began to gather as he drifted...

*Not into the usual scene of his recurring nightmare. Only a blackness, shrouded in fog.*

*He dug in his pocket, touched his watch.*

I'm dreaming.

*Out of the mist, she came sliding into concrete form, faster than she ever had before. Like a bolt of lightning streaking down from the sky, she landed on solid ground, striking the earth ten feet away from him. Striding toward him with a storm flying around her, she was all long legs, flying hair and snapping green eyes.*

*"You. Where the hell are my Gatekeepers? I want them back," she demanded, marching forward to grab him by the front of his shirt. She held it in her fist, staring up at him, fury swirling in those green eyes.*

*"Forget it," he said coolly, staring down at her.*

*"You don't think I can* make *it happen?" she said, lifting her chin a notch. "You have no idea what I'm capable of, angel. I'll make you come like you never have before, not even in your wildest dreams."*

*He pried his shirt out of her fist, shook his head and*

*pushed her away. "That's a kind offer, but I think I'll have to refuse."*

She ran her hand down his body, fingers skimming lightly down to the waistband of his jeans.

*"You don't even know what you want," she said. Her voice was a smooth purr that washed over him. "A man like you has probably never had the opportunity to explore his own desires. There are things I can offer you. You could have anything you want. You could live in a mansion much larger than my palace if you wanted. Drive a fleet of exotic cars. Own a yacht. Have women dangling off you at all moments. Women like me."*

At the last word, he flinched, although only very slightly. And then he froze, kicking himself for reacting, hoping she hadn't noticed. But of course, she had.

*"What's wrong, big boy? Got a monster under the bed? I'll chase it away," she whispered.*

He cleared his throat and said, "I'm not going anywhere with you."

*"You'd rather stand around and wait for your recurring nightmare, then? Do as you wish." She flicked her hand at him, dismissive. "If I were you, I'd rather take my chances with the unknown than stand around waiting to get shot."*

"Who told you about that?" he demanded.

*"Just a good guess. But* vediamo...*'let's see.' I already guessed during the fireworks that you were a gunshot victim. And the way you cower and hesitate ever so slightly when you enter certain alleyways...well."*

"And the dream?"

*She lowered her lashes, masking her eyes for a moment. "That part was a complete shot in the dark, so to speak."*

"You're the only one who has ever figured it out," he

*said, not quite knowing why he was telling her. "Other than Michael, you're the only one who knows."*

*"Perhaps I'm the only one who cares," she purred. "Come, let me take that pain away," she said, drawing away, sliding her fingertips down his arm. "Come with me."*

*"I'll keep my pain, thank you very much," he said, wanting to reach out and grab her.*

*"If you won't cooperate, that's fine. I don't need your permission. Where did we leave off the last time we were together?" she said, moving up against him. "As I recall, we were standing in a doorway near San Marco's when your boss interrupted us."*

*Around them, the dark mist began to solidify, the scene around them crystallizing into the place where they had stood last night. She pressed herself against him, backing him into the door this time.*

*"This is how it was, no?" she purred, smoothing her palm down the length of his torso.*

*"Knock it off," he growled, grasping her wrist and attempting to hold her at arm's length. Trying to remind himself of Michael's warning. "Not like this."*

*She paused, relenting a little. "What do you want, then? You angels are so bland. Your deepest, darkest sexual fantasy is probably a threesome in a haystack with couple of cowgirls. Let me show you the possibilities of what you can experience."*

*Around them, the environment dissolved, the colors of Venice blending into a whirl.*

*When the scene began to solidify, they were on a stretch of beach that curved into a long, deserted crescent, rimmed by palm trees. Two girls, a blonde and a redhead, frolicked topless in the ocean, beckoning to him from the waves. When he made no move to join them, they came out of the water, giggling as they walked toward him, their breasts sparkling with sea-water.*

*"This is not my fantasy," he ground out.*

*Luciana tilted her head to one side, her eyes poring over him. "Really? What do you want? More girls?"*

*Out of nowhere, a few more women appeared in the surf.*

*Brandon crossed his arms, making no effort to move toward them.*

*The scene shifted around them again. This time, Luciana had taken him to a sumptuous bedroom, with a woman and two men on a bed. The men were fit and well muscled, and they smiled invitingly as they saw Brandon.*

*"Why not come join us?" said the man.*

*"Or I could leave you boys alone, if you prefer," said the woman.*

*Luciana lingered in the background, raising her eyebrows questioningly.*

*"Sorry, wrong again," Brandon said.*

*"What do you want, then?" Luciana said, frustrated. "Tell me."*

All I want is you, *he thought.*

*The words, not spoken aloud, hung in the air between them, as visible as if they had been written in black and white. Shouted as loudly as if they had been screamed through a megaphone. Those words terrified her, he knew. Which was why she had tried to put so many people, so many creatures of pleasure between them tonight.*

*"Are you afraid of what will happen if we're alone together, just the two of us? Like it was last time?"*

When you pulled away?

*"Of...of course not," she said. But she was trembling, almost imperceptibly.*

*"I've had enough," he told her. "Take me back to Venice."*

*"Va bene," she said.*

*She swallowed. Something in those green eyes of hers seemed to waver in her resolve.*

*Once again, the scene around them shifted. And as it solidified, Brandon's heart began to pound so hard it almost broke through the confines of his chest.*

*When he looked down, the ground was at least three hundred feet below him.*

*And he was dangling in midair.*

# Chapter Ten

*The view at the top of the Campanile at midnight never failed to inspire.*

*"You nearly gave me a heart attack," he said, gripping his chest with one hand.*

*With the other, he clutched the brick ledge of the bell tower that had finally materialized.*

*"Wasn't that fun?" she said brightly. "Almost like flying."*

*"Where are we?" he asked, still dazed.*

*"Back in Venice," she said into the breeze.* And Venice itself is half the seduction.

*Below, the five domes of San Marco's Basilica glowed white in the moonlight. The curving, brown-roofed labyrinth of streets wound for miles around them. Where the city ended at the lip of the sea, the dark Adriatic stretched into the infinity of night. Overhead, the stars glittered, a brilliant canopy set against the black velvet sky.*

*Venice in the aggregate was more impressive than any single church or palace, no matter how architecturally stunning. More beautiful than any one painting, sculpture or jewel. More breathtaking than any individual violin concerto, dance, glass of wine or dish of risotto.*

"We are at the top of the most famous bell tower in the city," she said. "This is where Galileo first demonstrated his telescope to the Doge, more than four hundred years ago."

Brandon did not look impressed. He leaned out over the edge of the tall brick structure, looked down at the rectangle of the empty Piazza San Marco below and asked, "How do we get down?"

"Right now, we don't," she said. "Just enjoy the view. Almost nobody gets to come up here at this hour of night."

It was true that tourists were not allowed here after the official hours of operation.

But some of Luciana's most prized victims had been treated to this extraordinary late-night view. And every victim she had ever brought here had been impressed by the thrill of the observation platform and the massive iron bells hanging above, at this forbidden time of night. When each of those victims had died, each had departed his or her human life after a unique experience that only Luciana could offer them.

Brandon did not seem to appreciate the privilege.

No matter. She would make him appreciate it.

She launched into the same story she fed every victim she brought here.

"This is the special place I like to come to by myself, late at night, when I want to escape the world," she told him, peering up at him with an appealingly shy glance. "When I want to be alone. To clear my head, and to enjoy the beauty of Venice."

"So you've never been up here with another man?" he asked.

"Of course not," she lied, adding a tiny flutter of her eyelashes for effect.

*"Of course you have." His mouth twisted into a slow smile. "The question is, how many?"*

*"Why do you bother asking questions if you already know the answers?" she said, annoyed.*

*"At least there are only two of us here right now," he said, the smile twisting a little farther. "I expected there to be another orgy."*

*"There's nobody here except the two of us," she said.*

*She kept her mouth shut, and thought about the golden weather vane on top of the Campanile. In the shape of the Archangel Gabriel. She had always loved the irony of conducting her seductions watched by the figures of angels and saints crowding the city. But Brandon didn't need to know about that. Not now.*

*The wind swept through her hair. For a moment, she almost believed her own illusion. Almost fell into her own trap. Into believing that they were a pair of star-crossed lovers, escaping the impossibility of a situation. Not angel and demon. Not sworn enemies, sent to hunt each other down.*

We can't be both enemies and lovers, *she realized.* It's one or the other. We must choose.

*"Think of how beautiful your existence could be. You could live in splendor like this all the time," she said, trailing her fingertips down his chest. "You could travel the world. Own a pied-à-terre in London or Paris, in Hong Kong or Dubai. A Maserati or a Ferrari. The possibilities are limitless. You're so much more than just a supervisor at the Company of Amateurs. You could be an Archdemon."*

*Beneath her fingertips, she felt his entire body tense, steel ready to blow.*

*"Don't push me. There's nothing in this world that I want," he ground out.*

*"Isn't there?" she said, looking up at him.*

*He shook his head, but she could see the lie in those gray eyes of his.*

*"Mi arrendo—'I give up.' Tell me what you want. Just whisper it in my ear," she said.*

*He leaned in close, paused before whispering a single word in her ear. "Enough."*

*But he did not pull away. Instead, he drew her earlobe into his mouth. The softness of his tongue along her sensitive lobe was astonishing. She leaned toward him, the hard muscle of his chest beneath her palms. His breath warmed her ear.*

*Against the side of her neck, he murmured, "No more games."*

Arielle sat outside the door to the room where Brandon slumbered.

*Sleep.* The one thing Brandon had refused to do with Arielle when they had been together. While she waited for him to wake, she remembered the day he had first walked through the doors of her unit headquarters in L.A.

*A day so hot, the thermometer outside Arielle's office window had burst.*

*Brandon Clarkson had not been like any other neophyte angel. The moment he walked through the doors of the legal-aid clinic that doubled as unit headquarters, everything seemed to change. The clinic suddenly seemed impossibly small, as though it might burst like the tempered glass tube unable to contain the overheated mercury.*

*"Michael sent me," he said, knocking on the door. "I'm here to join the Company."*

*He was so different from any man she had ever seen.*

*His shaved head, his impressively muscled physique did not intimidate her, but caught her interest immediately. Back then, he had only had one tattoo. On that first day, she had seen only the curl of a feather peeking out the neck of his T-shirt. Had figured that, like many members of the military and police, it was probably an American eagle tattooed on his shoulder.*

*"The air-conditioning broke down. I'm the only one here," she explained, sitting upright to dab the perspiration from her forehead and trying not to drool on her mountain of paperwork. "Everyone else has gone home, or they're out on assignment. There's a repairman coming in a few days, so we can get you started later this week."*

*She went back to work, expecting him to leave.*

*Minutes later, she felt a breeze cool the back of her neck.*

*He had fixed the air-conditioning.*

*"I'd like to get started as soon as possible," he said, leaning in her office doorway. "If there's anything you need a hand with, I'd like to stick around and start learning."*

*And so she had set him to work.*

*Brandon would do anything asked of him, she found, and didn't need to be told twice.*

*One week later, he had already completed his first official assignment as a Guardian, in a record amount of time for a fledgling angel.*

*He came into her office and shut the door.*

*"Do you mind if I show you something?" he asked, pulling down the window shade. "It's kind of personal."*

*"Of course," she said, trying to keep a straight face as he removed his shirt.*

*And showed her the little star tattooed on his chest.*

*A symbol of his first Assignee, a little boy with terminal cancer, whom Brandon had helped pass into the afterlife.*

*"Does this happen after every assignment?" he asked her. "I got it last night. I just woke up and it was there."*

*Then he turned around to show her the massive angel, wings outstretched across the broad muscles of his back.*

*"No," she said. "I've never heard of another Guardian with tattoos like that."*

*A gift. From the divine. She knew that when she saw them.*

*She had already begun to fall for him... And yet, it was not the tattoos that had struck her, and not even the impressive physique. It was the man underneath it all.*

*Two angels falling in love. The makings of a fairy tale...*

What had gone wrong, Arielle had never quite figured out.

Sitting in the heat of the ruined palazzo, she felt the moment he jarred awake.

Felt it, and she herself jolted out of her reverie.

When she opened the door, he lay sprawled on the cot, bare from the waist up, his ripped torso and arms adorned with those magnificent tattoos. He turned his head in the direction of the light streaming in through the open door. His sharp gaze fixed on her, as vast and inescapable as the sky before rain.

*Oh, but he's beautiful.*

He blinked, still half seeing whatever—whomever— he had been dreaming about. She read the naked desire in his eyes. Saw it wash away, like a stain washing off a sidewalk in a rainstorm. Watched him avert his gaze, cheeks flushed with color.

*What was he dreaming about?* she wondered. And as she watched him, she knew, *Whatever it was, it was not about me.*

He stretched his big body, sat up on the edge of the cot. Behind her, a few members of the Venetian unit hurried in to bring him a glass of water, a clean washcloth, satisfied that he had finally managed to get a full night's sleep after such a long stretch of wakefulness. Arielle tried not to stare at his sharply defined abs, or at the sprawl of tattoos, so many of them new since the last time she'd seen him.

She had lost the right to look. But perhaps she would win it back.

*Somehow, maybe,* she thought as he pulled a shirt over his head.

She turned and went back out into the large room where the Venetians sat quietly talking amongst themselves. When Brandon came out, she told him, "We were talking while you slept. The Company has come to a decision. What we have decided is in everyone's best interests."

"What is that?" Brandon said.

"Our plan is to dispose of Luciana," Infusino answered without hesitation. "Venice will be rid of that demoness at last."

"Disposal? You're convinced that's the right course of action?" Brandon said quietly.

The Venetian supervisor nodded. "Two hundred years we have battled with this woman. You have been called into this fight just a handful of days ago. I tell you, it is impossible. Luciana must be returned to the source of all life. She will rest in peace at last."

Brandon's gaze shot to Arielle. "I thought you believed that everyone deserves a chance at redemption. Don't they?"

She could feel her face flushing red. She did not reply.

"Perhaps you have become too personally involved with the situation," Infusino suggested. "It is difficult to see clearly when we are in the thick of things. We all understand that."

"No, you don't understand. You know perfectly well that you need the approval of the Archangels before you start talking about disposal. They will never agree without the unanimous support of the Company. And I will never allow it."

"We'll see," was all Infusino said.

The others went on about their business, although quietly and with their heads bowed.

Brandon sauntered over to Arielle, leaned in close. "I know exactly who is behind this. Make no mistake, you and I will never be together. No matter who you schedule for disposal."

"But, Brandon, I..."

"Don't you get it? It's never going to work out between us," Brandon snapped. "Even if Luciana had never been born, there is no way I would be with you."

Then he stormed toward the door.

"Wait," she called after him. "Listen to reason. These Guardians have been dealing with the demoness for far longer than you or I. She is truly dangerous, Brandon. You need to know that disposal is in everyone's best interests. In the best interests of humankind. Luciana cannot be allowed to continue her evil."

He didn't say a word. Just stood there and looked at her with those eyes, cold as stone.

"You don't see how she's beginning to affect you," Arielle said.

Then he slammed out of the building.

Arielle knew the moment she lost it. The moment everything slipped, and the world went sideways. The moment she went into the room where the Gatekeepers were kept, and unleashed her wrath on them.

"Take them away," she said to the Venetian angels, who stood silently, regarding her with their luminous eyes. "We'll petition for their disposal, too."

She shivered, recognizing the seed of something that had been growing in her for a long time.

*Vengeance.*

That which she had hated so much in Luciana was beginning to grow in herself.

Arielle saw it, but she had no idea how to stop it.

Brandon half hoped that the rickety old building would fall down and crush the lot of them.

He hadn't gotten far when a wordless scream came out of the building he'd just exited. Not a human scream, but something animal.

The scream of something—*someone*—being tortured.

He rushed back into the building, up the stairs, bounding toward the room where the Gatekeepers were held. Arielle was just exiting it, wiping blood from her hands onto a cloth.

"The big one's not talking anymore," she said.

"Why not?"

Arielle said nothing, that inscrutable expression on her face. Brandon went into the room. There was blood all over the floor, running down the Gatekeeper's chin. He went over to the demon, opened his mouth.

The Gatekeeper no longer had a tongue.

Brandon bolted down the stairs. Arielle looked at him calmly, perched on the ledge of a windowsill, looking out at the early morning light bouncing off the canal.

"I may have been a little overzealous. Sometimes these things are necessary," she said.

"Necessary," was all he could say.

"It's not like he's human," she said, turning to look at Brandon. "If you begin to sympathize with these demons, you'll never get the job done."

Across the canal, everyone in Ca' Rossetti heard the scream.

"That was Giancarlo," Luciana said to Massimo, looking up from her worktable. "I know it."

"Giancarlo and Antonio are old souls in strong, young bodies," Massimo assured her. His face, however, had gone as white as the arsenic he was measuring. "They can fend for themselves. The likelihood that something has happened to them…"

"Screw likelihood, Massimo. I *know* what I heard."

Fury welled up in her. She set down the flask she had been holding.

They stood looking at each other, not speaking. A staff of Gatekeepers that had taken her centuries to collect, decades to train. Ruined. By that damned angel.

Massimo's frown deepened. Finally, he said, "Perhaps now would be the time to…"

"Go. Take the others and go to Tuscany, or go to Naples. Go somewhere and don't tell me where."

Massimo fell silent for a moment. Then he said, "I'm not leaving you. You need protection, more than any of us. We swore an oath."

"You're just getting in the way here, and presenting

more targets for those damned angels," she said irritably. "We cannot remain cooped up in this house. I would leave, too, if I could. But I have responsibilities here in Venice. I must stay. Go, Massimo."

"No, *baronessa*. Not unless you can convince me that it is absolutely necessary."

There was a terrible silence between them. Something of which they never spoke.

"I cannot tell you that, Massimo. Not right now."

"Then I'm staying."

Death was not the end. They both knew that. The soul was never destroyed.

They had both died before, as humans.

But torture at the hands of the Company of Angels... neither of them knew exactly what that meant. Except for the scream they had both heard carry across the water, a wordless sound that could mean no good.

## Chapter Eleven

Brandon stormed away from Arielle, slamming out the back door of the dilapidated building for the second time.

Moments later, he scaled the side wall of Luciana's palazzo, climbing easily up the ornamental columns and cornices. What impelled him to do so this time, he wasn't quite sure. Nor did he care. He only knew that he was past thinking.

What drove him now was pure gut feeling.

Luciana's home was like the rest of her, Brandon thought as he popped the lock on her bedroom window and stole inside. *Opulent. Luxurious. Sensual.*

Nudes adorned the frescoed walls, satyrs and nymphs in risqué positions, their partially clothed flesh portrayed in sensual colors that looked almost touchable. Swathes of silk and velvet curtained the windows and draped the large, gilt bed that stood in the center of the room.

*But where is the demoness?* he wondered.

The presence of her remaining Gatekeepers and the possibility of capture, he had totally pushed out of his mind.

She came into the bedroom after a bath, dressed in a black silk robe, drying her hair with a thick white towel.

When she saw him, she dropped her towel, stumbled a few steps toward the door.

"Wait," he said, blocking her way. "Don't call for your Gatekeepers."

"Why shouldn't I?" she said, narrowing her eyes at him. "How do I know that you're not planning on torturing us all?"

Any explanation, any words he wanted to speak were stuck on his tongue.

The message he had come to deliver hung in his mind, unspoken.

*The Company is planning on obliterating you.*

Too late already. He was dragged off course and drugged into senselessness, merely by her presence. He was losing his edge, and wandering into dangerous territory. She had some strange hold over him that he could not explain.

"What is it you want?" she asked, the question that had been burning between them all this time. "You said no more games. We could play at this forever, waiting for the other to give in. We will be sitting here for another century. Stuck in this stalemate of wills. Or we could simply give each other what we both want. But you have to tell me what that is."

She thought he had come for seduction. Maybe he had.

Whether he had really come to warn her, he doubted severely.

He resisted. And yet, somewhere deep within him, the answer to her question surged up within him. What he desired was simple.

*You.*

Luciana was the only thing he wanted at this moment.

She was what he wanted most, and what he absolutely could not have.

"Say it," she whispered.

What he wanted could not be voiced, at least not to a lady. She might not be a lady, but she was still a woman, and at that moment he was struck wordless by an odd silence that had nothing to do with mere shyness.

No, he was flat-out shocked by his own desires.

He wanted to plunge into her.

To take her against the wall like a wild animal and not stop, to take her in every way he knew and in ways he had not yet begun to imagine. To let go of his angelic nature for just one instant. To give in to the desires of his physical body. Desires that had not been truly sated for a very long time. Desires that could not be fulfilled with the politeness required of intimate relations with other angels.

"Enough talking. Let me show you what I want."

He kissed her, far more urgently than he ever had before.

In that kiss, he felt her response, every bit as demanding and impatient as his.

He pulled open the silk tie holding her bathrobe closed, letting the garment fall open. His hands moved over her body, exploring its contours, fingers dragging on her still-damp skin. Moving up her back, he reached up to cup her breast, caressing, testing its heaviness in his hand. He fondled her, felt the nipple tighten beneath his thumb. In his pants, his cock throbbed, at maximum pressure and ready to explode.

She moaned, a sound that vibrated all the way into his gut as she moved against him, arching up into him, offering herself to him.

In that moment, he felt the possibilities open up, as

though the universe were cracking wide-open and offering itself along with her. As he gazed into the green depths of her eyes, he saw infinite possibilities.

Perhaps things could be different between them. That possibility arose in his mind for the first time.

*What if...?* he asked himself. *What if the woman standing before me wasn't a demon? What if we weren't mortal enemies on opposite sides of a never-ending war?*

Julian Ascher had been a demon. He had found redemption in the arms of his lover.

Was it possible...? Brandon's mind began to churn through the possibilities, contemplating exactly how he might be able to reform her. It wouldn't take much, he reasoned.

She already seemed amenable, responsive to his lead.

She ran her hand down the front of his jeans, fingers teasing open the button of his fly.

*What are the consequences of sleeping with her, anyway?* he wondered fleetingly. *Serena St. Clair survived, although barely....*

But he was not Serena. He knew that if the woman who had her hand on his most vulnerable appendage chose to sink her claws into him, it would be game over.

"That's it. It's just a matter of getting it out," she whispered.

"Getting *what* out?" He held her at arm's length, separating them a little, his eyes flickering nervously over her half-bared body as she stood in front of him.

She ran a finger down his chest. "The darkness in you. You're not like the other angels. You pretend to be at peace, but inside you, a storm is raging. I've seen it."

She had hit a nerve. She saw it in the twitch of his jaw, the stone-hard stare of his gray eyes. Heard it in the low rumble of his voice, as he said, "Luciana, you're treading on dangerous ground."

"Why not let it out, that rage inside you?" she whispered. "You don't know how much pleasure darkness can bring. Or how beautiful a storm can be."

Her hand reached out, down. Stroked his thigh, once, twice.

For an instant, he considered it. She saw that hesitation in his eyes, the momentary pause. The yearning. The need.

Gently, oh, so gently, he put his hand on top of hers. And pushed it away.

"This isn't the way," he said. "*I'm* the one who came to save *you.* You've got to realize that. It's the only way things can work between us."

"Oh, you're so mistaken," she said, leading him to her bed. "Let me show you exactly how mistaken you are."

He said nothing. She watched him swallow, the delicious movement of his throat, the dryness of his mouth audible.

And that was the moment she knew she had won.

In the corner stood an elaborate mirror, nearly the height of the room, framed in gold.

He caught her gaze in it, staring back at him, so very green and glittering in the semidarkness. He saw himself reflected, leaning over her, as she half turned and looked over her shoulder. He turned her, so that the front of her spectacular body was reflected, and himself behind her.

"Look," she told him, nodding toward their reflection. "Watch us. You'll see that we're the same, creatures of pleasure, both of us. You're no different than I am."

He ran his hands over her body, fever-hot and lush.

Held her in front of the mirror, staring into her eyes as he felt her gyrating slowly against him.

"Don't make this into something ugly," he told her. "I want you to realize how beautiful you are."

"I'm beautiful in body. But not in soul," she said.

"You're beautiful in both. Every soul is beautiful," he whispered. "Some just don't realize it."

She opened her mouth to protest, and he cut her off with a kiss.

"Don't argue. Just let me make love to you."

In the mirror, he watched every reaction as it crossed her face, watched their two bodies as he knelt behind her on the bed. His view of her from behind was of the toned, perfect muscles of her back. Gently, reverently, like a man worshipping at a temple of her body, he ran one of his big hands up to cup her breast. Held its heaviness in his palm, spilling out of his hand.

God, she felt good.

Rubbing himself against her, he felt himself harden; he had thought he could not get any harder.

In his arms, she turned, his partner in an intricate dance, still watching themselves doubled in the mirror. They writhed, slid around each other and then somehow she was on top of him, straddling him, lowering herself over him.

He entered her, feeling her stretch as he eased her open.

He waited, easing his way in by fractions of inches, holding himself back, mentally steeling himself to go slowly. To enter her fully would take such a simple movement, an upward thrust of his hips he fought against. Otherwise, in an instant, he would come inside her.

As he buried himself to the hilt, he felt her relax. Felt her sink down onto him, melting around him.

In that moment, he knew the absolute and utter rightness of sexual connection, of the pure and unadulterated pleasure of it, a celebration of the divine. Demoness or not, she was still essentially a part of the divine, irrespective of who or what she *thought* she was.

He exploded inside her, emptying himself into the vessel of her body.

At that moment, it did not seem to Brandon that she was herself at all, but some female incarnation of an urge much more primordial that had emerged at the beginning of time. She existed beyond the binary oppositions of angel and demon, good and evil. She was a conflagration of innocence and temptation that spun around him and melded in his mind.

She was Eve in the garden.

She was the forbidden fruit, ripe and temptingly lush on the bough of the great tree.

And she was the green-eyed serpent, all at once.

He felt her tremble on top of him, quiver around him. The sensation brought him reeling back to consciousness, tumbling back to earth and to the certain knowledge that whatever else she might be, she was a woman.

Flesh and blood, with a heart beating beneath the perfect breast around which his fingers still remained curled.

Luciana had the moment of orgasm down to an art. She knew exactly when to moan, how to writhe at just the right times, which muscles to tense and when to collapse, seemingly out of exhaustion.

*"Mio caro, I'm coming,"* she purred loudly, at exactly the right second.

He lay half sprawled over her afterward, utterly spent, with a small, satisfied smile on his face. For an instant, she resented him, because it was clear that the sex had been much better for him than it had been for her.

And while Brandon was busy thinking of Eve, Luciana was thinking about Lilith.

Before there was Eve, there was Lilith. Poor Lilith did not show up in the official versions of any religion. Her life was relegated to folklore, her history passed down through hearsay and whispered stories. According to these stories, she was Adam's first wife, created at the same time as he was, out of the same earth. Created as equal, and not lesser than. Lilith had gotten tired of their banal monogamous sex life, and had run away from the Garden of Eden to seek a more exciting time among the demons.

Lilith was not afraid to do what she wanted, to fuck whom she wanted.

Lilith was known to attack men in their dreams.

*What would Lilith do now?* Luciana wondered.

Undoubtedly, Lilith would end Brandon. Swiftly, and without regret. She would reach under the bed, to where Luciana always kept a little bit of cyanide stored, for just such occasions. When a man was either asleep or nearly asleep beneath the silk coverlet of her sumptuous bed.

And she would inject that poison into him.

Even if he did not die, Lilith would have kept him captive until she could solve the problem with finality. Until she hit upon whatever she needed, until she found a way to do away with him permanently.

That was what Lilith would do.

But Luciana was not Lilith. Even after all the deaths she had caused, over hundreds of years, she still felt remorse.

Here in her bed, Brandon's big body rested beside her. Moonlight splayed over him, and in the dim light he looked almost like a young god sent down from the heavens.

And yet, there was something so earthly about him, something so very nearly human.

He was not the brute she had thought him to be the first time she had seen him.

*What is wrong with me?* she thought, furious at her own reasoning.

She reached under the bed, her fingers just brushing the plastic tube of the syringe tucked there.

And at that moment, he pulled her toward him.

"That was intense," he said, burying his face in her hair. "It was mind-blowing."

"Mmm, yes," she said, making a few vague sounds of agreement, trying to mask her ambivalence, thinking about making a second grab for the cyanide. "Like the fireworks all over again."

He sat up, his gray eyes illuminated to silver in the moonlight. "You didn't come."

If she had not, it had not been his fault.

In her experience, sex ranged from slightly uncomfortable to sometimes painful. With Brandon, she had hoped it might be different. The fact that it wasn't was disappointing, but no great surprise.

"Of course I did," she said quickly. "You're a phenomenal lover."

"That's not the issue," he said, something like anger edging his voice. "Don't lie."

She shrugged, rolling over to reach under the bed once again.

He stopped her, with a strange urgency in his voice. "Why did you fake it?"

*Because I always do.*

"Whether I did isn't important, so I don't know why you're harping on it." She sighed. "It was very pleasurable, *mio caro.*"

"What the hell is that supposed to mean? There are two of us in this bed. Sex is about connection. If you didn't enjoy yourself…"

"I enjoyed myself very much, *amore mio.* Thank you."

*What about the cyanide?* she wondered. She lay quietly on her side for a moment, still facing away from him. If she just reached a little farther, she could grab the syringe, and…

"You know what they say," he said, interrupting her thought. "If at first you don't succeed, try, try again."

She frowned. "That really isn't necessary."

"Necessary? Not so long ago, you were the one talking about pleasure and letting go. Maybe you're the one who's all talk, after all."

"I might not be able to—"

"Shh," he whispered into her ear from behind, flicking the lobe with his tongue. He sucked the delicate little bud of flesh, tugging it as she felt the heat of his mouth, the gentle nip of his teeth. Felt the exhalation of his breath in her ear. She shivered, and he murmured, "Whether you come or not, there's so much pleasure we could discover in each other."

As lightly as if he were running a feather along her skin, he trailed his fingertip all the way from her earlobe down the long column of her neck. Along the sweep of her collarbone and down the center of her chest. Then he traced the outline of her breast, until all of her was shivering in anticipation. By the time his fingertip neared the nipple, she was aching for his touch, straining toward the promise of that caress.

She dared not move, lying still on the bed, not wanting to give him any sign that his tactics were working.

His fingers stroked the underside of her breast, playing there. Squeezing a little, ever so gently. His hot breath fanned down her neck, seemed to skim along every nerve ending in her body, to set every cell of her quivering.

*Don't move,* she told herself. *He mustn't win.*

Her mouth went dry and her lips parted. She heard her own breath quicken, ran her tongue along her lips to moisten them. Sank her teeth into her bottom lip to keep herself from making a sound that might betray her. Squeezed her eyes shut, but that only intensified the pleasure he was teasing out of her. A melting sensation tingled through her, radiating out from the place his fingers were stroking. From the nipple he was now touching. Which hardened at his touch.

Her body was a traitor, responding to enticement by an enemy.

But her mind was still free.

She bit harder on her lip. Even that did not stop the tiny sound of pleasure in the back of her throat, a sound so quiet it was not even a moan. Yet more genuine and more telling than any of the loud exclamations of faked pleasure she had manufactured just moments ago.

He whispered in her ear. "See what I mean?"

She heard the smugness in his voice and shook her head. She sat up blinking, breathing hard. *I must get away. It is imperative that I get away.*

"Oh, I know you see," he murmured, pulling her back into his arms. He reached to pull the tangle of her hair free from her neck so he could kiss her there, running his lips along the sensitive flesh where her pulse beat its quickened cadence. "You know exactly what I mean."

His hands roamed the curves and valleys of her body, seeking, exploring. His lips followed, his mouth hungry to explore. His tongue flitted over one nipple, then the other. She bit her lips again—both of them this time—to keep from arching into the sensation.

He eased her back on the bed. She reached out desperately, gripping the silk sheet to pull herself out of the breaking storm. Instead, that hand seemed to anchor her, gripping to hold her in the middle of that maelstrom, waves of pleasure washing over her, threatening to drown her.

Reaching down, he stroked her belly, teasing. He shifted his own body, kissing her stomach in the wake of his fingers. All the way down to the most sensitive place of her, a place he had already been. But this time he lingered, stroking the closed lips of her sex before he coaxed her legs open. With his fingers and tongue, he stroked lightly, ever so lightly, so that she finally let herself go.

When she realized she was writhing on the bed, she sighed out her defeat.

He raised his head and she saw his gray eyes shining with satisfied victory. "Do you still want me to stop?"

"I want you to…" she began, gasping a little. The syringe of poison had slipped out of her thoughts completely.

She lost the ability to think entirely when he dipped his head again, returning his attention to her, plunging a finger into her darkness. She tensed around him, her body on the brink of climax as it had never been before.

He was on top of her then, entering her as she climbed toward her peak. He inched into her slowly again, as hard as he had been the first time. But now he kept his finger on her clit, continuing to stimulate as he pushed into her, each stroke seeming to stretch into an eternity of pleasure.

She was full of him, matching his rhythm, caught in his silver-gray gaze as he watched her face, his attention unwavering for even a moment.

He was a man utterly set on his task. A man deep in the eye of the storm, unfazed by the tempest he had unleashed in her body. A tempest he was intent on mastering.

A sheen of sweat covered his massive, tattooed body, muscles flexing as he moved in her, working her with an expertise that was sinfully divine.

She came then, the waves of her orgasm washing over her, ravished by the wild bliss he had orchestrated inside her. Pounding over the rock-hardness of him.

He had always appeared as an enemy to her. That was what she knew of him: that he was a Guardian. But in the ecstasy of her orgasm, she *saw* him for the first time. Saw him for what he really was. Saw into his soul and saw the flare of brilliant light there that could only be one thing.

*Divine.*

In that moment, he thrust deep inside her. As she looked into his eyes, she knew that he was with her in that place of untamed rapture she had never known existed.

Then they lay joined together, gasping for breath as the storm passed into stillness.

In her bed, beneath the canopy of silk where she had lain so many nights, lonely and unfulfilled, she trembled, unable to control the shiver that ran through her, sure in her knowledge that the devil himself would find some way to intervene.

Finally seducing him ought to have been a great accomplishment. The possibility for finishing her sacrifice to the devil was laid out before her. A mere brush of her fingertips away. Yet, now that she had him here, draped over her, his hand still closed over her naked breast, she found herself completely unwilling to carry out those plans.

Under the bed, the syringe of cyanide remained untouched.

As he lay in her bed, in the jumble of silk that tangled around them, drowning in the aftermath of their lovemaking, he knew the possibility that love with a demoness might well unleash some uncontrollable dark side of him. Just as Luciana had said.

He was a millimeter away from falling.

"Just think. It could be like this forever," he said.

"I don't know how you dreamed you could change me. Just by fucking me?" she whispered, smiling a little in the darkness. "You don't have that kind of power over me. Not like that insipid little Serena has over Julian. Your heart is so much darker than hers could ever be."

And at that moment, he knew she was right.

He might not be a rookie angel like Serena St. Clair.

But he had so much more resentment in him. So much more anger.

He had somehow expected Luciana to soften, and she showed no sign of it.

"Get out," said the demoness.

He felt the prick of a needle at the side of his neck. Saw her thumb hovering on the plunger of a syringe, poised, ready to inject.

"Whatever you wanted to accomplish tonight is never going to happen. Go, before I shoot you full of poison. While you can still walk out of here on your own two feet."

After he left, she capped the syringe and placed it back under the bed, still full of cyanide.

She lay in the darkness, listening to the rapid beating of her own heart. She heard the flutter of wings and the coo of a pigeon departing from the balcony outside her window. And she knew that the sense of peace he had brought had departed with him, drained from her body.

But it was not replaced by the same centuries-old bitterness as before.

The desire to kill had also been drained out of her. The desire for revenge was dull and sluggish, her mind grasping for the memory of it. Merely a few days ago, that desire had raged in her bloodstream. Now it was more like a distant trickle.

*All because of Brandon.*

She shivered, the implications of such a change crashing over her.

*I cannot let go of that which keeps me alive,* she thought. *There is only one place left to go. One person left in Venice who can help me.*

She rose from the bed, dressed herself and went to cut some roses from the courtyard, to take as an offering to the darkness she would now call upon.

Brandon climbed back down the darkened facade of Ca' Rossetti and slipped into the night.

*Lucky.*

That was all he could think. Why she had kicked him out, he had no idea.

But it was the only thing that had saved him.

Returning to the Company's encampment across the canal was out of the question. He had been cooped up in there for far too long. Tossed out of Luciana's bedchamber after intercourse with the demoness, it would be impossible for him to face Arielle.

Not now. When the feeling of the demoness's body was still hot on his skin. When his body still sung from the nearness of her.

In the absence of a car to lose himself in the power of driving, he walked. He wandered for a long time, thoughts churning as he crossed bridges and navigated narrow lanes, until he was lost in the tangle of streets and water.

*Someone who has brought me so much joy, if only for a brief moment...she couldn't be all evil, could she?*

He looked up at the sky, at the multitude of stars above. Nothing had been resolved. If anything, their interlude had complicated things beyond imagining, the dreamed quality of their encounters brought into flesh, brought into reality.

And the demoness herself. His mind had difficulty pinning her down. The thought of her was elusive, shifting, transitory. Maiden, dragon. Seductress, Madonna. It seemed as though every thought he had ever conceived about womanhood existed inside of Luciana. All of those images and feelings, shifting and changing beneath the surface of her skin.

Maddening.

An old iron gate caught his eye. It seemed to pop out of the laneway, the ornately wrought metal appearing to glow a little, the vines curling up it seeming to beckon to him, swaying a little in the breeze. He walked toward it, looked inside but could not see.

Pushed it open, heard the creak of its disused hinges, and walked into a garden.

Inside, fireflies clustered over a statue in the center of the garden.

As he walked toward it, he saw a statue of St. George slaying the dragon.

What it meant, he had absolutely no idea.

Because the most maddening part of the whole situation, he realized, was that at this point, he was nearer to being swallowed by the dragon than slaying it.

## Chapter Twelve

Massimo steered the boat across the dark lagoon, into the marshy waters near the island of Sant' Ariano. The mysterious little island had been deserted for centuries, since the sixteenth century, when the city of Venice decided to use the island as an *ossario,* an "ossuary."

A dumping ground for the bones of dead Venetians.

Luciana had first come here as a young human woman, searching for snakes on the island rumored to be infested with them. And snakes were vital in the formulas for poisons she had researched in old apothecaries' handbooks. But she had found something else here.

*Someone* else here. Someone who had helped her master the art of poison far beyond what she could have learned on her own.

"Wait here for me," she told Massimo, embarking from the boat and taking the flowers with her. "This is a matter I must resolve on my own."

A strange mist drifted on the surface of the lagoon, unusual for high summer in Venice. Luciana's shoes crunched over the earth. She steeled herself against the knowledge of what was crushed beneath her hard soles. Until about a century ago, bodies had simply been dumped in piles. Then the city officials decided to flatten these piles, leaving bone chips and shards all over the island. A wall had been erected around the island, hiding its contents from public view.

Walking over the uneven ground now, Luciana sensed the energetic trace of thousands of people who had lived and died, their bodies ground into shards and composting quietly with the earth here. Something less than ghostly, the bare essence of them left behind, a fine sort of memory etched on the air.

She forged farther, until she found a small, broken-down building. The roof had long been torn off, and overhead, tree branches interwove to form a natural roof, moonlight shining through the gaps. Spiders had taken up residence, the sticky residue of the webbing pasting itself to her fingers, attaching itself to her hair.

*Disgusting,* she thought as she pushed her way into the small, enclosed space. *What a terrible idea it was to come here.*

"Zitella?" Luciana called.

Perhaps the old crone was gone. It had literally been ages since she had been there, ages since she had needed the kind of help that this woman could give. Perhaps she was not there.

But among the rotting walls, she recognized her old mentor.

The master alchemist, the master poisoner.

Seated in a chair, exactly the way she had been two hundred years ago. Her white hair piled into a neat bun at the back of her head, her black widow's weeds unchanged in style, shapeless and covering her frail body. Decrepit. Her bony fingers pointed up toward Luciana, thin and spindly in the moonlight, beckoning her closer.

Zitella's age was impossible to guess. Even two hundred years ago, when Luciana had come here as a young widow, desperate for a way out of a terrible situation, the old crone had already been decrepit.

Back then, Zitella had spent her day grinding human bones to sell for use in refining sugar. What the old woman did now, Luciana had no idea. What she *was* now…that was equally a mystery. Whether demon or ghost or something caught in between, Zitella was definitely not alive.

Zitella stopped humming and looked up. "Luciana Rossetti? Is that you, child?"

Luciana stepped forward.

"Come closer, child. How long has it been? Centuries…"

She laid the offering of flowers in Zitella's lap.

The old crone picked up the roses, sniffed them briefly before casting them into the darkness behind her. "Do not try to bribe me with such trifling gifts."

"There's something else, Zitella," Luciana said hurriedly. "I've brought another gift for you."

She placed the vial in the old woman's hand.

Zitella closed her bony old fingers over it. In the faint light, she held it up, uncapped the cork stopper from its top. Inhaling deeply, she said, "Yes, that's more like it. The blood of an innocent, the essence of a recent death. Yes, I am pleased. What have you come to trade this for?"

"Whatever you wish to give to me, ma'am," Luciana said, knowing better than to ask for what she wanted.

Carefully, Zitella recapped the vial and tucked it into a fold of her black garments. Then she fished into another unseen depth of her clothing and handed over a small bottle of blown glass, with a dull-looking powder inside. "This is what you seek. Ground bones from the most evil beings that walked the streets of Venice.

Murderers' bones and rapists' bones, bones from sellers of children and purveyors of lost souls, ground to powder. Prepare a base of venom, hemlock and cyanide. And then add the blood of the innocent. Lastly, mix in this powder. Then, you will achieve what you need in such a formula—the ingredients to kill both the body and the soul."

Luciana accepted it, curtsied a little out of habit from the old days. "Thank you, Zitella."

"Use the techniques exactly as I taught you, those many years ago. Then you will be able to kill any demon on earth."

*And if it can kill a demon, surely it will also kill an angel,* Luciana thought.

"I will be eternally grateful to you for all that you have passed on to me, both then and now," said the demoness. She bowed her head in reverence, then turned to leave.

The old crone stopped her, reaching forward to grab Luciana's hand with surprising strength. The grasp felt strange, and the demoness almost recoiled from the feel of the old woman's skin, hardened into bone itself.

The old woman pulled her so close that they were looking into each other's eyes. "Wait," said Zitella. "I have one more question for you. Who is this man who has come to you? Your lover?"

"I have no lover, Zitella. No one more than there ever was. You must be imagining things," Luciana said, trying to pull away.

"Don't lie to me, Luciana Rossetti. Someone has entered your life."

"Perhaps," she relented a little, "there is a man. But he is of no consequence. The relationship is doomed. There are vast differences between us."

"Don't fool with the angels. Yes, I know. It is obvious. I can smell him on you. He has seen within you." The old crone jabbed a bony finger into the left side of the demoness's chest with such force that it hurt. "He knows your heart. Knows you have one."

And she laughed, a cackle so loud it disturbed some of the branches of her makeshift roof, causing a hole to break into the ceiling. Moonlight streamed in, shining on Zitella's wizened old face.

"Go now," said the old woman. "What you intend to do with this substance is beyond my control. But have a care where you use it. And remember. Sometimes it is what we fear most that we need most."

*Crazy old hag,* Luciana thought to herself, stumbling back toward the boat in the darkness. She picked something out of her hair, expecting it to be more of the disgustingly sticky spiderweb from Zitella's hut, or perhaps a twig that had fallen from the roof.

It was a feather.

"Bring me one of the goblins," Luciana instructed Massimo much later that night when the sun was about to rise.

She finished the last essence she was distilling as Zitella had instructed, had finally gotten the mixture to a point where it seemed stable. Took some of the new poison. With shaking fingers, she drew some of the liquid into a syringe.

Shot it into the goblin.

Massimo released it, setting it on the floor to watch it scramble madly around.

"Maybe nothing will happen," Luciana murmured. "Zitella is ancient, and clearly quite mad. Maybe she gave me a bottle of dust."

The creature on the floor let out a vile cough, and a jet of crimson blood spewed out of its mouth, the spray making a disgusting mess on the floor. The thing fell sideways, a red foam spilling from its mouth.

"Then again, maybe the old woman is not insane after all," the demoness murmured.

"That's promising, certainly," said Massimo. "I've never seen one of your poisons kill that quickly before. Or that violently."

"But does it have the power to kill an angel as powerful as the one who watches us?" Luciana mused. "We can only determine that by trial and error," she said. "There's no guarantee. I would like to test it before I try it on the angel."

"How can we do that?"

"Perhaps Carlotta will help us out. She always knows the location of a Gatekeeper who can be gotten cheaply. We shall go see her."

"And risk being caught by the Company?"

"It is worth the risk this time, Massimo. We will arm ourselves."

She handed him a syringe full of the poison, capped it. "Be very careful. I trust you with this. You must promise not to misuse it. It is probably the most dangerous thing we have ever handled. This could change everything."

The party at Carlotta's was finally coming to an end, after five long days and nights of debauchery.

Up in Carlotta's rooms, Corbin and the madam were wrapping up their own private party. Strewn on the floor lay discarded lingerie and high heels from the various women he'd screwed over the past handful of days, as well as empty champagne magnums, a half-eaten platter of caviar and foie gras.

"I've had a hell of a time," Corbin said. "But now it's time to say goodbye."

"Where's the money you owe me?" Carlotta said, sitting up with her hand out. "You said you were going to pay for all of this."

"Did I really?" he stated, his amber eyes boring into her. "Nobody likes a greedy whore."

"And nobody likes a has-been," she flung out casually.

"I've killed for lesser insults," he said.

Inside him, a quiet fury flooded up. He reached into his pocket, where he had kept the little vial of Luciana's poison since taking it from her. He popped open a new bottle of champagne, poured them each a glass.

Into hers, he slipped the poison.

"*Cin cin,* darling," he said, raising the glass.

"I really don't feel like it," she said.

"Humor me. The last drink of a very enjoyable party."

She drank.

Then she set the glass on the table and turned. He watched her closely, saw her hand touch her throat. She whirled back to look at him, her eyes wide, and choked out, "What the hell did you put in there?"

He did not bother to answer, but sat down in a chair and finished his own champagne.

She fell onto the thick patterned carpet, limbs thrashing wildly in violent spasms.

Finally, she was quiet. Corbin stood, surveying the wreckage of the party.

And in the middle of it, Carlotta's body.

Poison was such a clean kill. *Too clean,* he thought.

And that was when he set to work.

When he finished dismembering her body, there was a large pool of blood in the middle of the carpet. He opened the door and called down to a couple of his Gatekeepers.

"What happened to her?" one of them asked as they stared at the remnants in the center of the room.

Hired to replace the ones who had defected in Vegas, these Gatekeepers still had not learned how to keep their mouths shut. But they would learn. Even if he had to teach them the hard way, Corbin knew.

"Nothing you need to know about," the Archdemon said, pouring himself another glass of champagne and sipping.

He felt like toasting himself. It was his first kill since his spectacular defeat at the hands of Julian Ascher, and he felt a sense of triumph rushing through his body. Even if she had only been a second-rate Rogue demon, killing Carlotta brought him a renewed sense of power.

"If I feel like killing, I kill," he said. "I don't need a reason to do it."

He wished the same applied to killing angels.

But there would be consequences that even he could not risk facing.

The two Gatekeepers stood looking grimly at Carlotta's body as Corbin drank the champagne. He could see it on their faces—they were undoubtedly thinking of the brothel keeper's hospitality. The phrase *she did not deserve this* probably floated through their minds.

Corbin didn't care.

"Get rid of the corpse," he said. "In fact, help me get rid of them all."

# *Chapter Thirteen*

*Chiuso*—Closed.

That was what the glass gallery door sign read when Luciana and Massimo arrived the next morning. At ten o'clock on a weekday.

"How strange," Luciana murmured.

Yet when she twisted the doorknob, it was unlocked and the door swung open easily. The bell above the door tinkled. Inside, the shop stood silent and empty. The colorful rows of blown glass stood on their pristine shelves, sparkling in the morning sun.

But no salesgirl manned the shop. No customers perused the displays.

She looked back at Massimo, who merely shrugged as he followed her in. She led him into the back room, through the door and up the dark passageway.

"Girls? Carlotta?" she called as she climbed the stairs. "It's me, Luciana."

*Nothing.*

No horrible nicknames shouted down from the floor above. No sound of women's laughter rang through the large rooms, no raucous celebrations like the other evening. No soft murmuring of whores to their clients. Not even a whisper.

"That's odd," she commented. "It's very quiet."

*Too quiet.*

At the top of the stairs, she stopped so suddenly that Massimo almost bumped into her.

The brothel was a disaster. On the floor, debris lay scattered, the aftermath of a wild party. Empty bottles lay discarded, glasses broken and ground into the carpet. Tables were overturned, chairs broken. Bits of clothing were flung everywhere, even dangling from the banister above. The chandeliers lay shattered; their crystal prisms littering the floor like the leftover wreckage of a plundered treasure chest.

But there wasn't a person in sight.

Not a body, not a limb, not a digit. Not a single hair remained of any of the girls.

Not even a hint of ghost lingered, no scrap of a soul left behind.

"Perhaps there's someone upstairs," she said, clinging to her last vestige of hope as she mounted the curved staircase. In Carlotta's office, she made her way among more strewn bottles, navigating the upended furniture and the half-eaten trays of delicacies.

In the middle of the lush carpet was a deep red stain.

In the center of that stain lay a ripped silk garment, soaked in crimson.

In the folds of that garment rested a single emerald earring, a bright green teardrop still wet with blood.

Luciana took a handkerchief out of her pocket. She bent and picked up the earring, tying it carefully into the fabric. Pressed her fingers closed around it, as if she could squeeze some remnant of Carlotta out of that hard, old gemstone.

A tear slipped down her cheek.

"I wanted these earrings back," she muttered aloud. "But not like this."

As horrible and backstabbing as Carlotta had been, she had not deserved *this*.

Luciana slipped to her knees, bracing herself against the floor to keep upright. The urge to vomit washed over her in a wave, almost tipping her over.

"Let's get out of here," said Massimo, lifting her up by the arm. "We can't risk becoming victims of who-ever has laid waste to this whole establishment." But there was no question in either of their minds. This was the work of Corbin Ranulfson.

Luciana leaned against him to stand, shaking on her feet as she tucked the earring into her pocket. Massimo was right. She could not afford to stay here and mourn. "I will bury the only thing that remains of her. And re-member her as she should be remembered."

They waited until after sunset, when the cover of night would help conceal their movements. The salt spray of the Adriatic misted Luciana's face as Mas-simo chauffeured her to the outlying islands once again.

Not to the wild, haunted dumping ground of Sant' Ariano this time. But to the more civilized place Vene-tians took their dead. Where Venetians had been ferry-ing corpses since Napoleon had invaded and declared their traditional practices unclean, shocked at the habit of burying the dead within the city itself.

Instead, the dead were brought here.

To the island of San Michele.

Named for the Archangel Michael, this *cimitero* had not existed when her family had died. Not the first time, anyway. To purchase this plot fifty years after their death, to build this memorial to her dead family…it was Luciana's way of sending a clear message to the divine.

*Nothing is sacred.*

"Eternal rest is a myth," she said to Massimo as he

pulled the boat up near the entrance to the walled cemetery. "And anyone who believes in it is a fool."

Now, in the middle of the night, the burial ground was still. Stately cypress trees loomed overhead, guarding the silence of the dead. Luciana swept past crowded tombstones, past long stretches of white crosses and stacked mausoleums. Among the monuments she stumbled, overwhelmed for a moment by the masses of flowers laid atop the graves, by the scent of decaying petals, by the dank smell of foliage rotting in the heat of high summer.

For a moment, she thought she might faint. She swayed and almost fell, catching herself on the cool face of a marble tombstone, fingers fumbling against its solid smoothness. Righting herself, she soldiered on.

Massimo trailed after her, following slightly behind her in case she should collapse.

Until she came to the place she sought.

In the moonlight stood a solid block of old white marble, topped by a winged figure that might be angel or demon at this point, eroded by time into a grotesque creature. She bent, running her fingers over the grooves of the text engraved on the stone.

*Lorenzo Rossetti, 1727–1784. Padre.*
*Maria Elena Rossetti, 1732–1787. Madre.*
*Carlotta Rossetti, 1761–1783. Sorella.*
"Father, mother, sister."

An empty grave, an empty monument. The sole record of three souls whose human remains were lost, perhaps buried beneath the city's paving stones, or perhaps in the public wells, as bodies of the poor often had been.

Whose existence had been wiped out of human memory by the hand of the devil.

Luciana dug a little hole in the earth and placed the earring into it.

She said a silent farewell as she covered the small object with earth.

"Now that earring will rest with two of the women who wore it," she explained aloud to Massimo. "They were my mother's before they were mine. And then Carlotta wore them. At least they stayed in the family."

He did not answer, but stood silently by, his face as still and white as stone.

"One way or another, I will avenge her death," Luciana swore. "This act will not go unpunished."

"Do you really think you can best Corbin, *baronessa?*" Massimo asked quietly.

"I have to try," she ground out.

"The question is, who do you hate more? Corbin or the Company of Angels?"

"I hate them both equally. And so I must try to avenge myself equally on both of them. But you're right. We must pick our battles, Massimo. And since the Company is our most pressing concern, we will concentrate our efforts there. But mark my words. The time for a reckoning with Corbin is coming."

She and Massimo turned at the same time.

Behind them stood the angel. His gaze tracked to the disrupted earth at the base of the monument, then upward to read the names on the stone.

"Irony of ironies, for a demoness to consecrate her family on holy ground," he said.

"You angels are such wimps. None of you have ever raised so much as a whisper about it in all these centuries. Where is your precious Michael now?" she hissed.

"He may not be here," said Brandon. "But I am."

"And why have you come? To torture me? There isn't any point. Isn't it enough that she is gone?"

"What happened?" he said.

She reached out, touching the last name on the monument, fingers drifting over the engraved grooves. The explanation stuck in her throat. She only managed to shake her head as a single, angry tear slid down her cheek. She swiped it away.

"You can put a stop to all of this, Luciana," he said. "I can help you."

She was so tired, so weak. She wanted to believe what he said.

"Come with me now, only for a little while. There must be somewhere we can go. Where we can talk, just the two of us."

She sagged forward, bracing herself against the monument, leaning on the strength of the old stone. She, who prided herself on her strength and her ability to survive, felt so fragile now. Dried out like the petals of the decaying flowers left on the graves around her. As though she might break apart at a single touch.

Turning to the Gatekeeper, she said, "Massimo, leave us. Take the boat and go home."

*"Baronessa?"* he said.

"Go," she said, waving him away. Then she said to the angel, "Yes. There is a place."


In the boat, Massimo worried.

He watched the Guardian take the *baronessa* away in another boat, toward the Lido.

Briefly, Massimo contemplated following, but thought better of it. Although the Gatekeeper worried for himself, he worried for the *baronessa* more. She had suffered through much. *Things no one ought to bear.*

What she was doing now, Massimo had no authority or desire to question.

*Let her have her moment of happiness with that angel,* the Gatekeeper thought. *Love has no place among demons, but at least she might know a moment of peace. If only a moment.*

Luciana took Brandon to the Lido, the long stretch of sandbar where tourists sunned themselves, packed as tightly as sardines washed up from the Adriatic. Now, at night, the beach was deserted and lit only by a few flickering lights.

As the boat veered along the shoreline, she looked behind them, to the receding lights of Venice sparkling in the distance. The city floated like an illusion, like a dream. *Like a hallucination.*

*Am I really awake?* she wondered.

As Brandon steered, she ran her fingers along the muscles of his arm.

In no dream had he ever felt so real. In no dream had she ever felt so vulnerable.

*Please. Let me have a little time with him. Just a little...*

Luciana did not know to whom the words were aimed.

She only knew that her most fervent wish was to be here, with him.

*Anywhere, with him.* Without the Gatekeepers and the rest of the Guardians watching, she and Brandon could be alone. If only for a moment, a stolen little bit of time.

She directed him to a place where they pulled the

boat up on the sand. She slipped off her shoes to walk across the beach, retrieved a hidden key near the front door of her little summer villa.

"This really is the place where I come to be alone with my thoughts," she said as she unlocked the door.

"The last time you said those words—" he began.

"I was lying. Not this time."

She led him inside, standing in the doorway of the place that had lain dormant for years. She opened her mouth to tell him how her sister had finally been destroyed, after centuries of hard survival at the brothel. But all she wanted to do was forget. To fill the void in her gut—the big, black, gaping hole of fear and grief that threatened to swallow her from the inside out.

"Luciana, you're in a fragile state of mind," he said, holding her at arm's length. "I don't want to take advantage of that."

She looked up at him, choking back tears. "I need you. I need this."

His hands were in her hair, tilting her face up toward him. "No more illusions. Just us."

He kissed her, the force of his passion bearing down on her so fast she no longer had time to think. On the cool floor of the villa, they were on each other, inside each other. Without language, without words. Without hesitation. Skin sliding on skin, muscle pulsing against supple muscle. Water lashing on rock. Waves breaking on sand. Two forces of nature, so physical and so violent in opposition. Yet so dramatic and so beautiful in their joining.

Rain falling on fire, clashing together to make steam.

Afterward, she traced a finger over his shirtless chest, mapping the tattoos covering his arms and torso.

Slowly, she followed the lines etched in ink, the dragon's head curving over his heart.

"Do they hurt, these tattoos of yours?"

He shifted a little under her touch, but said, "No."

"I want to know more," she said, tracing the edge of a gray feather along the trapezius muscle at the top of his shoulder. "Tell me about this one."

After a pause, he said, "That was the first one I got, just after I died. I was shot in the back. My flesh exploded, torn into a thousand shreds. When I was sent back to earth as a Guardian, the tattoo was there. A constant reminder of what had happened."

"Not every Guardian has such markings," she said.

"The Archangels wanted to remind me of what I'm doing here," he ventured. "Maybe they thought I had a higher chance than the other Guardians of straying."

*Maybe they were right,* he thought.

"Most of the tattoos depict different Assignees I've had over the years," he said. "In some form or another. Some of the animals represent the spirits of people I've helped."

"Am I supposed to end up there, too?" she wondered aloud. "Perhaps after you've dealt with me, there will be a spear through this dragon's head. That's what you were sent here to do, wasn't it? Destroy me."

She said it as a fact, not a question.

One that he denied, shaking his head. "I told you, I came here to apprehend you, not to harm you. And I have obviously not been successful at capturing you."

"But you were successful at every other assignment you had. Isn't that right? You've saved hundreds of people. Maybe thousands," she said, stroking his skin.

"I wouldn't say I saved them. You can't save someone

who doesn't want to be saved. All of my human Assignees have saved themselves. I just showed them the way."

*You can't save someone who doesn't want to be saved.* Brandon's words circulated in Luciana's head. She wrapped herself in a blanket and went outside to sit on the beach, looking out into the darkness of the Adriatic. He came up behind her, kissed her shoulder as she looked out to sea.

"Tell me what happened to your sister."

"Corbin killed her," she said, not knowing what else to say. "He wanted to hurt me, and he knew where to get me."

"I want to know everything, from the beginning," the angel insisted.

"You already know about me. You were given a file on me, were you not?"

"I don't know your side of the story. I want to hear the words from your own lips."

"That's a very long story," she said. "I don't even know where to begin."

"Begin at the beginning," he told her. "I want to hear everything. Especially why you hate Julian Ascher so much."

She sighed. "The beginning. If you insist…

"I was born in 1756, the daughter of a rich silk merchant in a city blooming with gilded lilies. Surrounded by the pleasures of festivals and Carnival, showered with gowns and jewels supplied by the wealth of my father's silk trade. My sister, Carlotta, was five years younger. I loved her, even though she could be very spoiled and sometimes acted like a brat.

"All of Venice celebrated in those days, but the city was going downhill. After its military and political position slipped, trade began to decline. Our father invested everything he had in a shipment of silk from the Far East that he thought would bolster our family's depleted finances. The ship sank, and we lost everything. Our parents panicked.

"I was seventeen years old when our world of luxury was torn apart. Little by little, the house was stripped. First it was the Tintorettos and the Tiepolos, and then the antique furniture. Then the silver services and the Murano glassware. Our mother's jewels, our father's collection of pleasure boats.

"Our father ordered me, 'You'll have to marry, and soon. We've no time to spare.'

"The man they picked for me was my worst nightmare, a man who knew our family through my father's business connections. Old, fat and degenerate. I had feared him since childhood—he had been leering at me since early adolescence. Since our youth, Carlotta and I had secretly nicknamed him *'il vecchio pedofilo.'* 'The old pedophile.'

"When I heard the news, I cried for three days, sobbing without end on the silk carpet of my bedchamber. My mother tried to bolster me, saying, 'You'll ruin your eyes if you cry like that, darling. Then your husband-to-be won't want you at all, will he?'

"I hoped that would be the case. Fleetingly, I contemplated slitting my wrists or disfiguring my face. But ultimately, I was too afraid of God to carry out such a death or even to harm myself.

"'It's either marry or go to work in the Arsenale,' my father joked, referring to the famous shipyard where workers were employed to build Venice's naval fleet. 'Or you could become a courtesan.' When I realized he was only half joking, I cried even harder.

"In the end, I realized I would have to find another way.

"I went to the Redentore Church and lit a candle. On my knees, I begged in prayer, *'Please, God. Send me a way out of this. Give me a sign.'*

"On the way home from the church, I saw Julian Ascher sauntering beside the Grand Canal. I thought God had answered my prayers.

"As it turned out, he had not.

"I loved Julian. Even though I was in a desperate situation, my heart was pure. But Julian used me. He took my virginity. Then he discarded me like a broken piece of glass, a trinket that had outlasted its novelty. The last time I saw him before he departed for England, I wept, begging him to take me with him. He refused. He left me to fend for myself.

"Although Julian had already left the city, the rumors spread. Venice is a small town, and it was even smaller back then. Soon the whole town was chattering about it, and *il vecchio pedofilio* found out that I was a ruined woman.

"The only people who had not heard about the scandal were foreigners. I found an Englishman named Thomas Harcourt, who seemed like a fine prospect for a husband, although in reality I knew nothing about him. I was a good enough actress that I could counterfeit love, enough to fool him into thinking I was a virgin. That part was easy. A little slit of my hand, a few drops of blood on the sheets. Harcourt did the gentlemanly thing and married me.

"Once he took me back to England, I saw another side of Harcourt that was far from genteel. A cruel, perverse side that was drunken and harsh, that thought nothing wrong with beating me until I bled. But in those times, if a man had wanted to beat his wife, there was nothing she or anybody else could do about it.

"And it was all for nothing.

"As soon as I left Venice, Carlotta was married to the decrepit old pedophile in my place. *Il vecchio pedofilio* had gotten his beautiful bride in the end, after all. One that was even younger than he had hoped for. My sister was only twelve years old.

"I had thought I would have time to figure out a way to help her. But I was wrong.

"In Venice in those days, marriage was often delayed into the twenties, not like it had been in earlier centuries. My sister's wedding was not illegal. But to me, my parents had committed an act of monstrosity. In hindsight, it was an act of desperation.

"The old pedophile was every bit as bad as I had feared. As the years ticked by, Carlotta's innocence ripened into maturity. She was no longer the child bride the old pervert had paid for. He took to frequenting whores, the younger the better. He contracted a bad case of syphilis and passed it on to Carlotta. She suffered a string of miscarriages due to the illness. She wrote me letter after letter detailing her misery, but there was nothing I could do. I was helpless, trapped beneath Harcourt's petty despotism.

"Ten years after I had come to England, I ran into Julian Ascher in a ballroom in London. I hated him, but I hated Harcourt more. I threw myself on Julian's mercy. Begged him to kill Harcourt in a duel. I had thought it would be a sure thing. My drunkard husband was normally incapable of walking a straight line, much less shooting straight. But the duel didn't go as planned, and both men were killed.

"I buried Harcourt and bowed my head at his funeral, as a good widow should. But I did not truly mourn him. Nor did I feel badly for Julian. I didn't regret the way that he died, nor the fact that his death solved my greatest problem.

"I rushed home to Venice, hoping to finally help Carlotta. She was heavily pregnant again with a child she thought would survive. But I was too late.

"She died in childbirth, and the baby died shortly after taking its first breath.

"I survived for a year after that, a free woman at last…. Until Harcourt clawed his way out of hell and strangled me."

The sun began to creep over the horizon, spilling light into the room and washing over his face. She saw the tiredness in his eyes; she was tired, too. Too tired to recount anything more. There was too much, too many years…

"What happened then?" he pressed. "How did you get out of hell? How did Carlotta end up at the brothel?"

"That's a story for another day, *caro*. You asked why I hate Julian Ascher so much, and there is your answer. Tonight, we have already run out of time. The rest will have to wait for the future."

*The future.* What a ridiculous notion, she chided herself. The idea of a time between them that would be peaceful enough for the telling of stories…that was more nonsensical than a fairy tale. She reminded herself, *Demons don't live for the future. Not a real future. We might be greedy for something we want. But mostly, we are trapped in the past. Or we live for the moment. But if we are swayed by considerations of the future, those considerations have only to do with revenge.*

"Come with me. You know you can. It's the right thing to do."

"I can't just waltz out of Venice with you," she laughed softly, laying her cheek on his broad chest, tracing her fingers over the images of ink drawn over his body. "The demon hierarchy will be out for my head. It is impossible. Corbin would retaliate. He would take revenge. There is Ca' Rossetti to consider. I have worked for centuries to preserve it. It has been the seat of my family for over a thousand years. And there are other things…" she said vaguely.

"What? What is there that ties you to this city?"

Her eyes wide, she didn't answer.

"You know it's possible," he said. "If Julian Ascher can change his ways, you can, too."

At the mention of his name, she flinched. "Don't talk about him."

They sat for a long while, staring out to sea together.

"If it happened, I would have to make preparations. At home," she said, very tentatively. "I cannot make any promises. There are others at stake, still. Other considerations, other people. My Gatekeepers…" she said, looking out to sea, wondering where Massimo had gone, whether he had enough sense to make it home without her.

"That you consider the possibilities is all I ask," Brandon said.

She thought of Violetta, and the sad singing that rang through the halls of Ca' Rossetti. Wondered if Violetta would ever find a way to let go of this world, and if Massimo had spent the night listening to that melancholic singing.

"Meet me at the opera," she said, flinging the suggestion out, reminded by that thought. "Tomorrow night. I will consider it…."

* * *

Back at Ca' Rossetti, Massimo and Violetta sat on the rooftop. He watched her wistful, young face as she watched the sun rise over the rooftops, unfurling the city into daylight.

"I wonder when she's coming back," he said.

"I don't really care," said Violetta. "I'm glad we have a little time to ourselves. A stolen moment, without her. Where did she go?"

"With her lover," he admitted.

"The angel?" Violetta asked. "But she always says that demons are incapable of love."

"Her whole way of thinking is unraveling," he told her. "Everything she has worked so hard to accomplish is falling apart."

"That is the nature of time, my love. The old falls apart. So the new can grow." Violetta moved her hand to his cheek, mimicking the gesture of touch although the connection was impossible.

"How did you get so wise in such a short time on earth? And so brave? I've never seen anyone stand up to the *baronessa* like you, even when your life was at stake."

She shook her head. "I'm not wise and I'm not brave, Massimo. I don't even know if I can bring myself to do what is necessary…."

"What do you mean?" he said. "Have you figured out what you need to do to let go?"

She did not say anything, but bit her lip and let her long, brown hair hang forward; a sheer curtain covering her sheer face.

"If you know what to do, then do it. You must. That, or remain a ghost forever. Is that what you want? It's not what I want for you," said Massimo.

"Of course that's not what I want," she whispered. "I want to touch your face. I want to hold your hand and feel your breath when you whisper in my ear. I want to *be*. I want to stay in this world with you, forever."

"We will see each other again, Violetta," he murmured, closing his eyes and wishing he could hold her. "I know we will. After you leave this place. We will find a way."

But he knew no such thing.

He only knew that he wanted what was best for her, and that it did not involve him.

Very late at night, when Luciana stole back into Ca' Rossetti, she heard the singing. So poignant and sad that she almost wanted to weep at the sound of it, right then and there.

*Escaping with Brandon is impossible,* she realized.

Dragging herself up the staircase of her beloved home, she had made up her mind.

To flee. Alone.

Because it was the only way she could think of to lessen the risk to those she loved.

## Chapter Fourteen

In her bedchamber, Luciana pulled a box out from her dressing table. Hands shaking, by the dim light of her lamp she sorted through her best jewelry. She put aside only the best of the old family pieces that she had painstakingly recovered after her mother had sold them to various pawnbrokers around the city.

She would not let these treasures go again. Not even at the risk of getting caught. Especially not after what had happened with Carlotta's earrings last night.

"Going somewhere?" a familiar voice said behind her.

She jumped, the jewels spilling from her hands.

She pivoted to see Corbin, leaning against the wall, watching her.

"I knew it," she said flatly. "I knew you would come. I knew you would find some way to intervene and spoil everything."

"But what are you talking about, Luciana? Are you planning a vacation, my dear? Perhaps you feel like you need some time away after you deliver the angel. Tonight's the last night, you know. I would have expected you would have finished the job by now."

"I was simply looking through some of my things.

Don't worry, Corbin. You'll get what's coming to you," she said.

"Are you having second thoughts? From my point of view, I can't see that you've made any progress toward your goal. The Guardian is still out there. I have reason to believe you've been meeting with him in secret."

"There's no secret to the fact that I've been meeting with him," Luciana scoffed, mustering as much bravado as she could, although she was shaking inside. "How else do you expect me to seduce him?"

"Are you falling in love with him?"

"Of course not. Not after I've had *you*," she simpered.

"I'm not fooled by you, Luciana. I know you used me to get to Julian. You're a liar and a whore. However, the fact that you've fallen in love with a sworn enemy is unexpectedly pathetic, even for you."

She raised her chin and stared back at him. And dared to say, "What would it matter to you if I *was* falling in love with him?"

That was a mistake.

Corbin grabbed the jewelry she had dropped onto the bed, hurling it on the floor. Some of the more delicate pieces smashed apart, pieces of gold and precious gems rolling across the hardwood. A lump rose in her throat.

*Do not cry,* she told herself. *He will destroy you if you cry.*

"You've got a job to do. I told you to kill that angel. Tonight, the clock runs out," he said, his voice terrifyingly normal.

"Brandon…he's not nearly ready," she protested weakly.

"You've gotten into his dreams, haven't you?"

"Yes, but… I'm not even close. He's strong. Too strong."

Corbin slammed his fist into the wall beside her ear. She froze.

"There are rules in the interactions between angels and demons," she said, closing her eyes, swallowing down her fear. "Rules that cannot be broken."

"Rules can be bent," he said, moving to loom over her. "You've said so yourself. Don't forget what you are. What you've always been. A demoness and a whore."

She opened her eyes and glared at him. "I know what I am. The task you set me hasn't been easy, but I agreed to it, didn't I? I will deliver the angel by the end of tonight. I hit some unexpected roadblocks, as I'm sure you know. There have been some deaths amongst the demon community here in Venice."

"I wouldn't know anything about that," he said, straightening. Completely toneless, he continued, "But let me just say that those who deserved it got their end. Don't fret about Carlotta. She spent a long time on this earth. Longer than most ever dream of. It was time for her to go."

"So you did kill them," she accused.

He came up, grabbed her by the throat. "Why would I ever need to admit to such a thing?"

The sensation of choking was unbearable.

Like death all over again. His eyes, as cold and as unfeeling as a serpent's, bore into her.

*No,* she thought. *A snake would have more feeling.*

She felt herself fading, her vision filling with stars, a billion dots of light.

"I remember what it's like to die," she choked out, her voice barely rasping past her lips. "Just do it." She let her eyes close, willing him to finish it. "Kill me."

"Kill you, my dear?" he snarled. "I would never dream of making it so easy. No, darling. I'm taking you on a tour of your own private version of hell. Just to remind you exactly what's at stake. Open your eyes."

*My own private version of hell. I can't go back there. I won't.* She willed herself, *Don't...don't...don't open your eyes.*

He shook her just once, but so hard she thought her eyes might snap right out of her head.

Very quietly he said, *"Open your eyes,* or I will open them for you. I will rip your eyelids off, and it will be unutterably painful."

She had no doubt he would do it.

When she looked around, she and Corbin were no longer in her palazzo. They stood on the steps of the Redentore Church. Not the *real* Redentore Church. One that existed in the deepest reaches of her wildest fears. One whose pristine marble facade had been desecrated, the saints and angels beheaded and smeared with a black, oozing substance that seemed to slither toward her.

"Welcome back to the underworld," Corbin said smoothly. "We've missed you down here."

The sky was a mottled red, with dark scarlet clouds streaming overhead in clots, like a sped-up film shot through a bloodied lens. Thunder rumbled from above, and the ground beneath her feet trembled as though it would split open. But she knew there was no farther down she could go.

"Release me," she demanded. "You have no power over me."

"On the contrary, my dear. I have all the power in the world over you, until you manage to fulfill your end of the bargain. And until then, it's in my hands to motivate you. Besides, didn't you just invite me to kill you?"

He dragged her into the church. It was empty and

decrepit, the long nave strewn with rotting leaves and broken plaster. The great crucifix loomed over the altar, the figure of Christ missing and a giant crack splitting the wood in the middle.

"On your knees," he thundered.

"Not for you," she ground out. "Not this time."

He slapped her then. The sting of it reverberated in the space of the church and knocked her to the floor. She looked up toward the rounded space of the dome overhead. And closed her eyes, silently begging. Just one word: *please*.

"Do you think it'll do you any good to start praying at *this* point, my dear?" he laughed. "Haven't you learned anything after all this time? Do you think your saint is going to come save you now? That big, tattooed freak of yours isn't coming to redeem you. I've told you so many times. It's the other way around. Your job is to bring him down here."

He grabbed her by the hair, hauling her to her feet.

"Your little tour doesn't stop here. Let's jog your memory some more. This is the little hotel where Julian had his rooms. Where you gave up your virginity to him. And there's…"

She knew what was coming next.

The thing she always tried to forget.

The thing she hadn't found the courage to tell Brandon.

"…the place where you tried to hang yourself after he abandoned you. But you didn't succeed, did you? When you realized there was nothing you could do to save your family after all. When you realized you had failed. Admirable that you tried again, even after that disaster. Look, here's the sucker you got to try to help you out of that. Harcourt. My, he hasn't aged well, has he?"

She had not seen Harcourt in over two hundred years, since she had clawed her way out of this hell. His skin looked withered, shriveled, older than anything she had ever seen before. His head creaked as he turned to look at her.

"Ah, my dear," he said, reaching toward her. "Luciana, my lethal little bride. I have been dreaming of what I would do if I ever saw you again."

His ancient, clawed hand reached for her, grasping her around the arm. She almost screamed, but she knew such a sound could trigger a frenzy in Harcourt from which she would not escape. Forcing herself to swallow the scream, she shuddered, feeling the bony claw scrape its way across her chest to close over her breast.

"So fresh…" Harcourt groaned.

"Perhaps we can arrange a reunion between you two later," Corbin chuckled, jerking her away. "But right now, we must move on," said Corbin. "There's one more thing I'd like to show you."

Pulling her by the hair, he dragged her into another room, this one a distorted version of Carlotta's brothel. There, in the middle of the blood-spattered room was a pile of dismembered corpses. Among them, Luciana spotted the battered, bloodied faces of some of the girls she'd worked with years ago; others she hadn't known personally but still recognized, girls she'd seen around Venice. They were mostly girls she'd seen at Carlotta's only a few days ago, girls who had been laughing and cavorting, and *breathing*.

And among them was her sister's face, her green eyes staring straight ahead.

"Even in hell, Carlotta is dead," he said. "Nothing you ever do can get her out of here."

Luciana looked at the pile of bodies, death piled upon death, stacked up.

She saw *herself* for what she was: a bringer of death.

One who brought nothing but suffering. She may not have killed these women herself, but she had killed plenty of women and men in the past.

And now, sent by the devil himself to perform the most sacrilegious and heinous act.

To kill an angel.

Not simply an angel, but a man who had grown to trust her.

A man who had grown to love her.

"What's the difference between this version of hell and the one on earth?" she asked Corbin, genuinely puzzled.

He slapped her. Full across the face, so hard that she felt the inside of her mouth split open and the coppery tang of blood flow down her chin. His neutral expression didn't even shift as he said, "Watch your mouth."

She glared up at him. "Seriously. I don't know. Whether being a slave in this hell or a slave on earth… both of them involve just as much suffering. What have those girls done to deserve this treatment? Nothing. Some of them weren't bad people. Some weren't even demons. They were human. Who gave you the right to take their lives?"

"I have every right in the world. I am an Archdemon."

*And perhaps if I stay down here, Brandon will just leave,* she thought suddenly. *Go back to America, realizing that I've gotten what I deserve. That his assignment has been finished, although not in the way he anticipated.*

"Oh, no, you don't," said Corbin, guessing her

thoughts. "You're not staying down here. You still owe the devil a sacrifice, and you're going back up there to get him. If it's the last thing you do on earth. Which it might well be."

He pulled her back upward. Toward the surface.

When reality stabilized around them, they were back in her bedroom, amid the ruined jewelry scattered on the floor. And then he let her go. She fell to the floor, gasping for air and clutching the burning-raw place where he had held her neck.

He dropped something next to her, a small object that hit the floor just inches from her face.

A single emerald drop earring, twin to the one she had buried last night.

"Why did you do it?" she said, tears finally spilling from her eyes.

"Why?" he hissed, bending down to look at her. His amber eyes nearly glowed with the fervor of the kill, the spark of recognition kindling in their eerie depths. "Because I could, *baronessa*. Because I have the power. I don't need poison. It doesn't take me a week to kill. I can kill in the blink of an eye, without consequences and without recrimination from anyone."

"Maybe you can kill any human or any demon without answering for it," she rasped out. "But you can't kill an angel."

He went wild, grabbed the chair from her dressing table and smashed it against the wall. Around her, shards of wood splintered and fell. He knelt low to the floor, near her ear and growled, "Those whores are all back down in hell now, where they belong. Let it be a warning to you. Your time with that angel is almost up."

"I can't," she said. She closed her eyes, wishing she would just disappear.

"My dear," he said, his voice all the more terrifyingly for its calmness, "that's simply not an acceptable answer."

He yanked her off the floor, pulling her into her closet, where he leafed through the racks of her evening gowns.

"Most of these are far too trampy. You'll never catch an angel in any of these." Onto the bed, he threw a floor-length white evening gown. "This one's appropriate. White. How virginal. Like a sacrificial lamb. He'll like that. And it's quite ironic, wouldn't you say?"

She stripped quickly, hating the feeling of him watching her, taking in the details of her naked body.

He picked the emerald earring up from the floor, pushed it roughly through her pierced ear. Then he held her body against him. "Yes, very ironic indeed. I could fuck you right now if I wanted. But I'd rather wait until after. When there's time to really enjoy it. When you've destroyed that angel and gotten all that pathetic *hope* out of your system."

He pushed her away. She resisted the urge to vomit.

"Now, show me the poison you're going to use on him."

Immediately, she reached under the bed for the syringe of cyanide she kept there.

"Of course. Trust you to keep your most dangerous poison under the bed. Now, was that so difficult? I hope for your sake that you're not too attached to this angel. Once I have his body, I plan to cut those tattooed wings off of him."

"What, do you mean *skin* him?"

Corbin smiled, and the urbane, unfeeling look on his face made even her blood run cold.

"Of course," he said.

She shivered at the thought of it, the image of that magnificent body defiled in such a way. There was no doubt in her mind that Corbin would carry out his threat. That he would revel in doing it.

"Don't come back until you've done your job," Corbin said blandly. "What a shame it would be if a pretty girl like you were sent back to hell, even if you think it's a better alternative to being up here. The Gatekeepers down in the underworld will love it. You should last about thirty seconds intact."

He ran his hand down the front of her body.

She drew back and slapped him.

For a terrified moment, she waited, as something dangerous rippled in those eerie amber eyes of his. He said, "You don't know what kind of war you've started, my dear."

Then he shoved her roughly onto the bed.

"Don't waste any more time. The devil doesn't wait for anyone. Stop stalling, and don't come back until you've done your job."

Massimo watched Corbin walk down the staircase of the palazzo. As he passed Massimo, who stood on the landing, he nodded cordially and then exited the house.

A few minutes later, Luciana came out of her bed-chamber, dressed for the evening.

*"Baronessa?"* he asked, noting that her throat was bruised and a little blood seeped from her left ear. "How may I assist you?"

"You must go, Massimo. Leave here now, and don't come back. You must forget you ever knew me. Promise me you will go."

She stared at him with her intense gaze, and he nodded.

Then she walked down the stairs and out the front door.

Massimo watched her leave, and said to Violetta, "She's heading to La Fenice. That's your territory. Go and watch over her. Please, even if you hate her, do this for my sake. If she needs help, come back and get me. I'm not leaving her. Not when she needs me."

"Of course not," the girl said without hesitation, pressing a ghostly finger to his lips. "If we don't get another chance, then let this be our goodbye."

"We will see each other again, my love," Massimo promised her, even though he knew with an aching certainty that they would not have another moment together. "But until then, know that I love you with all of my dark heart."

Across the canal, Brandon readied himself for his rendezvous with Luciana.

He showered in the makeshift shower the Venetians had rigged in the back of the house, grateful for the rudimentary plumbing job they had done. The cool water put him at ease, soothing his anxious mind in the relentless humidity.

No, this was a different kind of stakeout entirely.

There was still so much at risk.

"Why did she ask you to meet her at the opera?" Arielle wondered aloud, standing in the doorway with her arms crossed. She watched him as he stood shaving over a stone basin and a propped-up mirror. "That's such an odd meeting place."

"Honestly, I think she just threw it out there. I don't know how her mind works. But you wanted me to win her trust, right? That's my job, isn't it? That's what I was sent here to do," he said grimly. "I've got to change, so do you mind giving me some privacy?"

Arielle's idea of privacy was to turn around, going to look out one of the windows on the pretense of looking at the canal below. She said, "It's nothing I haven't already seen."

*Not for a long time, you haven't,* he thought.

One of the larger Guardians from the Venetian unit had contributed a black suit and white shirt. Brandon deliberated arguing with Arielle, but thought better of it. Shedding his jeans, he pulled on the dress pants, the shirt.

"I don't know how the Italians stand dressing up in this heat," she said, turning around. She touched the open shirt at the neck. "You look like a different man. Not like the usual Brandon I know."

He pushed her hand aside and headed for the door.

"Are you falling in love with her?" Arielle asked, stopping him in his tracks.

He turned. It was perhaps the first time he had ever seen real emotion on Arielle's face. Real lines on her forehead, creasing her brow. Real pain.

"Of course not," he lied. The lie burned in his mouth, and he hated himself for telling it.

"Good. I know you might not agree with our plan to dispose of her. But it will take an eternity to reform her otherwise."

"I see," Brandon said. He knew already what was coming.

"It's the best thing for her."

He said nothing, but picked up his suit jacket and stepped out the door toward his rendezvous with the demoness.

# Chapter Fifteen

"*Singing inside La Fenice is like being inside a diamond,*" a famous diva had once said.

The opera house's interior sparkled like a diamond. A gold-and-crystal chandelier flowered from the sky-frescoed ceiling. The velvet-covered seats and tiers of mirrored boxes ascended in layers of gilded splendor. The acoustics allowed the bright, beautifully polished voices to ring through the theater with matchless clarity.

*Like being inside a diamond.*

*Trapped inside something beautiful and glittering, yet hard and lifeless.*

That was what the phrase meant to Luciana.

In the Royal Box across from center stage, the demoness sat in the very heart of this diamond, looking as flawless as a gem in her white silk gown. Every operagoer milling in the seats below and the boxes around her craned their necks to get a look at her. Of all the things that sparkled inside La Fenice tonight, Luciana shone the brightest.

Yet, all she could think of was death.

She ignored the open stares of her fellow operagoers, not seeing them. The fluttering scores of richly dressed Venetians and tourists who had come to the opera in their summer evening clothes. Drifting layers of cleverly designed chiffon and jewels draping the women. Crisply ironed white linen beneath the dark suits of the men.

*One day, sooner than they think, each and every one of them will die.*

*No matter how beautiful.*

They all admired her, of course. They coveted her beauty and the exclusivity of her place. But what these mortals thought made no difference to her.

None of them could alter fate.

Not their own. Not hers. Not Brandon's.

And she hated this feeling. Of being exposed. A sitting duck.

A pawn of men.

"With the devil as my witness," she muttered under her breath, "I will never let this happen again."

She looked at the program, blindly browsing through its pages. *La Traviata.*

*Of course,* she thought. *The opera with a heroine named Violetta.*

Luciana had seen this opera dozens of times, with numerous stars over the years, each more brilliant and more lucid than the rest. *In the Royal Opera House in Covent Garden. At the Met in New York. At La Scala in Rome. At the Opéra Bastille in Paris...*

But never waiting for a man like this.

She set her gaze on the stage, listening to the music and losing herself in the world of the opera. She loved opera not only because she adored the beauty of the singers' voices. Not only because she loved to sink into the richness of these stories she had watched so many times, and knew so well.

For Luciana, opera was like traveling backward in time. Through music, she felt as though she could almost return to the past. To a time when she had been innocent and unhindered by the knowledge that death touched everything. Untouched by the reality of being a bringer of death herself.

There was only sound.

When the door opened behind her, a strange sensation throbbed in her chest, a kind of ache she remembered from human life. Something like regret.

She had felt many things before a kill.

*Fear. Elation. Anger. A desire for vengeance.*

But never anything like this.

*I have no choice,* she told herself. *I must perform my duty.*

Inside the opera house, Brandon felt her dark energy smoldering. Unsettled. He tracked that energy up to the second floor of the small opera house, where he could feel the sensual pull of her, simmering.

He entered her box through a small door. Closed it behind him.

Alone, on a red velvet chair, sat the demoness.

His first impression was that he had slipped into another era, two and a half centuries ago. Before his eyes a vision of Luciana drifted. Of the demoness as a very young woman, still human, attending the opera with her family, happy amongst the companionship of others.

The mirage glimmered for an instant and then evaporated, shifting back to the present.

She turned slightly toward the noise of the door, but did not meet his eyes. Her luxuriant, curling hair was upswept, leaving her shoulders and back exposed. Her dress, elegant, bias-cut white silk, poured like water over her bare skin. Along the long column of her throat, he saw her throat tighten, his heightened awareness of her tiny swallow, a motion so subtle, yet so sensual. He wanted to reach out, run his fingers along the length of her neck.

In a dream, he might have done so.

But this was no dream. There was no watch in his pocket.

He checked. He double-checked.

*I'm awake.*

He took a seat beside her.

"Did you know," she murmured, without turning, "La Fenice burned down not once, but twice? In the end, the opera house survived, rebuilt by us Venetians to rise again from the ashes. She is a true phoenix."

Luciana turned to look at him fully then, those emerald eyes of hers glittering in the darkness, so green against the dimly lit gilt and mirrors decorating the interior of the box.

"You are like a phoenix, too, rising every night after your repeated death," she said quietly. "And you will continue to rise. On your own. You must know that I can't go with you. It is completely impossible."

"You're making this more difficult than it has to be," he said. "It can be easy."

"Easy?" The single word, spat, her brow furrowed. "I will make it easy for you. Go back where you came from. Leave now. Before something disastrous happens."

"Never. Now that we're here, let's at least be honest with each other. We both know that I won't go home. That I will never leave you alone. And the reason I came tonight no longer has anything to do with the assignment the Company sent me to accomplish. Nothing to do with my mission."

"Look around you," she said, ignoring his comment. "There are more demons in the world than humans could ever imagine. We run rampant in this city. We are responsible for everything. From corrupt politics to overcharging tourists for mediocre food in the *caffès.* From natural disasters to picking pockets on the vaporetti. We are everywhere."

Brandon stared back at her. "So are angels."

"We are inescapable," she said, barely hearing him, staring out over the audience of the opera house with wide, frightened eyes.

"Are you talking about Corbin?" he asked. "Because the Company can find a way to protect you from him."

Her mouth set into a stubborn line. She shook her head, her dark curls tumbling around her. "We'll win in the end. You know it. My kind always do. We barely have to lift a finger. Humans do it to themselves."

He couldn't speak past the lump in his throat. He wanted to bolt the door shut and keep her in here for eternity, in their own little bubble of gilt and mirrors. It wasn't exactly his taste, but with her here, he would capture this moment forever.

*Forget the war between angels and demons,* he thought.

The war going on inside him was a thousand times more dangerous.

*There's no point in arguing with him,* she thought. *It always results in the same thing.*

*An impasse.*

So instead, she smiled and said, "Let's not argue about it. We have this time together. After the opera is over, we will say our goodbyes. But until then, let me love you."

She rose, pulled the curtain shut across the front of the box.

"I didn't know you could do that," he said. "What's the point?"

"In my day, we shut these curtains all the time. The opera was a lovely place to come to have a little party with the people you knew. Half the time, we only listened to the arias."

To lose herself in his arms. That was all Luciana wanted.

Sorrow. Melancholy. Regret.

These things welled inside her, untouched for so long. His mere presence stirred them.

Her hands reached up to caress his neck.

"I'm sorry," she whispered.

*What do you have to be sorry for?* he wondered.

He was about to speak the thought aloud, but the words never made it through his lips.

Instead, he felt the prick of something sharp sliding into the carotid artery. Felt the cool rush of the foreign substance entering his bloodstream. He knew instantaneously what she had done.

*Poison.*

Releasing itself into his bloodstream. He blinked, holding his hand to his neck.

In that instant, he realized just how mistaken he had been. How badly he had missed his mark. He had sorely underestimated the speed with which Luciana worked, the ruthlessness with which she performed her set task.

Brandon felt the nearness of death. Knew that whatever poison she had shot into him was working its way through the pathways of his body. Through veins and arteries, until it reached his heart. Once there, the heart would stop pumping, the chambers of it cease the circulation of blood. His breathing would stop. The flow of blood, that precious substance, would stop entirely.

Whatever he had expected, he had not been prepared for this. He had made a stupid mistake, coming here. Expecting that what they had shared together had actually meant something to her.

*Fight,* he told himself. *Get up off the floor and take her down.*

But he couldn't. Couldn't move his limbs. Couldn't marshal his arms to push himself upright, nor his legs to support him. His muscles seized again, his body going rigid as the poison worked its way through his nervous system.

"What did you shoot into me?" he muttered, furious that his control was fading fast, his vision blurring. Even with his reduced capacity to think, he was more furious at the fact that, whatever she had done to him, it was ultimately his own fault.

Didn't expect an answer, wasn't surprised when she simply smiled, as angelic as the mother of God herself. She stroked his head and murmured, "There now, *tesoro mio.* It is time to say our goodbyes."

"Did you stick me with your goddamned poison?" he ground out.

Strychnine, arsenic, cyanide...whatever earthly poison she threw at him, he could handle. He would recover from those things. But none of the angels knew for certain what her special concoction contained.

It had killed a demon. That much, he knew.

Brandon felt himself slipping, his mind fighting to keep control.

He had to trust that in the end, there was a reason for everything. Knew that whatever happened to his physical incarnation, even if this particular body died again, well, he would be recycled.

He forced himself to let go.

Brandon was stuck in a haze.

*Am I dreaming?* he wondered.

There was no alleyway. No smell of squalor. No shock of bullets entering his body. Instead, a moment of confusion, caught between two worlds, conscious and unconscious.

He faded into darkness. Dreamlessness.

Heard her bend down and whisper, "Hush, now. Just let it take you."

*Screw that,* he thought. *I'm not going anywhere.*

The small door behind them burst open.

One of her Gatekeepers—*Massimo,* Brandon thought—stumbled through it. Near exhaustion, his face smudged with ash, his clothes singed. He choked out, "*Baronessa.* Ca' Rossetti is on fire."

Her face, those glittering green eyes trained on Brandon with absolute hatred.

She was out the door in a flash, not bothering to utter a single word to him.

The look alone had conveyed everything.

Luciana ran out into the mezzanine, down the marble staircase, the quick series of taps that her high-heeled shoes made on the stairs as she ran down them, delicate and light.

Inside the opera house, the first act was ending. Amid the shouts and the cheering, she and Massimo crossed the foyer.

Out into the cool summer night. To the boat tethered not far from the entrance.

He did not question her, but leaped into the boat behind her.

Neither of them spoke as she drove, cleaving down the canals, veering around corners and finally, nearing her home.

She felt the heat of it from fifty yards away as they approached. The roar of it, as if a dragon had come thundering up from the depths of the canal to scorch Ca' Rossetti with its fury. But her own heart thundered much louder. She felt the weight of that organ dropping into her stomach, through the bottom of the boat, down into the dark waters of the canal.

Ca' Rossetti burned.

Violetta stepped into the box, knowing why she had come to La Fenice tonight—and it had nothing to do with the demoness.

She had stayed on earth to accomplish this single thing before she went into the light.

To love Massimo, and to be loved by him. Perhaps that had been part of her lesson here on earth, in the very short but very sweet time they had shared. But she knew that the more important reason for her stay, and maybe the whole reason she had died in the first place, had been for this.

This single moment, so brief but so important.

*I may no longer have a body, but I have a voice.*

Looking at the angel on the floor, she bent down, and shouted into his ear with all the force of her classically trained lungs.

"Wake up!"

He didn't move, so she shouted again. And again.

Until she watched his eyes flicker open. Until she was sure he was moving back into consciousness, his hands fumbling for something in his pocket that wasn't there, then pushing against the floor.

And then she spiraled upward.

Upward, departing through a rain of applause, the audience inside La Fenice clapping at the end of the opera, shouts of "Bravo!" creating a tunnel of sound around her. Pushing her, propelling her up.

*Into the light.* Past the tiers of boxes and their glittering wall sconces. Past the gilt-and-crystal chandelier she had always loved so much. Past the winged angels frescoed on the sky-blue ceiling. She departed the world from the theater that she loved so well, the place that would forever hold a part of her soul.

How long Brandon had been lying there, he didn't know.

He awoke to the horrific sound of a ghost screaming in his ear.

When his head finally began to clear and he sat up, she was gone.

The demoness was nowhere to be seen.

But she hadn't killed him, after all. Hadn't injected him with the special concoction that could have ended his existence on earth, could have taken away his immortality and wiped out his physical existence.

*What was in that syringe? Cyanide? Strychnine?*

He didn't know. But where she had gone, he knew instantly.

He rubbed the side of his neck. Checked his limbs. With an effort that would have rivaled any Herculean act, he climbed to his feet.

And went to find her.

## Chapter Sixteen

Flames licked the night sky. Playing a dangerous game of tag with the buildings around Ca' Rossetti, fire streamed out the windows of the palazzo, threatening to catch the walls and roofs of neighboring palaces. Thick smoke and the smell of burning hung in the still air. The sound of crackling sent a cold sweat down Luciana's exposed back.

She slipped to her knees, barely conscious of Massimo taking the wheel of the boat as she collapsed, clinging to the side of it. And then she was over the side of the boat, leaping onto the pavement.

She ran into the house.

The bottom floor had not yet begun to burn—the fire must have started upstairs. Perhaps there was still some way to stop it, she thought wildly.

*But how?*

Then she felt the heat billowing down the staircase, the flames still out of view but so hot it was like the inside of a wood oven. The palazzo was beyond saving, she knew. The only thing she could do was to take what she could carry and run.

*But what to take?*

Her mother's jewelry lay broken and scattered on the floor of the bedroom upstairs. The Tiepolos and

Tintorettos were huge canvases, too large for her to pry off the wall by herself and carry outside.

And more precious than any single item of art or jewelry was the palace itself...the frescoes she had painstakingly and lovingly restored, the plasters and the stonework repaired by the teams of artisans she had brought in, the delicate applications of gilt on the front facade...

There was no way to save it all...no way...

She charged up the stairs, heedless of the heat. Like an inferno. Like the flames of hell.

Every which way she turned, she did not know what to save, how to save anything.

No single item could preserve the memory of her family's lost legacy.

Pushing open the door to her workroom, she saw the vials of poison she had so painstakingly created, lined up on the table. She grabbed a fistful of them.

The flames came barreling their way down the hallway, roaring toward her.

She no longer wanted to be a part of this world.

It had beaten her. She sank to her knees, ashamed of herself. Ashamed that the only thing she thought to save when her ancestral home was burning was the most evil thing in it, apart from herself.

That her first and only impulse was to grab the most important thing to her.

*Poison.*

With all the strength she had left in her, she crawled toward the fire.

*Let it take me.*

And then she was pulled by a force greater than anything earthly. Not the fire. Not the heat.

But him.

Through the flames he emerged, big and brash and fearless as ever.

When she saw him, she knew beyond a doubt why he had been resurrected as a Guardian. The fact that he would risk himself for a woman who had just shot him full of cyanide and left him to suffer.... It made her want to weep, right there in the middle of the fire.

"There's only one way out," he shouted over the roar of flames, his voice, roughened by smoke, ground in her ear. "You've got to come with me."

She knelt there, paralyzed. What would happen if she simply gave herself over to him?

*Disaster.*

His fingers pried her hand open, forcing her to release the vials of poison she still clutched. And then arms were clamping around her, and a single word, an order. "Come!"

He dragged her back toward the stairs, but they were blocked. No way to get down. The only way to go was up. And so they went. Up toward the roof. Dragging her, he pulled her through the house. Outside, to the air. Cool air that burned her lungs.

On the rooftop, it was like standing on top of a bonfire, on the last log that was yet to be consumed by the flames. Beneath them, the building was going to collapse. He pulled her toward the edge of the roof.

"Jump!" Brandon shouted over the noise of the fire beneath them.

The roar was deafening. She thought of what she had seen in hell. The image of Harcourt flickered before her. Of the pile of dead girls. Of Carlotta.

"Don't just stand there! Jump!"

In the end, it wasn't her who made the decision. It was all him.

Flinging himself off the roof, he pulled her through the air with him. He leaped from the top of the building just as it exploded into flames, the burning heat shooting up into the night sky behind them.

They fell in a graceful arc that seemed to last forever. She wished it would, the two of them plummeting downward amid a gray rain. Not feathers this time, but the ashes of her home littering the night sky.

He knew the moment he lost her. Not in body, but in soul.

It was the moment he jumped off the rooftop, pulling her with him.

*You can't force someone to take a leap of faith.*

But he did, grabbing her in his arms and flinging them both into the dark space over the canal, half expecting them to land in a dreamscape.

Instead, they landed in the real world, in the murky water of the Grand Canal.

Down, down they plunged.

So far down, so cold, so dark that she thought she might as well stay here instead, beneath the water. Waiting for the dragon she might call up from its depths to drag them away, to join the corpses of so many victims she had dumped here over the years. Or to meet the devil's ferryman, who might arrive in his black funerary gondola to row their bodies away to the underworld.

Whoever came for them, their final destination would remain the same.

But Brandon would not relent. There was something so unbreakable about this man. He pulled her up, upward, until the air singed her lungs and once again ignited in her somewhere deep down the will to exist.

But that existence was not without pain.

When she screamed, nothing came out of her but a thin wail. So whisper-fragile that it was as if her voice, her very soul, had been sucked into the flames along with her home.

Vaguely, she heard Brandon's voice above her, comforting, rationalizing.

Whatever he said didn't even register.

Centuries of history. History for which she had fought. The last remnants of a family legacy she had struggled to preserve. Gone. Burned to ashes.

She screamed again, wordless rage drowned by the frenzied human activity around the building, the Venetian firemen already rushing to the scene with their hoses, pumping water from the canal onto the burning building.

And *them*.

The goddamned Company of Angels.

Standing up on the rooftops around Ca' Rossetti. Watching it burn.

In the late evening, lit by the flames that consumed her ancestral home, stood a line of half a dozen figures dotting the neighboring rooftops. She recognized most of them, but her attention swung like the scope of a rifle, fixing on two figures in particular, two Company supervisors she had not expected to see here tonight.

Arielle, the bitch who had thwarted her plans in America, supervisor of the L.A. unit.

Infusino, her old nemesis, supervisor of the Venetian unit.

Brandon hauled her out of the water, into a boat that someone had pulled up beside them. Covered her with a blanket, rubbing the canal water out of her despite the fact that her most pressing need at this moment was far from dryness.

It was revenge.

The flames of hell were green. Brandon was sure of it when he looked into her eyes.

When they had gotten far enough away from the building that the fire was no longer visible, she turned toward him.

"Angels," she hissed, spitting the word out. An accusation, a swear, a profanity. "You fight dirtier than any demons I've ever met."

"I'm not sure who set your palazzo on fire," he said. "It certainly wasn't anything I had planned, nor was I involved."

As they navigated down the Grand Canal, they saw another figure, amber eyes glowing in the dark. Corbin Ranulfson smirked down at them from the balcony of one of the grand hotels.

"This is not our doing," he said. "You saw yourself. It could very possibly have been Corbin."

"Even if it was, he would never have done this if you hadn't appeared in the goddamned Redentore Church, you wingless sewer rat. If you had never come here, I would have completed my sacrifice for the year. I would be relaxing on my rooftop, enjoying a cocktail and my victory over your wretched kind."

"Perhaps," he said. "But you might be in a worse situation."

"Worse," she said, her voice flat. He knew what she meant. In her estimation, there was nothing worse than being captured by the Company of Angels. A moment later, she said, "Where are you taking me?"

"Back to the States," he answered.
*Back to America.*

Luciana turned away, completely wrung out. Not an ounce of strength remained in her to run away. Not an iota of energy to resist capture. As Brandon steered the boat through the flat lagoon in the dark of night, the only thing she could do was glare at him in the darkness.

If hate was tangible, she could feel it now, pulsing inside her.

Huddled against the seat, she clung to that hate. Would never let go of it. The possibility of relenting, once so close, seemed completely impossible now. She had almost done so, and it had quite literally backfired.

At least there was one consolation. In America, there would be plenty of time to get revenge.

Brandon would pay.

Julian would pay.

The entire Company of Angels would pay.

# *Chapter Seventeen*

Brandon drove Luciana's boat through the dark lagoon, toward the airport.

In the back of the boat, Luciana huddled in the silver-foil emergency blanket he had pulled out of the vessel's first-aid kit. Beneath the blanket, her ruined silk dress clung to her magnificent body. Her dark hair streamed with water from the canal. She turned her face to stare at the flat sea, making no effort to escape, but refusing to look at him.

He had finally captured her.

Yet, he felt no satisfaction. Instead, an odd feeling of loss gnawed inside him.

He pulled up to the dock at the Marco Polo Airport, removed her from the boat. And when he walked the demoness toward the Company plane that waited on a strip of runway, she made no attempt to resist, clutching the square of foil around her like a child huddling under a security blanket.

"Are you all right?" he asked, guiding her up the retractable stairs to the small plane.

She didn't answer. And her silence was deeply disturbing.

He expected a curse. A wordless accusation. A glare at the very least. Some form of resistance, not this blank acquiescence. Not this crumpling of her spirit that seemed at once fitting, yet unnerving. Instead, there was nothing. Just a flat expression, more frightening than the shrillest scream or the angriest evil eye. When her gaze passed over him, there was a look of absolute emptiness in her green eyes.

They boarded the small private plane. Infusino and Arielle were already seated there, along with a few members of the Venetian unit as backup. Brandon took her to a seat and buckled her in. Still, she betrayed no sign of reaction, made no effort to resist.

The plane taxied down the runway, and her gaze fixed on the dark window. Her face was blank, whiter and paler than he had ever seen it.

Across the plane, Arielle leaned over to whisper something to Infusino, covering her mouth with her hand. Beneath the noise of the plane's engine, he caught the name of Luciana's home in that covert whisper.

*"...Ca' Rossetti..."*

The demoness heard it, too.

In one smooth motion, Luciana flipped open the buckle of her seat belt, lunged forward and leaped out of her seat. Brandon grabbed for her, and caught her just in time. But she came so close to raking Arielle across the face that her manicured fingernails grazed the edge of Arielle's meticulous hair, swiping a fraction of an inch away from the angel's unflinching face.

Arielle didn't even blink. She simply said two words as Brandon pinned the demoness back down in her seat. "Restrain her."

He wrestled Luciana into compliance, handcuffing each of her wrists to the arms of her seat. Then he left her staring out the window, down at the lights of Venice as they faded into the distance below. Finally, he sank into a seat across from Arielle, buckling his own seat belt.

"You should have secured her the minute you brought her onto this plane," Arielle noted.

"Enough," he said, closing his eyes and shutting her out.

Exhaustion took hold of him. His aching body shifted, seeking what comfort it could in the rigid confines of the seat.

"I don't mean to criticize. Of course you deserve to relax for the moment," said Arielle, reaching over to pat his arm. "She's in good hands now. Once we get her back to Los Angeles, we'll take her to the new retreat center we've just acquired. You're going to love our new facility."

*Los Angeles... Retreat center...*

His eyes snapped back open.

Arielle was smiling contentedly, clearly pleased with herself. "Didn't I tell you? We're expanding into a new compound."

"Where did you get the money for that?" he asked. "The L.A. unit has been notoriously underfunded."

She smiled, but said nothing. He knew the answer. *Julian Ascher.*

"I'm taking Luciana back to Chicago with me," he said. The roughness of smoke lingered in his lungs, abrading his throat as he spoke. He cleared it and said, "I captured her. She's my detainee."

"Your contribution has certainly been commendable," Arielle told him, with that placid smile fixed on her face. "But the demoness is technically the responsibility of the Company as a larger organization. Considering the amount of...ahem...personal interaction you've had with her, you wouldn't want anyone to think you were biased, would you?"

Something gleamed in the corner of Arielle's eye.

If he didn't know her better, he would have said it was something evil.

In her own seat, the demoness sat absolutely still. Restrained by the cuffs, both her hands were clenched into fists.

"Forget it," he said. "I've cleaned up your mess, Arielle. Now I'm going home. Back to my own unit. Back to my own team. You're no longer a part of this assignment."

The blonde angel leaned forward and stared him evenly in the eye.

He shivered, overcome by the sensation that he was staring into a block of ice.

"That's not your call to make, now, is it?" she said. "Given that this plane belongs to the L.A. unit, you don't have a lot of say in our destination."

Brandon sighed, too exhausted to fight. "Why are we arguing about this, Arielle? Let's just contact Michael and ask him for our next instructions."

He pulled his wet cell phone out of his pocket. Trying to power it on, he realized it was waterlogged and defunct.

"Give me your phone," he told her.

"It's not safe to use cell phones during flight," she admonished, with that trademark smile of absolute neutrality. "Besides, does Michael know exactly how personally close you've gotten with the target?"

"Don't threaten me, Arielle," he growled.

She sat back in her chair, crossed her legs. Folded her hands on top of one knee. "The plane is on course for Los Angeles. You'll see once we get there. It really is the best place for her. It's so secure and secluded. We'll have a proper chance to discuss the option of disposal," Arielle said sweetly. "And we can interrogate her."

"Interrogate her?" said Brandon, his hoarse voice rising, attracting the worried glances of the other angels. He didn't care. "That wasn't our assignment. Our assignment was to capture her, and to make sure she didn't circulate any more poison. Those goals have been accomplished. Michael never said anything about interrogation."

"We'll see about that," Arielle said, "once we land in L.A. Luciana is a source of information, and there are still so many unanswered questions. Luciana has not yet disclosed whether any poison still exists. Nor is there any guarantee that she'll refrain from using her considerable skills to concoct more poison in the future. We must ensure that she is neutralized. The Archangels left this with us to resolve."

"We *will* see about that," he growled.

But short of hijacking the plane, Brandon realized there was no point in arguing with Arielle any further.

Even if he wanted to, he had no energy left to do so.

All he could do was lean back and battle sleep with every ounce of energy he had left in his body.

*This is utter humiliation,* Luciana thought to herself as the angels bickered over her. *Not since my human life have I been shamed in such a manner. I have not been taken against my will for over two centuries.*

The last time she had been held captive, she had vowed she would never let a man seize the vantage point again. Between Julian and Harcourt, the bowels of hell and the brothel, she had endured enough hardship and betrayal for a dozen lifetimes. Being chained to a bed alone with Brandon was one thing. Deep down, she had always known that there was a way out. But now, staring out the tiny window of this little plane, in the company of these assholes, chained to the seat?

There was no escape this time.

*America represents abject failure,* she thought. When she had last left American soil, she had crept away a broken woman, barely alive, having escaped by the skin of her teeth. She had to clench her jaw to keep from screaming out what was going through her mind. *Whether it's Los Angeles or Chicago, it hardly matters.*

Brandon and Arielle stopped fighting, and the plane lapsed into hushed whispers. Brandon sat silently with his eyes closed, but the rest of the angels continued to murmur about the Guardians who would be waiting for them in L.A.

*Serena St. Clair...Julian Ascher....*

*Mother of Lucifer, let me out of here,* she pleaded. *If I could only open a window right now, I would gladly pitch myself from this aircraft at ten thousand feet and spare these celestial vermin the trouble.*

"Serena is a yoga teacher whom Luciana had almost succeeded in killing only weeks ago," Arielle explained to Infusino, who was nodding, taking in the information.

*Hearing that girl's name is like fingernails on a blackboard,* Luciana thought. *But Serena is merely an annoyance, not a serious challenge.*

"And then there's Julian Ascher," Arielle said. Her voice dropped. "He's Luciana's ex-lover. The reason she had become a demoness in the first place."

Then, Luciana really did stop listening.

She did not need to hear the details as Arielle murmured them to Infusino.

It was a story the demoness knew by heart.

A heart that had long ago been crushed into dust.

The plane jolted and Luciana's stomach churned, but whether it was from the turbulence or the thought of Julian Ascher was difficult to tell. The last time she had seen Julian, only a couple of weeks ago, her plan for revenge had been horribly spoiled. Perhaps now there would be another chance.

Now, she had nothing to lose.

Luciana smiled to herself, turning her head to conceal the smile.

From across the plane, Brandon saw her and frowned.

*Let him wonder,* she thought. *He, too, will pay.*

That thought churned in Luciana's head for the next dozen hours as she stared miserably out that little window. It churned and churned, until the plane landed and she found herself staring at the hazy-dry landscape of the San Fernando Valley in high summer. In only half a day, the angels had transported her a world away from her cool marble palazzo in Venice.

A palazzo that was no more.

Brandon watched the demoness stare out the window, taking in every detail of their early morning arrival. Sunlight spilled over her features; he was struck by how beautiful she remained, even in the midst of her exhaustion. Still lovely despite her despair, despite her fury.

He refused to feel sorry for Luciana.

*She deserves to be brought to justice for what she has done,* he reminded himself. *Whether that's here in L.A. or in Chicago will be for Michael to decide once I contact him.*

He saw the clarity of her green eyes as she gazed out

the window, sunlight slanting through her irises. Her gaze flicked to him.

There was war in those eyes.

Despite that, Brandon knew that abandoning the demoness now was not an option.

"Let's go," Arielle instructed.

Heaving a sigh, he uncuffed the demoness. Led her down the metal stairs and into the July heat, through the terminal and out the other side, where an SUV was waiting for them. Brandon pushed her inside and sat down next to her, while Arielle piled into the seat behind them.

Watching the scenery roll by outside the car, in the strange peace of the early morning, none of them spoke a word.

"No doubt, we're heading to another hovel," Luciana muttered, after an hour of silence in the car. "You angels and your sanctimonious poverty."

Like Luciana, Brandon had expected the compound to be a modest affair. By "retreat center," he imagined a run-down operation that was poorly maintained. A few rustic cabins a step up from camping. Bathrooms with mildewed walls. Primitive cooking facilities with communal food preparation responsibilities. Lots of fireside sing-alongs.

Not a gated compound, whose sprawling, multilevel buildings might have been conceived by Frank Lloyd Wright.

A strange chill passed over Brandon as the driver pulled through the iron gates and into the compound. As those gates clanged shut behind them, Brandon realized why Arielle had picked this place. Not because it could have been on the cover of *Architectural Digest*. The clean lines of the whitewashed walls fairly glowed, pristine beneath the soft glow of the coastal sunset. But despite the smooth strokes of its architecture, despite the natural harmony between the structures and the environment, the compound was built like a bunker.

Fort Knox with sand.

Originally, those gates had obviously been designed to keep people *out*.

Under Arielle's direction, they would now be used to keep people *in*.

"What is this place?" he said as he looked at Arielle's pristine blond hair and the content little smile on her face as they pulled up to the main building. He had no doubt it really had once been a retreat center, the kind of high-end health resort where wealthy ladies forked over thousands of dollars to be taken on "nature hikes" on dirt trails for hours and then served a few leaves of lettuce for lunch.

"It used to be a residential health spa," she confirmed. "We were very lucky to get it. We're still deliberating about the name. But we're thinking of calling it the Center for Redemption."

"Sounds like a recycling facility," Brandon said. Remembering the angels' old joke that when a Guardian's physical body happened to be killed, it could be "recycled" and sent back to earth, he shuddered.

"In a manner of speaking, I hope it will be," Arielle replied.

The blonde supervisor led the way, waiting for Brandon to escort the demoness out of the car. Hauling Luciana out, he cuffed her to himself. "Let's go, *principessa*."

She offered little resistance, wide-eyed as she stepped from the car.

They entered the building, into a lobby that could have belonged to any institution with money, a richly

endowed museum or an ultramodern theater. The white-
ness of it almost overwhelmed him, its blank paleness
broken only by the enormous panoramic wall of glass
with an unobstructed view of the ocean.

The building was absolutely deserted.

No staff stood behind the reception desk, no guests
or patrons milled in the lobby. Instead, emptiness hung
beneath the soaring ceilings, and the sound of their own
footsteps echoed against the marble as they followed
Arielle.

As they rode up the elevator, Brandon took note of
the security measures. The card-swipe and electronic
combination locks, the surveillance video cameras everywhere. The heavy bars on the doors they passed as
they walked the demoness down a hallway.

And he wondered what Arielle was really planning
to do here.


"Is this the Company's idea of heaven?" Luciana
muttered. "Everything sterile and completely colorless? Perfect."

Nobody answered. Instead, they marched her through
the building and brought her to a stark, white cell of a
room. The only furnishings were a single bed with a
white duvet, and a white plastic chair. Both of them were
bolted to the floor. The small, antiseptic-looking bathroom was also entirely white, with nothing in it except
a toilet, a sink and a shower stall.

Brandon uncuffed her. Then he pushed her gently
into the room and shut the door. She heard a series of
electronic beeps and the slide of a heavy metal bolt.
Locking her into this high-end version of solitary con-
finement.

"I should have killed you while I had the chance,"

the demoness hissed, running to the door to slam the butt of her fist against the small window. "I could have done it easily."

Brandon didn't answer. He just stood there and looked at her through the small square of reinforced glass, his rainy-gray eyes overflowing with anger.

"Now, now," Arielle chided brightly. "Think how lucky you are. People have paid a veritable fortune to come here and stay in the very same room you're in right now. The Company has been working overtime to prepare these accommodations especially for you. We put a lot of effort into modifying these facilities. We hope you'll enjoy our hospitality and have a very relaxing stay with us."

"I'm going to make sure every last one of you suffers hideously by the hands of Satan himself," Luciana screamed, pounding the window. "The Prince of Darkness will disembowel you with his own bare hands. And I will be there to watch."

Arielle's mouth curved into an infuriating smile. "Make yourself comfortable here, dear. You're going to be staying with us for a very long time."

*"Mezza stronza, mezza strega,"* Luciana cast at the window before spitting on it. *"Andare all'inferno."*

The angels walked off, leaving her in the prison cell alone.

But she heard the end of their conversation as they walked away.

"'Half witch, half bitch.' That's what she called you," said Infusino. "And then she told you to go to hell."

"Thank you, Infusino," Arielle said, pursing her lips tightly. "In future, if I want a translation, I shall ask for one."

## Chapter Eighteen

In the bright sunshine of the perfect SoCal summer day, an eerie feeling swept over Brandon as Arielle led the rest of the Guardians through her new property. As they walked, he only heard fragments of what she said. Something in his gut churned, but he couldn't identify what. A feeling of suspicion, perhaps. He didn't trust Arielle, but he didn't quite know why.

"…security cameras monitoring every inch of the detention facility…"

"…converting this into a training area…" she said, pointing to a large grassy field.

"…the helicopter pad for emergencies…"

"Where's Michael?" Brandon demanded. "We don't have time right now for a guided tour. There are important matters to attend to."

"Patience is a virtue," she admonished, pursing her lips at the interruption. "Look, here we are. This is our new boardroom. It's a change from the legal-aid clinic, though we plan to keep the old headquarters, too. But it was time for an expansion."

On the second floor of the main building, the room she led them into was large and impressive, with soaring ceilings and a view that overlooked the wide expanse of lawn that stretched to the ocean.

At the head of the long, rectangular boardroom table sat Michael.

The rest of the members of the L.A. unit sat assembled around him. Brandon recognized Julian Ascher and Serena St. Clair, and two dozen other faces, all of them calmly waiting.

He took a seat in one of the empty chairs at the end of the table.

"Congratulations, Brandon, on a job well done," Michael said. "I speak for the entire Company and all the Archangels when I say that we recognize and appreciate your hard work in finally capturing Luciana Rossetti."

All pairs of jewel-bright eyes fell on Brandon, all of them shining with gratitude.

The angels clapped and nodded vigorously, smiling their approval.

"Thanks," Brandon said. "But we need to talk about what we're going to do with her."

"We'll discuss that now," said Michael.

Arielle cleared her throat, rising to stand at the other end of the table. "If I may speak frankly, I think we can all agree that this is a strong case for disposal."

"Forget it," snapped Brandon. "We don't all agree."

Michael sighed. "We cannot let such things divide us as an organization. We must work together at all times to achieve our goals. I know every person in this Company has different opinions and different beliefs. But we're all working for the same thing. For the greater good and protection of humankind."

"Yes, Michael," Arielle said. "What do you propose?"

"We Archangels are against outright disposal in all but the most extreme cases," said Michael. "We don't judge that Luciana has been proven to be such a case in this time. We will revisit the case in the future, once more evidence has been compiled and a period of observation has elapsed. If she shows signs of remorse and the possibility for redemption, we must pursue that path. We Archangels trust you Guardians to deal with Luciana in the meantime, until we have determined the best course of action."

"Seriously?" asked Brandon. "Keeping her here indefinitely isn't an option."

"Come, now," Arielle chided. "It won't be forever. We can reform her at our own pace."

"How do you plan to do that?" Brandon challenged. "What are you going to do when she tries to escape?"

"She won't. This place is airtight. But just to demonstrate, I think we should stage a little trial run. Won't that be fun?" asked Arielle.

A set of monitors lowered from the ceiling. As they flicked on, what they showed was footage from the security camera in Luciana's room.

Where the demoness sat on her white bed, still dressed in her ruined silk gown, looking miserable.

Arielle pressed a button. And the door to Luciana's room swung open.

Luciana stared at the open door.

*That's a trap if I ever saw one,* she thought. But the open door called to her. *What's the alternative? Sit here and wait for them to wear me down?*

She got up. Took a step toward the door. Then she ran as if she still had a life that depended on it. Down the length of the long, white hallway. Down the curving staircase. Through the empty lobby and out into the blazing heat of the midday sun.

She bolted, barefoot, racing across the vast stretch of lawn, not knowing where she was headed. Yet certain that anywhere was better than that stark little room. Her lungs burned, but she did not stop running.

Heading to the left, she ran toward the wide-open space, toward what looked to be an undeveloped area. If she could just get herself out of here. Back to Venice. Somehow, she would cut a deal with the devil. She would complete this year's sacrifice—maybe throw in another victim just to smooth things over. She would make things right again.

Nothing was going to keep Luciana down.

She reached the fence, looking up at it, studying the ornamental wrought-iron spikes at the top. It was about a dozen feet high, difficult to climb under the best of circumstances. And now, exhausted as she was from this whole ordeal, it would be impossible.

That fence stopped exactly where the lawn ended and gave way to a small stretch of sandy beach. Straight ahead lay the open ocean. But the waves were turbulent, and the beach was bordered on both sides by craggy rocks. Luciana had thought simply to slip around the end of the fence. But as she touched it, she felt a flash of pure energy that blinded her as though she'd run into an electric current. She fell to her knees, clutching her head. Between her temples, a blinding white light pulsed, combined with the most powerful pain she had ever felt.

She screamed, a shriek that must have carried up to the heavens and down to hell. But not a soul came to aid her.

She looked up, toward the main building.

Where the ethereal beings who held her captive stood in a long row, looking down at her from the vantage point of a wall of glass that stretched along the second story.

Watching.

The Company of Angels had her penned in.

"What was the point of that?" Brandon asked, standing with the rest of the angels at the window as they watched Luciana writhing on the ground. He started toward the door, determined to go get her. "It was just unnecessarily cruel."

Arielle put a hand on his arm, stopping him. "There's no need. I've sent a couple of my people out to take her back to her room."

The Company watched as two of the Guardians went out to collect the demoness.

"The point of that was to prove that we do, in fact, have the facilities to keep Luciana securely locked up. And to teach her that there's no point in trying to escape," Arielle said calmly.

Brandon looked toward Michael, challenging. "I cannot believe you're letting this go on."

"I agree," said Michael. "That did seem unnecessary. Arielle, in future, please refrain from any needless disturbances to the detainee. Your track record is spotless. I know you understand your responsibilities in terms of safeguarding the best interests of everyone involved."

"Yes, of course," Arielle said smoothly.

"For now, this meeting is adjourned," said Michael.

The Company began filing out of the boardroom, the angels muttering quietly to each other about what had just happened.

"Wait," Brandon said, turning to Michael. "What about me? What is my role here?"

"That is your own decision. The Chicago unit is functioning well at the present time. No problems have been reported. You may stay or go as you choose," said Michael.

Then he, too, turned and walked out of the room.

Leaving Brandon staring out at the spectacular view, wondering what the hell he was going to do.

"I need to talk to you," said a voice behind him, startling him. "Man-to-man."

Brandon turned to see Julian Ascher standing there.

"Man-to-man, I think you've got your head shoved up your ass," Brandon said. "At least when it comes to Luciana."

"You may well be correct. So I need you to listen."

"Why would I do that?"

"As Michael said, we're all working for the same thing. The greater good of humankind."

"I don't buy that for a second," Brandon said.

"Call it guilt, then." Julian sighed. "There are things I was never able to admit to before. There are things you don't know about Luciana. Things that are important."

"I'm listening."

Julian held his head in his hands for a moment. When he raised it, he looked squarely at Brandon. "This isn't easy to say. But I have made some terribly bad decisions when it came to Luciana."

The story Julian spun out before him was a tale of a young English lord, a future duke, who had traveled to Venice on his Grand Tour. Who had stayed because he was mesmerized by the beauty of the city and its people. Fundamentally, it was the same story Luciana had told Brandon only a few nights ago on the Lido.

Except when Julian told it, he did not blame himself entirely for what had gone wrong.

"We were two young people who had fallen madly in love. But then I, arrogant young man that I was, began to doubt and then test that love. I found Luciana's attentions lacking, and thought she did not truly care for me. I ultimately made the decision to leave her to fate, and left to go home to England.

"I had not seen Luciana for ten years when I spotted her in a crowd in London. Luciana came to me with a story of a difficult marriage, of beatings, of desperation. And we resumed our affair. Soon after, she asked me to kill her husband. I challenged Harcourt to a duel. Neither she nor I expected her drunkard husband to show up sober, nor that Harcourt would be such a good shot. Yet with a miraculously steady hand, he hit his mark. And I hit mine.

"Both of us bled out on the winter snow of an empty field.

"In hindsight, I have finally come to a place in my life where I can take some responsibility for what happened. I no longer blame her for the choices I made."

"Maybe you should tell *her* that," Brandon said.

"If you think it will help, I will go talk to her. But I doubt she'll listen to me."

"Even if she doesn't listen, it's something she needs to hear."

Luciana huddled inside her cell of a room, miserable and still filthy from her capture and her attempted escape.

*For celestial beings, these angels have no sense of decency,* she thought.

She glared up at the video camera in the corner of the room.

Going into the small bathroom, she finally stripped off the ruined silk gown and threw it in the garbage bin. Stood in the shower and felt the comfort of hot water pouring down over her tired body. There was a folded outfit on the bed, a modest white dress that reminded her of a hospital gown. She put it on. Then she sat down on the bed, wondering where Brandon had gone. Wondering what these angels planned to do with her.

*What do they expect me to do? Curl up in the fetal position and give up?* she thought bitterly. *I have survived for over two hundred years. I am not giving up now.*

She knelt and began to examine the chair, contemplating whether she had the strength to unbolt it and throw it through the window.

The series of electronic beeps sounded. The metal bolt slid open.

The man standing at the door made her wish she had unbolted the chair.

So she could smash it over his head.

*Julian Ascher.*

When they had said he was a changed man, they had not been kidding. The difference in him was palpable on his face, on his body. As long as she had known him— and it had been a long time—he had always been smug, arrogant and self-absorbed.

Now, he seemed lighter, somehow. Brighter, somehow. It made her sick.

"I don't believe it," she said flatly.

Julian sat on the edge of the bed.

She recoiled, moving away from him.

His hands shot up in a gesture of pacifism. "I didn't come to hurt you, Luciana. I came to ask you to consider what the Company is asking of you."

"Why should I?"

"A lot has passed between you and I. There's something I need to say to you." He paused. "I need to ask your forgiveness."

She blinked, the shock of that word hitting her, slamming into her like a slap in the face.

*Forgiveness.*

A word more profane than any curse she had ever heard.

That word was like a sucker punch to the gut.

Drawing in a deep breath, the words that poured out of her seemed so inadequate, so profoundly failing to express the utter fury that burned inside her. But she let them stream out of her anyway.

"How dare you," she ground out, advancing toward him in the small space. "After what you did to me? To my family?"

"I am deeply regretful for the harm I caused you. Looking back, there are many things I would have done differently, if I could. If I could change things now, if I could only go back in time…" Julian paused. "But I can't. So I hope you'll accept my apology."

"*Complimenti* to the Company for brainwashing you so thoroughly," she said. "Serena St. Clair must have gold between her legs. Because the devil knows that you would never have spoken such words as *apology* or *forgiveness* before. Not in the more than two centuries I've known you."

"Luciana, I truly—"

"*Vaffunculo,*" she hissed in the instant before launching herself at him. "And in case you forgot what that means, it translates to 'go fuck yourself.'"

When Julian came out with three bloody lines raked down the side of his classically handsome profile, Brandon was unsurprised.

"There is a reason she carries out these sacrifices each year, a reason her hatred has escalated over time. You must find out her side of the story. Get her to confess everything to you. She must make the transition to our side. That is the only way to end this. Because if you don't, Arielle will dispose of her as she sees fit. Luciana has done some inexcusable things in the past, but I still believe there's good in her. You've seen that. I know you have."

As Julian left, one thing was clear to Brandon.

Julian Ascher was not telling the whole truth.

But he was right. There was a reason Luciana believed she had to remain a demon.

A secret she was hiding deep within herself.

And Brandon meant to find out what that secret was.

When he entered her room, she was sitting at the head of her bed, looking out the window into the darkness, staring out over the ocean. Outside, the moon and stars were so bright that the light flooded into the room and illuminated her pale face.

It was an image that was entirely in keeping with the rest of his experience of her.

*Ethereally beautiful, but absolutely miserable.*

In the stark emptiness of the room, the vibrancy of her beauty was more stunning than ever.

"Go away," she said without turning to look at him. "You should have left when you had the chance. Did someone order you to stay?"

He didn't answer.

"It couldn't have been the bossy one," she said quietly, still staring out the window. In the moonlight, her profile was delicate, the vulnerable lines of her difficult to reconcile with the woman who, twelve hours earlier, had injected him with poison. "Tell me, was she always an ice queen, even when you were sleeping with her?"

"What makes you think that?" he growled.

"Spare me. You angels are incapable of telling a decent lie," she said.

"I came to check on you. I thought you might need a friend."

Luciana rolled her eyes, finally turning to address him, her green eyes almost leeched of their spark. But not quite. She told him, "You're not my friend, and I don't need your pity."

"There's a difference between pity and compassion."

"Please. I don't need a lecture right now. What would someone like you know about pity, anyway? You're as smug and perfect as the rest of them. Dressed up like a bad guy with your tattoos. Beneath that tough-guy exterior of yours beats a pure heart. It's the same story for all of you. I bet you lived like a monk before you died. Isn't that what it takes to be an angel?"

He didn't answer, refusing to let her goad him into anger.

He wanted to tell her that he knew the difference between pity and compassion, because he had given and received both.

To be perfectly honest, he didn't know how to help her right now.

He hadn't even figured out how to help himself.

But he asked anyway. When he did, it came out entirely wrong. Perhaps because he was tired. Perhaps because her anger touched something in him that was still raw.

Whatever the reason, even as the words came pouring out of his mouth, he regretted them.

"What is it you want so badly that you're willing to sell your soul to the devil for it?" he said. "Is it that you love power? The thrill of killing? I don't believe that for an instant. What is it you don't have? What is it that you want?"

*You. You are what I don't have,* she thought, looking at him. *Well, that and revenge.*

"Julian told me his version of the truth," he said. "About what happened between the two of you. It seems like perhaps the two of you have just come to a 'he said, she said' disagreement about events."

"Julian is fundamentally incapable of telling the truth about our relationship."

"Whatever you want to tell me, I'm willing to listen."

But there was nothing.

Nothing she could think of that she would want to say to Brandon. Nothing she had to say about Julian that didn't involve entering into a world of bitterness and regret. What would she say? That Julian had treated a seventeen-year-old girl with casual disregard, stripping her of her virginity and abandoning her to fate. That, over the centuries, he had toyed with her emotions time and again, causing her to hope each time that he cared about something more than just her body or the power she could bring him in the demon world.

"Nothing," she said. "There is nothing I wish to tell you."

*Nothing you would understand.*

"Have it your way," Brandon said. Under the scrutiny of those piercing gray eyes, she felt like she had been shrunk to the size of a pea. "But for your sake, I really hope you'll reconsider. There is more at stake here than you can begin to guess."

*Let them take me,* she thought, closing her eyes. *Perhaps it will be a relief after all this time.*

"Forget about forgiving Julian. I don't think that's the real issue. The question is whether you can forgive yourself for all the suffering you've caused. If you were given the chance, could you let go of your guilt and start over again?"

"The world doesn't work like that," she said. "I know Julian was redeemed. That the Company *saved* him. Now he gets to sleep with an angel every night, and go to bed scot-free. Good for him. I don't know how Julian got over his guilt, but I know that's not going to happen to me. Redemption is not an option."

"You're wrong about that. If you give me a chance, I'd like to show you how wrong."

"That's impossible," she said.

"Why are you so quick to believe in tragedy over miracles?" he challenged.

She knew the answer to that immediately.

Because her entire life had been steeped in tragedy.

Because what little grace she had experienced during her brutally short human life had been ripped away and buried in an unmarked grave. Because everything and everyone she had ever loved had been destroyed or had soured against her. Because in the time since then, a very long time indeed, she had neither seen nor experienced anything that told her anything different.

Because she had laughed at redemption, had mocked those who sought it.

Because nobody had ever offered her redemption before.

There was a myriad of reasons why she could not be redeemed. But how could she express that to Brandon, who seemed to have an infinite capacity to try to forgive, even if he never quite accomplished that task? Who was haunted on a nightly basis by the most unspeakable act a human being could do to another. Who simply bore his excruciating nightmare and got up the next morning, went on about his day.

But she didn't have the strength to explain any of that to him.

Not now. Not tonight.

"I don't know why you stayed," she said instead. "Now you're stuck here with this lunatic band of rabid do-gooders. I know you dislike them. Not as much as I hate them, but you understand."

"True. But I'm also stuck here with you," he said. "Good night, *principessa*."

He walked out and closed the door gently behind him.


Brandon was beginning to question his sanity and his motives.

That night he lay in the room next to hers, which mercifully had not been converted into a prison cell. Separated only by a few inches of drywall, timber and dead air, he lay in the comfortable bed. The real barriers, the psychological, emotional and spiritual barriers between them were being stripped down to thin slivers that barely held them apart.

*Leave. Just get up and leave,* said his brain. *This is no longer an assignment. Let Arielle deal with Luciana. The demoness is not your problem anymore.*

What kept him there was the knowledge that beneath it all was a terrorized young woman whose life had gone badly off the rails at the age of seventeen.

He closed his eyes and slipped into sleep.

*Sliding into dream, she came for him, grabbing him by the arm and yanking him with her.*

*"I've had enough of revisiting* my *past for one day. What about* your *past?"*

*Luciana took him to visit his wife, Tammy.*

*"Don't visit your loved ones," was the order Michael had given him.*

*Not every Guardian was given that advice.*

*Many of them went back, to check up and to watch over their loved ones.*

*Why Brandon had been forbidden from visiting was a mystery to him. But he had obeyed nonetheless. Now, with Luciana standing beside him, he felt vaguely guilty for disobeying, even though he had no control over where she chose to take him.*

Besides, *he told himself,* it's only a dream.

*Tammy still lived in the house Brandon had bought for them, a few years after joining the Detroit P.D. Standing across the street from the house, he saw Tammy come out and speak to two little boys playing in the yard. Brandon smiled, happy that she was happy.*

"Let's go," *he said to Luciana.* "I don't want to stick around in case she sees me."

"It's just a dream," *said the demoness scornfully.*

"Still," *he said.* "She might remember."

"Wait. I think you'll find this interesting."

*He saw a man drive up.*

*Get out of the car and kiss her.*

*Something bittersweet twisted inside Brandon as he watched them.*

"Who is that?" *Luciana asked.*

"My wife, Tammy," *he said.*

"The man, I meant," *she said flatly.*

"My best friend and partner, Jude," *he ground out.*

"Did you know?" *Luciana asked.* "That they were together?"

"I had no idea. I was told to leave it alone. And so I did."

*Her eyes sparkled in the light, and what he saw in them was pure, green evil.* "There you go. Learn your own lesson in forgiveness. I dare you."

## Chapter Nineteen

Brandon awoke, sweating and sick with the knowledge that more than a wall separated him and Luciana. Not just wood and drywall, after all. But the fundamental core of what they were.

Angel and demon.

*She's pure evil. I would never have done such a thing to her. Would I?*

His heart pounded as he lay in the bed.

*What did she really do, except reveal the truth?* he argued with himself.

He shot out of bed, threw on his clothes and tore into the hallway.

The noise of it woke Arielle, who was sleeping in a room across the hall.

She opened her door and stood there in her night-gown, white and ethereal.

"What's wrong, Brandon?"

He needed to drive, to get far away from this insane asylum full of immortals. His palms tingled for a steering wheel. His foot yearned for the press of a gas pedal. He needed speed to rid him of the desire to crawl out of his own skin. Before that desire drove him crazy.

And Arielle knew it.

"Just a minute," she said, going into her room. When

she returned, she handed him a car key and said, "Outside. In the driveway."

Veering along the Pacific Coast Highway, he drove until he reached Zuma Beach, Malibu. Where he stood on the sand, looking out over the still-dark ocean. Listened to the sound of the waves. Asked for guidance. And what—who—he found there was Michael. High on a cliff above the beach, the Archangel waited, his massive wings extended out behind him.

He launched off the cliff and circled down, toward Brandon, landing on the sand.

"I take it the current situation has exceeded your capacity to text," said Michael.

"Seriously, I need help. But not from you."

"You're stuck with me," said Michael. "So talk."

"What am I doing here?" Brandon asked. He did not whine. He never whined. But the frustration had become so intense, it threatened to explode out of him if he did not give it voice.

"What do you mean?" Michael asked quietly.

"I should not be involved in this assignment anymore."

"You can leave. You have that choice."

"I don't trust Arielle. But that's not the whole problem. I had a dream last night. Not the same dream. And I saw something I had never seen before."

"What was it?"

"It had to do with Tammy. And her husband."

Michael let out a sigh, compassion on his face. "There are circumstances beyond your comprehension. There are reasons for things that even we Archangels do not understand. But I warn you, Brandon. You must forget about this entirely. Leave it to divine justice to handle. Don't throw away everything you've worked toward for your entire existence. This, like everything else, is merely a test. You have a choice. The best option is to leave it alone."

"I'm worried about Tammy," he gritted out.

"Are you worried about Tammy, or are you angry with her? Brandon, let it go," Michael warned. "You have your instructions. You have been a good Guardian all these years."

"So I think I deserve to know. How long have Tammy and Jude been together? Since my death?"

Michael answered, "Yes."

"Since before my death?"

The question hovered between them.

Brandon was certain Archangels were physically incapable of dishonesty. Michael's mouth contracted, but he didn't deny it. All he said was, "We can't control the actions of anyone but ourselves."

Fury burned inside him. Hurt. Sadness.

His mind flipped back through all the events of his past. Jude, his partner and best friend. Older and wiser. Giving advice. Hugging Tammy. Hugging her a little too tightly, Brandon realized now.

"Let it go," said Michael again. "You are not to pry into the lives of your loved ones."

*Let it go.* Brandon had said essentially the same words to Luciana. But now he realized how difficult, how agonizing that suggestion was.

"How?"

"You'll find a way," said Michael.

"And this demoness?" he asked. "What am I to do about her?"

"Slay the dragon."

"Wait. What the hell does that mean, anyway?"

"That's for you to find out."

* * *

When Luciana awoke in the early hours before dawn, Arielle was standing over her.

"Where's Brandon?" the demoness asked.

"He went for a little trip. It will give you and I an opportunity to talk," Arielle smiled. "To get to know one another."

Luciana almost snorted. "My kind do not *get to know* your kind. Serpents do not get to know the rats they devour. Even when the rats gang up and gnaw the snake to death."

"I'm going to ignore that comment because I know you're under a lot of stress. Look, I've brought you some breakfast," said Arielle.

There was an assortment of breakfast foods laid out on a tray.

Cereal, scrambled eggs and bacon. A cup of coffee.

"American food," said Luciana with a flick of her hand, looking over the food. "This is clearly part of my torture, no? A choice between cardboard and a heart attack? No, thank you."

"Cut the crap, Luciana. This isn't *la dolce vita.*"

"Really? I think you'd be a lot happier if you learned the art of *la dolce far niente*. 'The sweet art of doing nothing.' Either that, or maybe you could get laid once in a while," she said, smiling her sweetest, sunniest smile. "And maybe then you wouldn't need to pimp out members of your Company."

Impervious to the insults, Arielle merely picked up the cup of coffee, set it in front of her. "I trust you slept well."

"*Grazie,* I slept tolerably enough," Luciana said, taking a sip of the coffee and grimacing. "But not as well as I slept after I made love to Brandon."

Arielle still didn't move a muscle. "I understand that you're frustrated and I imagine it's not very pleasant for you to be kept against your will. But if you cooperate, then we can all accomplish our goals. We know you created a very special kind of poison."

"Perhaps," Luciana drawled.

"You will tell us where it is. You will tell us how you made it."

In her blandest tone, the demoness said, "No wonder it took you two hundred years to reform Julian. If this is your idea of how to negotiate, I can't blame him. It's too bad that the best you can offer demonkind is a good screw from your underlings."

"Where's Corbin?" the supervisor asked, switching subjects abruptly.

"I have no idea where Corbin is," said Luciana, studying her fingernails.

"You must know. You were lovers. You spent three months living with him in Las Vegas."

"Truthfully, I really don't know where Corbin is. I don't care. He's no longer my lover, and he's certainly not my friend."

"Play these games," Arielle said coolly. "Laugh at me all you want. But in the end, I'll have the last laugh. I have the power to keep you apart from the only thing that matters to you."

"You don't know what you're talking about. My home was destroyed in a fire two nights ago. There's nothing more that I want."

"Well, now, that's not true at all, is it?"

It was not an angelic halo that radiated out from this woman, but an aura of smugness.

"This is a totally different approach than you took with Julian," Luciana said instead, broaching a subject that genuinely piqued her curiosity. "You went to such lengths to reform him."

"Of course," Arielle said. "Because Julian was my very first Assignee. When I was ordained as an angel, two and a half centuries ago, the first person I was sent to guard was Julian. But you know how things went with him. He got extremely out of hand, especially when you entered the picture. Why, all those years ago in Venice when you were seventeen, I told him to leave you. If you had just stayed out of the picture, everything would have been fine."

Arielle smiled as the morning sunlight broke into the room.

And Luciana understood everything.

Julian had been a priority for Arielle because he had been a personal mission.

The one who got away.

And Arielle had been responsible for guiding Julian's decision to leave Venice two and a half centuries ago. That decision had ultimately ruined Luciana's human life.

"You're not interested in reforming me, are you?" Luciana said finally.

"Not you. The idea of *you* joining the Company is intolerable. You will never become an angel," said Arielle evenly.

"I have to hand it to you, Arielle. There's more to you than I thought."

"*Grazie*. I take that as a compliment," said Arielle.

"There is no more poison. It burned to the ground with Ca' Rossetti," the demoness said truthfully.

"Good," Arielle said. "That's all I really wanted to know."

"Yes, that's the truth," Luciana said. And for once, it was.

"No, actually it's not."

"I swear it all burned. I tried to save some of it, but your colleague stopped me."

"Well, no. There's still some of that poison left. Do you want to know how I know?" Arielle smiled, infuriatingly neutral.

*It's eerie the way she sometimes reminds me of Corbin,* Luciana thought.

"I found this in your home before I burned Ca' Rossetti to the ground."

She held up one of the little glass vials, which held the poison Luciana had concocted in her workroom in the days before she had left Venice.

It was empty.

Luciana looked down at her coffee cup. "American coffee really is poison, isn't it?"

*Is this how it feels?* Luciana thought. *I had forgotten.*

The pain of dying was unbearable.

The poison Arielle had fed her burned through her veins, killing parts of her physical body as it went.

"How strange to be poisoned yourself, isn't it? Imagine, after you've done the same to so many others," said the angel.

Luciana tried to answer back. The word *bitch* formed on her lips even as she convulsed, caught in a spasm as the cyanide burned through her veins. Arielle looked down at her, that infuriating coolness of hers unchanging as she surveyed the results of her work.

"Who do you think ordered the burning of Ca' Rossetti? You may have thought it was Corbin, but I doubt he would ever be so destructive. No," Arielle said, "I was the one who did it. The reason should be perfectly clear to you. I did so in order to save human lives."

Luciana looked up at her from the floor.

"I think you did it for your own satisfaction," she managed to gasp. "For revenge."

Arielle shrugged. "The reason hardly matters now. What's more important are the consequences. By burning down your house, I was also able to ensure that you wouldn't be able to manufacture any more poison. From what I hear, you had quite the little laboratory set up there."

The demoness stumbled away, about to vomit.

"We're working toward the same thing here in the Company of Angels. Only we call it by a different name." Arielle smiled. "Disposal."

The thought that ran through Luciana's mind was, *I wish it had been different.*

A thousand thoughts and a thousand images rushed into her mind, flooding through her like a wave that washed over her, took her breath away, swept her into unconsciousness. *Her parents' faces...her sister... Julian...the fallen republic of Venice and all the citizens plunged into poverty and humiliation...every face of every human victim she had ever killed...the Gatekeepers she had raised like children...*

*And Brandon...*

As the tide of darkness rolled over her, she smiled, suddenly grateful that she had gotten the chance to know him at all.

A single word rushed into her mind.

*Peace.*

How much time passed as Luciana lay on the floor of that horrible little room, fading in and out of consciousness, carried on the tide of the poison, she had no idea.

She only knew that when she opened her eyes, Arielle was standing over her, looking down, her blond hair lit by a blaze of fluorescent light from the ceiling above.

"Get up," said the angel.

"You killed me," Luciana accused, coughing out a little blood.

"No. I shot you full of cyanide, just like you did to Brandon. You should have figured that out by the time you didn't go to hell. And you should have figured out that I'm not a murderer. Not like you."

"What do you want?"

"Oh, there's a lot I want from you. I know you have a lot of knowledge, and I hope we can channel that knowledge, together, for the greater good of humankind. Perhaps once we've gone through this poisoning process a few more times, you'll begin to work with me."

*Torture,* Luciana thought wildly. *She plans to torture me.*

"Brandon will never let you get away with this," she managed to choke out.

"Brandon is going home to Chicago," said Arielle. "You're going to tell him you want him to leave. He is far better off without you, in any case."

*That's the one thing you've got right,* the demoness realized.

Arielle held up a fistful of Luciana's vials.

"I've got half a dozen more like this, stashed away," said the blonde angel. "You know exactly what is in them. If you dare disobey me, I will hunt down everything that is dear to you and obliterate it from the face of the earth forever. Those Gatekeepers of yours, especially that big one. What is his name? Massimo?"

Luciana closed her eyes and swallowed back a cry, refusing to give the angel the satisfaction of an answer.

"And just think. If you ever did escape, wouldn't it be terrible to worry that perhaps Brandon was at risk, too?" asked Arielle.

"They say the line between angels and demons is a fine one," said Luciana, finally turning her head to stare up at her tormentor. "You're starting to sound exactly like Corbin."

"Now, now. There's no need for name-calling. Since you're going to be spending a long time with us here, you'll have to learn to be more civil. *Mezza stronza, mezza strega,*" said Arielle as she loomed over the gasping demoness. She kicked her once, in the center of the gut, so hard that blood spilled out of Luciana's mouth. "You don't know the half of it."

# Chapter Twenty

Brandon bore down on the gas pedal, veering along the curves of PCH as he raced back toward the retreat center. He cranked the stereo up. The entire car rattled with the pounding beat, the screaming guitar riffs from a heavy-metal radio station threatening to blast out the windows and his eardrums.

No music was loud enough to drown out his memories.

A babble of conversations with Jude flooded into Brandon's mind.

Now, he could not help but dwell. Not just dwell.

*Seethe.*

In the hours before Brandon had entered that alleyway, he had fought with Jude.

*"We need to go down there tonight,"* Brandon had insisted.

*"Buddy, we're off duty."*

*"We have a job to do,"* Brandon insisted. *"I have a hunch about this."*

*"Suit yourself,"* Jude said angrily. *"I thought you were going over to play poker with the guys. I had other plans for tonight. But if you really want to go, then so be it."*

Of course, they had gone. And Brandon had never

gotten a chance to set things right with Jude. Had never gotten to tell him how much he had appreciated his friendship over the years. How much he missed the guy. Loved him, even.

He had always regretted not telling him that.

Jude Everett, the hero.

Who had captured and arrested his shooter.

*Am I still supposed to feel grateful? What were your plans that night, Jude? Were you planning on banging her? Are you still a hero if you were sleeping with your dead partner's wife all along?*

Jude's grinning face floated in his mind's eye.

Brandon floored the gas pedal. The car shot forward.

The rush of speed accelerated his anger. Fed his frustration. The next turn came a little too fast, a little too sharp. The car swerved out of control. He slammed on the brakes. The wheels spun out under him, sending the car rotating 360 degrees…720 degrees…how many revolutions it spun, he lost count…the palm trees and scrubby landscape and ocean blurred together into a dizzy splotch. The front bumper—or was it the rear?—bashed against the guardrail, sending the car flying across the road diagonally.

And then it stopped.

The radio was still playing something loud and thrashing.

He shut it off, sat in silence.

Mercifully, he had not crashed through the guardrail and ended up in the ocean.

Thankfully, there were no other cars on the highway.

No one else he could injure while he worked out his own horrific issues.

He looked at the tattoos covering his arms, the multitude of designs and images interwoven as if they all fit together somehow. Right now, he didn't want to think about any of it. Not about any of his past Assignees, not about any of the angels, not about the inked wingspan sprawling across his back. He wished he could crawl out of his own skin right now. And leave it all behind.

*Pull your shit together,* he told himself. *Because if you don't, the rest of the Company is going to do it for you. And Arielle will be the first in line.*

Go back to Chicago. Stay in L.A. It hardly mattered. All the things he had counseled Luciana to do—*forgive*—he would have to figure that process out for himself.

How he was going to do that, he had no idea.

But he was going to have to start somewhere.

He turned on the ignition again, and headed back toward the Center.

Arielle came out to look at the car, her mouth pressed into a thin line when he pulled into the driveway. The early morning sunlight glinted off her perfect hair as she eyed the large dent in the rear bumper, shaking her head with disapproval.

"When I let you borrow that car, I trusted you would drive it responsibly," she said.

"Now is not the time," he growled.

"Come into my new office and we'll discuss this like rational beings," she said, crossing her arms. "If you're dealing with something, perhaps I can help you."

*I seriously doubt that,* he thought. But he went anyway, too tired to resist.

"I'm afraid you're becoming exhausted, Brandon. I think it would be best if you went back to Chicago. As much as I appreciate having you here, I'm sure your own unit needs you more."

He stopped listening as she enumerated a number

of other concerns she had about him. His head began to ache.

"I need to clear my head before I make any decisions," was all he said.

He stood up to go. Arielle bent over her desk, attending to her endless pile of paperwork.

But as he was about to leave her office, he spotted something in Arielle's garbage can.

A little glass vial.

Plain, innocuous.

Empty.

Exactly like the ones Luciana used.

*Is she okay?* he wondered frantically.

*If she is, I've got to get out now and take her with me*, he told himself. *But how?*

Without saying a word to Arielle, he slipped out of the hallway and walked briskly to the surveillance room. Where the video monitors showed Luciana in her room, lying on the bed. She lay there, still and bleeding.

*Is she dead?*

The tips of her fingers began to curl, and she reached to wipe a little blood off her mouth.

*Still alive. She survived whatever Arielle did to her while I was gone.*

The Guardian on watch duty turned around. "May I help you?"

Brandon just smiled, his eyes flickering away from the monitors. "Just checking things out," he said, hoping he sounded as banal as he intended. "Pretty impressive setup."

Julian was the first person he ran into as he stepped out of the surveillance room. Brandon tried to blow by him, fully focused on getting to Luciana. But Julian caught him by the arm.

"Where are you going in such a hurry?"

Brandon dragged him into a corner and told him in a hushed voice, "I have no time to explain. I think Arielle has gone crazy. I saw something in her office. I can't tell you everything now. But man-to-man, Luciana's in danger."

Julian did not seem surprised. But he said, "Arielle is my supervisor. Technically, she's also my Guardian."

"You ignored her for over two hundred years. What's another half hour? I swear, that's all it will take. Help me. For Luciana's sake. She needs our help," said Brandon. "Now.

Julian paused, frowning. "All right. But Arielle will crucify me if she ever finds out."

"No, she won't. Because you're footing the bill for this place. Now think. How can I get Luciana out of here?"

"As you saw yourself, Arielle has this place surrounded by an energy field, like a giant fence. If you try to break Luciana out of that wall, her head will all but explode."

"So is there any way out?"

"You can't break her out by going through the fence. But theoretically you can go *over* it. Way over it. My helicopter is parked on the launchpad outside. Take Luciana. I'll distract Arielle for as long as I possibly can."

"I've never flown a helicopter," Brandon said.

"You don't have to fly it for long. Just get over the fence and far enough so that you have enough time to get away. Then ditch the helicopter and find a car."

He rattled off a list of instructions, and Brandon tried to commit the details to memory.

"Press the red starter button on the left-hand side,

master avionics switch on, fuel valve master on, roll on the throttle to power the engine…"

Brandon blinked, trying to absorb it all.

"Just remember, too much throttle and the helicopter will get too much liftoff."

"What would happen?" Brandon asked.

Julian grinned, giving him a hearty pat on the shoulder. "Don't worry about it. That's the beauty of being immortal."

*Whatever,* thought Brandon. *I just hope this works.*

Luciana was still lying on the bed, feeling nauseous when the series of electronic beeps sounded again. She thought, *God, who is it this time?*

Brandon rushed in, yanked her up by the arm. "Come on. I'm getting you out of here."

"Where are you taking me?" she asked, not moving.

"Now is not the time to ask questions," he barked. "We don't have time. It's your choice. You can either come with me, or you can stay here with Arielle. But you've got to trust me."

In her gut, something flickered, a tiny flame of hope. She leaped off the bed.

He twisted her arms behind her back, secured her wrists together with a plastic tie.

The little flame of hope flickered, dimming inside her. She resisted, trying to twist away. "Not this again!"

"I told you," he said. "You've got to trust me."

He led her out into the hallway, where a few Guardians strolled, going about their assigned tasks. He marched straight ahead, head up, not bothering to hide from any of them. One of the angels stopped him at the end of the hall, just before a set of locked doors.

"Where are you taking the detainee? Do you have clearance to move her?"

"Arielle asked to see her," he said. "In the main office."

The angel nodded and buzzed them through the door.

"You're crazy," she muttered. "She's going to flay us alive if she catches us."

"Be quiet. Keep walking."

He marched her down the staircase, out the back exit.

To a helicopter that was parked on the round slab of concrete. He opened the door and shoved her in, strapping her into the passenger seat. When he took the pilot's seat, he started muttering to himself, flipping a number of different switches. In an alarmingly random fashion.

"Have you ever flown one of these before?" she asked, her heart faltering a beat.

"No, but what's the worst that can happen?" he grinned.

He eased a lever forward, powered the helicopter on.

The rotor blades began to rotate, the noise drowning out any possibility for debate.

Arielle came running out of the main building, waving her arms at them. Brandon saw her, but did not stop. He pulled up on the control stick. The helicopter jerked off the ground, lifting off in a crazy circle like a broken midway ride. Arielle ducked, running back toward the building for cover.

For a moment, Luciana felt certain they were going to crash.

*Better to go down fighting,* she thought, holding her mouth shut.

Sweat dripped down Brandon's face as he gripped the control stick, struggling to get the helicopter stabilized. His gray eyes pored over the instruments with intense concentration, flicking switches as he tried to figure out the complex machine. The look on his face was one of sheer determination. Why and how he had deemed *her* worthy of such an effort and such an immense risk, Luciana didn't quite know.

Finally, they swung up and over the wide lawn, pulling smoothly into the air and away.

On the ground below them, Arielle looked up, shielding her eyes from the bright morning sun with her hand, her meticulously styled blond hair blown terribly out of place, whipped by the draft of the helicopter as they flew away.

"Let them run," Arielle said calmly to the Guardians who gathered around her, watching the helicopter make its wobbly escape. "There's no point in tracking them. I already know exactly where they'll both end up."

*"Zuccolo,"* Luciana muttered, clenching her jaw as she sat immobile in her seat. "You are completely crazy."

He landed in a field with a bump, breaking one of the landing skids on the bottom of the helicopter so that they ended up lopsided.

But still intact.

In the stillness, he began laughing. Out of shock, she thought.

Her hands were still bound behind her back. "Let me out. Now."

He obliged, muttering about needing a car. She jumped out of the broken helicopter and collapsed on the ground, inhaling deeply. After a few moments of recovery, she got up. And headed toward the highway.

"Stay here," she told him. "I'll take care of the car."

"Wait, Luciana. We can't steal—"

He was shouting something, but she ignored him.

A moment later, she returned in a little black BMW Roadster.

"Get in. Don't ask how I got it. Nobody was hurt. I don't want any more discussion, not after you almost crashed us back into the afterlife. And this time, I'm driving."

Without a word, he folded his big body into the passenger seat and she took off, heading north. Away from L.A., where Arielle would have the city crawling with her own people, every Guardian within her control likely on high alert.

"If Arielle catches us, it will be worse than death, just so you know," she said, gripping the steering wheel. "She's probably planning to waterboard me in her new meditation pond. And she'll scrape off your hide and fly it on the flagpole in front of her center as a warning to the others."

"Then we'd better not let her catch us," he said.

He turned around and checked out the rear window, looking back every thirty seconds.

"Quit it," she told him. "You're making me nervous."

"I've never run from anything in my life," he said. "Plus, I'm used to being in the driver's seat. Distract me. Tell me the rest of the story of how you became a demon."

"We're not on a road trip where we share bagged snacks and our most intimate secrets," she said irritably. "Why do you want to know? That's all in the past."

"It's part of you. It defines you."

She sighed, checking the rearview mirror herself.

There was no one following them. No one above them. And the road ahead was straight and clear.

"Fine," she relented. "Where did I leave off?"

"Julian and Harcourt killed each other in a duel. What happened after that? I want to know how you died. How you came to be what you are."

She heard him shift, searching for a comfortable position in his seat.

"Oh, that," she said, exhaling deeply. "Let's see…

"I buried my husband in his birthplace in England. And then I went back to Venice. I expected to find my parents and Carlotta. But I returned to Venice too late.

"When I arrived at Ca' Rossetti, it was a stranger who opened the door. My parents were no longer living there. They had sold the palazzo when they ran out of money. I finally tracked them down in the poor quarter of the Campo San Barnaba, where they were living in destitution in a single room above a tavern.

"They told me that Carlotta had died in childbirth, not long before my arrival. Her last baby did not survive, either, my parents told me. They also said that the old pedophile remained as wealthy as always, and had refused to help them when they had asked for his aid.

"Soon after my return to Venice, the old pedophile died, too. But not of natural causes.

"He became my first victim. In Carlotta's name, I learned the art of poison. I began to study on my own, through books and experiments. But on the island of Sant' Ariano, I found a woman who taught me far more than I had ever imagined. Her methods were ghastly. But after ten years of being beaten by my husband, after knowing my sister suffer so miserably, after she and I had spent so many years as chattel, shuttled from one miserable fate to another…well.

"I had never dreamed that a mere woman could feel such a power.

"After my revenge on the old pervert, a kind of satisfaction settled over me. But it was not enough, I knew. I felt a sense of elation then. Of knowing that there was justice in the world. And that it had nothing to do with God. Over the next year, I honed my skills, searching for other victims, seeking out ways in which I could increase my power.

"In the end, who came for me was not God, but Harcourt.

"Harcourt, like so many other men I have known, blamed me for his death. He strangled me, dragging me down into the bowels of hell with him. I did what I had to do to survive. I took my revenge on my husband yet again, making a deal with the minions of hell to ensure that he was permanently left in the lowest reaches of hell. In order to do so, I used every resource I could to barter and trade. Eventually, I clawed my way out of hell and became a Rogue demon.

"The brothel above the glass gallery was the first place I was sent. To my shock, when I arrived there, Carlotta was already working there.

"During her life, she had taken her own revenge on the prostitutes her husband had hired. She blamed the women for infecting her with the disease that killed her unborn children. My sister was too much of a coward to take care of the real culprit, her husband. As her punishment, she was sent back to earth into an existence of prostitution herself. It was a ghastly situation.

"I knew I had to get myself out somehow. And that's when I made the bargain with the devil.

"One single human soul per year, delivered during the Festival of the Redeemer. The devil was so pissed off that the Venetians had found a way to cheat him of his beloved plague that he wanted to find a way to desecrate the church they had built in honor of the Redeemer. To me, one sacrifice per year did not seem like a large price to pay in exchange for my freedom.

"While I was struggling my way up through the ranks of the damned, Julian Ascher had already gained a position of prominence in the demon world. From time to time, we crossed paths, but it wasn't until recent years that I began to think in earnest about destroying my former lover. I traveled to Las Vegas and took up with Corbin Ranulfson, specifically to find a way to take Julian down. I failed, quite miserably. That was when I ran into the Company and met your friends. And the rest," she said, "is history."

Brandon was silent, twisted in the passenger seat of the small car to look at her, to listen.

"There is more, of course," she said. "Behind every story is another story. There are infinite layers of stories, as many stories as there are stars in the sky. But for tonight, that's enough, *mio caro.*"

"I have one question," he said finally. "Do you think you could ever be good?"

It was her turn to fall silent.

At last, she said honestly, "I *want* to be good."

Whether she was capable of being good was another question entirely.

She drove until dark. All the way up the coast of California, until they crossed the state line into Oregon. Sometime in the middle of the night, she finally ceded the driver's seat to him, and hours later they crossed the border into Washington State. They drove into the next day, until neither of them could keep their eyes open.

When the sun began to dawn on the horizon, they had almost reached Canada.

"We have to stop and rest," she said. "We can't just keep driving forever."

They found a cheap motel, paid cash that Luciana managed to pickpocket off an unsuspecting motorist at a gas station. Parked the stolen car behind some bushes around the corner. Went inside and shut the curtains.

"I suppose this is as good a place as any to hideout for a while. Until Arielle cools down," he said.

Lying on the hard motel-room bed beside her in the darkness, Brandon tried to sleep.

All he could think about was the story she had told him in the car.

How difficult her human life had been.

And how things could have been different for her.

*I want to be good,* she had said. He believed she could.

If only…

She turned her head to look at him.

"I must be dreaming," she murmured, lifting one hand to trace the side of his face. "To be here with you now, seems unreal. I want every minute to count. I want to be here with you."

By moonlight, he worshipped her, in awe before the grace of her.

A cathedral of flesh and bone, her clavicles like buttresses, the architecture of her as fine and as strong as old stone. He found the altar of her spine, traced the path of it with his fingers, a pilgrimage of her body. Bent her backward into his hands. Kissed the tips of her nipples, her breasts, those fragile domes. Her body was his sanctuary. He entered, reverently, so quietly he might have been a penitent come to lay offerings at a shrine.

A prayer dropped from his lips. Her name.

Whispered as devoutly as if it were the name of God.

By the time they were finished, he knew without a doubt that she was a part of the sacred, as much as he was, as much as any of them were, and that she would always be.

"I want to slay dragons for you," he said as they lay in the darkness, their sated bodies pressed against each other. His breath burned in his lungs, but whether it was from exertion or from anguish, he did not know. "I want to scale mountains and swim oceans."

She shifted uncomfortably, pushing out of his embrace. "You don't need to do that. I'm right here. And I can fight my own battles. I'm strong enough to do that on my own."

"Yes, but are you strong enough to walk away from the fight? You could turn your life around if you were willing to let go."

"Stop preaching, *angelo mio*. Don't you think I've heard centuries of it? Do you think I'm going to change now?"

"Julian reformed himself. With Serena's help."

"Don't speak their names," she said, infinitely sad. "Not at a moment like this. Even if that's true, I don't think it's possible for me."

"Arielle isn't the absolute authority on such things," he said.

"Shh. Don't speak of it. Just let me love you."

She pored over every inch of him, wanting an explanation for every stroke of tattoo on his body. She wanted to know them all, to memorize the map of ink that covered his skin, a map of his history and his unspoken bravery.

"I want to remember your body," she said. "I want your skin to be the last thing I know before I..."

"Before what? You're not going anywhere. Not if I can help it," he said gruffly.

Afterward, he found he could not sleep. He lay staring at the ceiling, wondering if the unfinished business of his own life would ever be resolved.

"What happened when you died?" she asked as they lay in the darkness, insomniacs together.

"You've seen it yourself, in my dreams," he said. "Don't pretend you haven't."

"Yes," she admitted finally, sighing. "I suppose I have."

He sat up suddenly on the bed and asked, "Why do we have this strange bond, the ability to enter each others' dreams?"

"Evidence of a cruel and ironic God," she said.

He suspected there was more to it than that. Suspected that she had the ability to enter his dreams on purpose. That she had explored the sleeping minds of many other dreamers, for purposes that were far from innocent. However, he put that out of his mind. Right now they were here, far away from Arielle. Safe.

They lay together, the rhythmic flow of their breath perfectly in sync.

"Did they ever catch your killer?" she asked.

In the darkness, Brandon nodded. "They arrested two men, the drug dealers I was hunting. But they always swore they didn't do it. Said they were nowhere near the alleyway when the shooting went down. They ended up in the Baraga Max—that's a maximum security correctional facility in Michigan. They were put away for life."

"Do you think they really did it?"

He froze, silence thickening in the space between them. "Why do you ask?"

"You still dream about it every night. It's obvious there's unfinished business."

Perhaps some part of Brandon remained a part of the human world because of this unfinished business. As he lay in bed, Luciana's head on his chest, he stared at the bright stars outside and thought of that.

And wondered how in the world his unfinished business could be finished.

*"I still can't sleep," he said after a long while.*

*She laughed. "You're already dreaming. You just don't know it. Come, I'll show you."*

*"No," he gritted out. "I want to wake up. There's no need to go through this again."*

*"You need to see this. You need to know for certain who killed you, and you need to confront him."*

*It was the same old nightmare.*

*The one he'd relived thousands of times. The one he could never avoid.*

*Down the dark alley, past the spilled garbage, the toxic ooze of leaking slime, stench of rotting food and other decomposing filth strewn across the pavement. He followed, unsure of where this was leading. Unsure of exactly what Luciana wanted him to see.*

*"I've got your back," she said. "I promise you. You're not alone. I will not let you die here tonight."*

*They walked into the alleyway, angel and demon together. Back-to-back, his big hand clasping hers, pale and fragile yet strong as silk-covered steel. He reached into his shoulder holster, pulled out the gun. Held it at eye level as he moved forward.*

*And when the shooter arrived, time seemed to slow as he raised his gun. But Luciana was faster, somehow behind him, blocking him from moving. The man turned to uncover a face Brandon knew well. A face he had loved.*

*The face of his best friend.*

*His wife's second husband.*

*The father of her children.*

*Jude raised his gun, ready to fire. Not into Brandon's back this time, but point-blank, aimed toward his chest.*

*The shots rang out, as they always did.*

*First one, then the other, the same familiar noise he had heard so many times before.*

*But not the same pain. No doubled flare of pain exploding in the back of his body.*

*Because they were fired into another body instead.*

*Faster than a human, Luciana had launched herself in front of him, taking both of the bullets. One of them hit her square in the middle of the chest, the other in her throat.*

*He caught her as she fell.*

*Held her as though he would never let her go. Even as she bled out on the concrete, and he was unable to do anything to stop it. She smiled as her eyes fluttered shut.*

And then Brandon awoke, sweating in fear as he had done every night for the ten years before he encountered the demoness. Awoke with a pain and a knowledge that, at that moment, felt heavier and more terrible than death.

He fought through the haze of confusion, trying to recount the facts to himself.

*You can't die in a dream.*

He definitely knew firsthand that it wasn't true.

She had taken a bullet for him. It had *only* been in a dream. But it had happened. She had experienced all the same suffering of death as he had.

He bolted upright. Beside him, the bed was empty.

He remembered where she had gone.

Remembered the last words she had said in the dream, after closing her eyes.

*"I'm going to kill that bastard."*

# Chapter Twenty-One

*Vengeance.* If Brandon wouldn't seek it on his own behalf, Luciana would do it for him. She would slay this one last dragon of his human life, and put it to rest finally. Because Brandon was too good a man to do it himself.

As Brandon slept, she picked up the car key from the dresser.

Slipped out of the motel room, quietly closing the door. And drove.

As Luciana boarded a plane from Seattle to Detroit, she felt a pang of something that felt almost like sadness. She, Luciana, was not good. Brandon might be convinced otherwise, but she was evil at the core. She had been for centuries, and she would continue to be, until the end of time.

*There's not an ounce of forgiveness in me,* she thought.

The strange part was that she no longer cared about Julian.

Staring out the window at the urban sprawl below as the plane descended toward the Detroit Metro Airport, she pondered it. The lightness within herself. The refreshingly peaceful feeling when she ran the syllables of his name through her mind. For the first time in centuries, she no longer felt like vomiting when she thought about him.

*Well,* she thought to herself, *that has nothing to do with forgiveness and everything to do with Brandon.*

It took Luciana the better part of a day to arrive at Brandon's former home, a small bungalow in a suburb of Detroit in which his wife still lived. A pair of small blond-haired boys roughhoused in the yard outside. Children who, under different circumstances, might have been Brandon's.

"Are your mama and papa here?" she asked them with her sweetest smile.

"Mommy's at the store," the younger one said.

"Don't talk to her," said the older boy, a child of about six. He squinted up at Luciana with an ornery look on his face. "We're not 'posed to talk to strangers."

Sighing patiently, she said, "This time it's okay, darling."

The littler boy peered at her and said with the brutal honesty of the very young, "You're prettier than Snow White from the movie. But you're badder than her evil mommy."

"Well, now, that's not fair. Even at my worst, I have never laid a hand on a child," she told him.

Two pairs of small blue eyes squinted up at her, relentlessly accusing. If Brandon had melancholy thoughts about missing out on fatherhood, he ought to take a look at these two, she thought. It would cure him of those thoughts immediately.

She smiled pleasantly and said, "But you could be the first, little man."

The small one screamed then, a high-pitched sound that Luciana had only ever heard come out of malfunctioning electronics and once when she had jammed on the brakes of a car. The bigger one joined in, belting out, "Daddaaaaaaaaay!"

The screen door banged open and a big, burly man came out. "Boys? Who you talking to out there?"

*Jude,* she thought. *The man of the hour.*

"Hello there, sir. I was just having a conversation with your *bambini*...what is the word in English... I believe it translates to spawn," she said cheerfully. "But now I'd like to talk to you in private."

"You two boys run on back and play in the yard, now," he told the children warily. To Luciana, he said, "You here selling somethin'?" His leering gaze swept over her body.

"Not exactly. You have an object that belongs to someone else. I want it back."

Jude's face went ash white. He did not ask what the item was.

He simply reached into his pocket and pulled out a watch.

"Jude Everett, you're a sick bastard."

"Who are you?"

"Never mind," she said, easily overpowering his weak human mind. "That's of no matter to you. Just give me the watch."

She held it in her hand, the same watch she had seen Brandon reach for a dozen times. In his pocket, in his dreams. While awake, to make sure he was in the real world. On the back of the watch, as she flipped it over, she saw the engraving there of the Archangel Michael.

"Why did you steal this, you twisted, pathetic excuse for a man?" she said. "And don't lie to me."

"Because I like to remind myself of what I'm capable of doing," Jude said.

Of what he had done to his friend.

An image entered her mind, of Brandon's body lying on the ground.

Of Jude reaching down and taking the watch out of Brandon's bloodied hand.

"You did it because evil people do evil things," Luciana said, more to herself than to him. "That was why you did not simply throw the watch into the garbage. Even though you threw away Brandon's life."

He stared at her, his body pulling back in shock at the name. "How do you know about Brandon?"

"Never mind that now. Come with me," she said, staring deep into his eyes. "You will not resist."

In that instant, she knew she would make her sacrifice to the devil this year, after all.

Better late than never.

One step behind the demoness was one step too late. When Brandon arrived at his old house, Luciana was long gone. He could feel the dark pull of her, heading away from him. And he knew where she had gone.

*Back to Venice.*

But there was still unfinished business here. Brandon pulled into the driveway that he had driven up thousands of times before. Tammy was sitting outside, watching her children play in the yard. At first, he only saw the side of her familiar light brown hair, shining in the summer sun. As he approached, she turned her face toward him.

"Go in the house," she told the boys quietly, her eyes widening slightly.

"Where's Jude?" he asked.

"Went with the black-haired lady!" one of the boys shouted through the screen door.

"Stay inside!" Tammy told them.

"Oh, my God," she said, her dark brown eyes clearly revealing her confusion. She reached out her hand to touch Brandon's chest, as if expecting it would go right through him. "It really is you."

"I'm not a ghost," he said.

"What are you?" she asked.

"I'm something else," he said, not bothering to explain. "It's complicated."

"My God, it's like you haven't aged," she breathed, reaching out to stroke his face. "Like time has stood still."

"Trust me, time has passed," he said.

How odd. Seeing her for the first time in a decade… he had always assumed it would be different. He had stayed away all this time. Some angels didn't, he knew. Some of them were allowed to visit their loved ones, to watch over them. And some of them broke the rules and let themselves be seen.

But Brandon had always followed instructions.

Had resisted the urge to go back home and visit. Partly because he had thought that Jude, his best friend, would be there to take good care of her. Would console her.

*Well.*

"Did you know?" was all he said to her.

She didn't bother to ask what he meant. Merely shook her head.

"Not until after," she said. "I had no idea. I wasn't even really sure until…"

*Now.* The word hung between them as she stared up at him.

"Can you forgive me?" she said. "There are things

I did. Things that happened before you died. I have thought for the past ten years, if only…"

"You can't think like that. What's done is done." He smiled. "Forget about all of this. Forget I ever came."

He kissed her cheek, the feeling of it so familiar and yet so strange, the skin he had once known, now striated with fine lines at the corners of her eyes and mouth. And he left her standing there, his first love, pressing her hand to her cheek in the place where he had kissed her.

Getting Jude to Venice was so easy, Luciana could have done it in her sleep.

After dealing with the Company of Angels, manipulating humans was a walk in the park, the demoness realized. Human minds were so malleable. After dealing with stubbornly strong-willed Brandon and his complicated dream sequences, Jude was like dealing with a child.

Nor did the airport security present a problem, for the human security guards were just as easy to manipulate as Jude. Sitting on the flight home, she finally relaxed for the first time in a very long while, more content than she had been the last time she had departed from America.

"We're going to a very lovely place," she said aloud to Jude, who sat next to her.

Jude, eyes glazed over because she had temporarily suspended his brain functioning, did not answer. However, the fact that Luciana was conversing with herself didn't spoil her mood in the least.

*Prendere due piccione con una fava. Kill two birds with one stone.*

The expression arose in her mind again.

In one stroke, she would finally complete her yearly sacrifice.

*And* exact revenge for Brandon's human death.

A beat behind Luciana, Brandon arrived at the airport in Detroit and strode up to a ticket counter.

"I'm sorry, sir," said the ticket agent. "You just missed our only direct flight to Venice today."

His gaze skimmed the dozens of departures listed on the electronic board behind her. "There must be another way. What's the fastest connection you can get me?"

Her fingers rattled over her computer keyboard as her eyes scanned its screen. "I can route you through London. It's a very tight connection, but you might make it."

"Do it."

Sitting on the plane, he forced himself to sit still without fidgeting. Time was of the essence. His ability to guess Luciana's destination would determine if Jude lived or died.

Why Jude's life was so important to him, Brandon didn't know. He knew only that it *was* important, even after what Jude had done.

Brandon stared out the window, into the clouds.

*Where is she going?*

*The Redentore Church is too obvious. She'll never go back there.*

A voice drifted into his head. Not Luciana's voice, but the voice of her sister, the day he had met Carlotta in the glass gallery. *"...the pieces are lovingly crafted on the neighboring Island of Murano, where all the studios were originally established because of the risk of fire..."*

And he knew exactly where the demoness was headed.

* * *

On Corbin's yacht, still anchored in St. Mark's Basin, Massimo stood in front of the Archdemon, offering his services as a Gatekeeper.

"I'm so glad you've come around to my way of thinking," said the Archdemon. "Now we can work together, toward our mutual goal. The downfall of the Company. And more than that. The downfall of humankind."

"Yes, *signore,*" Massimo said.

"Luciana trained you well. But you must forget your allegiance to her. She abandoned you to run off with that brute of an angel, Brandon. You know he was responsible for the disappearance of your little girlfriend, don't you?"

"Yes, *signore,*" he repeated.

In Massimo's heart, revenge was brewing.

And it was only a matter of time before he would be able to savor it.

# Chapter Twenty-Two

Luciana dragged her sacrifice toward her destination. This time, it was not to the Redentore Church. On landing at the airport in Venice, she commandeered a boat and drove out to the nearby island of Murano.

To the place she had sworn she would never come.

To the place she knew she could finish off the sacrifice, once and for all.

"I'm taking you somewhere very special," she told Jude as she steered the boat. "We're going to visit a *fornace,* a glassblowing factory. You're going to get an exclusive opportunity to experience the glassworks as no other tourist has before."

Jude continued to stare blankly into space, not registering their surroundings or her words. She slowed as she approached the island, winding the boat through the canals until she reached the building she was looking for, where she pulled up and tethered the boat. She led him out onto the *fondamenta,* guiding him toward the *fornace.*

Like the glass gallery in the Rio Tera dei Assassini, the factory had a storefront where products were sold to tourists. Rows of glassware stood in the darkness. Much like the gallery at this time of night, it was totally quiet.

"I have always hated this factory just as much as I

hate the gallery," she said, shuddering as she tugged Jude through the storefront. She led him to a pair of large iron doors, framed by an archway of colorful mosaic tile. She knocked, and a burly Gatekeeper hauled one of the doors open just an inch.

"Yes?" he growled, peering through the crack.

"I need to speak to the maestro," she announced. "Tell him Luciana Rossetti is here."

The master glassblower appeared in the doorway a moment later. He was a ruddy-faced man dressed in a heavy apron with spatters of red. He frowned slightly, but bowed and said, "*Baronessa,* what a surprise to see you here. We never thought you would grace us with a visit."

*We never thought you would stoop to enter this place,* was his unspoken message.

Every demon in Venice knew that Luciana Rossetti disliked the heat and the noise of the *fornace.* That she avoided it because of its association with the glass gallery, and with Carlotta. But also, in Luciana's eyes, the killings that went on here lacked sophistication.

It had nothing to do with the art of glassblowing.

But with the maestro and how his Gatekeepers operated.

*I have no choice,* she knew. *I have to finish this task. For Brandon.*

"I have a very special guest with me," she said, ignoring the maestro's frown and its subtext. "He deserves to have a unique experience of Venice. One I know only you can give him."

"In that case, please enter," said the maestro.

"You'll want to be fully conscious for this," she said to Jude. Snapping her fingers in front of the human's face, she brought him out of his mental haze.

He blinked several times, trying to process his surroundings. The maestro towered over them, grinning in anticipation. The Gatekeeper hauled open the iron doors with a great screech, and a sweltering gust of hot air blew through them. Jude wobbled backward a step, knocked off balance by the heat.

And by what he saw inside.

The demoness pushed him through the doorway, into the factory. The raised metal platform on which they stood overlooked the factory floor. Hundreds of Gatekeepers stopped to look up at them. A hive of activity at the ovens froze momentarily as the demons stopped to see who had just come in. Some of them nodded to Luciana, acknowledging her entrance.

Then, as abruptly as the workers had stopped, they returned to their activities.

Some of the Gatekeepers were blowing glass. They stood at the burning ovens with their glowing-hot blowpipes, rods and tongs. Many stood shaping and twisting bubbles of glass into ornate sculptures, vases and stemware.

Others were forging weapons. Making various kinds of swords and knives, they heated the metal in the ovens and pounded it with massive hammers. The ring of the blows echoed in the large space of the factory.

Still other demons were busy burning things. A bloody mass of severed limbs—some animal, some human—stood heaped in the middle of the factory floor in a great pool of blood. A charred smell, the scent of seared flesh, hung in the air.

"In the traditional *fornaci* of Murano, in the ordinary glass factories, the ovens burn twenty-four hours a day, seven days a week," the maestro explained. "Human glass masters begin work at six in the morning and stop at four in the afternoon. However, we demon artisans work all hours. Here, the fires are kept burning for many different purposes, as you can see."

Jude's eyes went so wide Luciana wondered whether they might pop out of his head.

"Normally, the openings of the ovens are relatively small, only a few feet in circumference. We have modified these ovens somewhat, you'll notice," said the maestro.

*Large enough to fit a human body. Or several, if need be,* Luciana noted.

"Much of our operations are still in experimental stages," the maestro said. "We are preparing for what is to come. There is so much yet to accomplish. When it is finished, our humble *fornace* will be one more step toward reconstructing hell on earth."

Luciana leaned in close to Jude and whispered, "And guess what? You're going to be a part of it."

The human screamed. A very bad idea.

Hundreds of eyes swiveled back toward the platform. The demons had been relatively disinterested in the pair's arrival. But a screaming, terrified human was entirely different. Entirely more interesting.

"Well, now, Jude, it seems you have caught the attention of our hosts," she told him. "Why don't you run along and take a closer look?"

She pushed him, and he stumbled down a few stairs toward the factory floor. A few demons came to collect him, and Jude began to struggle, kicking and screaming. He grabbed on to the metal railing of the staircase, but the demons pulled him off and dragged him away.

*Good,* she thought. *He deserves to suffer as much as Brandon suffered. Jude deserves the equivalent of three thousand deaths.*

"Don't dispense with him too quickly," she called to them. "Be creative about it. Your glass creations are beautiful and so distinctive. I'm sure you can apply your inventiveness to this task, too."

Jude heard her, and screamed again, louder, begging God to save him.

"*He* is not exactly popular with this crowd, *mio amico*," she called down to Jude. Then she muttered, "This pathetic human is the most you're getting from me this year, *diavolo*."

The sound of the iron doors scraping open behind her made her look backward.

Corbin stood in the doorway, his amber eyes glowing with satisfaction. Behind him was Massimo.

"Oh, no, *caro mio*," the Archdemon said, grinning. "This scrawny little human won't do the trick. I thought I'd already made that very clear. You should have done your duty when you had the chance, *baronessa*. You were supposed to deliver the angel. *He* will accept nothing less."

Of course Corbin would come. She had expected it all along. Had known she couldn't outrun him. Had thought that avenging Brandon's death would be worth anything she would have to suffer.

*But Massimo?*

Her once-trusted servant stood behind Corbin with a look of barren anger in his eyes. The ache of his betrayal cut her deeply. She glared back at her former Gatekeeper, silently accusing him.

"I will never deliver Brandon to you, no matter how much you threaten me. No matter what you plan to do to me. I would rather rot in hell for the rest of eternity," she told them.

"You know what's in store for you. If you're not

afraid, you should be," Corbin growled. "I should have known you would never deliver that angel. You're in love. How sweet. We can all wait for your lover together, darling."

"He doesn't know about this place," she said, thinking back frantically. *I never mentioned it. Did I?*

"He's a smart man. He'll figure it out," Corbin laughed. He grabbed her by the hair, yanking her face to his so he could press his cheek against hers. "Shall we see?"

Arriving at Marco Polo Airport, Brandon sprinted down the pier to the line of water taxis waiting to be hired. His best estimate put him forty minutes behind Luciana. There wasn't a moment to waste. *If it isn't already too late,* he thought. He was in the middle of engaging one of the drivers when Infusino and Arielle pulled up in a blue-bottomed municipal police boat. In the vessel sat a few other members of the local unit.

"You don't know what you're dealing with, Brandon," Arielle said. "Come with us."

He glared at her for a long moment. "You must be insane to ask me that. You tortured Luciana."

"Brandon, I know you feel strongly for her," said Arielle. "But she is a demoness. She is part of something that could end us all. Not just the Company. Not just angels. But humankind. The world as we know it could disappear forever. We have received information that the demons here in Venice are preparing for something bigger than we had ever imagined. We must deal with Luciana. Tonight."

In that moment Brandon paused. The question in his mind was, *To whom do I owe allegiance? To Arielle or to Luciana?*

*To neither,* was the answer. *I owe allegiance to my duty as a protector of humankind.*

He got into the boat, needing to see for himself exactly what Arielle was talking about. He could not let Luciana murder a human. Even if that human was a murderer himself.

"Come," said Infusino. "We must hurry to the Redentore Church."

"She's not going to the Redentore Church," Brandon told them as Infusino started the boat. "She's going to Murano. To the glass factory that supplies the gallery her sister ran."

"What? How do you know?" Arielle asked, her intense gaze gleaming.

"Just trust me," said Brandon.

"I know where the *fornace* is," Infusino said, then revved the boat into gear.

As they cleaved through the water, Arielle radioed the Venetian unit for backup.

"Why didn't Luciana take *you* to this *fornace* if she wanted to finish you off?" Arielle asked him as they sped toward their destination.

"Because she never seriously intended to kill me," Brandon said. "Every attempt she ever made on my life failed miserably, because she could never bring herself to do it. But that's not the case with Jude."

Arielle fell silent. She pursed her lips and stared out over the passing lagoon.

Once they reached Murano, Infusino quietly ushered them out of the boat.

"We cannot simply pull up to the front of this factory," said Infusino. "We must be subtle. There is a back way."

They disembarked and followed Infusino through

a twisting passageway that led to the back of a large, brick building. Cylindrical chimneys billowed smoke into the night sky. Light spilled from the large windows into the darkness around them. From inside came the repeated ringing of metal striking metal, and the flaring roar of burning flames.

Infusino motioned for the rest of the group to stay behind, while he and Brandon crept over to peer through the brightly lit windows.

What Brandon saw there brought him to only one conclusion.

*They're preparing for the End of Days.*

*Torture instruments. Weapons. Ovens.*

*Piles of dismembered limbs.*

How many bodies were there, he could not even say. The flesh was skinned and bloody, an amalgam of limbs so disfigured it was impossible to tell whether they were human or animal or both.

*And Jude.* Trapped in the middle of a horrific scene, with demons all around him, prodding at him with burning-hot tools.

For an instant, a primal urge deep in Brandon's gut was finally satisfied.

*After all this time, my shooter is getting his punishment....*

He shook his head and squeezed his eyes shut, willing that thought away.

Forcing himself to remember.

*Who I am...what I am....is a Guardian.*

Whatever base emotion had swept over him, whatever satisfaction he had momentarily felt at seeing Jude in pain—that was all overridden by the conviction that his role as an angel outweighed everything else. Brandon's oath to protect humankind was more important than any revenge he could have wished on a miserable person like Jude.

Backing away from the windows, the two angels retreated to the rest of the group and described the scene to them.

Infusino said quietly, "We knew something like this was coming."

Arielle nodded in agreement. "We knew the demon ranks were massing, but we didn't quite know how. This is only the beginning. There will be other groups. More preparations."

Brandon felt queasy, wondering whether his recent suspicions about Arielle were right.

Whether what his gut told him was true.

Whether she really was *evil*.

Or whether Arielle was simply dedicated to her mission on earth—protecting humankind and fighting demons—and doing what she thought needed to be done.

"Is this why you're building the Redemption Center?" Brandon asked.

She nodded. "Yes, and you must help me. We members of the Company all need to trust each other if we have any hope of winning. I don't know how we're going to defeat these demons. We'll have to find a way. But we can't stay here now. We've got to leave, formulate a plan and return later."

*Later will be too late,* he knew.

"The rest of you can do what you need to," he said. "I'm going in. Now."

"Wait," said Arielle, reaching toward him. "You can't just walk into a swarm of demons unprotected. They will rip you limb from limb and then burn you alive, just like they're going to do to that human. Besides, he doesn't even deserve to be saved."

"We can't just leave him here," Brandon said. He looked at her pointedly. "Torture is never justified."

He turned, steeling himself for what he must do. Or perish trying.

Infusino grabbed his arm, holding him back.

He broke free, tearing toward the factory doorway, toward certain destruction.

A lone feather drifted into Luciana's view. The moment she saw it floating in the middle of the factory, a wisp of melancholy grazed over her. Because she knew that if the angel arrived now, Corbin would take him. And that would be the end.

*How can he have found me here?*

The iron doors groaned open once again. This time, every Gatekeeper in the factory turned toward the sound, the nearness of his energy pulling every gaze upward.

Brandon stepped into the factory. As he walked onto the platform, she saw how stunning he was, the ink-etched muscles of his arms glistening in the heat. Light poured from him, illuminating every surface. The fires in the ovens seemed to dim in contrast. As Luciana looked up at him amid the dull gray of the factory, his gray eyes radiated. Lucent. Fierce. Powerful.

But he had come alone.

And she knew all was lost.

As powerful as he was, a single angel against a horde of demons could not possibly win. Could not possibly even escape. Yet Brandon himself did not seem to realize that. His broad shoulders were set in a stance of absolute confidence, much like the first time she'd ever seen him.

"Stop!" the Guardian thundered.

All activity in the factory ceased.

Silence fell over the building. The muted rumble of fire inside the ovens crackled, waiting.

Then Jude's screaming commenced again.

Brandon descended the metal staircase, each footstep ringing in the large room.

The demons stood transfixed for another moment, watching him. Then they began to converge toward the stairway, gathering in a ring around it. Brandishing weapons glowing with the heat of hellfire, they circled slowly. But none dared touch him.

With bold strides, the Guardian headed toward Jude. Untied him.

Hauled his own murderer over his shoulder.

And strode back toward the staircase.

It was Corbin who stepped forward, blocking his way. "You think you can walk in here and take what belongs to us? Massimo, take care of this intruder."

The Archdemon snapped his fingers. Very quietly, Massimo stepped forward.

With a syringe in his hand and a quick flash of vengeance in his eyes.

A syringe she recognized. Which she had handed Massimo herself, along with the words, *I trust you with this.*

"If this is the end, so be it," Brandon said. "I have no regrets. I will not run from evil."

But Massimo did not move toward the angel.

Instead, he raised his hand and inserted the syringe into the side of Corbin's neck. In a smooth, deliberate motion, he pressed his thumb down and injected the contents of that syringe into the Archdemon's carotid.

Corbin stood, stunned for a moment.

"Why?" he managed to gasp out.

"For my mother," Massimo whispered.

"That bitch Luciana is not your mother," Corbin choked.

"I know," said the Gatekeeper. "Her name was Carlotta Rossetti."

Corbin swallowed, a simple movement of his Adam's apple. He touched the center of his neck, then coughed. A scarlet gleam of blood spattered on the ground. And then the death rattle began, moving up his windpipe. The sound of dying Luciana had heard so many times before. The Archdemon fell, splayed on the bare concrete floor, twitching out the last moments of his existence.

As he lay in his final convulsions, there was a momentary pause.

The Gatekeepers stood peering down at him, astounded, many of them expecting him to get up.

*So it works,* was what Luciana thought. *The poison works after all.*

And then one of the ovens exploded. Whether by some divine intervention or set off by some earthbound thing or creature, she could not say for sure. All she knew was that the oven flared apart with a burst of flame that shot out in every direction, blowing out the nearest windows and cracking the floor beneath it.

The blast of heat rocked them all: demons, angel, human, Luciana, Brandon, Jude.

But it was not fire that began to engulf the building.

The building shook beneath them as the cracked floor split open, a vein tearing open to become an abyss. Water gushed in. Faster than any surge Luciana had witnessed, even after centuries of living in flood-famed Venice. Water engulfed the factory floor, rising around the ankles and up the shins of the shocked demons standing inside.

The horde scattered, running through the now-knee-deep water, pushing and shoving toward whatever exit was nearest. Brandon grabbed Luciana, hauling her out the back door with Jude over his shoulder. Bolting down the *fondamenta* away from the *fornace,* so fast she wondered for a moment if they were actually flying.

Behind them, the water washed into the ovens inside, hitting the fires with a great hiss of steam that rose to the top of the building. Pressure built. And then it ruptured. The roof blew open and the air was filled with shattering glass. The walls shook, old brick crumbling like unfired clay.

Fifty feet away from the disaster, she turned to look back.

And like a carrion crow arriving at a scene of carnage, the devil's black funerary gondola came floating down the canal. Into the *fornace,* the dark vessel sailed on a river of flame. Death's ferryman extended his withered arm from within his black cloak, steering into the heart of the boiling inferno. Moments later, the boat emerged, and as it floated past them, Luciana looked down and saw the body of the Archdemon stretched along its floor. With a nod of his head in her direction, the demon gondolier gave a single push on his pole and drifted away.

Luciana almost collapsed on the *fondamenta.*

The stone walkway was solid beneath her feet, although it did not feel real.

And yet, there was one more thing to take care of.

Brandon set the miserable human down. Jude stumbled away, zigzagging a few steps. Where he was going, Luciana didn't care. She only knew that she wanted to stop him. She picked up a piece of pipe lying nearby and went after him. He fell, looking up at her with terrorized eyes as she held the pipe at his throat.

"Let him go. I have forgiven him," Brandon said, catching her arm.

"Why do you still care what happens to him?" she said, still gripping the pipe so hard her hand hurt. She ached to plunge it into the human's throat, to put an end to the injustice and suffering Brandon had endured. "He *killed* you. Don't you get it?"

"He's human," said the angel. "It's my job to protect them."

"Why do you defend them?" she said fiercely. "Humans are vile. Not even two hundred years ago, people were torturing each other in the streets. Public executions were a form of entertainment. Severed heads hung outside city gates, on bridges, in marketplaces. Don't think for an instant that this human would hesitate to parade your severed head as a trophy if he thought he could get away with it."

"You and I were both human once."

"We're not human anymore," she said quietly. "This man does not deserve to live."

"There's no justice here on earth that can judge what he's done. We were not sent here to judge. We can't presume to know the full reasons behind what occurs on this earth. Come with me now. Come. Walk away with me. And let him go."

Brandon held out his hand.

The pipe trembled in her fingers, poised at Jude's throat.

"Leave him," the angel coaxed. "He's not worth it. Not when he is all that stands between you and I. Come away with me now. We can be together."

An eternity seemed to pass outside the still-flooding factory as they stood amid the chaos of fleeing demons and panicking, newly woken humans running in all directions.

Almost imperceptibly, she nodded.

But she did not believe what he said.

*We can never be together,* she knew.

"Leave him," Brandon said. "It's not up to us to decide what happens to him."

"If that's what you want," she said finally.

She let the pipe fall, heard its clatter as it dropped to the ground and rolled into stillness.

He wrapped an arm around her shoulders and pulled her away, leaving Jude to stumble through the dark streets of Murano, relinquishing him to fate.

In the boat she had taken from the airport, Luciana and Brandon drove back to Venice. Hand in hand they walked among streets still quiet and dark as the humans lay sleeping safe inside their homes.

She wanted to collapse from relief, from the shock that Corbin was finally gone.

The reality of it had not yet sunk in, but she knew it would soon.

Along with the reality of leaving Brandon.

"I want to take you home, my love," he said. "To Chicago. To start fresh."

She smiled. There was no home for her but Ca' Rossetti, and that no longer existed. No life but the one she had known for hundreds of years. He did not seem to understand that now, but he would come to accept it sooner or later.

He would have an eternity to accept it.

*How strange,* she thought, *that although we cannot be together, I feel oddly at peace.*

He paused at an archway with an ornate, old gate curling with vines.

"I came here the night we first made love," he said, pausing for a moment to peer into the dark garden that lay within.

In the moment of his pause, Luciana slipped inside, slamming the gate shut behind her. The old latch fell shut with a *snick* that sounded eerily final. A fraction of a second later, Brandon reached through the wrought iron and grabbed her wrist.

With his free hand, he grasped the handle. Tried to open it. It would not budge.

"This is Venice, where things are very old," she said. "It seems to be locked shut."

Around her wrist, his fingers curled, holding her. "Even if it won't open, I'm not letting you go. We'll have to wait until it unlocks."

"We could stand here forever," she said. "Caught in another stalemate until we're both exhausted. Or we could do things the easy way and you could just let me go."

His fingers tightened. "I will never give up on you. On us."

"Get this through that head of yours—I am never going to change. There's no place for the two of us together, not in this world. Maybe in the distant future. But not now. You have to let me go. You know that. I won't let you give up everything that you have and everything that you are. Not for me," she told him. "Close your eyes."

"Forget it," he growled.

"Just close them. I promise I won't do anything stupid."

The image she sent into his head was of the two of them.

*Enclosed in each other's arms beneath a canopy of stars. The first man and the first woman. The last man and the last woman. Both. One. Always.*

"Let me go," she said. "I will come back to you. I promise."

He opened his eyes. Looked deep into her mist-green gaze.

Just for an instant, he relaxed his fingers.

And in that instant, she was gone.

It took only a moment for Brandon to scale the gate, to leap over it in pursuit of her.

Where she had vanished, he had no idea.

Here in Venice, he would never catch her. She would evade him forever, slipping through his fingers as she always had. He would search, but already he knew it would be futile. Like trying to grab a handful of moonlight from the surface of the canal.

Inside, on the grass of the garden, she had dropped a shining silver object. He picked it up, felt its familiar weight in his hand. Turned it over and ran his thumb over the engraving of the Archangel Michael there, slaying the dragon.

"Where were you tonight while this was all going down?" he said aloud.

Behind him, he heard Michael's voice say, "I knew you could take care of it, Brandon. You don't need a babysitter."

But when he turned around, Michael was not there.

Tucking the watch into his pocket, Brandon knew why Luciana had dropped it.

He wondered if she ever truly intended to keep her promise to come back to him.

He was left standing the middle of that empty garden, with a cluster of fireflies flitting among the wild, fragrant foliage. And the statue of St. George, frozen with his spear poised above his head, yet another warrior preserved in the moment of conquering evil.

# *Epilogue*

*One year later*

In the burned-out remains of Ca' Rossetti, Luciana sifted through the ashes of her ruined palace.

The fire-eaten remnants of furniture and household goods—the charred edge of a table here, a pile of broken dishes there—lay in a jumble amid blackened timber and chunks of fallen concrete. The outer walls, once three-stories high, were badly cracked and crumbling. The roof, torn away completely, gave way to the night sky. The skeleton of the palazzo threatened to tumble down around her.

Luciana turned to look out over the water.

The canal, at least, was unchanged and shimmering in the moonlight.

*No wind. No melancholy singing. Only peace.*

Through the empty opening where a wooden door had stood, Massimo appeared. As she knew he would.

He bowed. She nodded in acknowledgment.

They stood for a long moment without speaking, in the ruin of the grand palazzo they had both worked so hard to maintain, gazing at the brittle old bones of the home they had loved.

"Come, walk with me," she said, pulling him out of

the wreckage to stroll in the quiet streets. "Let us leave this place, and I will explain what you have waited so long to hear. I will tell you about your mother. What I know of her last days as a human I found out from my parents, your grandparents, when I returned to Venice, shortly after Carlotta's death."

His face betrayed nothing. He asked no questions, made no comments.

He simply listened.

And she began. "It was not customary for a Venetian woman to return to her parents' home to give birth. But Carlotta arrived nonetheless, soaking wet in the middle of the night, swollen with child. During that long night, after the agony of childbirth, she died. The son she bore was washed and swaddled in the only silk left in the house. Then the baby was taken to the Arsenale and given to a boatbuilder in return for a handful of ducats, just enough to feed the rest of the family.

"As soon as I was in a position to do so, I searched endlessly for you. It took me until after your human death to finally find you. By that time, you had already been claimed by the devil as one of his own," she said.

She remembered her sadness at discovering he had taken to fighting in his early twenties. That after killing a few other young men in fights, he had been killed in a knife fight in a local bar brawl.

"I negotiated the release of your soul from hell. As far as you knew, you were simply another minion, a Gatekeeper who kept order in one of the great houses in Venice."

"I always considered myself lucky to have such a post," he said.

*Lucky.* She had not anticipated that reaction. In the past two centuries, she had not been able to bring herself to reveal his true origins. In her mind, she imagined what her own reaction might be if she were told such a thing.

*Pure fury followed by certain retaliation.*

She had considered it from every angle.

Better to believe you had died the poor son of a boat-builder than the abandoned child of a bankrupt noble house, sold to the lower classes to get money for bread. Better to believe your parents were long dead than to know your mother had ignored you completely while existing in excess and debauchery a few miles away… for centuries.

"My mother is long gone," he said softly. "She died the day I was born."

"How long have you known?" she asked aloud. "That she…that Carlotta…"

He shrugged. "How could I not know she was my mother? It's something to do with instinct, I'm sure. I never asked, because I already knew."

Luciana groped for words, but they fell so short of what she wanted to express. "Your mother loved you dearly. When she was alive, she was something different. Death changed her. As it changes all of us."

Massimo nodded, and she saw in his eyes that he understood.

"I don't know where she has gone now," said Luciana. "There are a thousand possibilities, a thousand places souls go. Places of which even we have no knowledge. But I am certain that wherever Carlotta is now, she is finally free. She has gone beyond both hell and earth."

Massimo nodded, head bowed. "And you? What have you been doing this past year?"

"Searching for a way to exist on my own terms, not the devil's. I simply cannot do that anymore, Massimo," she told him. "However, you have to make your own choices. Ca' Rossetti is yours to rebuild if you so wish, along with the necessary funds. Our old enemies still exist, though, as they have for centuries. They will try to stop you, I'm sure. But you are a survivor. You have the strength to endure."

"What will you do, *baronessa?* Where will you go?"

She smiled, looking up at the moonlit sky. She would go on searching.

And she knew in that moment that every prayer to the divine she had ever whispered or even simply thought in the most vague and wishful sense…every desperate plea for mercy she had uttered in her basest moments of hopelessness…all the good she had ever wanted had finally been answered in the best way possible.

With one glaring flaw.

One monumental, heartbreaking flaw: she would have to live without Brandon.

Yet, it was still the best way possible.

Because an existence with Brandon was impossible.

A strange sensation tingled at Luciana's inner wrist. She turned her arm to inspect it. There, on her translucent skin, was a tattoo of a feather. An ordinary pigeon feather exactly like the one she'd picked up from the edge of her worktable when she'd first sensed Brandon's approach to Venice.

Gray at the tip, fading to colorless at the base.

The tattoo had appeared the night she had fled Venice a year ago.

She touched it and closed her eyes, flooded by the same sense of peace that Brandon's nearness had brought her during their brief time together. The sense of peace that still came to her whenever she thought of him.

*He is near,* she knew. *I must leave before he arrives.*

One day, she would find a way to atone for her wrongdoings.

Only then would she deserve to be with him, she knew.

*I know that day will come. As surely as I know that one day every creature on earth will find peace.*

Heading away from him, she walked quickly along the streets of Venice. Wandering with no particular direction, she walked until the sensation of tingling faded. She walked until she found herself standing on the lip of San Marco's Basin, where the stone met the edge of the water. She stood there watching a distant flutter of wings, a flock of birds on the edge of the horizon rising into flight.

Brandon felt her presence here, in this city she adored. But although the ashes of Ca' Rossetti seemed to pulse with the vibration of her, she was no longer there. There was no trace of her in the glass gallery. Nor in the abandoned rooms of the brothel above it. Her summer pied-à-terre on the Lido, too, sat in pristine silence. He roamed the twisting streets looking for her, hoping for a glimpse of her, but she was nowhere to be found.

The last place he looked was the Redentore Church.

*Same crowds of people,* he thought, working his way inside. *Same interminable heat.*

But Luciana was not here, either.

With a fool's hope, he had thought he might find her in one of the chapels, kneeling in repentance. In the midst of finding some way to forgive herself for her long catalog of sins. In the midst of an epiphany.

*Has she killed again?* he wondered. There was no way of knowing.

He went back to the place he had first taken her, to the ramshackle pensione where he had chained her to the bed, picked broken glass out of her back and watched the fireworks explode over a city into which she had completely disappeared. However, when he arrived at the old Company safe house, it wasn't Luciana he found there.

Arielle sat waiting in the modest foyer, as immaculately groomed as ever.

*The perfect angel.*

"I didn't expect to see you here," he said.

He wasn't kidding. They had not spoken a single word to each other in the past year. But he knew exactly what she was doing here. Considering that the pensione was no longer used as a safe house after what had happened last year, Arielle had no other reason to come.

*She's waiting for Luciana. Or waiting for me. Or both.*

"It's important for all of us to work as a team," she said, training her unwavering blue gaze on him. "To ensure there are no further insurrections in this area. I'd expect a bit more gratitude after Infusino and I blew up that factory last year and saved you."

"You?" he said, only mildly surprised. "All this time, I thought it was an act of the divine."

"Wasn't it?" Arielle smiled thinly. "We were extremely lucky. We fired the flare gun from the boat into the oven. Most of these buildings are extremely fragile, built on wooden piles that were driven into the lagoon, some of them over a thousand years ago. It didn't take much."

"Do you want me to thank you? You got me demoted afterward."

"Demotion is not permanent. In time, I'm sure you'll

work your way back up to your old position as a supervisor," she said evenly. "Besides, *I* didn't get you demoted. You got yourself demoted."

*Even if that was the case, it was worth it,* he thought. *Everything I did last year was worth getting Luciana out of your claws.*

As usual, Arielle wouldn't let up, but continued to lecture him. "You shouldn't have taken that helicopter. You shouldn't have absconded with a detainee. You should *never* have let her escape at the end of it all. I don't know how you managed that. There are a lot of things you shouldn't have done, Brandon."

"You weren't aiming to reform Luciana," Brandon said, looking down at her impassive face. "You intended to keep her and torture her. And use her for your own purposes."

"Don't be ridiculous. I would never do that," she said. She stood sharply, rising to leave. But just as her foot was poised on the doorstep of the pensione, she turned back and added, "Even if I did, there's no way you could prove it."

Her lips curved into a tight smile. For the first time as he looked into Arielle's blue eyes, he thought that her trademark neutrality was not a sign of equanimity.

But instead, a sign of something pathological.

In his room upstairs, he sat down on the edge of the hard bed, struck a match and lit a candle on the bedside table. He opened the window and stared out over the Adriatic by the steady flame.

Waiting.

*She promised she would come back.*

He lay down on the bed with neither fear nor hope.

In the past year, he had been completely cured of his nightmares.

Somehow, she had freed him from reliving the horror of his human death. His dreams had returned to normal, more like the dreams he'd had during his human life. Full of possibilities and impossibilities, experiences and oddities all mixed in together.

But he had not dreamed of her in the past year, either.

He closed his eyes.

*She came sliding into his unconscious—though not sharply, not vividly as she had done in the past. The image of her appeared, hazy and mystical, like a mirage flickering in the distance. As he approached her, she was only a phantom of a woman, the shivery touch of a hand and a glimpse of curved, ripe lips half-hidden behind a fall of dark hair.*

*She lingered for only an instant. But he felt her love radiating toward him, around him, into him. Heard her voice, faint but so ardent that he did not for an instant doubt the sincerity of the words she whispered.*

Ti amo.

*Even as she drifted into ether, he felt this vision of her more strongly than anything he had experienced while awake in the past year without her.*

But every dream must end. And every dreamer must awaken.

He awoke clinging to the memory of her, reaching for the feel of her. With the knowledge that, just as the dragon dragged up from the depths of the Venetian lagoon had no place in the everyday world, Luciana did not truly belong by his side.

And yet, he knew he would never stop looking.

*I will cross centuries and traverse continents to find you. I will scale mountain ranges and swim oceans to be with you. I will wait. Until the end of time if I must.*

He stood at the window from which she had once

leaped with her dark, wild hair streaming in the moonlight. He looked up into the night as fireworks exploded over her beloved Venice. Brilliant colors rained down over him, directly overhead. Tinny speakers broadcast rich arias from the neighboring balconies and rooftops. One emerald flare shot high into the sky to fracture into a million glittering fireflies.

*I will slay dragons to be with you,* he promised silently. *I will find a way.*

Until then, he would listen for the whisper of her honeyed voice in his dreams.

\* \* \* \* \*

# Acknowledgments

Thanks once again to my own set of earthly guardians:

Valerie Gray, executive editor at Harlequin MIRA. This novel exists because of your persistence and creative guidance. The book's dedication is a reference to T. S. Eliot's dedication of *The Wasteland,* "For Ezra Pound: *il miglior fabbro*" ("the better craftsman"). My gratitude goes out to *la miglior fabbra,* the better craftswoman, for helping me and many others write stories that would otherwise only exist in our dreams.

The team at MIRA. To the art department, *bravo!* Another gorgeous cover—your work inspires me. To editorial assistant Michelle Venditti and the Sales, Marketing and PR Departments, thanks for your hard work and dedication to entertaining, enriching and inspiring.

Kimberly Whalen. Agent *favolosa* at Trident Media Group, your advice is invaluable.

Patricia, Garyen, Johanna. Parents and sister, thank you for your encouragement and support. Thanks especially to my mom for my first, wonderful trip to Venice. And for passing on your creative spark.

Friends, teachers, fellow writers. For your generosity of spirit and the lessons you've taught me, I'm truly grateful. *Grazie mille* to Linda Hutcheon for your unflagging belief in me, and for sharing your love of opera (and SO much more) with so many of your students.

Readers and bloggers. You have my most sincere appreciation, especially those who have reached out with kind words to welcome me into the romance community.

Dexter the pug. Thank you for bringing us so much love with your big pug smile.

My husband, Ed. Last of all, but first in my heart, thank you to my real-life Guardian. I'm constantly humbled by your commitment to excellence and your contributions to humanity. Every moment with you is truly a gift.